HER LONELY BONES

BOOKS BY WENDY DRANFIELD

HER LONELY BONES

WENDY DRANFIELD

bookouture

Published by Bookouture in 2023

An imprint of Storyfire Ltd.
Carmelite House
50 Victoria Embankment
London EC4Y 0DZ

www.bookouture.com

ISBN: 978-1-83790-784-7
eBook ISBN: 978-1-83790-783-0

For Winnie.

PROLOGUE

FIFTEEN YEARS EARLIER

The young mother is beguiling to watch, even when she's not speaking. Sitting under the harsh fluorescent lights of this unwelcoming conference room, there's an innocence about Tiffany that suggests she's too young for this shit. That trouble made a mistake and knocked on the wrong door. At just twenty years old, she's going through the worst trauma any parent could ever suffer.

It doesn't seem fair to Officer Mike Bowers. He wishes he could ease her suffering somehow. "We'll be ready in just a minute," he says gently, handing her a box of tissues.

She looks up at him, shaking her dark brown hair away from her face. He sees panic in her eyes. Her hands are squeezed under her jean-clad thighs. She doesn't want to be here, that much is evident. She's probably wondering how her day went from ordinary to catastrophic in the blink of an eye.

"Can I get you anything?" he asks. "Water?"

She shakes her head and looks away, wanting this to be over with.

This isn't the first time Mike's helped a distraught parent, and it won't be the last. Even though he'll remember each parent forever, they won't give him another thought once the investigation is over. He's just a young officer, only present in case something goes wrong. But he wants to do more. His career goal is to eventually make detective. He wants to see cases like this through to the end. Bring the families some resolution. Get them the justice they crave and deserve.

The TV producer behind him addresses the cameraman. "Is the camera good to roll?"

"It's ready," comes the reply.

The producer listens to someone talk in his ear before announcing to the room, "Okay, people, we have twenty seconds until we're on-air." He turns to the detective sitting next to the distressed mother and, a second before they go live, gives him a thumbs-up.

Mike stares at the TV screen placed just right of the table where Tiffany sits. He watches as Detective John Ramsey clears his throat and focuses on the camera's lens. Ramsey begins by introducing himself as lead detective at Lost Creek Police Department before explaining to the viewing public that a baby named Grace is missing. She needs to be found. The police will be issuing an Amber Alert immediately. If anyone knows anything... yada yada yada.

Grace's mother sits in silence the entire time, holding back tears, until the detective eventually turns to her. "Tiffany? Is there anything you'd like to say?" he asks.

She wipes her runny nose with the back of her hand. Her face is flushed. Her blue eyes weary and fixed on the table in front of her. "Please bring her back," she mumbles. "I need my baby home. She's all I have. I'm not built for this kind of thing. My heart can't take it." Her hand flies to her mouth to catch a sob.

When it looks like she's done, she surprises them all by looking up so they can see the despair etched on her face. She radiates a quiet intensity as she stares directly into the lens. "If I don't get my baby home safe within the next twenty-four hours... I'll kill myself."

To Mike, still watching the screen, it feels as though she's talking directly to him.

The room is silent. No one seems to know how to react. How to end the disturbing press conference. The cameraman slowly and steadily zooms in to the young woman's face, then into her eyes. She's visibly trembling.

There's something in her look that disturbs Mike. He glances at Ramsey and can tell he's thinking the same. They both know she isn't screwing with them. If Tiffany doesn't get her baby back safe by the end of tomorrow, she'll make good on her promise.

And her suicide will be on them.

Mike sets the timer on his watch. Twenty-four hours to find Grace.

CHAPTER ONE

PRESENT DAY

Tires crunch over a gravel driveway as the vehicle creeps toward the wooden two-story house. Once parked, the twin boys in the back are out of their seats before the woman can even remove her sunglasses and cap.

As it's early Sunday morning, most people are still in bed, but the day is already bright with summer sunshine slowly peeking over the property's roof. She takes it all in. The peeling white paint, overgrown yard and broken porch floorboards suggest the place should be pulled down and rebuilt. Instead, they're moving into it.

As they emerge from the car, her tanned partner, wearing a red T-shirt and blue jeans, stretches his arms above his head and yawns before making his way behind the vehicle to the attached utility trailer. With a crack of his neck he says, "Let's see if we lost anything along the way."

The closer they came to their final destination—the small mountain town of Lost Creek in southwestern Colorado—the more winding the roads became, and the old covered bridge they crossed in order to enter the town felt as though it might collapse beneath them. Her partner had commented on the welcome sign they passed that proudly declared Lost Creek is *Where the lost are found.*

She's hoping the unnerving declaration is hokum.

She leans down and glances into the rear of the car before turning back to face the house. "Wait for us!" she shouts after the boys. "We don't know what condition the place is in. It could be dangerous inside."

She's worried there could be an unexpected resident inside, either human or animal, although she'd be surprised to see squatters out here. They did pass a few other houses on the street, but they're all well-spaced apart and from here she can't see any of them. Their house is surrounded by a wooded area. The fir and pine trees contrast against some striking aspens. In the other direction they have a view of the mountains.

It's truly breathtaking here. Especially on a warm mid-August day. There's no denying this land has a lot of potential for the right family.

Still, the property gives her the creeps.

The children don't stop running, despite her plea. "Well if you break your neck, don't come crying to me," she mutters under her breath.

At the top of the porch steps the oldest boy—by twelve minutes—finds the front door unlocked. With a heavy push, the door opens, revealing a pitch-black interior. The woman shudders when thinking about going inside. The house has sat vacant for months after the previous owner died. They don't know what awaits them.

The enormity of her situation suddenly hits her. *There's no turning back now.*

Her partner places the box he's holding on the ground at her feet. When he straightens, he places a warm arm around her shoulders and she can smell the sour sweat from his armpits. The car's A/C was bust, making the drive harder than it needed to be.

He slaps a kiss on her forehead. "I think this is just the kind of fresh start we need," he says. "I've got high hopes for this place. It's a real fixer-upper. Something I can get my teeth into. And the kids are going to love living in a mountain community, with all this space and fresh air."

She stands that way for a while, his arm around her shoulders, as they both gaze up at the house in front of them and listen to the children's footsteps running across the wooden floorboards inside.

She thinks about how, to onlookers, they would appear to be the perfect family.

The thought leaves her cold.

CHAPTER TWO

After a long and tiring Monday, Detective Madison Harper sits quiet and alone in the local cemetery, listening to the sound of birdsong coming from the trees around her. It's a balmy August evening and the sun is beginning to lower. This place is both beautiful and peaceful, but it holds a lot of heartache for Madison as it's where her father was recently buried. She's suffered too much loss in recent years, and now she's set to lose her son too.

She stands, trying not to think about it. As she meanders back toward her car, she comes to the headstone for Mike Bowers. Before Madison was promoted to detective, Mike was her sergeant. They worked well together and she had a lot of respect for him back then. He was caring toward victims, had a great sense of humor and she thought they were friends. She trusted him.

She shouldn't have.

Eventually he made detective, and that's when everything went wrong for Mike. He died young, at just thirty-eight years old.

She reads the inscription on the headstone, which is still in good condition as it's only been here just over a year.

In memory of Mike Bowers.
Loving father to his beautiful daughter.
You will be missed.

Given the way he died—and the reason for it—the inscription is brief.

Madison has unresolved feelings about his death. Because his life didn't have to end the way it did.

With a deep breath, she resumes walking. Once inside her car she pulls away from the cemetery and switches the A/C on. Just thirty minutes with the engine off has warmed the car considerably. On autopilot, she drives by the familiar sights of her hometown. While picturesque to look at, she's seen it all many times before, so she allows her mind to wander. She tries to think about work. Because if she focuses on work, she won't need to think about how her only child is leaving home and heading off to college at the end of the week.

Although it should be a happy occasion, Madison is filled with despair. Now eighteen, Owen has only been back in her life for just over a year. Thanks to a corrupt social worker, she wasn't allowed contact with him after being wrongfully convicted of manslaughter. She served six years in prison before she was finally reunited with him last summer. But Owen was no longer the ten-year-old boy she had left. He was a young man. Almost a stranger. It's taken time to get to know each other. And now she's about to lose him all over again.

"I need longer," she mutters. The sound of her voice makes her realize she's thinking about it again. She tries to concentrate on the road ahead. When her cell phone rings, she answers it hands-free.

"Hey, Madison, it's Stella." An experienced dispatcher, Stella Myers is Lost Creek PD's longest-serving employee.

Madison keeps her eyes on the road. "Hey. What's up?"

"Detective Adams has requested your assistance at a crime scene. A homicide. Can I send you the location?"

Despite being on her way home from work, Madison doesn't hesitate. "Go ahead." Her phone pings in seconds with a text containing an address.

"And, Madison?" says Stella. "He wants you to know it's a bad one. Multiple victims. He says to brace yourself."

Madison takes a deep breath. Detective Marcus Adams moved to town last year when he was offered the role after her last partner died. So far, he hasn't impressed her. He has a negative attitude and an unwillingness to take risks in order to keep the community safe. Adams isn't from here—he arrived from a much larger PD in Denver—and in her opinion, he isn't suited to the role or the community. He isn't used to small-town mentality and thinks everyone here is either inbred or has a few screws loose, sometimes both. That may well be true, but there are also good people in Lost Creek.

Madison suspected he'd skip town after the notorious Snow Storm Killer savagely murdered several young mothers here last Christmas. That case disturbed him to the point of inaction, and he wasn't much use to her during the investigation. But to his credit, he stayed put, and he's kind of growing on her the more she's exposed to him, like painful new shoes that need a lot of wearing in.

It's fair to say he wouldn't be her first choice of partner, but she probably wouldn't be his either. She wrecked his prized Chevy Camaro while in hot pursuit of the serial killer and, so far, he hasn't demanded any financial compensation. They tend not to talk about the car. It's a little awkward. Especially since, due to financial constraints that include a freelance writer for a wife and twin nine-year-old daughters, Adams has been forced to purchase a used Ford that he's ashamed to be seen with.

Hearing the scene she's about to race to is particularly bad makes Madison wonder whether this will be the case that convinces Adams that Lost Creek isn't for him. She hopes not. She doesn't want a third partner in less than a year. "Understood. Thanks for letting me know, Stella. I'm on my way."

She ends the call and hits the gas, changing direction in the mall's parking lot. Once downtown is behind her, she passes Fantasy World amusement park and reaches the White Woods and the rural tracks that lead to Grave Mountain. She can't imagine this crime scene being worse than some of the others she's attended since getting her job back last year, but the adrenaline kicks in anyway.

She reaches the dirt track out at the Clearview junction and carefully turns into it. It's another mile before she sees stationary flashing lights. Her heart flutters briefly. That moment before she enters a crime scene is the worst. She doesn't know what she's walking into. It could be anything.

Madison has a good imagination but nothing can prepare her for some of the things she's witnessed over the last twelve months. Just when she thinks people can't be any more depraved someone comes along and proves otherwise. It makes relaxing difficult in this job. Downtime is ruined with flashbacks of victims, their crime scenes and their killers.

With the sun lowering, Madison briefly hopes the attending officers have brought scene lighting for when they lose daylight completely.

She peers through the windshield looking for the correct turn. One cruiser is present, parked on a long gravel driveway, alongside Adams's Ford. No one is visible outside. A large steel utility trailer sits to the left of the property, unattached to any vehicle and missing a license plate. It doesn't look old like the house and it has something loaded onto it, protected by a black cover. She pulls in behind the vehicles, on the edge of some lawn, before killing the engine.

What strikes her first is the silence out here. There are no dogs barking. No traffic noise or kids bouncing balls. And although the property is surrounded by trees, the air is utterly still, with no breeze to make them rustle. Madison feels like she's in a vacuum.

She pushes her door open and steps out onto ankle-high grass next to the gravel. A cricket leaps out of her way, and a chorus of chirping erupts from all around her. The stillness ceases as the creatures dart back and forth over the grass, disturbed by her arrival. Slamming the car door shut, she looks up at the house. It looks as though it should've been torn down a long time ago as it's clearly in need of extensive renovation work in order to make it safe.

Could their victims have been homeless, perhaps squatting here out of necessity? Or contractors looking to tear the place down in order to build on the land?

"Detective!" Officer Luis Sanchez appears at the front door. At just twenty-six, Sanchez is currently their youngest officer. He looks up at the sky and takes some deep breaths before running a hand over his black hair.

Madison slips on two pairs of latex gloves. The top pair will be changed whenever she touches something, to avoid spreading DNA around the place. Next, she pulls protective shoe covers on before approaching the porch. The wooden steps creak as she climbs them and she has to dodge some gaps where the wood has rotted away.

Sanchez's expression is grave. Something's rattled him.

"What have we got?" she asks.

He turns to look at the house but struggles to find the words. Eventually he shakes his head and gestures inside. "I don't even know where to start. Sorry, I need a minute." He leaves the porch and heads to his cruiser. Slipping into the driver's side, he leaves the door ajar. "Detective Adams is inside," he says.

Madison suddenly wishes she'd switched her phone off after leaving work. She could be soaking in a hot bathtub with a cold beer right about now.

She steps over the threshold and it takes her eyes a few seconds to adjust to the lower light level inside. The first thing she notices is a smell lingering in the air. Someone has started decomposing in here.

The aroma of death always unsettles her. It's such an unnatural smell. It can't be confused with anything else as it's like nothing else. It's unmistakable, as well as difficult to forget.

Still, it's not overwhelming down here yet, which means the victims must still be relatively fresh. She moves farther into the house and walks through the mostly empty downstairs.

Furniture-wise, the living room contains just a worn leather couch and a coffee table. They're surrounded by boxes, some open, some closed. It suggests someone was either moving in or out when they were disturbed. One box has children's toys poking out: a large plastic ambulance and a small baseball glove.

Madison's heart sinks. There were, or maybe still are, children in here.

In the living room, the weakening sun streams in through the large window that faces the front yard. The kitchen beyond the living room sits in shade and the cabinets and countertops look old and dirty. It's missing the basics: a refrigerator and stove. Perhaps a removal company is set to show up soon with the rest of the furniture.

Madison spots an open loaf of bread near the sink, next to a butter knife. A tub of margarine has been left unsealed. Flies hover around it.

She doesn't hang around downstairs. She can't see any signs of a disturbance here. And no victims. She heads toward the staircase and hears Officer Sanchez on his cell phone or radio outside, but she can't hear what he's saying. Upstairs, someone is moving around.

As she climbs the stairs a fit of menacing laughter erupts.

"Holy crap!" Her hand goes to her chest where she feels her heart racing. Underfoot is a small toy clown. She must've accidentally set it off.

She pushes the toy aside with her foot and a look of contempt.

The closer she gets to the top of the staircase, the stronger the odor, but it's not the worst she's experienced. Another day or two in this heat and it would be unbearable. She's reminded of other victims from other crime scenes, in various states of decay, but she doesn't dwell on the images that flash up. They can be intrusive, arriving while she tries to sleep; or worse, when she's trying to eat. All she can do to stop them is to focus on something else.

She steps onto the landing. "Hello?"

"In here," comes the reply from the bedroom at the far end of the hallway.

Madison approaches the room, pinching her nose closed until she's able to tolerate the smell. A swarm of flies appears to have taken ownership of the room. As well as the live ones buzzing around, clusters of dead flies rest on the floor upside down.

Detective Marcus Adams sighs heavily. His shirt has sweat patches around the armpits and he needs a shave, but he's not unattractive for his age, forty-one. He takes care of his looks by dying his hair black, a little too black if you ask her, and he's a sun worshipper who sports a year-round tan that she suspects he gets from tanning salons over winter because she knows he can't afford exotic vacations, same as her.

"This window was already ajar," he says. "I've tried opening the others on this floor to clear the flies and the smell, but some of them are sealed closed with paint. There's zero breeze outside, so I think we're stuck with the odor."

Madison's gaze is drawn to a wooden-framed queen-sized bed on her left. It takes a minute before she grasps what she's looking at. On the bed are two Caucasian victims. From their bodies she can tell one is male and the other is female. But they don't look right.

A closer inspection reveals that's because the spot where their faces should be is just a bloody pulp. A chill runs through her. "You've got to be kidding me? Someone beat them so bad they're unrecognizable."

After a second she realizes that what looks like white rice covering their open wounds is actually fly eggs. "Oh God."

Madison takes a step back and tries not to heave. With a sense of urgency, she turns to Adams. "Whoever did this is dangerous. We need to secure the scene. I don't want any risk of DNA cross-contamination in this house. Protective suits and gloves should be worn by everyone who enters and for the whole duration they're in here."

"Got it," he says.

Madison turns back to the faceless victims. "I don't know what happened here, but these poor guys didn't stand a chance."

CHAPTER THREE

Footsteps closing in behind Madison make her turn.

"Alex is on his way," says Detective Adams, referring to LCPD's forensic technician. He hands over a protective suit retrieved from the trunk of his vehicle. "And I've told Sanchez to stay outside or suit up. I called the medical examiner's office but they said Dr. Scott's already left work for the day. They're going to try to get ahold of her on her way home." He rubs sweat from his forehead.

Madison knows how he feels. It's warm in here. The bedroom must've been in the full glare of the sun at some point as it's collected heat. The property appears to be without A/C.

"By the way," says Adams, "this isn't the worst of it."

Her stomach flips with dread as she zips a white protective suit closed all the way to her throat. Before she goes to see what else is waiting for her, she wants to be methodical and concentrate on one scene at a time.

She inspects the victim closest to her, on the left-hand side of the bed. The female is spread-eagled on her back, with one leg hanging off the uncovered mattress. It's clear she soiled herself at some point, maybe through fear, or maybe after death.

She's wearing a black T-shirt with black yoga pants and dark blue sneakers. The T-shirt is pulled tight across a generous bust. Her long platinum-blonde hair is matted with blood and tissue.

"She wasn't dressed for bed," says Madison.

The only bedding is a single white sheet pulled over the male but not the female. The pillows are uncovered, suggesting the couple hadn't even had time to make the bed yet. They were taken by surprise.

The mattress appears well used, dipping in the middle and bulging in places, leading her to believe it was left here by the previous owner. The wall behind the headboard, painted a pale blue color, is covered in blood spatter, as is the mattress.

Looking around the room, she says, "Any weapon found?"

"No," says Adams. "Nothing obvious in here."

Adams leans in to the male victim, who is resting on his side, facing away from Madison and the dead woman. His torso is bare. Adams lifts back the sheet, which reveals the only item of clothing the dead guy is wearing is a pair of boxer shorts. "He looks as though he was asleep when attacked."

Madison wonders if the couple came to bed for a nap due to the physical exertion of moving on a hot day, or whether they were forced to lie down before being killed. Whichever scenario is correct, this was a brutal, painful death. "It's odd that their killer didn't use a gun or a knife instead of bludgeoning them."

"I know, right?" says Adams. "No one would've heard a gunshot out here, and even if they did, they would've assumed it was hunters or kids. That tells me this was personal, not a random attack. The killer was obviously angry with them."

She nods, thinking the same. "Also, guns can be traced."

The only furniture in the room is the bed. A small lamp for a nightstand sits on the floor next to it, tipped over and switched off. The man's sneakers are spaced out on the floor, one almost under the wooden bed frame and one on the other side of the room, as if the killer kicked it out of the way or tripped on it as he worked. The male victim's clothes, a pair of blue jeans and a red T-shirt, are thrown haphazardly on top of a closed box in the corner.

"Who called this in?" asks Madison.

"A woman named Dawn Freemantle," says Adams. "She lives farther up the street and saw them moving in yesterday." He pulls his small notebook out and reads from it. "At approximately four o'clock this afternoon, she and her young grandson came by to welcome their new neighbors. She says she found the front door ajar and got no response when calling out; so, thinking they might be out back, she started walking around the side of the house and didn't realize her grandson had run inside and upstairs until she heard him hollering."

He slips the notebook away. "Dawn said the boy couldn't get out of here fast enough. He wouldn't tell her why, and she took her time deciding whether or not to call us about it. Instead, she waited and chose to drive by a couple of times later this afternoon to see if there were any signs of life. When it stayed quiet, she figured something was wrong and finally called it in."

Madison shakes her head. "That poor boy must've seen this."

"Yep. I've told Dawn to expect a visit from one of us at some point." He moves to the door. "Come see the other victim."

Madison follows him to the next bedroom. It's positioned at the front of the house and, with no drapes on the window, the evening light illuminates a small, lifeless body lying on a single mattress on the floor.

The mattress has no sheet, just a white blanket over the body. The young Caucasian boy lies deadly still. With no obvious injuries, his skin is pale and mottled, like his parents'. Flies hover nearby, ready to make their move.

Madison desperately wants to look away. To walk away even. No one should have to see a dead child. But it's her job.

With a tightening sensation in her chest, she forces herself to approach him. He's facing away from her and his shaggy brown hair covers his face. She'd guess from his size that he's around seven or eight. Lifting the thin blanket she sees he's wearing a green T-shirt and white underpants. A pillow sits next to his head, not underneath.

She gently pulls on his shoulder to peer briefly at his face. His eyes are bulging. His lips are blue. But there are no fly eggs evident yet. Probably because his skin is intact.

"Poor kid," she says, gently rolling him back onto his side. "I'm no expert but he looks as though he was struggling for breath. Although, I don't see any marks around his neck."

"He was probably smothered with the pillow," says Adams. "A horrible way to die." He shakes his head. "We're dealing with a monster here, Harper."

She agrees, but she can't let it rattle her. "The killer didn't bludgeon him. This was about the parents."

"Right." Adams nods. "Like I said, this was personal."

Madison looks around the room as she says, "That doesn't mean we should rule out anything else just yet. There's always a possibility this scene has been staged by the killer to make us concentrate on the victims' close circle instead of other possibilities. It could be a home invasion. Perhaps they had money."

Adams scoffs. "Are you kidding me? Look at this place. I'm going to go out on a limb here and say this family wasn't well off."

"Don't be so sure. Some people hoard money, saving it for a rainy day that never comes." Madison looks around the room for anything the killer could've used as a weapon on this boy's parents. She squats to carefully check underneath the mattress. The entire floor is empty. The poor kid didn't even live here long enough to scatter his toys everywhere or lose any socks under his bed. She stands.

"Want me to notify Chief Mendes?" asks Adams.

Madison nods. "She needs to be aware of what's happened here. Once you've done that, have Sanchez set up a boundary around the property because the press will find out eventually. They always do. Then I need you to question the woman who called this in and ask if she noticed any strangers in the neighborhood."

He nods slowly, but doesn't move. He just stares at the little boy, his shoulders slumped. Adams always acts defeated at crime scenes and it drives Madison mad. Of course this scene is shocking, but that should feed his energy. He should want to hunt down the killer as speedily as possible.

Instead, he eventually walks away like a child with a whole bunch of homework to complete.

Once Madison's alone in the room with the boy she looks at his small, lifeless body. He reminds her of Owen at that age. She thinks about how she had no idea where her son was and who he was placed with the entire time she was incarcerated. She would spend hours worrying he could be hurt in a stupid accident, or even killed, and she wouldn't be there for him. She even inquired with the prison warden whether she would be allowed out to attend his funeral should the worst ever happen. Thoughts like that left her in a deep depression for a long time. She felt overwhelming guilt because she couldn't stop anything bad from happening.

The same will be true again once he leaves for college.

Ever since he was accepted into Arizona State University, she hasn't been able to stop thinking about all the things she hasn't had a chance to teach him yet. And not just about household chores and how to pay bills, but about important things like how to trust your gut when it comes to new people in your life. How to help those less fortunate than you when you don't have much yourself. And how to stay alive in a world where there are people who would mercilessly kill this little boy in his sleep after brutally bludgeoning his parents to death.

She blinks hard. She mustn't think about Owen's departure. Not until Saturday, the day he's due to leave. She needs to toughen up this week and focus all her attention on finding the person who killed this small family.

Madison heads to the final bedroom on this floor. It's completely empty apart from a battered wooden closet. The doors are open so she checks inside. Empty, except for some wire clothes hangers. Parts of the room are missing drywall in places. It makes her question why this family bought this house.

She'll need to find out who they bought it from in order to get answers. But more importantly, she needs to identify the victims first.

Voices behind her make her spin around. She has company.

CHAPTER FOUR

Madison leaves the boy's bedroom and watches LCPD's forensic technician climb the stairs. Alex Parker is British and a walking encyclopedia when it comes to all things forensics. He's thirty-four years old but looks younger as he dresses like an emo kid from back in the day, complete with a slim build, black hair and pale skin. He's the most respectful and intelligent person Madison's ever worked with, and his dry sense of humor keeps her going some days.

"A date?" he says, talking to someone behind him. "Who's the lucky person if you don't mind me asking?"

"It was just going to be coffee," comes the reply. "It's the first time we—" Dr. Lena Scott, medical examiner, stops talking when she sees Madison. She looks flustered as she smiles and says, "Hi."

So Lena was on her way to a date when she got the call to come here instead. Madison wonders who she was planning to meet.

"Evening, Detective," says Alex with an end-of-shift weariness. "I had hoped I wouldn't see you again so soon. No offense."

She smiles. "None taken." They both left the station and said their goodbyes just two hours ago.

"Detective Adams said there are three victims, is that right?" asks Lena. Her long brown hair is tied back and, like Alex, she's wearing full protective gear over her clothes.

"Right. One young boy and two adults." Madison leads them to the adults' room first.

Alex approaches the bodies on the bed and raises his eyebrows at the gruesome sight. "Ah." After his initial surprise, he retrieves a camera from the case he's carrying and begins photographing the scene with a professional detachment few others could manage.

Lena moves to the other side of the bed and leans over the male victim for a good look. She seems interested in the eggs covering the victim's face. "None of the eggs have hatched yet," she mutters.

It means nothing to Madison.

"So it's probably less than twenty-four hours since they were laid," says Alex, pausing what he's doing.

Impressed that Alex's knowledge stretches beyond forensics, Lena smiles. "Right. It's likely we'd see maggots by now if these people had been dead any longer than that. And the visible eggs are only the tip of the iceberg. I don't want to think about what's already growing inside these two."

The thought turns Madison's stomach. "What about the bugs flying around?" she asks. "They don't count?"

"They're the ones who're laying the eggs," says Lena. "They can smell these bodies from outside, especially in this heat. If the windows were open, they probably started arriving within minutes of the murders. With this much exposed tissue, they hit the jackpot." She sighs. "I'll have to ask my team to use the heavy-duty body bags to contain the infestation."

Lena pulls the sheet off the male victim and takes hold of his left arm. She tries bending it at the elbow. "Huh." Once lowered back into place, she does the same with his left leg, flexing it at the knee. "Only slight resistance," she mutters.

"What are you doing?" asks Madison.

"Checking body temperature and muscle rigidity. Determining what stage of rigor they're in will help me calculate an approximate time of death." She moves to the other side of the bed and repeats her actions with the female's right arm and leg. They both appear flexible. Lena looks at Madison and says, "Where's the child?"

"Follow me."

In the next room Alex photographs the mattress and the dead child as Lena and Madison remain silent. The medical examiner doesn't have children, but you don't need to be a parent to appreciate how heartbreaking this scene is.

Madison knows she'll have to review Alex's photographs many times over the coming days. It's not a pleasant thought.

"Okay, done with photos," says Alex, putting his camera away. "I'll need to check the victims' bodies for possible trace evidence before your team can take them away, Dr."

"Of course," says Lena. She approaches the child and gently lifts the one accessible arm, before bending it at the elbow. She leans in to his face without touching it in any way. When she's done, she turns to Madison. "I'll be ready to examine all three victims first thing tomorrow. Do you want to be present?"

No, she doesn't. But it's her job. "Yes. I'll bring Adams too. What time do you want us?"

"I can start at eight if that works for you?"

"Sure. Thanks, Lena."

Once the ME has left, Madison leaves Alex to his forensic exam and carries on checking the property. Through the living room window she sees Officer Sanchez outside, briefing another officer who has newly arrived. There doesn't appear to be any media presence yet.

Madison checks her phone in case Owen is wondering why

she never made it home for dinner. No messages or missed calls await her attention. He's used to her getting tied up at work. Still, she wishes she could spend as much time with him as possible this week. Disappointed, she slips her phone into the pocket of her black pants and exits the house through the back door, which is unlocked.

A close look at the door and its lock reveals it wouldn't be difficult to break into the property, even if it was secured. The door is flimsy and the kitchen windows are single paned. None have been broken. This family might have known their killer and willingly let them in. Either that or they left their door open as they unloaded boxes from their vehicle.

The fact the front door was left ajar *after* the victims were killed, according to Dawn Freemantle, suggests the killer left everything unlocked as they fled, having completed their gruesome work.

She stops for a minute. Other than the trailer, there was no vehicle outside. If the killer took it with them, they might be easy to track through the license plates. The thought gives her hope. But they need to figure out the make and type of vehicle they're looking for first.

Madison enters the large, unkempt backyard. It stretches into the woods beyond, with no visible fence or border marking the property's boundary. Like the house, it's been neglected, and is made up of mature trees and overgrown lawn and brush. Sprinkled throughout are dry patches of soil where the intense summer sun has killed off the lawn in places.

She strips out of her protective suit and shoe covers before removing the latex gloves. It feels good to get them off and cool down.

An unexpected noise to her right surprises her.

She turns her head sharply, listening to see if it came from one of the officers out front and echoed through the trees.

When she hears it again, she thinks it's a cough. A weak, pained one.

"What the?" She drops the bundled protective gear onto the ground at her feet.

Another cough. Weaker still. It's definitely coming from the backyard.

Chills run down her arms. It could be another victim.

Before she rushes toward the sound, she hesitates. Because it could be the killer.

CHAPTER FIVE

Madison approaches the location of the coughing and notices shallow scuff marks in the dirt. It looks like someone's either crawled or been dragged out here. She can't understand how this was missed. Adams should have had the entire property searched as soon as he arrived on the scene.

She forces her way through thorny weeds, feeling them scratch her arms through her thin shirt as she goes. "Is anyone there?" she says.

Silence.

She pushes deeper into the brush, on her knees now, and comes across blood smeared along the dirt. It stops her in her tracks and the hairs on the back of her neck stand up.

"This is the police," she says forcefully. She feels for her service weapon in case this is the killer hiding from her. "Are you armed?"

Silence.

"I'm approaching you with my weapon raised. Make yourself known." Madison advances until she sees a foot poking out through the long grass ahead. It's small.

"Oh God." She slips her gun away and rushes forward,

parting the grass. It reveals a small boy, about seven or eight years old. He's wearing pajamas with cartoon dinosaurs on. His top is bloody, mainly around the stomach area. A pool of blood has formed in the dirt around him.

She reaches for his shoulder and gently shakes him. "Hey, sweetie. You're safe now. I'm a police officer. Can you hear me?"

His eyes flicker and he struggles to focus. When he musters the energy, he looks over her shoulder with frightened eyes. After licking his dry lips he whispers, "Where's my mom?"

Madison's heart breaks for him. He wants his mom. She doesn't even consider telling him his mom's gone. That his entire family is gone. "It's okay," she says with false reassurance. "You're going to be fine. I'm going to—"

His eyes roll back in his head.

Madison shakes his shoulders. "Hey, little man. Can you hear me?"

He goes limp and unresponsive.

"Shit." Madison tries to pick him up. He weighs next to nothing and his entire body is floppy in her arms. Her stomach fills with dread as she realizes there's a chance he won't make it.

"Help!" she yells. Crawling out of the brush, she barely registers the thorns that catch her arms and cheeks. The boy's head is protected against her chest. "I need help over here!" she yells.

No one comes. Madison finally manages to stand so she runs around to the front of the house with the boy in her arms. Officer Sanchez appears. He rushes toward her.

"We need an ambulance!" yells Madison desperately.

Sanchez immediately radios for EMS while Madison places the boy on the grass and checks for a pulse. She can't feel one. Officer Shelley Vickers steps in and takes over, checking his airway before starting compressions. She seems completely unfazed that this boy's life is in her hands.

Madison stands on shaky legs and watches Shelley work. She feels helpless.

"An ambulance is coming," says Sanchez.

She nods. Frustration builds in her chest when she considers how negligent Detective Adams was not to check the entire property for more victims when he arrived. "Sanchez? Did you or Adams search the area before I got here?"

"We checked inside." He shifts uncomfortably. "Sorry, Detective. I didn't see or hear anyone out here. I should've thought..."

Madison isn't accusing him of doing anything wrong. Adams was in charge. She orders Sanchez to check the entire property now. "There could be more victims out back."

He immediately disappears behind the house.

Madison crouches down next to Shelley who is still administering CPR. The fact the boy was outside suggests he was attempting to escape the massacre inside. He's deathly pale. His stomach leaks blood with every compression she makes. It's unbearable to watch. Madison can't tell if he's suffered a gunshot wound or something else. There's too much blood. She applies pressure to the wound, trying to keep out of Shelley's way at the same time.

After a while she takes the boy's wrist in her hand to feel for a pulse. There isn't one.

Shelley has sweat dripping down her face. She's panting from the effort. "Where's the damn ambulance? I can't do this forever."

Madison nudges her out of the way and takes over. "Take a breather."

The boy's chest feels impossibly small and delicate. Each compression leaves her feeling as though she's hurting him and doing more damage, but she has to keep trying. She can't let him die.

After what feels like an impossibly long time, they hear sirens wailing. Madison's arm muscles scream for her to stop.

Shelley gently clutches the boy's hand, her spare hand at his throat feeling for a pulse.

Madison hesitates as she hears the ambulance pulling up behind them. She looks at Shelley, who shakes her head. "He's gone."

Madison's shoulders sink. She moves over to make room for Jake Rubio, the first EMT out of the ambulance.

"How long have you been performing CPR?" he asks.

"Approximately four minutes, I think," says Shelley.

Jake's co-worker, Rita, joins them and immediately shoves a plastic device down the boy's throat to open his airway. Jake listens to his chest before restarting compressions. Madison notices Alex has taken a break from his forensic work upstairs to come and watch from the porch. He has his fingers crossed as he watches intently.

Time stands still and it seems as if even the crickets stop chirping as everyone waits with bated breath for Jake to work his magic.

When he slowly withdraws his hands and leans back on his feet with an air of defeat, no one asks any questions.

"Sorry," he says. "It's too late. He's gone."

CHAPTER SIX

Madison sits on the top step of the porch watching the sun set behind the mountains. Ignoring the trembling in her hand, she sucks deep on a cigarette while the ambulances drive away empty. Her hands, face and clothes have the little boy's blood on them to varying degrees. It's not drying because of how sweaty she is. She can't even bring herself to go and wash her hands in the house just yet. Her body won't move. It just wants her to sit here and process what happened.

The dead boy has been gently placed in the back of a vehicle from the medical examiner's office, awaiting the rest of his family.

The sound of a car engine makes her look up. A Chevy Traverse turns into the property and Madison watches as her friend Nate Monroe parks before getting out with his German shepherd-husky mix. Brody is a former cadaver dog who's useful not just for searches, but also as a companion to his beleaguered owner. Madison called Nate in the hope that Brody might be able to help the officers locate any other potential victims on or near the property, whether dead or alive.

Nate smiles as he approaches. Now dark out, the porch

light highlights his sun-kissed, light-brown hair. He's dressed casually in smart jeans and a dark blue T-shirt, and she can tell from the stubble on his jaw that he hasn't shaved today, maybe not yesterday either. He's only forty, but he has some specks of gray in his stubble and his hair. It's not surprising, he's had a stressful life.

Nate's one of Madison's closest friends but this is the first time she's seen him in a month. So much has happened since they met last year, after their traumatic pasts helped them to bond quickly. Because Nate was also wrongly convicted of murder. But he was on death row. Now he works as an investigator for a local lawyer, trying to help other people avoid wrongful convictions.

Madison has kept him at arm's length for a while because last Christmas she went through a traumatic time that no one could help her with. She lost her estranged father in devastating circumstances. Her only remaining family member, other than her son, is a sister who's currently incarcerated for various crimes. Now that Madison's lost both her parents, and her son is leaving for college soon, she feels lonelier than ever.

When Nate's close enough, he notices the blood on her shirt and the shallow scratches on her face and arms. His expression changes to concern. "What happened? Are you okay?"

She nods before standing. "Four people were found dead here today. Murdered. One of them, a young boy, had managed to get out of the house to hide. We didn't find him right away and because of that he didn't make it. I want Brody to see if he can find anyone else who might have escaped, because I'm not sure what we're dealing with yet."

Nate's eyes reveal he has plenty of questions, but he holds off for now. Brody has wandered over to sniff the blood on Madison's clothes. He's a large dog, with brown and cream-colored fur. He has intelligent brown eyes and he always knows when you're talking about him. Once he's finished sniffing her, he sits in front of his owner, alert and ready for instructions.

"Come on, boy," says Nate. "Let's see what we can find."

Nate leads him to the side of the house where portable lighting has been set up in the dark. The dog begins sniffing the ground and ducking under bushes. With no pattern to his work, he zigzags through the long grass and goes wherever he thinks he might smell someone.

Madison and Nate follow him at a distance.

"It's been a while," says Nate, stealing a glance at her. "How have you been?"

It's a difficult question to answer, so she says, "Fine. You?"

He sighs. "I guess. I still have good days and bad."

She drops her cigarette butt and stamps on it before picking it up and absently slipping it into her shirt pocket. She needs to quit again. "But more good days, right?"

He nods slowly, as though he doesn't want to talk about it.

The trial of the person who was responsible for putting him in prison is coming up in a couple of weeks. Father Jack Connor killed a twenty-year-old woman, Nate's fiancée, back in 2000. Nate was framed for the murder and sent to death row in Texas, where he served seventeen years. He was due to be executed in a matter of months before new evidence was found that proved he wasn't a killer. He was released three years ago, but it wasn't until he and Madison teamed up last year that they were able to finally catch Father Connor and have him arrested by the FBI.

The priest is an old man now. His trial is due to be held in Texas. Nate vowed never to return to Texas in case he's ever arrested and returned to death row. Even though it sounds unlikely, his paranoia is understandable. But the prosecution needs both him and Madison to testify. Madison has already agreed to attend because she wants the killer to spend the rest of his years behind bars, not just for his crimes, but for what he's done to Nate.

She doesn't know whether Nate can bring himself to attend the trial. The priest has an emotional hold over him that her friend can't seem to free himself from.

Madison's suddenly ashamed for isolating herself from him these past months. He's probably the only person in town she can fully trust, and he needs her right now. But she has a lot going on too, and her feelings for Nate are confused. They shared a kiss last Christmas. They could've shared more but his past got in the way, so she cooled things. And now they're in a weird space and neither of them is brave enough to mention it.

After a long search of the entire backyard and even part of the woods beyond, Brody hasn't located anyone else. He wanders off to sit in a dirt patch, where the hot summer sunshine has taken its toll on the lawn. He stares at the ground before lying down.

Madison walks over and checks the area. She can't see any blood or scuff marks, and it's far away from where the boy was hiding. She ruffles Brody's fur. "You tired, boy?" It's been a hot day and Nate has previously told her how a search can take it out of the dog.

She glances at Nate. He's distracted, checking his phone.

She hears movement from inside. Alex must have finished his forensic examination of the house. Nate follows her to the front of the property. The sun has fully set now and the house is illuminated from within, providing limited lighting out front. Madison switches her car's headlights on just as assistants from the medical examiner's office bring out the three other victims one by one. They're all bagged, sparing Nate a disturbing sight.

"Any clue who might've done this?" he asks.

"It's too early to tell." With the final body loaded into the vehicle, she says, "I think that's the whole family wiped out." Frustrated, she shakes her head. "We were so close to saving the little boy. If we'd just found him twenty, maybe thirty minutes earlier... If the ambulance had already been here when I found him..."

Nate rubs her back. "Don't do that to yourself. He could've still passed away."

He's right. The boy had obviously lost a lot of blood. But if he'd gotten to the hospital fast enough, there was at least a chance of a miracle, no matter how slim.

Once the victims are driven away, headlights approach. Detective Adams has returned from interviewing the woman who called this in. He gets out of his car and nods at Madison before holding out a hand to Nate to introduce himself. They've never officially met and Adams is so self-involved that Madison would bet he's never even heard of Nate or his history. "Marcus Adams. I'm Harper's partner," he says.

Madison scoffs. *Some partner.*

Nate shakes his hand. "Nate Monroe. Pleasure."

"You married, Nate?" asks Adams. "Kids?"

"No. It's just me and Brody." Brody sniffs Adams's shoes like he might urinate on them.

"Think yourself lucky," says Adams. "I've got a wife and two girls. The twins are nine going on nineteen." He laughs as if he's made a hilarious comment.

Madison rolls her eyes. He's pissing her off.

Adams notices. "What's the matter with you?" He looks at the blood on her shirt and face. "Did you help move the bodies or something?"

Her face flushes in anger. He has no idea what she and Shelley had to do. "No. This is a result of trying to save the life of the *fourth* victim. The one who was left dying in the back-yard because you were too sloppy to search anywhere but inside the house."

His face freezes. Looking mortified, it takes him a second to speak. "You're kidding, right?"

"I wish I were. He was young, with a stomach wound. He'd

made it all the way outside in a bid to—" Her voice catches and she turns away from both of them.

"Shit," says Adams. He runs a hand over his thick hair as he takes it in. "I'm sorry. I just assumed the officers would search the area. I mean, do we have to tell them everything?"

She turns back to look at him. "*You* were in charge. *You're* responsible for assigning duties. You should know that."

He wipes sweat from his brow. "It won't happen again."

"Somehow," says Madison, "I don't think that's going to help the little boy now, do you?"

"Alright, alright. I get it." He takes a deep breath. "I guess at least now he won't have to live with the fact his whole family died."

Disgusted by the comment, Nate walks away. He lets Brody into the back of his car. Just before leaving he looks over at Madison. "We should catch up properly. Let me know if you want to grab dinner soon."

Madison nods, but she can't think about that right now. She's trying to contain her anger at her partner. She's trying not to think of the little boy's final words.

Once Nate's reversed off the property, she heads to her car. Before getting in she says to Adams, "You're on duty, so I'm going home to get a few hours' sleep. Cancel any plans you have for the weeks ahead because this case is going to occupy all our time. And tomorrow morning we're meeting Lena at the morgue first thing. I expect to see you there no later than eight."

She doesn't wait for a response. She slips into her car and backs out of the driveway, relieved she gets to leave this horrific crime scene and spend some time with her son.

CHAPTER SEVEN

Madison arrives home to a dark, empty house. After dropping her car keys on the sideboard by the door she turns and trips over Owen's backpack, which has been carelessly discarded at the bottom of the stairs. She almost headbutts the wall before catching herself. "Dammit!" she mutters. "How many times have I told him not to dump that there?"

She switches a light on before removing her holster. Her reflection in the hallway mirror shows blood smeared across her cheek. It's even found its way into the hairline of her shoulder-length blonde hair. It's sad to think where this came from, but she knows she can't focus on the little boy, not if she has any hope of getting some sleep tonight. There will be time for that tomorrow when she visits him in the morgue.

The mirror is unforgiving. Her skin is greasy from the day's heat, with only the remnants of today's makeup visible. Nate must have thought she looked a mess. Not that it matters. She heads upstairs to shower and change. The hot water is comforting against her skin, and she has a few minutes' reprieve from the horrors of the day while she thinks of nothing but the heat soothing her back muscles. She doesn't bother blow-drying her hair before returning downstairs to check the contents of the refrigerator.

Lasagna ingredients stare back at her. She was going to cook for Owen and had expected him to be home before her, but truth be told her appetite isn't what it should be after witnessing the condition of the victims. She retrieves her cell phone and calls her son.

Owen answers on the third ring. "Hey, Mom." He sounds upbeat, like he's enjoying himself. But Owen's always been a positive kid and can make her feel better about any situation.

"Hey," she says with a smile. "Where are you? I was planning on making us some dinner before I got called back to work. I can still make it now if you're on your way home?"

"Sorry, I can't," he says. "Richie's keeping me busy."

Richie Hope is the lawyer Nate works for at Hope & Associates. In reality Hope & Associates consists of just Richie, as the only attorney; Nate and a guy called Frank Brookes, who work as investigators; Janine Blake, who runs the office; and Owen, who works as an intern. He's given all the jobs no one else wants: filing, running to the court house with important documents and keeping the office kitchen stocked with coffee and snacks for Richie. He accepted the job for work experience as he's planning on becoming a lawyer.

"What time do you think you'll be home?" she asks.

She hears Owen ask Richie how much longer he needs him, but she doesn't hear Richie's response. Owen comes back on the line. "About another hour or two. You may as well eat without me."

Madison hides her disappointment. Maybe him leaving home isn't as big a deal for Owen as it is for her. Maybe he still resents her for spending six years in prison and leaving him motherless. Or maybe she's overthinking it, as usual. She considers telling him about the crime scene she just left and what a difficult day it's been, but decides against it. She doesn't want to burden him.

"Okay. Hey, do you need any help? I could bring takeout."

"No, that's okay. Richie's ordered pizza. Sorry, Mom, I have to go. You'll probably be asleep when I get in, so I'll see you tomorrow."

"Sure. Bye." Disappointed, she slips her phone into the pocket of her sweatpants and looks around the kitchen. She notices Bandit, Owen's young cat, asleep on top of the clean pile of laundry that's sitting on the dining table, waiting to be put away. Without getting up he stretches out one paw and yawns. Then he meows at her.

"Hey, cutie," she says, going to him. He lets her stroke his silky white fur for a while and then stands, stretching his back. Once limber, he jumps off the laundry and heads to his food bowl. Madison laughs. "Dinner time again, huh? I swear you eat more than Brody does and he's gotta be ten times your size."

Bandit meows as if to confirm it, and Madison pours half a can of cat food into his bowl. The cat purrs as he eats. As soon as he's finished, he exits the house through the cat flap in the back door. Everyone has somewhere to be except her. She considers cooking, but she doesn't want to stay home alone. Plus she wants to avoid the dirty dishes in the sink, not to mention the stack of laundry now covered in Bandit's fur.

She heads to the hallway and grabs her car keys.

It's a short drive to Ruby's Diner and despite it being past nine o'clock the parking lot is full. She carefully squeezes between two trucks in her shiny new black Dodge Challenger Demon. It was a Christmas present from Nate. He spoiled her when her crappy old Honda finally died and she couldn't afford to replace it.

She'd felt guilty accepting it but he was adamant he needed something to spend his money on and wouldn't take no for an answer. She knows he can afford it thanks to his huge wrongful conviction payout from his time on death row.

Before getting out she quickly checks her reflection in the rearview mirror. She hadn't reapplied makeup after her shower and her hair is still damp in places, but it'll have to do. She doesn't intend to be here long.

Inside the diner she's greeted by Vince Rader, the owner. He's a good friend to both her and Nate, ever since they helped him locate his missing wife and grandson. "Evening, Madison. Good to see you." He appears a little on edge, his eyes looking everywhere but at her. "You want the special?" he asks, leading her to the far end of the counter.

"Depends," she says. "What's the special?"

"Our ultimate turkey sandwich with fries and slaw. You'll love it. I'll have it made to go. You just wait here." He disappears into the kitchen before Madison can tell him she wants to eat in. He seems to want to get rid of her.

With a frustrated sigh, Madison takes a seat next to a local man named Jim, whose eyes are fixed on the TV above the counter. She doesn't know him well but he has his favorite seat at the counter and always seems to be here after dinner. Probably for the company, like a lot of them. She doesn't think he's married as he wears no wedding ring.

He glances at her. "Evening, Detective." He's nursing a coffee. "How're you doing?"

She sighs. "Well, I could lie and say fine but it's been one of those days. You know what I mean?"

He smiles wearily. "After fifty-one years on this planet, I know exactly what you mean."

Madison recognizes the young woman seated on the other side of him. She's the relatively new girlfriend of Alex Parker, her forensic technician. Madison's only met her once, at someone's birthday drinks, but she was pleasant enough. She seemed perfect for Alex, intelligent but shy, and also a little geeky. She was hanging off of Alex's every word at the time. With dyed red hair and a perfect, pale complexion, she's certainly pretty.

Madison desperately tries to remember her name as the woman stops messaging madly on her phone and glances over at her.

"Evening," says Madison. Finally, her name comes to her. "How are you tonight, Samantha?"

"Please, call me Sam." She smiles. "I'm good. You?"

"Not bad."

"Is Alex still at work?"

Madison nods. "It's going to be a late one, I think."

"That's okay. I'll probably see him tomorrow." Being a social worker, Sam will know how it is. Her job requires long and unpredictable hours too. Madison's had a bad experience with social workers, but she doesn't let that ruin her opinion of Alex's girlfriend.

Sam finishes her soda then gets up and leaves with a goodbye. Once she's gone, Madison glances at the TV. It's switched to the local news channel, as always. They don't mention today's homicides, which means they haven't heard about them yet. It's just a matter of time before someone blabs to the press though. Her money's on the grandmother who called it in.

She looks around the diner, which is crowded. The waitresses are busy coming and going from the kitchen and the usual mix of locals are here, all avoiding cooking, like her. At the far end of the room she spots Lena, the medical examiner, sitting at a booth. Her back is to Madison, but her long brown hair is unmistakable as it's always impeccably blow-dried, to go with the full face of perfectly applied makeup Lena wears. Not that she needs it with her flawless skin. Some women just get lucky in that respect. Madison's not one of them.

She discreetly leans back on her stool, using Jim's back as

cover, to get a view of who Lena's with. Her eyebrows rise in surprise as she sees Nate sitting opposite her. He's smiling as he attentively listens to his coffee companion.

So this is who Lena was meeting for a date. Madison quickly leans forward, out of view. She rests her elbows on the counter and considers how she feels about it. They certainly make a good-looking couple. And it's time Nate moved on with his life. He shouldn't be alone anymore. But she would prefer not to have to bump into them around town if they're going to be a couple. It would be weird. Besides, she's a little jealous, even though she has no right to be. She can't help it. *She's* the one who brought Nate to Lost Creek. *She's* the one who's been helping him through his trauma. He's *her* friend.

She shakes the thought away. It's ridiculous. This isn't high school. And besides, she had her chance.

After he fixes his cowboy hat in place, Jim gets up. "Have a good evening."

Once he disappears, it leaves Madison visible. She cringes, suddenly wishing she'd stayed home, or at least thrown on something nicer than sweatpants after her shower.

It takes just seconds for Nate to notice her. "Madison!" he shouts.

She fixes a smile on her face and turns. Nate waves, so she waves back. Then he motions for her to approach them. Lena doesn't turn and Madison can imagine she feels a little awkward too.

"Hey," she says as she reluctantly approaches their table. She notices Brody on the floor at their feet, hidden under the booth. His tail wags slowly when he recognizes her. Not normally allowed in here, for obvious reasons, he's keeping a low profile and waiting for scraps. Madison spots the red bandanna around his neck. She's never seen him wear something like that before. It looks odd on a former police dog.

With a playful smile she raises her eyebrows at Nate.

"What on earth is Brody wearing?" she says. "He looks embarrassed in that thing. You realize all the other police dogs will mock him for that, right?"

Nate awkwardly clears his throat as Lena looks up at her. "I got it for him," she says. "I think he looks cute."

Madison realizes she's put her foot in her mouth. She laughs nervously. "He looks great actually. I was just teasing because I thought Nate bought it. Sorry."

Lena silently looks away and sips her coffee while Nate says a little too brightly, "Are you eating in?"

"No, I've ordered takeout. I couldn't be bothered to cook for one and it's been a long day. I just want to load up on carbs then pass out in bed." She anxiously glances at the counter. Thankfully Vince has reappeared and he's holding a bag of something. "Looks like my order's ready. You two have a good evening."

Nate nods and she can see in his eyes that he knows exactly how awkward she's feeling. He probably wishes he hadn't called her over.

To show Lena she's okay with the situation, Madison says to her, "I'll see you bright and early at the morgue. Don't stay out too late on a work night!"

She turns and cringes as she approaches Vince at the counter. Grabbing her food with one hand, she's thankful now that she didn't get a chance to order in.

"Sorry," whispers Vince. "I should've given you the heads-up. I panicked when you arrived." He glances at the couple. "I don't know what Nate thinks he's playing at. I can have a word with him if you like? Help him see that he's messing with fate."

She smiles, touched at Vince's emotional investment in their happiness. "It's fine, honest. Nate's a single guy, he can date whoever he wants."

Vince rolls his eyes. "You pair are going to be the death of me."

She laughs. "And each other, probably. Have a good evening."

Once she's safe in her car, Madison leans her forehead against the steering wheel and lets out a long sigh. "Well, that was awkward."

After a few seconds, she starts her car and heads home.

CHAPTER EIGHT

Nate discreetly slips Brody a couple of dog biscuits while listening to Lena chat about her day. His attention wanes now that he's seen Madison. She hadn't seemed bothered that he was here with Lena. He can't pretend he's not disappointed, and it's to be expected after the massive step back she's taken from him lately, but he misses being around her. Normally they end up working on the same case in some way. Nowadays he spends more time working with her son.

He realizes that, until today, Madison's stopped consulting him on her cases. She doesn't ask for his input anymore. He knows she's been struggling after the loss of her father, but now it feels like she doesn't need him anymore. Part of him is happy for her because it means she's stronger than she was when she first begged him to hire her as a private investigator, back in California, last year. The other part of him is disappointed, because he thought they made a good team, and he's developed strong feelings for her, despite never expecting to fall in love again after what happened to his fiancée twenty years ago.

His phone pings with a message from his boss, Richie Hope.

I know it's late but we're missing some documents. Did you take the Everett file home by mistake?

Nate thinks it could be in his car. He sends a quick reply.

Be right there.

"Is there a problem?" asks Lena, finishing her coffee.

"Sorry," he says. "My boss needs something." He holds up the text for her to read so she doesn't think it's a lame attempt to get away from her. "I need to drop by the office."

"Sure." Unfazed, Lena stands and picks up her purse. "I should probably get home anyway. Coffee's on me. After all, I invited you."

Nate smiles as he stands. "Thanks. And thanks for Brody's bandanna. I don't know how long it'll last as he has his own fashion sense, but he looks good in it."

They head for the exit and Nate sees Vince trying to get his attention. He pretends not to notice because he doesn't want a lecture about having coffee with anyone but Madison. Outside, he and Lena say their goodbyes from a distance and Nate lets Brody into the back of his car. He finds the missing client file tucked in the pocket behind the front passenger seat and makes his way to Richie's office.

When he and Brody enter the three-story brick building—formerly the town's jail back in the eighteen hundreds, according to Richie—the ancient ceiling fans are whirring overhead, spreading the tantalizing aroma of pepperoni pizza. Owen and Richie are in the front office working at the large oak reception desk. An empty pizza box tells Nate he's just missed supper.

"I can order another if you're hungry?" says Richie, spotting him eyeing the box. The white-haired attorney is surprisingly slim considering his love of takeout.

"That's okay. I'm good." He hands the file over. "Sorry about that. I don't normally remove them from the office, but I wanted to check something and must've taken it with me when I left yesterday."

"No harm done," says Richie. "Getting sued for breaking data protection laws is the least of my worries." He winks. Richie isn't always the most law-abiding person when it comes to the business side of running an office. His office manager, Janine, has tried to turn that around but it's a slow process.

Nate looks at Owen, who's leaning against the front desk, munching on a final slice of pizza while reading a document. Owen's tall with an athletic build that comes with youth. With his blond hair and blue eyes he looks more like Madison than his late father. He has an infuriating habit of constantly flicking his hair out of his eyes. It would drive Nate mad and he can't understand why he doesn't just get it cut. "How come you're not home yet?"

Owen looks up. "Richie offered double pay to stay late. Thought I'd make some extra money for college."

Even though Nate's paying Owen's tuition fees in return for good grades, the kid's still working hard while building himself a nice stash of cash for emergencies. Nate may not be the boy's father, but he's proud of him nonetheless. He has a good head on his shoulders and has overcome a lot. He just hopes Owen's smart enough to know he should spend some time with Madison this week.

"I saw your mom in the diner earlier. Looked like she'd had a tough day. She lost a young boy, despite her best attempts at CPR." He leaves Owen to catch his meaning.

Owen immediately nods. "I guess I should head home. It's getting late."

Richie closes the pizza box. "Oh shoot. I've been an idiot, haven't I?"

"What do you mean?" asks Owen.

"This is your last week at home." Richie slaps his forehead with the palm of his hand. "You should be spending it with your poor mother, not with me."

Owen looks away. "That's okay. She won't mind."

"Really?" says Nate gently. "Owen, she's devastated about losing you again. She's just good at hiding it."

The boy surprises him by turning his back on them. "It's not easy for me either you know. I'd rather not deal with it until Saturday."

Nate and Richie share a look.

Nate steps forward. "I know it's tough now, but once you're at college you'll have plenty of things to distract you. Lost Creek will become a distant memory. You just have to promise to come home and visit regularly." He smiles. "Otherwise I'll cut you off financially."

Owen snorts before grabbing his coat. "I'm beginning to wonder if it's worth letting you pay for college what with all these new conditions you keep adding."

Richie stands up. "Oh trust me, son, it's worth it. Once you see the costs involved, you'll soon realize that." He looks at Nate. "I heard whispers there's been a homicide nearby. Was the child Madison lost one of the victims?"

"Right. There were four altogether. The killer's escaped but knowing Madison, probably not for long. Which means you could have a new client in the next few days."

Nate offers Owen a ride home and they say their goodbyes to Richie.

In the car, Owen isn't his normal chatty self. He leans his head against the rest and remains silent for most of the drive.

When he's closer to home he says, "Maybe Richie would let me work for him full-time and I could go to an online college instead. I could study in the evenings while getting experience on the job. That way I wouldn't have to leave home."

Nate glances at him. "No, Owen. You worked hard for your place at college. You need to spend the majority of your time studying if you want to be a lawyer. This is your time to shine. You can't seriously want to stay in this deadbeat town working for Richie? He's a one-man outfit who barely makes enough to pay us. You could be working for any law firm in the country once you've graduated!"

Owen nods silently. They reach Madison's house and before he gets out Owen says, "It just seems so cruel, you know? To leave Mom all alone again."

Nate doesn't reply. Because soon she will be all alone. Her father's gone. Owen's leaving on Saturday, and she doesn't know it yet but Nate's leaving Lost Creek for good in a couple of weeks. His few personal belongings are packed up. He hasn't told anyone. He just knows he can't stay here anymore. There's no place for him.

With Madison pushing him away, and Owen moving on with his life, it's time Nate did the same.

He just doesn't know how to tell either of them, so he's planning to wait until Owen's settled at college.

"She'll get over it eventually," says Nate. "And it'll be easier once she sees you happy and doing well in Arizona."

Owen nods. "I guess. See you tomorrow."

Brody whines in the back seat as Owen slips out of the car.

Nate waits until he's safely inside the house. There was a time he and Brody would follow him in. But not anymore. Things have changed. Which confirms it's time Nate found somewhere else to start fresh. Someplace where no one knows his past, and wouldn't care if they did. He glances at Madison's bedroom window. The light is on.

He hits the gas and slowly drives away.

CHAPTER NINE

Madison fights the familiar urge for a cigarette as she waits outside the medical examiner's office for Detective Adams to arrive. She picked up the habit in prison and had successfully quit last year before again finding solace in nicotine after everything that went down with the Snow Storm Killer. She's determined to quit again, so as the early morning sun warms her face, she focuses on the mint-flavored candy in her mouth.

As it's just after eight o'clock, Adams should arrive any minute. Not one to be early for anything, he usually arrives at least ten minutes late. She usually gives him a pass as he has children to get ready for school, but school's out for summer. He should be here by now.

Her phone rings. Officer Shelley Vickers's name appears on-screen.

"Hey," says Madison. "How are you?"

"Not great," says Shelley. "I couldn't sleep thinking about that poor kid we lost. In the end, I called Jake. He came over and managed to convince me the boy probably would've succumbed to his injuries no matter how soon we found him after arrival."

That's a relief to Madison, but losing the boy still stings. "Are you and Jake dating?"

Shelley laughs nervously. "It's early days. I know I shouldn't go there again..." She trails off.

Jake Rubio is around thirty, two years younger than Shelley, and he has a reputation for sleeping around. Maybe he's calmed down now, but Madison's surprised Shelley is giving him another chance.

"I can't seem to resist the guy no matter how hard I try," says Shelley, feeling the need to explain.

"To tell you the truth I wanted to see you with Alex," says Madison. The forensic technician has had the hots for Shelley ever since he joined the department.

"I know you did, but it wasn't meant to be. In fact, Jake and I are going on a double date with Alex and Sam."

"Seriously?" says Madison, surprised. "Won't that be awkward?"

"No, it'll be fine. I like Sam. She's more suited to him than I am. I have to confess I don't know what he's talking about half the time." Shelley laughs. "We have *very* different interests."

Madison always suspected Shelley wasn't physically attracted to Alex. He's not exactly sporty, whereas Jake is a former high school football star and still spends a lot of time at the gym.

"By the way," says Shelley, "reporters have started showing up at the crime scene. It's just a matter of time before word spreads."

A minivan pulls into the medical examiner's parking lot and Madison watches as it stops near her. A woman is driving. She spots Adams in the passenger seat. "I expected nothing less. Listen, I have to go, Adams is here. I'll see you later, okay?"

"Sure."

Madison slips her phone away. She notices his twin daughters in the back seat. They look nothing like Adams. Instead of dark hair they're blonde with matching braids. Although one of the girls has pulled one hairband out so half her hair is in her face.

Adams's wife lowers the driver's window. "Madison? I'm Selena. Nice to finally meet the other woman in my husband's life."

She's an attractive brunette with mesmerizing green eyes. Madison wonders what this woman sees in someone like him, then feels bad for the thought. He's not *that* bad.

Madison steps forward and smiles. "Nice to meet you." She's actually spotted Selena around town a couple of times from afar but they've never been formally introduced. Madison peers into the back of the car at the girls. "And who are these two cuties?"

One girl giggles and waves enthusiastically. The other—the one with only one braid intact—shoots daggers with her eyes. It makes Madison laugh because she looks pissed off. She kind of hopes the girl gives Adams hell at home.

Adams gets out and approaches her. He doesn't say goodbye to his family, instead he heads straight for the beige office building. Perhaps he doesn't want Madison getting friendly with his wife. "Ready to go inside?" he says.

"Sure," she says. "Nice to meet you all."

"You should come for dinner sometime," says Selena. "I'd love to know what Marcus is like to work with." She says it with a glint in her eye, as if she's trying to affectionately embarrass him.

"Oh God," says Adams. "That's all I need, another female in my house when I get home from work."

Madison snorts, enjoying seeing him squirm.

Selena drives away with a smile on her face.

Catching up to him, Madison asks, "How come you needed a ride? You didn't trash your new car, did you?"

"Of course not." He gives her a sideways glance. "But *I* didn't trash my old one either, remember?"

She cringes inside but remains silent. There's an awkward few seconds as they pass her Dodge Demon, with Adams looking at it longingly. She wonders if he's noticed the black and ruby red leather interior, then feels guilty for wanting him to.

He sighs as he reaches for the door to the building. "It's in the shop this morning. Needs new brake pads. Now are we going in or not?" He's grumpy today.

Madison follows him inside.

The male stationed at the reception desk tells them Dr. Scott will be right with them.

Taking a seat, Madison wonders how Lena's date with Nate went, not that she has any intention of asking her. In fact Vince Rader texted her soon after she left the diner to inform her that Nate and Lena didn't stay long. Apparently, they left in separate cars and headed in different directions. It amused her to think Vince is so invested in her and Nate's relationship that he's running covert surveillance.

"Update me on the case," she says to Adams. "Did you find the victims' cell phones and wallets after I left the scene?"

"No, nothing. Sanchez and Williams were there all night searching for something that would help us identify the victims, but they hadn't found anything by the time I left at midnight."

Lena appears from a door on the right. She's wearing scrubs under a surgical gown and appears bright and alert. Madison wants to know her secret to never looking tired.

"Morning, guys," says Lena. "Follow me."

Detective Adams takes a deep breath, as if readying himself for seeing the victims again. He's not good with morgue visits. Few people are.

They enter the cool room. Lena has several assistants, and two of them are busying themselves with bringing out the bodies from the large storage refrigerator and preparing the tools required for autopsy. The usual aroma lingers in the air. A mixture of formaldehyde, decomposition and berries—from Lena's favorite air freshener.

The doctor slips an apron over her head as Madison and Adams mask up. "I won't make you watch the full autopsies as you could be here all day, but if I start with my preliminary external impressions and then send you a full report once I'm done, does that sound okay?"

"That would be great," says Madison.

"I guess you want me to focus on helping you identify the victims first and foremost?"

"Right," says Adams. "We don't yet know whether the family was local to the area. The state of the property suggested they'd just moved in right before they were killed."

Lena pulls on some latex gloves before covering her mouth and nose with a surgical mask. "Okay. Let's get started."

Adams nods. He's looking a little pale and Madison notices him shiver. It happens in here, since the temperature is deliberately kept low. The longer you're here, the more you feel it. He's wearing a shirt with no jacket, but Madison has come prepared with a thin sweater over her top.

Approaching one of the covered cadavers, Lena pulls the sheet back. The adult male victim is naked now. He has an athletic build, and is around five foot nine. Thick black hair covers his tanned body, with some grays evident on his chest. A lack of defensive wounds suggests he didn't see his killer coming.

Adams grimaces as what's left of the victim's face is revealed. "Gross." He covers his nose with his hand. Despite the low temperature, the bodies are still emitting certain odors.

"My team managed to suction off a lot of the bugs and eggs from their faces," says Lena. "And they attempted to kill what they could with bug spray, but don't be surprised if you see a few maggots squeeze out from somewhere. They're hardy creatures."

Madison exchanges a look with Adams.

"Okay," she continues. "Our victim is approximately thirty-eight to forty-two years old. As you can see, he has severe damage to his skull, neck and face, rendering him visually unidentifiable. I believe this was done with some type of heavy object such as a sledgehammer, given the amount of blunt-force trauma involved."

Madison turns to her partner. "Any sledgehammers at the house?"

"Not that I'm aware of. Let me shoot a message to the uniforms at the scene." He pulls his phone out. "They might be able to find something."

Madison leans in for a closer look at the victim.

Broken shards of skull fragments are visible in several places but his eyes and sockets are no longer distinguishable. The force of the sledgehammer has pulverized them. He still has a few teeth in place, but most of his jaw is crushed. He has a full head of black hair, and some of it is matted with his skin and what's left of his brain matter.

With some effort Lena rolls the body toward her, revealing blotchy red discoloration under the skin on the side he was found resting on.

Madison knows from experience they're looking at lividity in play. The victim's blood has settled after death. "Does that"—she points to it—"mean he died while on that side, suggesting he wasn't moved to the bed after death?"

"Right," says Lena. "The blood spatter at the scene looked consistent with that too, but Alex will confirm for sure."

"He must've been attacked while sleeping," says Adams. "He probably didn't even hear the killer coming."

Madison nods. "That's something at least."

"Okay," says Lena. "Let's have a look at the female. Hopefully we'll have more luck with her and she'll still have some identifying features left."

They move to the next table. When Lena removes the sheet, Madison can't stop her eyes from going to the woman's breasts. They're large, but also unusually rounded and pert, even though the woman is flat on her back.

"Implants?" she asks.

"I think so," says Lena. "I'll find out during the internal exam, but there are some telltale scars under her breasts here." She points to thin lines that appear paler than the rest of the skin.

The woman is slim and tanned like her partner, but with more moles. They cover her arms and torso. She might have been a sun worshipper. She's about five foot four. The skin around her abdomen is crepey, a telltale sign of pregnancy from having her sons. A prominent scar sits just below her bikini line. Madison knows from seeing this on other bodies that it's from a cesarean section.

Her eyes wander to the victim's hands. She hadn't noticed before but a platinum wedding band is still in place. She turns back to the male and checks his hand.

"What is it?" asks Lena.

"She's wearing a wedding ring but he's not. Can you tell if he did wear one but maybe took it off when he went to bed?"

Lena picks up his hand and looks closely at the skin. "It doesn't look like it. No indentation and no band of white skin. He's pretty tanned. If he wore a wedding ring, it would be obvious where it used to be when removed." She takes the woman's ring off and, sure enough, a white band of skin is evident where it's been protected from sun damage.

"Huh," says Madison. "Maybe they're not a couple."

"Or maybe she was cheating on her husband," says Adams. "A good motive for murder."

"Right. Unless our guy here is just one of those men who

refuses to wear a wedding band." Madison knows a few of them. She can't resist a sneaky glance at Adams's hand. His wedding ring is firmly in place.

Lena takes a closer look at where the woman's face should be.

Madison winces. There is nothing left of this woman's features except her forehead and lower jaw. The content of her skull is like mush. Her long platinum-blonde hair is matted in blood. There's a lot of it, with some tied back. Madison thinks she must be wearing hair extensions.

Lena moves the overhead spotlight closer to the facial area, carefully moving the woman's hair out of the way. "A lack of lines on her forehead makes me suspect she's a few years younger than her partner, but it's difficult to say. She has extensive tissue and bone damage, suggesting either she was hit harder or more times than her partner."

Adams raises his eyebrows. "Would that indicate our killer was there primarily for her?"

"Possibly," says Madison. "Or maybe she enraged the killer by fighting back."

"She has some defensive wounds," Lena confirms. "But nothing significant. Some bruising to the arms, and one of her fingers appears to be broken. Perhaps there was a struggle for the weapon. Alex is coming to take fingernail scrapings and fingerprints." She carefully rolls the woman toward her. "The pattern of lividity suggests she died on her back, where she was found."

After her external exam Lena returns to the male and checks him over for something. "Neither of them has any tattoos." She looks at Madison. "No tattoos, birthmarks, unusual scars or facial features. They're going to be tricky to identify unless you find ID at their house."

"If they've ever been arrested, we'll have their DNA and prints on record somewhere," says Madison. "But it would be quicker to find a driver's license or a bill in their name." She thinks about delivering the death notification to these people's families. How much detail she should go into about their injuries.

"What if they've never been arrested and we don't find anything at their house?" asks Adams.

"Then it's down to good old-fashioned police work. We canvass the neighborhood, hold press conferences, trace any vehicles they had and scour surveillance footage, and we hope in the meantime someone reports their loved ones missing. They'll be missed by their families and from their workplaces, so I'm confident someone will come forward eventually."

Adams silently nods, probably realizing how much work they have ahead of them.

Lena takes a deep breath. "Okay. Time to bring out the boys. You guys ready?"

Madison steels herself. "Let's get it over with."

CHAPTER TEN

Lena makes room for her assistant, Jeff, to wheel the boys over to them.

"We haven't had time to remove their clothing or wash them yet," says Jeff. "We concentrated on removing the bugs from their parents first. It took forever."

"That's fine," says Lena. Jeff leaves the room as she approaches the uncovered boys.

Madison has to stop herself from looking away. The little boy she found in the backyard, barely alive at the time, is still wearing his dinosaur pajamas. He looks vulnerable and devoid of all blood.

She turns to the other boy and, seeing his face properly for the first time, she gasps. "Oh God. They were identical twins."

Adams does a double take and groans. He must be thinking of his girls.

Lena peers into the boys' mouths to check their teeth. Then she measures their height and feet and compares the measurements to a chart on the wall behind her. "I'd age them at around seven or eight years old."

Madison nods. Seeing the entire family lined up next to

each other like this is tough. It hits home that the person who did this is cold and sadistic, and probably filled with rage. The killer could have easily left the boys unharmed, but he was filled with so much hatred for the adults that he probably enjoyed killing their defenseless children.

Lena turns to the boy found inside the house, on the mattress. She snips his clothes off and finds no visible scratches or lacerations on his body. There are several bruises on his legs, but Madison knows that's to be expected from a child this age. He probably enjoyed rough and tumble games like her own son did at seven or eight.

Lifting him forward, Lena examines his back before gently placing him on the table. She takes a light and shines it into his eyes. Madison sees a lot of red splotches in the whites of his eyes.

Checking inside his mouth again, Lena says, "I think he was smothered. Probably with the pillow. He has lesions in his mouth and trauma to his eyes, both consistent with smothering. I'll be able to confirm once I've performed an internal examination." She sighs. "From the way he was positioned on the mattress I think it's unlikely he saw his killer. He could've been taken unaware like his father."

"Do you think he died before his dad?" asks Adams.

"Yes, because otherwise he would've heard the attack on his father and attempted to hide."

Moving to the other boy, Lena cuts off his blood-soaked pajamas as they watch. This boy has a distinctive mole on the side of his nose, but it's the only real visible difference between the boys.

"This little guy was stabbed with a sharp blade to the abdomen," says Lena. "There don't appear to be any other injuries on him. It's amazing he survived as long as he did. He must've bled out slowly."

"The fact he was in the backyard suggests he wasn't in

either bedroom when the killer arrived," says Madison. "Maybe he was in the bathroom and came out to find his brother being suffocated."

Adams nods. "He must've been petrified."

Madison can't even imagine what he went through. "The killer must've spotted him, chased him downstairs and maybe grabbed a knife from the kitchen. What kind of blade did this?"

"I don't know yet," says Lena. "I'll check the depth of his internal injuries and get back to you on that."

Madison thinks about what took place. "It's unusual for a killer to use three different weapons. I mean, smothering, stabbing and bludgeoning seem so random, as if the murders weren't premeditated and he just used whatever he had to hand."

"He could've had an accomplice," says Adams.

She agrees it's a possibility. They could be looking for two or three different people. "Do you have any idea what time these murders occurred?" she asks Lena.

Pulling off her gloves, Lena says, "When we were at the house, I checked the adults for rigor mortis. The male's muscles were only slightly stiff, with returning flexibility, so I suspect rigor had been completed shortly before we arrived. Normally that takes around twenty to twenty-four hours. It would've completed quicker because of the warm day and the fact the whole family had likely been exerting themselves due to unloading boxes and moving into their new home. Physical exertion affects rigor mortis." She pauses with a frown. "But the female's muscles were stiffer than his, suggesting her rigor hadn't completed yet. She must've died after him. It might only have been an hour or two later, but it was definitely after him."

Madison doesn't want to think about what happened to the poor woman during that time. It's likely she was beaten unconscious, giving the killer time to murder the others first. Thanks to the condition of her face, they'll never know. "She would've been terrified and devastated. Her entire family was dead around her."

"It doesn't bear thinking about," says Adams. "I assume you'll check for signs of sexual assault?"

"If you want me to," says Lena. "She was fully clothed when found though, right?"

"Right. But it's still worth checking."

"Of course." Lena writes something down. "So, when considering all of the above, along with the unhatched fly larvae on their wounds, it suggests to me that they were killed the evening before they were discovered: Sunday evening." She looks up at them. "But you'd need a timeline of events to help pinpoint the exact time of death. Maybe someone saw what day and time they first arrived at the property."

"I tried asking Dawn Freemantle what time she noticed them move in," says Adams, "but she was distracted by her tearful grandson and couldn't focus on my questions. It would be worth questioning her again."

Madison agrees. "At least we have a starting point. Knowing they were likely killed Sunday will help get the ball rolling." She looks at Lena. "Thanks for your help. Keep us updated." She and Adams head for the door.

Once outside the building they both take a deep breath of fresh air. Madison notices Adams appears agitated. "You okay?" she asks.

With a shrug, he says, "I don't know. Each case feels like it's worse than the last. Like we're not even making a dent in the number of psychos in this town. I mean, what's the point, right? We catch this guy and then what? Someone even worse comes along?"

Madison's getting a little sick of his defeatist attitude. Maybe it comes from self-doubt. Maybe he doesn't feel confident enough in his own abilities to find this killer.

"Listen," she says, "if that's genuinely how you feel, then

why are you even in this job? Why aren't you pushing paper in an office somewhere instead? Or selling used cars downtown?"

He appears offended at the second suggestion.

She softens. "I feel the pressure too you know. Knowing that everyone's putting all their hope in us can be overwhelming. But I just take it one step and one clue at a time. And we're not alone in this. The whole department is there to support us. This is a team effort. Use whoever you need to help you." She smiles. "Hell, I call on the help of outsiders all the time, and I'm not too proud to admit it." She thinks of Nate and Brody.

Adams scowls at her. "I didn't say I was overwhelmed. I just said it was pointless." He heads to her car, needing a ride to the station.

Madison sighs. It's going to be a long day.

CHAPTER ELEVEN

FIFTEEN YEARS EARLIER

22.5 hours remaining

Officer Mike Bowers watches with interest as Detective Ramsey pulls back the screen door and knocks loudly on the open door behind it.

The sound appears to startle Dennis McKinney. They can see him at the end of the hallway, washing dishes with his back to them. He turns around to see who's interrupting his day. With a look of trepidation he drops the plate he was washing back in the sink and dries his hands before taking a sip of beer from the bottle next to him.

Taking his time, Dennis eventually puts the bottle back on the counter before approaching them. His sleeves are rolled up and he has sweat patches under his arms due to the heat that lingers into the evening. "Help you?" he says.

"I'm Detective John Ramsey. This is Officer Bowers. Mind if we come in for a second?"

Dennis is in his early thirties and Mike knows him through a friend of a friend, although not very well. They've never hung out.

After a puzzled glance at Mike, Dennis steps out onto his porch, closing the screen door behind him. "Here's fine," he says.

Detective Ramsey smiles, but the corners of his eyes don't wrinkle. "Sure, no problem. I just have a few questions then we'll be on our way. We're speaking to all your neighbors too."

Mike leaves his sunglasses on and remains silent while he quietly assesses Dennis's body language. He doesn't appear to be nervous or carrying a weapon.

Ramsey pulls out a photo. It's of a little girl, practically still a baby at just sixteen months old. Her blonde hair is in tiny pigtails and she's grinning at the camera, exposing her tiny teeth. "You know this kid, right?"

Dennis crosses his arms. "Sure. Grace lives right up the road. She okay?"

His question goes unanswered. "Her mom says you dote on the girl. You bought her a doll recently and you teach her nursery rhymes. That correct?"

Dennis narrows his eyes as he tries to read between the lines. "If you're asking whether I'm nice to my neighbors, the answer is yes. It's not a crime, is it?"

"No, it isn't," says Ramsey. With forced laughter he adds, "But the way the world's going, who knows. Am I right?"

Mike shifts position but his eyes remain fixed on Dennis.

"Is the girl okay?" asks Dennis.

Pocketing the photo, Detective Ramsey says, "Her mom tells me you may have been hanging around her property earlier this afternoon. That correct?"

With a confused expression, Dennis denies it. "No, that's not correct. I've been home all day. It's my day off."

Ramsey nods, then writes something down. "And I'm guessing you've been alone all day, right?"

"Right."

Another nod while Ramsey concentrates on his pocket notebook. "So you haven't seen this girl today at all?"

"Correct."

Ramsey looks up. "When *did* you last see her?"

Without hesitation Dennis says, "A few days ago. I keep chickens and Tiffany brought her by just before lunchtime to purchase some eggs. They were here for no more than eight or nine minutes."

"Uh-huh," says Ramsey, still taking notes. "That's pretty specific. You sure it wasn't ten minutes?" He has a patronizing smirk on his face that would annoy Mike if he was in Dennis's position.

"Get to the point, Detective." The guy's patience is running thin.

Mike can't help but chime in. "Don't you watch the news? A few hours ago we held a press conference with this girl's distraught mother. Everyone else seems to have seen it."

"I don't care for the news," Dennis replies. "Depresses me. Why? What's happened?"

Ramsey straightens before taking a deep breath. "She's cute, ain't she?"

Dennis frowns. "What are you talking about?"

"The mother, I mean. She's pretty hot with curves that won't quit and those big round eyes. What is she, twenty? And you're around thirty-one, thirty-two? That's still an appropriate age gap, I'd say. You ever dated her?"

"No."

"Ever wanted to?"

"No."

"Her kid is obviously going to be a looker too."

Mike shifts uncomfortably next to Ramsey. He's wondering where the hell this is going.

Dennis holds Ramsey's gaze. "She's a baby you sick bastard."

"Did you spot that about her, Mr. McKinney? That little Grace is going to be just like her mom? With her pretty face and little button nose. Hell, she probably walks around half naked due to the heat. Were you tempted by the pigtails and the angelic—"

Dennis lunges forward and punches Detective Ramsey square on the jaw.

Mike jumps in and pushes Dennis face-first against the wall of the house. "Stay exactly where you are!" he shouts while handcuffing him.

Cuffs secured, he steps back and raises his weapon at Dennis but, truth be told, he's not surprised the guy was offended. Ramsey took it too far.

Detective Ramsey steps forward, rubbing his jaw. "Where is she, Dennis? Can she still be saved? Can I take her home to her mother intact and stop that poor woman from killing herself tomorrow like she plans to?"

"I haven't touched Grace!" he yells. "I didn't even know she was missing!"

"You sure that's your story?" Ramsey leans in close to his face. "Because confessing early on can mean the difference between death row and life without parole. Choose wisely, my friend."

Dennis is clearly pissed, but also panicking. Sweat beads on his forehead. "I don't have a damn clue what you're talking about. I haven't harmed a hair on that girl's head."

Ramsey crosses his arms and sighs.

"And I'm not saying another word without a lawyer present."

After a long silence, Detective Ramsey says, "Get his sorry ass out of here, Mike."

Mike pulls Dennis roughly by the arm, not even giving him the chance to lock up his house before forcing him into the cruiser. There's no point.

His house is about to be searched from top to bottom in the hope they can find the baby alive.

CHAPTER TWELVE

PRESENT DAY

LCPD's conference room is slowly filling up but quickly becoming warm. Madison opens the only window in here and watches as Alex enters. White wireless earbuds indicate he's listening to something on his phone, probably a forensic podcast, knowing him. Three officers follow him in but Madison knows Officers Sanchez and Williams are busy at the crime scene.

Sergeant Steve Tanner appears. He nods at Madison. Nearing his mid-forties, Steve's been with the department for a while now. He's hardworking and a real asset to the team. Madison hopes that if Detective Adams ever decides to quit, Steve will take his place. He's single, lives alone and spends all his time at work. He glances behind him at the last person to arrive: Chief Carmen Mendes.

Mendes is dressed sharp, as always, in a silk shirt with smart pants and black heels. She closes the door behind her so they can get some reprieve from the constantly ringing phones in the office.

"Okay," she says, before stopping to frown. "What's that behind you, Madison?"

Madison turns to look at a whiteboard. It has all the victims listed on it with placeholder names: John Doe, Jane Doe, and for the infants; Johnnie Doe and Jake Doe. Each has a photograph under their placeholder names, except that the photographs of the adults are each covered with a sheet of white paper. The words *Caution—don't look while eating!* are written on them.

Madison glances at Alex. "Was this you?"

He pockets his phone and earbuds in his skinny black jeans. The dress code here is pretty relaxed as long as everyone does their job properly. With a smile he says, "I didn't want anyone losing their lunch. After all, not everyone has my strong constitution."

Chief Mendes walks over and lifts the first piece of paper before letting it drop back into place. "I wish I hadn't looked." She turns to Madison and Adams. "What do we know so far?"

Madison stands straight. "The victims' cell phones and wallets are missing, which means their IDs are missing. We need to check all their belongings for photographs, diaries and paperwork. There must be something in that house that can tell us who they are." She crosses her arms. "Adams and I have just returned from the morgue and the situation is grim. If we don't find any ID at the victims' property we'll need to see if we can use DNA to identify the adults, assuming we can locate a relative to obtain a comparison sample, that is. If not, maybe we'll get lucky and one of them has been arrested in the past so we can match their prints."

"They were that badly disfigured?" asks Steve. He obviously hasn't looked at the photos yet.

"They were," she says. "Even a facial reconstruction expert would be useless in this case as there's too much trauma. My hope is we either find something at the house that identifies them, or someone files a missing person report that matches."

"What about the children?" asks Chief Mendes. She glances at the whiteboard. "They weren't disfigured."

"No, but I'd be reluctant to get a sketch artist involved at this stage. Releasing images of them seems too..." She struggles for the right word.

"Invasive?" suggests Steve.

"And upsetting for anyone who might recognize them," she says. "Imagine their grandparents or older siblings see them on the news and realize their family members have been killed before we had the opportunity to support them. I don't want to traumatize anyone."

Alex speaks up. "I know an excellent forensic artist in Denver who could produce a 3D computer-generated image of the adults' faces. It's not a cheap option but if we still find ourselves at a loss to their identity after a week or so, it's worth considering."

With a puzzled expression Adams says, "How does that work if their skulls have been beaten to a bloody pulp?"

"It's a highly specialist skill," says Alex. "They would liaise with Dr. Scott and use whatever details she can give them to help reconstruct their features," he adds. "The images could then be shared widely through media outlets and online, along with any pertinent identifying features such as whether they have their ears pierced, or any tattoos and birthmarks."

Madison's impressed. "That's something to consider if all else fails, although I know for a fact our victims don't have any tattoos or birthmarks. One of the boys has a distinctive mole on his nose, but that's not that unusual. Anyway, I'm hopeful it won't come to that as someone's got to miss them eventually. A family of four can't just vanish with no one noticing."

Steve says, "If these murders were personal to the family in that house, it could mean the killer might go after the victims' wider family too. They could be in danger."

There's a hush around the room as everyone considers the implications.

"We need leads ASAP," says Chief Mendes. "We can't risk this happening to anyone else. When do you want to hold a press conference? Is it too soon?"

"I think so," says Madison. "Reporters have only recently started showing up, so we have a little longer to investigate before the community starts demanding answers. Also, I don't want to scare anyone."

The town was left reeling after the Snow Storm Killer's rampage. She could do without anyone jumping to conclusions about this case. "We don't know yet that the killer will target anyone else. Let's see how far we've gotten by the end of the day before we speak to the press."

"Fine," says Mendes.

Madison turns to Alex. "Did you find anything at the scene that could help us identify the killer?" she asks.

"Not yet," he says. "But it's a big property and I'm going back after this so I can continue dusting for prints and searching for trace evidence. I'll also visit the morgue and obtain some fingernail scrapings and fingerprints from our victims."

"Great," says Madison. "Lena thinks the female might have put up a fight, so hopefully she touched our killer at some point."

"There was no vehicle present at the house," says Steve. "If they had just moved in, wouldn't there be a U-Haul or a car present?"

Madison remembers seeing the utility trailer next to the house. It had looked out of place on its own. "Maybe the killer used the victims' vehicle to get away." To Adams, she says, "See what CCTV you can find on the routes around the area. We might get lucky and spot the family traveling toward the house, or the killer getting away. If we can check license plates, we can see who the vehicles are registered to and narrow down our search that way."

"Sure." Adams writes something down. "We can't ping their phones for location information until we find the phones, right?" he says, thinking aloud.

"Not unless we find something with their cell numbers on," says Steve.

"Right, of course." He looks at Madison. "I know schools are closed for summer but how about I try to speak with someone from the local elementary schools and see if they had twin boys in their classes?"

Madison's impressed he's being more proactive but suspects it's for Chief Mendes's benefit. "Good idea." She checks the clock on the wall. It's eleven already and she's eager to get moving. "I imagine someone will come forward by the end of the day to report their loved ones missing. In the meantime we need to concentrate on finding their killer. They gave themselves a lot of work by killing four people in three different ways. Hopefully that means they were careless and left something behind."

"We think they could've had an accomplice," Adams explains.

Steve nods. "That would make sense. They could've shared the work; one killing the boys while the other killed the parents."

"Right," says Madison. "But that doesn't mean it wasn't possible for a single individual to do this. Lena thinks we need to be looking for a sledgehammer and a knife, but she isn't sure what size knife yet. She thinks the boy found inside the house was smothered with a pillow."

Alex says, "I'll take the pillowcase and check it for DNA."

"There wasn't a case on the pillow when we were there," she says. "Either the killer took it with them or it didn't have one. I also noticed the bed in the adults' room wasn't made up." She sighs. "Just see what you can find."

"Of course," says Alex.

"Steve? Would you update dispatch and the patrol guys so they know the latest?"

"Sure thing."

"Thanks," says Madison. "I'm going back to the property, but first I want to speak to the other residents on the street to see if they saw anything. Keep me updated, everyone."

Knowing what they need to do, everyone quickly disperses. Madison feels under pressure to catch the perpetrators as fast as possible, but it feels good to know she has the support of her entire team.

CHAPTER THIRTEEN

The warm midday sunshine streaming in through the car's windshield makes Madison's journey pleasant, a stark contrast to what brings her out here. She has everything crossed that one of the victims' neighbors saw or heard something useful that will give her a starting point in her hunt for the killer.

As she drives, she finds herself wondering whether she'll see her son at some point today. Her plan is the same as yesterday: to have them eat dinner together tonight, so she can check how prepared he is for Saturday. Owen doesn't appear to have packed anything from his room yet and it's bothering her. As much as she doesn't want him to leave, it's Tuesday already and he's choosing to work instead of getting sorted for the biggest upheaval he's had since she was arrested.

She lets out a long sigh as she mutters, "I'll probably end up doing it for him."

After turning onto Blackwater Lane she continues slowly past the crime scene. Two cruisers sit in the driveway and the property is taped off. Three news vans are parked by the side of the road, with reporters standing nearby, exchanging facts about the case. Madison's high school friend Kate Flynn is notably absent. Kate's taking some time off work to be with her husband and children. Last Madison heard they were cruising around Barbados, which sounds much more appealing than being here right now.

Once the news vans are in her rearview mirror, Madison keeps going until she comes to the first house nearby. It's some distance away from the crime scene, which isn't visible from here on account of the trees. She pulls up outside the property and assesses the place. It's smaller than the victim's home, and single-story. The front yard is tidy and the house looks freshly painted. Faded yellow CCTV signs are propped against the inside of the windows, which raises Madison's hope that they might have captured a vehicle driving by around the time of the murders, despite this being the wrong direction for them to enter and leave the area.

The front door opens and an old man appears. With a scowl he yells across his lawn at her. "What do you want?"

A small, gray muzzled dog joins him on the step and begins howling. He looks like some kind of dachshund mix, with impossibly short legs.

Madison gets out of the car and approaches them. "Hi." She holds out her hand but the homeowner ignores it. "I'm Detective Harper from LCPD."

"Good for you," he says. "What's that got to do with me?" Dressed smart in ironed blue jeans and a pale blue shirt buttoned almost to the top with a white T-shirt poking out from underneath, he gives Madison the impression of being ex-military. His gray hair is clipped close to the head. She'd guess he's in his mid-seventies, due in part to the age spots around his forehead and the way he stoops forward slightly.

"Sorry to bother you, sir, but there's been a homicide in the area and I need to ask you some questions if that's alright with you?"

"I wondered what all the fuss was about," he says. "And

why I had a note through my door to contact you guys. I suppose you'd better come in." He turns and slowly leads her inside. The dog follows them.

The heat inside is a little stifling but the whirring ceiling fan provides some relief. The home is as neat as could be despite it being obvious no woman lives here. She suspects he could be widowed as there are black-and-white framed photographs on the walls showing a happy young couple posing together. She recognizes the younger version of the man in front of her.

The living room is so tidy that she notices the TV remote sits perfectly straight on the cheap coffee table, which looks to be the exact distance between the couch and the TV. The rugs and floor are recently vacuumed and Madison doesn't spot dust anywhere. It puts her house to shame. She was expecting the place to smell of dog but it doesn't, which is impressive. Even Nate's home smells of dog thanks to Brody's love of water and mischief.

"I've just had coffee," he says, "but I suppose I could go to the effort of pouring you a cup."

Madison smiles. "That won't be necessary, but thanks for the offer."

He shakes his head. "What are you, crazy? Who turns down free coffee? Give me a second." He shuffles into the small kitchen.

Something about his prickly personality reminds Madison of her father. Bill Harper was an FBI agent working in Alaska. He wasn't one for small talk. He liked to get right to the point and was direct with it. Madison prefers direct people. She knows where she stands with them.

An unexpected wave of grief suddenly hits her as hard as a physical blow to her body. Her heart pounds too hard and she goes dizzy. She panics at the thought of breaking down in front of this stranger and has to momentarily lean against the wall as she fights back tears. She's completely overwhelmed with a desire to see her dad.

The older man appears from the kitchen holding a mug and notices her panic-stricken expression before she manages to contain it.

"What's the matter with you?" he asks, his brow furrowed with concern. "You're not going to keel over on me, are you? I don't want to be accused of murdering a cop."

She tries to laugh it off but her nose is running now as well as her eyes and she can't find a tissue in her pocket. She can't stop picturing how her father looked as she held him in his final moments.

"Oh my God, I'm so sorry about this!" She clears her throat, trying desperately to stop crying.

Instead of patting her on the back or leading her to a seat, the old man disappears into the kitchen and gives her a minute. When he returns, he has tissues for her. "Here you go."

She uses them to wipe her eyes and nose. She could kick herself for being overwhelmed like that. It's not the first time grief has taken her unaware, but it's been eight months since her father's death. She thought this would've stopped by now.

"Sorry about that," she says again. She manages to compose herself and tries to focus on what she's come here for, which is nothing to do with her father.

Her companion ignores it, which she thinks is his way of helping to put her at ease. If she were indulged right now, she might never stop crying.

"I don't buy sugar," he says, handing her a cup of coffee. "So if it's not sweet enough for you, you'll just have to deal with it."

"I'm sure it's fine. Thanks."

He points to an armchair, so Madison sits down. After a deep cleansing breath she's relieved the feeling has passed. She sips her coffee, which tastes perfect. She doesn't put the cup down on the coffee table for fear of leaving watermarks behind so she holds on to it as she balances her notebook on her knee. "For a minute there you reminded me of my father. I lost him recently." That's all she manages by way of explanation.

He brushes it off, to show he understands. With all gruffness now gone he says amicably, "So what can I help you with, Detective?"

Madison takes another deep breath. "Before we begin, I didn't catch your name."

"That's because I didn't give it to you." He drops heavily onto the couch. The dog uses some purpose-built wooden steps to reach his owner, then flops onto his lap, panting from the effort. "The name's Richard. Don't call me Dick. That's not my name. It's Richard."

Madison can't help but smile. She's warming to him. "Got it. Let me get straight to the point, Richard. A family of four were found murdered in the house along the street. I believe it happened on Sunday evening. You're their closest neighbor, so I'm hoping you saw or heard something that could provide a lead."

He leans back and strokes the placid dog. "Sunday evening, you say?"

"Right. Were you home?"

"You fishing for an alibi?" he asks.

"No. I'm fishing for leads. I saw your CCTV signs. Are they real?"

Richard shakes his head. "Nope. Merely a deterrent. Same as the dog."

Madison has to stifle a laugh because this dog wouldn't even deter a cat, never mind a home invader.

"What about your vehicle?" She noticed a battered pickup truck outside. "Does it have a dashcam?"

"Do I look like someone who can afford fancy gadgets, Detective?" He coughs long and loud into his hand before reaching for his shoulder with a wince. "Damn arthritis." After rubbing it for a minute he says, "What time do you think they were killed?"

She checks her notebook. "We don't know for sure. It looked like they might've only moved into the house the day before they were found, so we're guessing it was that evening. Have you noticed any activity at the property lately?"

"Can't say I have, but I don't really care what my neighbors are up to as long as they don't bother me. I thought the place was still empty. Why anyone would want to live in that dump is beyond me."

"How long had it been empty?" she asks.

"Oh, a few months. Ever since the dragon died."

Madison tilts her head. "The dragon?"

"Sure. She went by the name of Linda something. A real piece of work. If you listen to the rumors, she died alone with no family around her. Let the house go to ruin. I hadn't seen her in years by the time she met her maker."

"Do you know her last name?"

"Not anymore. I probably did once. I never saw any realtor signs go up, so I'm surprised someone new moved in. I guess they saw the place was empty and decided to squat there. Damn freeloaders."

"We don't know that," says Madison. "Maybe Linda left it to someone in her will." She finishes her coffee.

"Maybe she what?" He leans forward, cupping his left ear.

She raises her voice slightly. "I said maybe she had a will and left the house to a family member."

"Nah, she never had visitors. What little family she had left town years ago. A good indicator of what she was like, if you ask me. None of them wanted to be around her. She had to call an ambulance herself when she took a funny turn, and then she died alone in the hospital. At least that's what I read in the paper."

That's sad. But Madison knows family estrangement

happens for all kinds of reasons. Sometimes it is because the person was so abusive or intolerable that they'd used up all their family's goodwill. If that's the case, it's likely the victims weren't related to the previous owner. They might well have decided the house was available for free since no one cared what happened to it. "So you can't tell me anything about her?"

He takes a deep breath and thinks for a second. "I know there were rumors she owed money to a loan shark. She refused to work, you see. Just wanted to sit at home all day and watch daytime TV probably."

Madison leans forward. "Who did she owe money to?"

Richard looks away, suggesting he doesn't want to snitch on anyone. "None of my business."

"That may be so, but it *is* my business." She's considering whether the loan shark came back to settle a score and picked on the wrong residents.

The old man appears to chew on it for a second. "Draper."

Madison frowns. It's not a name she recognizes. "First name?"

"Doug. Last I heard, although that was from some asshole in the diner, Doug and his wife live out in Gold Rock now."

Madison makes a note of the name. "Thanks. Have you seen him around here lately?"

"Nope. But I don't sit staring out my window all day, Detective."

"Sure. And as far as you're aware, nothing out of the ordinary occurred around here on Sunday or Monday? Specifically, Sunday evening."

He considers it for a minute. "I fall asleep early. I'm in bed by eight. Then I get up four times every night to use the bathroom. Five, if I'm stupid and I allow myself a beer after dinner. And why shouldn't I? There's nothing else for me to do at my age." He coughs harshly into his elbow before continuing. "I didn't see or hear anything that night. I didn't go out that day either, so I didn't happen to drive by the place. I used to go to church on Sundays until the priest was accused of fraud. He was pocketing donations. I always wondered how he could afford all the vacations he took."

Madison smiles diplomatically. It's clear she won't get anything else from him. "Well, thanks for your time, and the coffee." She stands and takes her mug to his kitchen. It's as neat as the living room. Signs of his single life greet her: one cup and plate in the sink, a mini loaf of bread on the side, a wall calendar empty of appointments and engagements. It reminds her she'll be in the same situation soon enough. The thought is depressing.

Richard walks her to the front door, the dog trailing behind him. "Think the killer will go after anyone else?" he asks.

Once outside she turns. "I'm hoping to catch them before that can happen, but I'd always advise to keep your windows and doors locked regardless, and if you're concerned, invest in some security." She can't resist a quick glance at the tiny dog.

"I thought I was doing that by paying your wages all my working life," he grumbles.

Madison doesn't react. It's a line you get used to hearing in her job. "Thanks again, sir. You have a good day."

This time he shakes her hand before she returns to her car. She can feel his eyes on her back. Despite his initial hostility she feels for him living alone with the dog. He seemed to judge his neighbor for dying alone, but she can't help wondering where *his* family is.

The next house appears to be closer in distance to Richard's than his is to the crime scene, so, as it's a pleasant day, Madison decides to walk over.

CHAPTER FOURTEEN

A topless male with shoulder-length bleached blond hair who looks to be around Madison's age, mid-late thirties, is mowing the grass in Dawn Freemantle's yard.

Madison always loved the sound of a lawnmower when she was a kid. It was the sound of summer for her. And nothing beats the smell of freshly cut grass. Except maybe freshly baked bread. Her stomach growls at the thought, probably because it's past lunchtime and she hasn't stopped to grab anything yet.

She approaches the stranger. When he spots her, he immediately stops work and the mower falls silent.

"Hey, Detective," he says with a confident smile.

He must recognize her from seeing her on the news. She's held a lot of press conferences over the past year, so it's not unusual to be greeted like this. "Afternoon," she says. "I'm here to speak with Dawn. Is she in?"

"Sure. Let me go fetch her for you." He heads inside the house through the front door.

Madison waits outside. She can hear barking out back, which sets off some chickens nearby. The loud barking pierces her brain.

It takes a while for Dawn Freemantle to appear and, when she does, she's holding hands with the younger guy. They walk toward Madison. She watches as the guy kisses Dawn's cheek. They smile at each other, giving the impression of newlyweds.

Dawn has white hair and looks to be in her late sixties. She greets Madison warmly. "Hi there. Your handsome partner told me you'd be along soon."

Madison smiles. "I understand you were unable to speak to Detective Adams because your grandson was still upset at what he saw at your new neighbors' house?"

"That's right. He's fine now though. He's out back shooting butterflies with his BB gun." She says it with a proud smile on her face. "Come on round." Dawn leads her around the side of the house to the large backyard.

Madison doesn't see the dogs coming from the far end of the yard until they're closer. Two overweight rottweilers with shiny black coats head straight for her, still barking. She freezes. She didn't grow up with dogs and it took a while for Brody to grow on her. It's not like she's afraid of them, but she *is* cautious. She's witnessed the aftermath of vicious dog attacks on kids, and while harrowing, she knows it was always one hundred percent the owner's fault, not the kid's or the dog's. "They friendly?" she asks.

"Oh, they won't hurt you," Dawn says with a laugh. "They just want to smell you, that's all."

The dogs come alarmingly close, with one jumping up and putting his paws on Madison's shoulders, forcing her back a step with his hefty weight. "Jeez, he's heavy."

"They're both girls," says Dawn. "Duchess! Delilah! Now you girls leave the detective alone, you hear me?"

The dogs quickly lose interest in Madison and run indoors, where they start barking intermittently again. Maybe it's their lunchtime too.

Dawn ignores them. Instead, she addresses her grandson. "Timmy, sweetheart, we've got a visitor."

A young boy sits on freshly cut grass. He's holding a magnifying glass over a bug. The sun is lighting it up. He peers up at Madison.

"Hi," she says brightly.

Timmy ignores her and goes back to burning bugs. Madison knows not to judge. Owen was the same at that age, or he was until she explained how much pain he was causing the creatures. He never did it again after that.

"Take a seat, Detective," says Dawn, settling into an old plastic patio chair.

Her lawn-mowing companion squeezes her shoulder. "I'll go finish up," he says.

Dawn pats his hand tenderly. "Okay, baby."

Madison keeps her expression neutral as she pulls out her notebook. "Sorry to have to make you relive this again, but I'm obviously here to listen to what happened over at your neighbors' house."

"Sure, I understand." Dawn pulls out her cell phone and Madison can make out black-and-white video footage of an older gentleman lying in bed.

"I'm just checking on my husband," says Dawn. "He has dementia. I could put him in a home but it's cheaper to let him stay here."

Madison has many questions, the first of which being: if that's Dawn's husband, why was she holding hands with the gardener? But, unless they've broken the law, other people's personal lives are none of her business. "It must be difficult for you."

"Oh, not really. Kai helps me out." She nods behind them to indicate Kai is the guy out front. "He's been such a blessing. I really don't know what he sees in an old fool like me."

Madison could hazard a guess, but she keeps her thoughts

to herself. She could be misjudging their relationship. She looks at the boy. "Does Timmy's mom live here with you?"

Dawn's face clouds over. "Nope. She's dead. Along with his dad. Crazy bastards OD'd within five months of each other. They were hooked on meth. I've raised Timmy ever since."

"Sorry, I didn't realize." Wanting to change the subject so as not to upset Timmy, Madison gets down to business. "Tell me why you went over to the house in the first place, would you?"

Putting her phone away, Dawn nods. "Sure. I was coming home from church on Sunday afternoon when I saw a car in Linda's front yard. I realized someone new was moving in. Now, I've only lived on this street for just over a year myself, so I didn't know Linda before she died. I just know the rumors about her being miserly and unfriendly. I never actually met her myself. So when I saw activity over there, I was relieved to have some fresh blood in the neighborhood. I heard young boys laughing and thought they might become friends with Timmy."

Timmy looks up at hearing his name mentioned. "I don't need friends, Grandma."

Dawn humors him with a smile. "Well, it doesn't matter now 'cause they're dead, ain't they?"

Madison's taken aback by her comment. It seems incredibly uncaring.

Timmy looks away.

Madison prompts her to continue. "So you went to introduce yourself?"

"Right, the next day. Figured I'd let them get settled before I bothered them. I went over at around four o'clock yesterday. Their front door was ajar, so I called out but no one came. I started walking around the side of the property, thinking they could be out back, taking a break, but little did I know that Timmy slipped inside without me even noticing."

"I saw a box of toys," the boy mumbles.

"Did you go upstairs, Timmy?" asks Madison.

He nods. "I heard flies buzzing. It smelled weird upstairs."

Madison's stomach turns at the thought of what he witnessed. "Which bedroom did you go into?"

Without looking at them he says, "The one with them people on the bed. Their faces looked like rice with tomato ketchup all over."

Puzzled, Dawn looks at Madison. "I don't know what that's supposed to mean."

Madison does. The description makes her queasy. She's no longer hungry for lunch. "What did you do next?"

"I ran out of the house," says Timmy. "I didn't touch anything."

"I've never heard him holler so loud," says his grandmother. "He just about scared the life out of me, so we hightailed it out of there. I thought he had the heebie-jeebies about something stupid so I didn't think any more of it, except it kept bothering me. Eventually I drove back over to see whether anyone was about, but the place was just as we'd left it, with the front door ajar and eerily quiet. That's when I called you guys."

Madison knows the call came into dispatch at five sixteen yesterday evening. "And you said you noticed a vehicle at the property when you first realized someone was moving in on Sunday. Can you describe it for me?"

Dawn takes a deep breath as she thinks. "I only saw the back of it as I drove by. All I remember is that it was dark colored."

"You didn't recognize the make or model, or catch any of the license plate?"

She snorts. "No, ma'am. I'm not good at that kind of thing. I've always got too much going on up here." She taps her head before something occurs to her. "Huh. You know, I don't believe the car was present the next day, when we went to say hi to them."

Madison makes a note that the vehicle was removed

between Sunday afternoon and Monday afternoon. "Was it a truck or a sedan?" she asks.

"Definitely a sedan, but that's about all I can tell you."

That will be helpful in narrowing down potential vehicles on surveillance footage. "Have you noticed any strangers in the neighborhood lately?"

Both the dogs suddenly stop barking and reappear at the back door. Dawn calls them over and they settle next to her feet. One rolls onto her back, exposing her plump belly. "Listen, Detective, half my neighbors are strangers. That's why I wanted this new family to work out. No one speaks to anyone anymore. And there's always someone up to no good in this town." She sighs. "How is anyone supposed to know who the bad guys are when we don't even know who the good guys are anymore?"

She makes a valid point. Still, shouldn't she be worried about her safety? Living so close to the crime scene with a young child, Madison would expect her to be more concerned. More afraid. Perhaps she's not the type to scare easily.

She thinks of what Richard said about the loan shark who may be operating in the area. "Does the name Doug Draper mean anything to you?"

Dawn shakes her head.

Madison plans to look into Draper regardless. She glances at the backyard, which looks like it needs more work than the front. "Was Kai here with you on Sunday?"

Shaking a cigarette out of its pack Dawn says, "He came over later that night. He doesn't do church." She snorts. "Thinks all organized religion is some kind of cult." Her eyes narrow as she realizes why Madison asked. "He spent the night with me, so don't go looking at him for this. He's a gentle soul who wouldn't hurt a fly."

Madison's eyes go to Timmy, who's hurting a fly as they speak. "What's Kai's last name? And don't worry, I'm making a note of everyone's details, not just his."

The older woman seems reluctant to give it up; she focuses on her phone. Her energy has changed and one of the dogs sits up, staring at her owner. Maybe she's sensed it too. "I can't remember."

"Really?" says Madison. "You two seem very close to not know his last name."

Dawn doesn't look at her. "Bishop, I think."

Madison watches her closely. If Kai has something to hide, maybe Dawn is in on it. Maybe *they* killed the family down the street. Nothing would surprise her anymore.

She stands. "If you think of anything else, give the station a call. It's important we find who did this. They're incredibly dangerous."

Dawn stands too, along with both dogs. "If they try entering my home, I'll shoot the assholes."

With raised eyebrows Madison says, "You have firearms on the property?"

"Damn right we do. Six of 'em."

"Are they licensed and locked away?" she asks. When Dawn's smile fades, she adds, "I'm sure you wouldn't want Timmy to get ahold of one."

"Timmy knows not to touch them." Dawn's eyes harden as she crosses her arms. That'll happen when someone thinks you're going to take their guns away from them. "They're licensed. That's all you need to know. You have a good day, Detective."

She's being dismissed. The dogs are silently staring at her. It's unsettling. "Thanks for your help, I appreciate it." She looks at the boy. "Bye, Timmy."

He watches her without replying. The empty look in his eyes gives her the creeps. There's something not right with that kid. In fact, everyone here seems a little odd.

Madison walks around to the front of the house and

approaches Kai before leaving. "Just confirm your full name for me, would you?"

He stops what he's doing. "Kai Bishop."

"Thanks."

He offers a disturbing smirk as she heads for her car, still parked outside their neighbors' house.

Kai's strange demeanor makes her determined to run a background check on him. On Dawn Freemantle too.

CHAPTER FIFTEEN

Nate's phone pings with a message from Madison.

On my way.

He's at her house with Owen. They were working together at Richie's office all morning and came up with the plan of making lunch for Madison. Nate's trying to get Owen to spend some time with his mother before he leaves for college.

"She's on her way," he says, slipping his phone away.

"Cool." Owen's carrying a bunch of different food they fetched from the diner.

Nate spreads a picnic blanket over the grass in the backyard, and Owen unpacks the food. It immediately attracts bugs, as well as Brody.

"Get back." He gently tugs Brody's collar, redirecting his face away from the quiche. "It's not for you, buddy."

"Didn't you just feed him?" asks Owen, amused.

Nate sighs. "Like that matters with this dog."

Owen pours three glasses of soda. "I bet Mom can only stay ten minutes. She always rushes off."

"Well, ten minutes is better than nothing. Cut her some slack; she's working a homicide case."

Owen sits cross-legged on the blanket, checking his phone and helping himself to chips and dip while they wait for her to arrive.

When Nate hears a car pull up out front, he stands. "I'll get her." He enters the house through the back door and walks through the kitchen. He finds Madison entering the front door.

"What's going on?" she says. "Is everything okay?"

He sees trepidation in her eyes. She's so used to being on high alert for work that she always expects the worst. "Everything's fine. We've prepared lunch outside. Owen wanted to spend some time with you."

Her eyes well up and she turns her face so he can't see. He hates it when she tries to hide her emotions from him. It shows she still doesn't trust him enough to let her guard down. He suddenly wishes they were here alone so he could lay his cards on the table and tell her how he feels. How he'd unpack all his belongings in a second if she'd just give him a chance.

Instead, he says, "I hope you're hungry. We went a little overboard with food."

Madison smiles; she seems bemused that they'd go to all this effort for her. Nate leads her out into the backyard, where Brody greets her excitedly.

"Where's his neckerchief?" she asks.

"Don't tell Lena, but he lost it in the creek by my house when he went for a dip this morning."

She laughs before taking a seat on the blanket next to Owen. She puts an arm around her son and hugs him briefly before pulling out a small bottle of hand sanitizer and cleaning her hands. "Wow, a picnic," she says, beaming. "I can't remember the last time I had a picnic."

"It's not as fun as it sounds," says Owen. "There are bugs literally everywhere."

Nate notices Madison eyeing a fly that's walking over the quiche. She turns pale at the sight of it. Eventually she helps herself to an egg salad sandwich. "Did Vince make all this?" she asks.

"Yeah," says Owen. "And he said it's about time we did something nice for you."

Madison laughs. "Ain't that the truth."

Nate smiles as he watches them both. "Are you driving Owen to Arizona on Saturday?" he asks.

Her smile falters. "No. I'm not allowed to go. He thinks I'll cause a scene."

Owen rolls his eyes and talks with his mouth full. "That's not what I said! I said you won't be able to drive straight for all the crying you'll be doing."

Nate laughs. "That sounds about right. Do you need a ride then?"

"No," says Owen. "Jason's dad says I can ride with them." Jason is Owen's closest friend. It's good to know he won't be completely alone in a new state.

"Let's not talk about it," says Madison. "Why spoil a nice lunch?"

They eat in silence for a while. The sun feels good on Nate's skin. There was a time, when he was locked up on death row, that he never thought he'd feel this sensation again. Then, once released, he quickly learned his skin was no longer used to UV rays, so he's had to wear high-factor sunblock every summer since getting out.

A sharp screeching sound comes out of nowhere behind him. Owen's cat appears.

"Hey, Bandit!" Owen feeds the cat tuna, sending Bandit's purring into overdrive. Sensing he's missing out on something, Brody reappears.

Madison covers her mouth as she laughs. "They're getting more food than we are!"

Nate pulls his phone out and snaps a photo of mother and son. If he could stop time right now, he would. Because, come Saturday, everything will change. He can tell Madison's thinking the same thing. Her eyes are watery but she's doing well to hold her feelings in.

He can't imagine what she's going through. Cheated out of seven years of being a mother affected her badly. To have to lose her son all over again, albeit in more positive circumstances, has got to be difficult. Nate's going to miss the boy too and he's only known him a year.

"So, Owen, when are you coming home to visit for the first time?" he asks.

"You better be here for my birthday next month," says Madison.

Owen downs some soda before responding. "Listen, guys. I can't make any promises. I mean, I could hook up with some hot chick right away and be forced to spend all my spare time with her."

Madison gently backhands his knee. "Hey! That's not allowed."

"What?" Owen laughs. "You want grandkids, don't you?"

Incredulous, she says, "No! Not for at least another twenty years. I'm far too young to be a grandmother! I'm actually still young enough to give you a brother or sister, so think about that when you're hooking up with the ladies."

"Eww, gross."

Nate leans in to Owen and says, "You know you're going to college to study law, not women, right?"

Owen grins as he stuffs as many potato chips into his mouth that will fit.

Madison grimaces. "Looks like we don't need to worry about you attracting the ladies if you eat like *that* in front of them." She finishes her sandwich before checking her phone, probably to see how long she's been gone. She rarely takes lunch breaks.

She must decide she can spare a few more minutes as instead of getting up she fixes her blue eyes on Nate. "What are you working on right now? Is Richie keeping you busy?"

He slips Brody some ham. The dog takes it gently, despite the size of his jaw. "Actually, I've set up a website to attract some new clients. Owen helped me."

Madison frowns. "For people who want to hire a private investigator?"

"Right. Richie doesn't always have a lot for me to do and I need to stay busy because... well, you know." Nate's prone to depressive episodes if he dwells on the past. They've eased off considerably since settling in Lost Creek, but he needs to keep busy and focused on the here and now. He's learned that working, and helping others, is the best therapy for him.

"I thought I could take on a client or two at the same time as working for Richie," he adds. What he doesn't tell her is that he's planning on traveling the country, going where the clients are. That's why he thought a website would be a good idea. Since he's not staying in Lost Creek, he can go wherever he's needed.

"Has the website had many hits?" asks Owen.

Nate scoffs. He missed the digital revolution while he was in prison, so he's not exactly a whizz on computers and smartphones. "I have no idea. You'll have to remind me how to check that."

Exasperated, Owen says, "Dude, I've shown you like fifteen times already!"

"Hey, I'm old. I need written instructions."

Madison's expression suggests she's thinking about the website. Nate hopes she isn't catching on to what it means.

"You're just taking on local clients though, right?" she asks.

He nods, then changes the subject. "So Father Connor's trial is coming up in a couple of weeks. Are you going?"

She sighs. "I have to. I want to see him pay for what he did to you and, besides, being a cop means I couldn't get out of it if I wanted to. But I understand if you don't feel able to attend, what with it being in Texas and all."

Owen looks at him. "You still refuse to set foot back in Texas, huh?"

Nate takes a deep breath. He may have vowed never to return to the state that incarcerated him, but he also wants Jack Connor to spend his final years behind bars. It would be poetic justice if he found himself on the same death row where Nate spent seventeen years.

Just thinking about the trial makes his heart beat a little too hard in his chest. It's the thought of Connor getting a not guilty verdict. The former priest would see it as vindication, despite knowing he's guilty as hell. If he gets released, Nate's torture would begin all over again.

Sweat pops up on his brow.

"Let's change the subject," says Madison. She can tell it's bothering him. She stands. "Unfortunately, I have to get back to work."

Owen gets up, dropping so many crumbs from his lap that Brody immediately moves in. They magically disappear within seconds.

"Thanks for this, you guys." She pulls Owen in for a hug. "It was just what I needed."

Nate slowly stands and is surprised when Madison embraces him next. He can smell the scent of apples on her hair. She holds him longer than necessary and whispers, "It'll all work out. Don't dwell on it, okay?"

He nods and offers a weak smile as she pulls away. He doesn't have as much hope in the judicial system as she appears to.

"Keep yourself busy instead. You can start with tidying all that away." She smiles playfully.

Nate looks at the picnic blanket behind them. Brody and Bandit are working their way through the leftovers. He shakes his head with a smile.

Owen picks up his cat as Nate turns to watch Madison walk away.

CHAPTER SIXTEEN

Madison returns to the crime scene a little less stressed than she was earlier. Taking a breather has cleared her head. The picnic was thoughtful and has left her feeling better about her relationship with Nate. It felt like old times and it's comforting to know he'll still be here once Owen leaves.

As she approaches the house on Blackwater Lane, she finds more vehicles, and reporters waiting on the sidewalk outside. Local television stations have sent news teams to cover the homicides. Officer Sanchez ushers them aside so Madison can drive onto the property. She ignores their questions for now. They all know the drill: when she's ready, she'll give them what they want.

Steve's outside the house checking his cell phone, and she notices a large area of exposed dirt, where the gravel driveway ends, is taped off to stop it from being walked on.

Madison parks on the overgrown lawn and steps out of her car. "Hey, Steve," she says. "What's this for?" She nods to the tape.

He looks up from his phone. "Alex was casting tire impressions. He told me why, but I've got to admit I zoned out while he was talking. You know what it's like."

She smiles. Sometimes, with Alex's longwinded forensic explanations, it's hard not to zone out, especially since so many of his tests and experiments result in dead ends. As long as Alex knows his reasons for taking the tire impressions, that's good enough for her. "This morning I knocked on doors," she says. "Spoke to all the closest neighbors. One or two seem questionable, including the woman who found the victims: Dawn Freemantle. I'll probably want to interview her further at some point."

She had also managed to visit three other neighbors after Dawn, before Nate texted about meeting her at home. They were all too far away from the crime scene to be much help, but they did provide one useful piece of information. "Someone told me the previous homeowner's last name was Hendricks. Linda Hendricks."

Steve writes it down.

"Someone else mentioned Linda might've owed money to a loan shark: Doug Draper."

Steve raises his eyebrows in recognition of the name. "I dealt with a complaint about him once. Last year, I think. A woman said Draper seized her car as compensation for not making a loan payment, but the woman dropped the complaint before I could do anything with it."

"That's interesting. Maybe he threatened her."

"Could have. Want me to check him out?"

"Yeah," she says. "Run a background check then get me his address. I'll pay him a visit."

"Take Adams with you in case Draper's an asshole."

She nods. "Has anything come into dispatch yet?" she asks. "Any missing person reports?"

"Nothing." He rubs the back of his neck. "No one's missing them yet, but that's not unusual. With school out for summer their neighbors probably assumed the whole family is away on vacation."

It's frustrating as Madison would like to think someone would be concerned, but she knows many people don't trust law enforcement and would rather wait as long as possible before reporting someone missing. Many hope they'll just reappear, having forgotten to say they were going out of town. Others are just so self-involved they don't notice any difference. That's how so many people can lie dead in their homes for weeks before anyone notices something's wrong.

"Have we found anything in the house that identifies the family?" she asks.

"Afraid not." He sighs. "There's a distinct lack of anything inside, including paperwork or personal belongings. It's odd."

Madison doesn't think so. "Most paperwork is sent through email these days," she says. "I don't get much mail anymore. And when you move, you tend to declutter beforehand. No one wants to pay to move a bunch of junk."

"Sure, but there aren't even any photographs from what I've seen so far."

Madison realizes she doesn't have a single photograph on display in her own house. "Framed photos are dying off thanks to smartphones. I mean, when was the last time you printed out a photo from your phone?"

"Never have," he admits.

"They sure traveled light though," she says. "I think the few pieces of furniture inside are leftovers from the previous owner, which means they only brought whatever could be boxed up."

"Who travels that light with kids?" he says.

She thinks about it. "People on the run, I guess."

Steve mulls it over for a minute. "Think they were in trouble somewhere else and came here to hide?"

"It's sure looking that way." She bats a bee away from her

face. "Unless they really were so down and out that they couldn't afford to bring furniture with them."

Steve rolls his sleeves up. It's hot in the sun. "We haven't found a sledgehammer on the property. The killer must've taken it with him. And it doesn't look like the family owned any firearms."

Madison looks up at the house. "If they weren't on the run, I'm struggling to understand why they wanted to move into this house. It's not exactly a family's dream home, right?"

Steve considers it. "They could've been into those fixer-upper shows and thought they could work their magic here. Or maybe they really were just plain broke. Do we know who sold it to them?"

"That's just it," she says, "the neighbors told me the previous owner was an unlikable recluse with no family contact. She died a while ago. They didn't see any realtor signs go up but I guess it could've gone to auction, or maybe it hasn't been sold yet. We need to check."

"Sounds to me like they thought they could live here rent free without anyone noticing or caring," says Steve. "And why not, right? It's not like there was anyone to claim it."

"True. Rent isn't cheap these days. They could've been just trying their luck." She chews her lip while she thinks. "When you get back to the office would you see if you can find out whether Linda Hendricks left a will and who legally owns the place? Maybe her kids inherited the house and sold it, or are planning to sell it. If they did, they could've withheld the proceeds from potential creditors like Doug Draper. Things like that can get messy after a person dies, and if we've got a case of mistaken identity here, our victims could've paid for Linda's debts with their lives."

He nods. "I've got some more boxes to check downstairs first. Do you want to see what you can find upstairs?"

"Sure."

She enters the house. The sickly sweet odor isn't as strong as it was when she was here last night, mainly because the bodies have been removed, but it'll take a lot more than a few open windows to eradicate it completely. It permeates everything around it, including wooden floors and soft furnishings. If Madison owned this place, she'd tear the house down and sell the land to property developers.

Steve wanders off to the living room as she takes the stairs. The toy clown she stepped on yesterday is gone, probably kicked out of the way by Lena's team as they removed the bodies.

Madison's drawn to the children's bedroom. Everything has a fine layer of fingerprint powder over it where Alex has been at work. Although probably not necessary now, Madison wears gloves to avoid contamination. A couple of unopened boxes reveal several toys when she pulls them open: Spider-Man figurines, a large plastic T-Rex and some remote-control cars. The boys were probably too young for cell phones, but she would expect them to have tablets to play on. She doesn't find any. It suggests the family moved quickly, leaving things behind, which means they're right to assume this family was in trouble.

The adults' bedroom is practically empty, so Madison heads downstairs and outside.

The afternoon sun beats down on her as she approaches the steel utility trailer. It must have already been given a cursory check over by someone as the black cover is untied and open at one corner. Madison wonders why it hasn't been properly searched yet. With some effort she pulls the cover off completely and finds a motorcycle secured underneath. Its license plates have been removed.

"Huh." For some reason she wasn't expecting that. She knows nothing about motorcycles but it looks to be in good condition. If the killer's motive was robbery, they probably would have taken this whole trailer with them when they took the victims' car. It leads her to believe the killer only removed the car to avoid easy identification of the victims.

The rest of the trailer has already been emptied, presumably by the family, except for two sealed boxes wedged behind the front wheel of the motorcycle. With some effort Madison pulls them toward her and tears the tape off the first one. When she sees what's inside, she frowns. It takes a second for the implications to hit her, and when they do, her blood runs cold.

"Oh God. No."

She pulls out a small yellow T-shirt that says *Daddy's Girl* across it. The age on the label says it will fit a child of two to three years old.

Madison's heart races. At the bottom of the box sits a stuffed unicorn, with a shaggy gold mane, underneath a stack of brightly colored clothes. Frantically, she pulls the other box toward her and rips it open. She's greeted with more pink, yellow and white clothes including some cute pink dungarees with a daisy embroidered across the front, again for a child aged two to three years old.

Madison spins around and runs toward the house with the dungarees in her hand. "Steve!" she yells.

She finds him in the kitchen.

Alarmed, he steps forward. "What is it?"

She shows him the dungarees. "There's another child! I think the victims have a little girl."

The blood vanishes from his face within seconds. "Holy crap. Are you sure?"

"Why else would they have two boxes of toddler's clothes with them?" Her mind is spinning. "I found these outside on the trailer."

Remaining calm, he says, "Let's not jump to conclusions. There's no bed or crib for another child upstairs. Wouldn't they at least have a mattress for her?"

She doesn't know what to think. "They didn't bring any

furniture with them. Maybe they were going to have her sleep in their bed with them until they got settled."

"Or," he says, "maybe they once lost a child and kept some of her belongings as a reminder of her."

Madison tries to slow her pounding heart by taking a deep breath. "I seriously hope you're right. Sad as it would be, I'd rather that was the case than the alternative." She turns to leave. "Come take a look."

Steve follows her out into the sunshine and she shows him the toys and the clothes. "There's no photographs of her," she says. "If they'd lost her and kept all this to remember her by, wouldn't they have photographs of her too? Wouldn't we find her death certificate? Drawings she did, birthday cards she got? I can't imagine any parent would get rid of those things after losing their child. I mean, there would be *something*. Not just clothes and this." She picks up the unicorn.

Steve seems reluctant to believe the worst has happened. "Why wasn't this trailer checked sooner?"

Madison runs over to Officer Williams, who's watching the reporters. Leading her away from the mics and cameras she says, "Gloria? The entire residence and the surrounding land have been checked for more victims, right?"

"Yes, ma'am," says Gloria. "If there was anyone else here, we—or your friend's dog—would've found them." Puzzled, she asks, "Is there a problem?"

"Yeah, there is. Do you know who was searching the trailer?"

Gloria nods. "Sure, it was Detective Adams. He said he'd take care of that."

Steve joins them. "He must've been distracted by something else."

Madison could tear her hair out in frustration. "Dammit! If we'd found these clothes right away, we could've found the child by now. Instead, the killer's been given a massive head start!" Her chest fills with dread. Every single second counts when a child is missing and now they might be too late to save her.

Her mouth goes dry and she turns to Steve. "Whoever took her could have done anything to her by now."

CHAPTER SEVENTEEN

"Marcus, it's me." Madison took a couple of minutes to calm down before calling her partner. She'll try not to lay into him, and she's using his first name to soften the delivery, but she needs to be honest and Adams is not going to like it.

"Hey," he says with a sigh down the line. "I'm checking for surveillance footage, but I'm having one of those days. No one's being cooperative."

"You're a cop, *make* them cooperate."

He scoffs. "No one respects cops anymore."

"Threaten them with a warrant. That usually works." She steels herself to change the subject. "You were the one who checked the trailer at the crime scene, right?" She wants to make sure Officer Williams has her facts straight.

"The trailer? Oh right, yeah. I started checking it, but then my phone rang and..." He doesn't finish his thought.

"And what? You were distracted?" Madison keeps her tone even.

"Selena called me about something. Why? What's happened?"

She shakes her head. There's nothing wrong with taking

personal calls while at work—you have to in their job because you're *always* at work—but he should've immediately returned to what he was doing. "I just found clothes and toys for a female toddler in the boxes that were stacked on the trailer. We think this family has a daughter as well as the twin boys."

It takes a second for Adams to put two and two together. Once he does, he sounds horrified. "Oh shit." He goes silent for a second. "I've given the killer time to get away with her, haven't I?"

"Yes. You have."

"I'll come straight there."

"No!" It comes out more forcefully than she intended. "There's no point. You're better off searching for surveillance footage because that's probably the only way we're going to find out who was coming and going from this area on Sunday." Madison takes a deep breath. "You're making this so much harder than it needs to be. You *have* to see things through in a case like this. If you get called away from a task, you should immediately ask a uniform to take over. Or you focus on one thing at a time. Got it?"

It takes a second for him to reply and when he does, he's defensive. "I know that, and I don't appreciate being schooled. I've worked in law enforcement a lot longer than you have, Harper."

"Not as a detective you haven't." He was a sergeant before coming to Lost Creek. "If you don't want to be here, then quit already so we can give the job to someone who wants it. Because if you keep making mistakes, I'm going to have to tell Chief Mendes you're compromising the investigation, and I don't want to be that person. I *want* to have your back and I want *you* to have mine. So get busy working or get busy quitting, because I want to catch this bastard before he hurts anyone else."

She's not trying to make him feel bad, but someone's got to tell him he's not performing.

With an even tone, he says, "I hear you. I'll get the surveillance footage and get back to you."

He doesn't wait for her to respond before he ends the call. Madison looks at Steve and shakes her head.

"He's still not working out, is he?" says Steve.

"I can't understand why he stays here when he clearly hates it." She slips her phone into her pocket. "I really wish Mendes had given you the job."

Steve had applied for it, so had Shelley. For some reason Mendes gave it to an outsider instead. Apparently, Mendes worked with Adams's brother at the Colorado Bureau of Investigation and thought Adams would be as good as him. Madison doesn't want to be the one to tell her he isn't.

Steve's looking at her weirdly. "You'd prefer me over Adams?" he says.

Madison snorts. "It's not really a compliment given I'd prefer anyone over Adams."

He nods with a faint smile. "Fair enough."

She looks at the reporters waiting behind the yellow tape and decides to hold an impromptu press briefing. "I'm going to speak to those guys in the hope we can get people looking for the girl as fast as possible."

Pulling his car keys out of his pocket Steve says, "I should get back to the station to brief Chief Mendes and the team. I'll send you Doug Draper's address as soon as I have it."

"Thanks."

Madison watches him back out of the driveway before approaching the crowd of reporters. The media could help her locate the missing toddler faster, so it's best she lays her cards on the table. She can't risk any delay now a child's life is at risk.

"Hey, everyone." She knows most people present, although the local newspaper appears to have a new journalist, a tall, skinny male who wears glasses with the thickest lenses she's ever seen. His eyes appear huge behind them. He's holding out his cell phone ready to capture what she says. His employee badge tells her his name is Burt Taylor.

Madison gets right to the point. "I have some disturbing information to give you, so I'd appreciate it if you'd share what I'm about to say all over your social media, and make it your leading stories. You'll understand why in just a second. Everyone good to go?"

The whole crowd is holding out smartphones and mics. Video cameras sit on shoulders and, once everyone hushes, Madison chooses a camera to look into and begins. "I'm Detective Madison Harper from Lost Creek PD. On Monday evening, dispatch was contacted by a member of the public, who asked if a welfare check could be carried out on the residents of the property behind me. Shortly after arriving on scene we found a family of four deceased. The two adults appear to have been bludgeoned to death. They had twin boys around seven or eight years old. One of the boys suffered a stab wound to the stomach, the other, the medical examiner believes, was smothered to death."

The reporters stare at her, their expressions blank. No doubt they'll dwell on the shocking details later, once they've completed their broadcasts and articles.

"This is a brutal attack on a family who had only very recently moved into the property," she continues. "I want to appeal for information about the family's arrival at the residence; specifically what time they arrived and what vehicle they arrived in. That vehicle is now missing. I also want to hear from anyone who saw anything out of the ordinary on Sunday. We believe the family was killed Sunday evening. If you saw anyone driving around this area Sunday night, or you witnessed erratic behavior, or saw bloodstains on someone's clothes, get in touch with LCPD immediately. Alternatively, if you saw a family with twin boys filling up at a gas station or stopping for snacks on their way through Gold Rock heading into Lost Creek, tell us about it."

She takes a deep breath. "Further to this incident, about thirty minutes ago, our searches revealed there may have been another child in the house at the time of the murders. We believe the family has a little girl, between two and three years old. She has *not* been located at this time."

Finally, the crowd displays some emotion: animated glances all around. They know this will attract viewers and readership and keep them busy over the coming days. The public likes nothing more than trying to help find a missing child.

"I'd like to appeal to the public to keep your eyes open for any neighbors, friends or family members who suddenly have a young female toddler in their care. If that's unexpected for the person, get in touch immediately. Our goal is to locate the toddler alive as fast as possible, and to find the person or persons who took her and killed her entire family." She pauses. "Any questions?"

The reporters stumble over each other in their bid to ask questions. Madison can't understand them. "One at a time!" she yells.

"Have you issued an Amber Alert?" asks Burt.

"Not yet because we've literally just found this out. We don't have a description of the child, but Chief Mendes will no doubt arrange for an Amber Alert to be issued as soon as possible."

"What are the names of the victims?" asks an older female reporter named Jess.

"Unfortunately, we haven't been able to identify them yet. Nothing has been found in the property to help us with this, so please, check on your loved ones and your neighbors. If you know a family of four or five who you haven't seen since Sunday, call them. If they don't respond, get in touch and we'll follow it up. We want to identify them as fast as possible in order to notify their loved ones what's happened, and to look into who was in their close circle of friends and acquaintances."

"Does that mean you suspect the killer knew them and this isn't a random attack?" asks Jess. "Because this is obviously going to frighten the community."

Madison nods. "I understand this is alarming news, and I have no guarantee this couldn't happen again, so the public should remain vigilant at all times. However, I will say that at this stage in our investigation, I believe it's unlikely the killer will strike twice here. If it wasn't personal to these victims, the killer has probably already left town, but I can't make any promises and everyone should be on high alert for behavior that's out of the ordinary. The public should *not* approach any suspects directly as they will more than likely be armed and dangerous. Contact LCPD. That's our job."

A young true-crime fanatic called Rory pushes his cell phone forward. Madison's seen some of his YouTube videos over the last few months, as the dispatch ladies like to watch him between calls. "Do you know if the victims are even from Lost Creek?" he asks.

"No, I don't. And I can't issue photos because of their physical condition." Madison reels off the best description she has of the adults: their heights, approximate ages and physical features. "If they sound like anyone you know, get in touch. Remember; we're looking for a female child between two and three years old."

She's eager to get to work so she wraps things up. "Someone from the department will keep you all updated with any significant developments. Thanks, guys."

They turn from her and start doing pieces to camera. Burt shoots off on his bike, presumably back to the newsroom.

Madison turns back to face the house, her mind spinning with everything she needs to do.

CHAPTER EIGHTEEN

The sun is weakening by the time Nate leaves the office to head home. He finished the case he was working on for Richie and spent a lot of the afternoon trawling through emails that have come in via his new website. Some were just spam, but he was impressed by the overall response rate. It reminded him just how many people hire a private investigator.

A lot of the genuine emails were from people desperate to find out if their partner is cheating, and that's not really what Nate's hoping to focus on. He wants to help people who are in serious trouble. Maybe those who have been wrongly convicted. People who have no one on the outside to investigate for them. No families fighting their corner. Nate had his father by his side during his own murder trial, but it had aged his father and he eventually succumbed to cancer just a few years after Nate's conviction.

His siblings—a brother and sister presumably still living in Kansas—stopped all contact once he was arrested for murder. They were never particularly close, but it hurt. It hurt having no family to stay in touch with during his slow-moving time inside. He occasionally thinks of tracking his brother down to see if he'd want to meet and catch up, but he doesn't want to reopen old wounds. Nate's obviously the black sheep of the Monroe family and he doesn't want to put his brother or sister through any more heartache. It must've been difficult living in his shadow, even after his exoneration. After all, not everyone believes he's innocent of killing Stacey Conner. Her real killer has plenty of followers willing to believe the priest.

Brody jumps into the open door of the car and settles on the back seat. Nate's tried keeping him in the trunk but the dog has his own ideas on how to travel. As a result, Nate's missing half of the headrests in the back of the car. Apparently, they're fun to chew.

With his seatbelt secured, Nate checks his cell and realizes he has a couple of missed calls from his contact at the FBI. He'd set his phone to silent while in a meeting with Richie and a client this afternoon.

Special Agent Lisa Baxter keeps hounding him for an answer as to whether or not he'll attend Father Connor's trial. Apparently, their case isn't as strong without their star witness.

Even though he doesn't feel comfortable returning to Texas, he knows it would be the right thing to do. Despite that, he can't bring himself to confirm one way or the other and hopes he can leave town and go off-grid before he has to commit either way. Realistically though, he knows there's no way of getting out of it. He seems destined to spend his life talking and thinking about the so-called priest.

As he pulls away from downtown and begins the journey home, his phone rings in the holder, making him jump. A quick glance tells him it's the FBI again. He rejects the call, but immediately it rings again. Nate lets out an irritated sigh.

He rejects it, and again the woman calls him right back.

"That's it." Nate pulls off the road and keeps his engine running as he answers the call. "I'm driving. Can't this wait?"

"Hi, it's Lisa Baxter."

"I know. I'm busy."

"You're always busy. But what I have to tell you can't wait. Pull over and switch your engine off. You're going to want to hear this."

Nate's heart skips a beat. This can only be bad news. Several thoughts rush through his head; has Connor come up with new accusations against him, in a desperate bid to deflect attention from himself? Has he killed again while inside? Has he made a new threat to Nate's life?

He switches the engine off with trembling hands. He just wants this whole sorry affair to be over, but it never is. It just gets worse and worse and it's been going on for twenty years now.

"You pulled over?" she asks.

Nate fights the urge to hang up, throw the phone away and drive right out of Colorado, never looking back. But part of him knows the Father Connor drama would follow him one way or another. Because it always does.

Brody sits up on the back seat and stares at him in the rearview mirror. He looks inquisitive. He can always tell when Nate's agitated. Maybe he can smell it on his sweat or something.

"Yeah. What is it?" asks Nate. "What's happened now?"

"Actually," she says, "I think you might be pleased about this latest development with Father Connor's case."

He remains silent. He can't imagine the words *pleased* and *Father Connor* being used together. Not unless he's been convicted without Nate needing to take the stand.

When she realizes he's not going to speak, the special agent says, "Mr. Monroe, Jack Connor passed away in the early hours of this morning."

Nate's mouth drops open and everything around him goes silent. It's as if time stands still. Not a single car passes him as he sits there, numb, while cold goosebumps cover his arms.

After a few seconds his eyes unexpectedly well up. He can't believe what he's hearing. He dare not believe it for fear they're lying to him. It could be a trick.

"You okay?" she asks.

He clears his throat. "Was he killed?"

"No. He was found unresponsive in his cell with no injuries or signs of distress. Looks like he just slipped away peacefully in his sleep. The guy just turned eighty, so the coroner doesn't think an autopsy is necessary. Let's just say he had known heart problems."

Nate closes his eyes against the rush of emotions surging through him. He thinks of his fiancée, Stacey, whose death was so brutal. And of the years of torment Connor put Nate and those around him through. He killed Rex Hartley, Nate's closest friend upon exoneration, and he badly hurt Kristen Devereaux, the woman who got Nate out of prison. Yet the guy gets to just slip away in his sleep like he wasn't a monster who deserved a worse end? It's a sick joke.

"He'll never be convicted now," Nate whispers.

It's a devastating blow. Because Connor got exactly what he wanted; in the eyes of the law he died an innocent man. His guilt was never proven. The thought is unbearable for Nate. It's like the priest won. After everything that happened, he got the ending he always wanted. Nate grips the steering wheel.

"No, he won't be convicted," admits Lisa. "But he's dead. Isn't that enough?"

Nate doesn't think it is. Not right now anyway. "I have to go." He doesn't wait for her response. He ends the call.

Brody leans in and forces a paw on Nate's arm. He barely registers it. His whole life has changed in one phone call.

It'll take a while to sink in that, for the first time in twenty years, he's finally a free man.

CHAPTER NINETEEN

Madison's driving through town and heading back to the station when she gets a message from Steve. It's busy on the roads with people finishing work, so she pulls over to read it.

Doug Draper has DUIs but that's it.

That doesn't mean he's clean. He might just be good at intimidating his victims enough to stop them from filing charges.

Her phone pings again.

I checked his address. Looks like he bought your sister's ranch.

She stares at the message in disbelief. She hadn't known anyone moved into Angie and Wyatt's empty ranch. It makes sense Angie sold it, considering she's locked up and needs money for lawyers.

Shall I send Adams to meet you there?

Madison considers whether to go alone. It's seven p.m., the sun is setting and her sister's ranch is in Gold Rock, which is a half-hour drive away if you obey the speed limit. The missing toddler could be there, so she doesn't want to wait for Adams to turn up. That guy would be late to his own funeral.

No need to send Adams. I'm near the One-Way Bridge already.

Then, because she knows he'll worry if she goes alone, she adds:

Will check in with you as soon as I'm done.

Steve replies with a thumbs-up.

She hits the gas. The fact that Doug Draper purchased her sister's ranch and is said to be a loan shark fills her with dread. Could he be as corrupt as her sister and brother-in-law were? Did he know them? Is he working for Angie? Her sister could easily be running something from the inside. She has enough contacts.

By the time Madison reaches the tiny old ghost town, she's assuming the worst. She hates this place. It's stuck in the past with its lack of sidewalks, run-down saloon and just a handful of old stores, mostly selling guns. No one from out of town ever moves here, so she can't see why Doug Draper felt compelled to. Giving him the benefit of the doubt, she supposes he could've bought the property for the business opportunity. There's money in junk. But it also provides a money laundering opportunity.

Pulling up outside the auto repair business that comes with the ranch, Madison's stomach is filled with nerves. She hasn't been here in a while and it looks exactly the same as the day her brother-in-law died a gruesome, painful death. It was the same day she lost a former co-worker too.

Detective Mike Bowers shouldn't have died that day, but there was nothing she could've done to stop it from happening. She knows that now.

With daylight diminishing, some super-bright outdoor lights are switched on throughout the salvage yard, reflecting off the metal and glass from the scrapped cars. She has to squint to see anything. Even at this time in the evening she can hear the car crusher working hard, and the sound of a couple of guys shooting the shit as they work.

On the other side of the generous property, the large horse paddock sits in semidarkness, but she can still tell it's empty. Maybe Angie's horses were sold at auction, same as the rest of the place.

Madison takes a deep breath before getting out of her car. A quick touch of her weapon reassures her as she closes the door and approaches the porch steps. Before she even gets to the top, someone yells out, "Can I help you?"

She turns away from the front door just as a man appears behind her from the direction of the repair shop. His face is in shadow until he gets closer. He's tall, maybe around fifty years old and tough looking. She can see his biceps through his greasy T-shirt.

"Hi," she says as she descends the steps. "I'm Detective Harper from LCPD. I'm looking for Doug Draper."

He stops a few steps away from her and casts a critical glance over her entire body. With no ounce of friendliness in his voice he says, "What can I help you with, Detective?"

Unfazed, she says, "I'm working on a homicide case in Lost Creek. It took place at the home of Linda Hendricks. Does that name mean anything to you?"

He doesn't stop to think. "Nope. Can't say it does."

She likes it when people incriminate themselves by lying to

her right away. It makes her job so much easier. "What do you do for work, Mr. Draper?"

He crosses his arms. "What's that got to do with anything?"

"Do you work in the salvage yard full-time? Because I can't imagine that brings in too much money."

With a crack of his knuckles he looks her dead in the eyes. "I guess you'd know, seeing as your sister and her husband started this business."

Madison doesn't react, but it confirms he knows about Angie and Wyatt. The question now is whether he's picked up where they left off. "That's right," she says. "I understand they had to supplement their income by numerous illegal means."

He remains silent.

"Did you know them well?" she asks.

"Never spoken to either of them. Bought this place through an online auction, sight unseen."

She considers whether he's lying to her. Even if he is, it would be easy to check how he bought the property. "Well I'm here because I've been told Linda Hendricks may have owed you some money. Could you confirm that for me?"

"How could she if I didn't know her?" he says. "I'm not in the habit of loaning strangers money, Detective."

"I understand." Changing tack, she says, "Where were you all day this past Sunday?" She watches closely for his body language. It doesn't change. His arms are crossed tight and he's careful not to show any anger.

"Sundays are my day off. I was here with my wife."

"Is it just you two living here or do you have kids?"

His expression is guarded as he says, "Just us."

"What's your wife's name? I'm going to need to speak to her."

Finally, a flicker of annoyance crosses his face. "Nancy. She's probably in bed now though. I'll ask her to call you tomorrow."

Madison turns to the house and makes for the porch. "That's fine, I won't keep her long."

Doug runs ahead of her and blocks her passage to the front door. "I don't want her woken. She doesn't sleep good at the best of times. She'll call you tomorrow."

Madison's not surprised by his reaction. He probably wants time to get his alibi straight with his wife. To coach her on what to say. But she doesn't have any grounds to barge into this couple's home and demand to speak to his wife. She listens quietly for a second for any children's voices coming from inside, but there's nothing.

She pulls out her card and hands it to him. "I'd appreciate that. She can leave a message if I don't answer."

As she turns to leave, she hears the front door creak open behind her.

"What's going on?" asks a woman.

Doug answers. "Not now, Nancy."

Madison turns to face her. Nancy Draper looks a little older than her husband, with a heavily lined face and dark circles. She has the weary look of an insomniac, and is in her pajamas despite it not yet being eight p.m. A large gold crucifix hangs around her neck.

"Sorry to bother you this late, ma'am. I'm Detective Harper from LCPD."

Her face lights up and her hands go to her chest. "My God! Have you found her?"

Madison frowns. Maybe Nancy's been watching the news. "Not yet, I'm afraid, but we're working on it. I just wanted to ask you some—"

Doug interrupts her. "I told you *not now*, Detective." He enters the house, shuffling Nancy backward and keeping the door as closed as possible while he enters. "We'll call you tomorrow," he barks over his shoulder.

With that, he slams the door shut.

Madison's left confused. The fact that Nancy Draper asked whether she'd found the missing girl suggests she's not here. Maybe Doug wasn't involved after all. He denied lending Linda Hendricks money, but she doesn't know how she'd prove he did, considering the woman's dead and buried.

But if he has nothing to hide, why won't he let her ask his wife about his alibi? The woman did seem a little confused. Maybe she has an illness and he didn't want her bothered.

She walks away from the house toward her car feeling even more uneasy about Doug Draper. But until she can prove he's doing anything wrong, she won't be able to secure a search warrant for his home. Which means she's back to square one.

CHAPTER TWENTY

The sun has set by the time Madison arrives at the station, and she's tired. It's been a long day and she needs dinner and a shower. But she can't go home yet, there's too much to do. She attempts to speak to Chief Mendes on arrival, but Mendes is on the phone. While she waits, Madison heads to her desk and uses the time to run a background check on a few people she's spoken to today, including Dawn Freemantle and her partner Kai Bishop.

She learns Dawn is seventy years old and comes with a long history of driving offenses. Kai is thirty-seven and has a previous conviction for domestic battery from a decade ago.

"That's interesting." She leans into her computer screen and reads the notes on his case. It appears he's not as easy-going as he tried to portray at the house. Apparently, he beat the crap out of a former girlfriend. He claims he acted in self-defense because the girlfriend was stealing from him and when he found out, she threatened to kill him. "Sounds like a healthy relationship," she mutters.

Kai served two years in prison for it but was released eight years ago and he's not been in trouble since then.

It's something to bear in mind. Living in close proximity to the crime scene means he can't be ruled out. Maybe he got drunk or high and decided to walk over there to introduce himself to the new neighbors. Maybe things took an unexpected turn for the worse while he was there. Although, Dawn didn't appear to mind Madison visiting her earlier, so she clearly wasn't hiding a toddler for her boyfriend. Not unless the girl was bound and tied somewhere out of view.

A chill goes through her. It doesn't bear thinking about.

She checks Kai's registered address and it's showing as Dawn's place. He's living there with Dawn, her grandson and her incapacitated husband. It's a strange set-up.

As soon as Chief Mendes is off the phone, she comes to find Madison. Madison updates her about the missing toddler. She leaves out the part where Adams could've found the child's clothes sooner if he'd finished searching the trailer. There's no need to throw her partner under the bus. "We need to issue an Amber Alert as fast as possible."

With her arms crossed, Mendes says. "We need her name first, or at least a photograph and a description."

Frustrated, Madison sighs. "We don't have any photos. I think we can assume she's a Caucasian girl judging by her brothers and parents, and I know her clothes suggest she's two to three years old. That's literally all I have so far."

"And nothing else has been found at the house?"

"Not that would identify any of the family, no," she says. "It's bizarre. They must've been on the run from someone to travel with so few personal belongings."

"You think that's why they chose that property?" asks Mendes. "Were they squatters?"

Madison leans back in her seat. "I've been thinking about it a lot, and that seems like the only explanation to me. They probably weren't planning on staying long, which means they must've been trying to get away from someone. And let's face it, their killer wouldn't have taken the time to hunt through all their possessions in order to steal every identifying document and photograph. There's no way! Cell phones, sure. And their vehicle, because that could be sold or traced back to them. But the killer would've wanted to get straight out of there the minute they were done killing. Which leads me to believe the couple didn't bring any identifying documents with them in the first place."

Steve joins them. "I agree with Madison. Records show the house was still in Linda's name. I don't think the victims were from here. If you ask me, I think they traveled here incognito to get away from someone."

"But if they were on the run, who were they running from and why?" asks Mendes.

"Oh man, it could be anything," says Steve. "Financial difficulties, an affair, trying to avoid prison time... The list is endless."

Madison fills them in on her visit to Doug Draper. "It looked like he was hiding something because he wouldn't let his wife speak and he wouldn't let me in the house. I don't think the child was there though. Maybe Doug was up to something else on Sunday that he doesn't want us to know about." She looks at Steve. "Could you try to track down the woman who told you he seized her car when she couldn't pay him back?"

He nods. "Sure. It shouldn't be too difficult."

Not wanting to focus too much on one person, Madison considers other motives for the murders, such as an affair. When visiting the victims in the morgue she'd noticed the male wasn't wearing a wedding ring. If he was having an affair with the female victim, they could've kidnapped the children from one or both of their spouses in a bid to start fresh somewhere they couldn't be found.

It seems a little too outlandish to be true, but not impossible.

Although, if they were killed because they kidnapped the kids, then how come the children's lives weren't spared?

"I wonder whether there could've been a custody battle going on," she says.

"Because one was taken and the other two killed?" says Mendes.

"Right. They could be a blended family who absconded with the girl against the other parent's wishes."

Steve nods. "Wouldn't be the first time that's happened. At least if that's the case, she's unlikely to be harmed, plus there will be some record somewhere of the custody case. Once we know their names, we could be on a fast track to finding the person who did this."

The thought gives Madison a boost but they're a long way from identifying the victims. "Without their names we can't even check if they ever filed a protective order against someone." Looking around the station she asks, "Is Alex in?"

"I saw him at the front desk a few minutes ago," says Steve. "He was talking to his girlfriend. I get the impression she turned up unannounced."

Chief Mendes looks across the office, unimpressed. "He should be working."

Madison stands. "I'll go find him. I want to see whether he's fingerprinted the victims yet."

Chief Mendes heads for her office. "Let me look into getting that Amber Alert issued."

Once she's gone, Alex appears with a sullen expression. He makes a beeline for the hallway that leads to his office, clearly trying to avoid them.

Steve calls him over. "Alex? Got a second?"

Madison senses something's happened between him and Sam. "Everything okay?" she asks as he approaches.

Alex shrugs unhappily. "Let's just say everything's going exactly as I predicted."

"What does that mean?" asks Steve.

With a glance around the busy office, Alex leads them to the small kitchen nearby so they can talk in private. It's empty when they arrive and the strong smell of coffee beans makes Madison's stomach yearn for a drink.

Alex faces them. "Sam just dumped me."

"That sucks," says Madison. "I'm sorry. Did she say why?"

"She did, but now I'm even more confused." He reddens slightly as he says, "It seems Sam's realized she's attracted to women. She said being with me has helped her accept the fact."

Steve winces. "Ouch. Sorry, man."

Madison doesn't know what to say.

"She's thirty years old," says Alex, looking at Madison. "What do *you* think? Does it really take that long to realize you're attracted to the same sex?"

Madison shrugs. "What do I know? I've been single so long I'd sleep with anyone at this rate."

She's joking, kind of. She's always known she was bisexual. She's attracted to someone's personality initially. She has to be able to trust them and they have to make her laugh, because her job can make her world too dark. The only girlfriend she ever had was killed last year, and despite their relationship ending eleven years ago, it was the last relationship Madison had. Spending six years in prison will put a dampener on your love life. And it's bound to be a turn-off for any potential love interest in the future. She knows she could be single forever but chooses not to dwell on it.

A fragmented memory of a dream suddenly comes back to her. She looks at Steve and smiles. "Oh my God, I had a dream about you the other night!" She blushes hard. It was pretty sordid.

Steve's face lights up. "Me? Really?"

"Yeah, but don't get too excited. I've had hot dreams about Mendes too."

Someone is hovering behind them in the doorway. They clear their throat to make themselves known. Madison turns and sees Chief Mendes staring at her, empty coffee mug in one hand.

Shit.

"Hey," she says casually. Her face reddens more by the second, so she turns back to Steve and Alex and silently cringes.

Steve stifles a laugh while Mendes fills her cup and leaves without saying a word.

Mortified, Madison says, "I can't believe she heard that."

Ever since Chief Mendes joined LCPD last year, speculation has grown that she could be gay. But that kind of speculation over someone's sexual preferences isn't unusual here. If you've never been seen with a partner, the rumors soon begin. It's done in jest, as a needed distraction from the daily horror of their jobs, and they wouldn't do it to anyone who couldn't take it. LCPD's current team is unusual in that no one has a problem with other people's sexuality. It's refreshing.

Alex, absorbed by his own drama, is oblivious. "I suspect Sam just said that as an excuse to dump me." He sighs. "You know, even though she's the only girlfriend I ever had who was actually interested in hearing about my job, I knew she was too good for me. I expected this to happen sooner or later."

Madison pats his shoulder. "Listen, you're a great catch. It's her loss. She sounds like she doesn't know what she wants. Maybe you're better off without her."

He nods, but he doesn't seem convinced.

She pours three mugs of coffee and, in an attempt to take Alex's mind off his love life, she asks what potential evidence he's found so far. After all, forensics is his first love.

"Well," he says, coming to life, "I've fingerprinted the victims and run the prints through the database, but neither of the adults has a criminal record, so I haven't been able to identify them."

Madison shoots Steve a disappointed look. "Dammit."

"Dr. Scott will provide some DNA samples that the lab can cross-reference with CODIS, but it's unlikely that'll be a successful route given the fingerprints aren't."

"Great," she says with a sigh. "We have an entire family we can't ID, which means we can't speak to their friends, co-workers or relatives. We have their DNA but nothing to compare it to. We have a potentially missing child who we can't release an Amber Alert for because we need her description for that. And we don't have the murder weapon, or the motive." She takes a sip of hot coffee and winces when it burns the back of her throat. When she's stressed, she gets acid reflux.

Footsteps behind them makes Madison turn again. Detective Adams has arrived. "Hi," he says with a sheepish look. He probably thinks they're talking about him.

She nods at him.

"Hey, Alex," he says. "I just saw your girlfriend leaving the parking lot. How the hell did you manage to hook up with her, man? What's your secret?" He grins like a moron. For some reason Adams finds pleasure in busting Alex's balls.

Madison coughs, trying to get his attention so that he'll stop talking.

Of course, Adams doesn't notice. Instead, he continues. "Have you forensic guys come up with some kind of high-tech body spray that lures the women in? Something that drugs them into thinking you're hotter than you really are? Because if you have, you need to sell us some. Right, Sarge?" He looks at Steve and laughs at his own joke. He does that a lot.

Steve crosses his arms. "Zip it, Adams. They just broke up."

Alex lowers his eyes. "No, Detective. I can't say I've ever resorted to drugging a lady."

"Ah, shit. Sorry, man." Mortified, Adams says, "I was just screwing with you."

An awkward silence falls over them. With no one

attempting to speak, Madison changes the subject. "Did you find any surveillance footage?"

Adams pulls two flash drives out from his shirt pocket. "I have the footage from two cameras at the gas station on Twin Pines Road. I need to watch it all through, unless someone else wants to do that?" He looks at Alex, hopeful that he'll volunteer for what is a notoriously boring job.

"I have enough to do," says Alex.

Madison thinks he probably would've agreed to do it if the guy hadn't just mocked him.

"And I'm looking into the original homeowner of our crime scene," says Steve. "Would you rather do that?"

Shaking his head, Adams says, "That's even more dull than watching footage."

Alex heads for the exit. "I better get to my office. I have several items to send to the lab for analysis."

"Oh yeah?" says Madison. "Like what?"

"The pillow we think one of the boys was smothered with. Plus, I found some hairs and fibers around the adults that looked promising. I need to get them compared to the victims' DNA. After all, if we can't identify the victims, we can at least concentrate on identifying the killer."

Madison feels a flurry of excitement in her stomach. "Alex? If you manage to work wonders, *I'll* be your girlfriend."

He blushes. "That might make Sam jealous if nothing else."

"Get them to fast-track *all* DNA results," she says. "Tell them a toddler's life is at risk."

He nods before disappearing.

Aware it's getting late, Madison leaves Steve and Adams talking in the kitchen as she considers going home. She approaches the dispatchers' cubicle on her way. Dina's taking a call, so she approaches Stella.

"Hey, Stella. Has anyone called in with any tips or leads about the homicides?"

Stella lowers her headset. "No, I'm getting calls from people asking what's going on. Apparently Channel Nine has just aired your piece to camera from this afternoon, so it's about to get busier on the lines."

That's good news. The more people looking for the killer and the girl, the better. "Fingers crossed we're not inundated with time wasters."

Dina finishes her call and takes a sip of something from her pink plastic bottle. "Think the killer could be gone by now?" she asks.

Madison hopes not. "We have no idea. I need you guys to take every single call seriously and get patrol to check out any credible tips. Contact me or Adams right away if it sounds like we need to arrange a search of a particular location or if we need to follow up with anyone acting suspicious. Adams is on duty tonight, but if you can't reach him for whatever reason, call me. Okay?"

"Got it," says Dina. With a smile she adds, "How you holding up about Saturday?"

Madison's stomach flutters with nerves. Being busy today has meant she hasn't had much time to think about Owen's departure. "Can't say I'm looking forward to it. I just feel like I'm going to make a fool of myself, you know? That I won't be able to hold everything in long enough to wave him off."

Stella nods sympathetically. "It's hard. I cried for weeks after every single one of mine left." Stella was a foster carer in her younger years, so she's been through this many times.

Dina says, "I wouldn't worry too much about him leaving. Kids are like boomerangs; they always come back. It'll get to the point where you'll wish he stayed away longer between visits because you'll be enjoying your freedom so much."

Madison can't imagine ever feeling that way.

Dina's attention returns to her computer screen as she takes another incoming call. "That's right," she says to the caller.

"We're looking for a female toddler. Why do you ask?" She rolls her eyes, indicating she has a time waster on the line.

Stella looks at Madison. "The poor child is so young to be out there with some stranger who's killed her entire family. I'll be praying for her before bed tonight."

Madison wishes prayers were enough to find this little girl alive.

CHAPTER TWENTY-ONE

FIFTEEN YEARS EARLIER

21.5 hours remaining

Just an hour after they dragged Dennis McKinney out of here, Mike's been asked to help the other uniforms tear apart Dennis's home for any evidence that he might be involved in the missing baby's disappearance. The guy lives with his father, who's away on business and has no idea what he'll come home to in a couple of days' time.

In the meantime, Dennis has lawyered up. He's not talking to Detective Ramsey at all anymore.

Tiffany's provided a description of what her daughter was wearing when she vanished earlier today: a yellow T-shirt, pink shorts and a pair of white plastic sandals. Her hair was tied back with a yellow ribbon, to keep her neck cool.

On the one hand, Mike's hoping he's not the one to find something. He could do without the nightmares. On the other hand, the baby's poor mother needs answers, and he wants to be the one to help her. Because Tiffany looks like she's not used to getting much help and may not have had the best start in life.

Mike's been watching Detective Ramsey's investigation into

Grace's disappearance closely, as he hopes to one day make detective and focus on missing person cases.

For a child to be safe at home one minute—happily playing in the yard—and then gone the next is a common occurrence in some parts of America, but not here in Lost Creek. At least not while Mike has been an officer. It's shocking. But he knows it's on the rise everywhere. There are some sick bastards getting away with horrendous crimes against children all around them, and the threat of a lengthy prison sentence is no longer a deterrent.

With two other officers searching the living room and kitchen, Mike heads for Dennis's bedroom. The guy's computer and cell phone have already been seized so that Ramsey can search for child abuse images. The heat in the house is stifling, with no evening breeze sweeping through the open windows yet.

Mike lifts the wooden bed, looking for pornographic magazines. Nothing there. In the old days, that's where guys would keep them. These days it's all online. They don't even need to pay for it. And you can watch it anonymously. Gone are the days where you had to select it from a shelf while women and children breezed past you, then take it to a female store clerk and hide your embarrassment while she wrapped it in a brown paper bag. In Mike's opinion, that's half the problem.

He lifts the mattress just to be sure. Nothing there. The reason he's checking is to see what turns this guy on, and what else he might be hiding. If Dennis is stashing pictures of naked kids under his mattress, then it's more likely Grace is already dead.

When he finds nothing, he focuses on searching the bedroom furniture. The vanity is full of clothes. With gloved hands Mike rifles through but finds nothing of interest. The closet has no secret compartments or hidden children's toys. In other words nothing that Dennis could have used to entice little Grace over to him and away from the safety of her home.

Also lacking are signs that the guy has a girlfriend, either live-in or otherwise. That doesn't mean anything. Detective Ramsey likes to remind the team that married men are just as likely to be sex offenders as single men are.

Dennis does have a collection of baseball cards that could be worth a lot of money. Mike's careful not to move them. In another room, the landline rings. Its shrill tone calls out unanswered. It's no wonder people are ditching these things faster than ever. They seem so archaic in the age of cell phones. After a while Mike can't bear it anymore so he locates the phone in the living room and answers. "Hello?"

"Who the hell is that and where's my brother?" yells a man.

Mike stands a little straighter. "The owner of this property is under arrest on suspicion of child abduction. He's being held at the station. If you want to talk to him, I suggest you contact his lawyer." He hangs up.

He knows the caller is in for a whole world of pain when he has to consider what his brother might have done to a baby.

Mike heads outside for some fresh air. He looks under, in and around bushes, trash cans and outbuildings while the sun beats down on him. His uniform is made of polyester. He can feel sweat running down his back the longer he searches. The sound of clucking chickens reaches him and he stops what he's doing. Despite the high temperature, goosebumps break out over his arms.

What if Dennis hid the girl's body in the chicken coop?

Mike gets off his knees and looks toward the far corner of the property. Several plump birds dig for food on the ground with their beaks. He slowly walks over, his chest growing tight at the thought of finding little Grace inside. His mind flashes up all kinds of images of her badly beaten body. Or maybe she was strangled. Perhaps stabbed. It would've been something quiet so that Dennis's neighbors, and Grace's mom, wouldn't be alerted to the child's demise.

He lifts the latch on the coop's perimeter fence. The birds become shrill in their excitement. Maybe they're expecting to be fed. He makes a mental note to ask someone to figure out what needs to be done to keep the birds alive in Dennis's absence.

Stepping over the birds, he reaches the wooden coop. It's not huge, but large enough to store a baby's body. It has a door. Mike reaches forward and gently pushes the door open. It's dark inside, and his eyes take a second to adjust.

Once he can see clearly, he realizes the coop is empty apart from some eggs, a lot of straw and a couple of sleeping hens. He breathes out, relieved she's not in here.

There's still hope she can be found alive.

A commotion near the side of the house makes him spin around.

One of the other officers steps away from Dennis's pickup truck, looking for Mike. "Officer Bowers?" he shouts when he sees him.

"What?" says Mike.

"I've got something." He holds it up for him to see.

It's a small white sandal.

Mike's heart sinks. He pictures Tiffany's face when Ramsey delivers the devastating news.

CHAPTER TWENTY-TWO

Madison's up at dawn, watching the sun rise lazily over the cornfields beyond her backyard as a breeze rattles the wind-chimes hanging from one of the tall fir trees to her left. The sound is calming. Raindrops glisten on the growing corn. There must've been light showers overnight.

She enjoys sipping coffee in her backyard before the madness of the day takes hold. The peace and quiet brings clarity before she has to launch herself back into the joint homicide and missing person investigation.

Owen had stayed out late again, but not to work this time. A bunch of his high school friends had planned one last party before they all disperse across the country to start their new lives. Madison stayed up and read a book in bed, waiting for him to return. In case he or his friends got into any trouble. Given their age and the occasion, she knows alcohol would've been flowing, so she was worried in case anyone was stupid enough to drink and drive.

The thought of any of them crashing their vehicles had filled her with dread. She attended too many teen RTAs during her time as a patrol officer. She still remembers her first ever one. She'd had to accompany a previous LCPD detective—John Ramsey—to notify the girl's parents. Not only had the high schooler's out-of-control driving killed herself, she'd killed five of her young friends too. They'd all been squeezed into the vehicle and they all had blood alcohol readings off the charts.

Detective Ramsey had handled her parents well. He knew exactly what to say and when. He comforted the girl's mother and stopped the girl's father from driving to the scene of the crash. He wouldn't have wanted to see what Madison and Ramsey saw. It took the fire department four hours just to cut the driver free.

Madison shudders. It doesn't bear thinking about. She's been lucky with Owen. He's a levelheaded kid. He's had to be with his upbringing. She heard him get in after midnight and he was banging around in his room for a while before she fell asleep. Perhaps he was packing at last.

She glances at her phone. Last night she'd texted Nate, just to check in and see how he is. Unusually, she hadn't gotten a response.

The back door behind her opens and Owen steps out, shielding his eyes from the bright morning sunlight. Maybe he did drink after all. He hands her the newspaper. The front page screams:

FAMILY OF FOUR SLAIN AS THEY SLEPT
Third Child Missing, Feared Abducted

They've depressingly referred to the victims as the Doe Family, since they haven't yet been identified. A photo of the family's house sits under the headlines. Officer Sanchez stands next to the yellow tape, and a shadow figure can be seen with their back to the window upstairs. Probably Alex performing his forensic exam.

Madison stops reading and looks at her son. "Morning," she says with a smile. "Did you have fun last night?"

He leans against the porch railing and nods but he looks exhausted and in need of a shower. His hair is all messy and he has some angry-looking pimples on his chin. "Kind of. It's depressing saying goodbye to everyone, you know?"

She knows too well. "You'll keep in touch with them though, right?"

Owen stands straight. "In theory, sure, I'd like to. In practice, we'll be making new friends at college, so we'll see. I'm guessing we'll all forget about each other pretty fast once we leave this place."

That must be a horrible feeling, to know you're about to lose contact with all your childhood friends. "Are you going to forget about me too?" she says, only half joking.

He smiles wistfully, but he doesn't reply. He looks like he wants to. As if he came out here with something to say. He seems to think better of it and goes silent.

"Did I hear you finally packing for college last night?" she asks.

"Yeah. Just clothes. I don't know what else I'm meant to take."

"Imagine you're going on a long vacation. Just take your favorite and most useful belongings. But don't stress about it. It'll all still be here when you come visit. I'm not going to clear your room out and turn it into a gym. Not yet, anyway," she jokes, her smile masking her pain. When unexpected tears rush to her eyes, she abruptly turns away from him. "Well, I should get to work. I guess I need to find my perp before you leave on Saturday, otherwise I'll be a mess at work."

"Sure," he says, turning to look at her. "I hope you find the girl today."

"Me too."

She enters the house through the kitchen and tries to

contain her emotions long enough for him not to notice she's on the verge of breaking down.

CHAPTER TWENTY-THREE

Once at the house, or *the murder house* as it has now been dubbed by most people, Madison sucks on a candy while squinting into the sunshine as she watches a team of officers and volunteers disperse. They're ready to begin searching the woods behind the victims' property. She ordered a ground search in case the murder weapon was discarded nearby in the killer's haste to escape. The search team has also been told to look for discarded passports, driver's licenses, wallets, cell phones and children's clothes. No one knows what the toddler was wearing when she was abducted, so every item found needs to be considered potential evidence.

Reporters wait patiently behind the yellow tape, no doubt zooming in with their cameras to see what's going on.

Madison's phone rings, distracting her. "Hello?"

"Hi, it's Lena."

She wonders whether the ME has found something useful. "Hey. How are you?"

"Good. Do you have time to talk? I've completed the autopsies on our victims."

She heads to her car and leans against the hood. "Sure. Go ahead."

"Okay, so you won't be surprised to hear my original causes of death remain the same: head trauma and loss of blood caused by blunt traumatic injury killed the adults, asphyxiation by smothering killed one twin and sharp force injury to the abdomen with loss of blood killed the second twin."

The words roll off Lena's tongue as if it's all in a day's work for her, and it is, but Madison finds herself wincing at the brutal descriptions.

"Also," Lena continues, "I checked to see whether our Jane Doe was pregnant when she died—just in case—but that was negative."

"That's a relief," says Madison. At least they won't have to add feticide charges when they catch the killer.

"I found no signs of recent sexual activity or assault on any of the victims."

"Understood." That's good for the victims, but it's one less avenue that could've provided the killer's DNA.

Lena asks, "Have you been able to identify either of the adults yet?"

"No. Their prints don't lead anywhere. Alex has sent a bunch of stuff to the crime lab to be tested, but no one in town has come forward about a missing person yet."

"Well I might have a way to help. Jane Doe had breast implants and those implants come with serial numbers. Maybe your team could use the serial numbers to track down the manufacturer and ask them which surgeon's office purchased them. You could see where that leads you?"

Madison frowns. "Do you think they keep records of that kind of thing? I mean, what if she's had them for years?"

"I agree it's a long shot, but I thought I'd mention it, just in case."

"You're right. Text me the serial numbers and I'll ask Adams or Steve to check it out."

"Sure. I also considered a number of different knives to see what type killed the boy found outside the house. The wound looks consistent with any regular steak knife that can be purchased for the home. Keep an eye out for that at the crime scene and, if you find it, I can compare it."

Steve was sure nothing of interest had been found but it's good to know what they're looking for. She'll update the search team. "Understood. Do you have any opinion on what order the victims were killed in now you've finished the autopsies?"

"I'm as confident as I can be. I believe the male was killed first, followed by the boy in the bedroom, then the boy found wounded outside, and then the female."

Madison nods. That would make sense given intruders usually disable the strongest-looking person at a scene first. The female was shorter and weighed less than the male and was therefore, presumably, less of a threat to the killer.

"I'll have the autopsy reports written up by the end of the day so you can review everything."

"Thanks, Lena."

"Before you go, I just wanted to ask you about Nate Monroe."

Madison's taken by surprise. "Nate?"

"Yeah." Lena takes a breath. "I know I've asked you in the past whether I'd be stepping on your toes if I got to know him a little better, and you said to go for it, but I got the impression the other night in the diner that things might not be as straightforward as they seem between you two."

Madison doesn't know what to say.

"I'm not prying," says Lena. "I just don't want to chase someone who's not really available. My last relationship was... violent, so when I meet a guy like Nate, it gives me hope that I don't have to be alone forever. You know what I mean?"

Madison didn't know Lena had a troubled past. "I'm sorry to hear that. You're right, Nate's a good guy." Feeling a little awkward, she chooses her words carefully. "There's nothing going on with us, but we are obviously friends. If Nate took you out for coffee, then I would assume he wants to get to know you better." She'd really rather not be having this conversation.

"Actually," says Lena, "it was *me* who asked *him* out. And I haven't heard from him since. So I guess I was trying to see whether that's because he's not interested." She doesn't wait for Madison to respond. "I think I'll just assume he isn't. Leave the ball in his court, right?"

"Right," she says. "Who knows what's going on in that head of his."

Lena says goodbye and Madison's left looking at her phone, thinking about how awkward that was. She needs to tell Nate to figure it out because she doesn't want any more conversations like that and he shouldn't screw Lena around.

She shoots him a message.

Would you please put Lena out of her misery? She's quizzing me on whether you're interested in her and I'd rather not be your wingman.

She adds a smiling emoji to soften the message.

The sound of a car engine reveals Detective Adams's Ford approaching. The vehicle is covered in dust and in desperate need of a wash. He used to keep his Camaro waxed to perfection, further confirming he really hates his replacement car.

Madison feels a pang of guilt.

Adams gets out of the car as she slips her phone away. "Hey," he says. He has bags under his eyes as if he hasn't slept. "Has the search begun already?"

"Only just." She fills him in on the latest from Lena before asking, "How did last night go?"

"Fine. I managed to track down administrative employees from the local schools. No one knew who the twins could be. The only twin boys they have are older and accounted for."

Disappointed, she asks, "What about the surveillance footage? Did you find anything on that?"

"Not last night, no, but I was watching the rest of it over breakfast this morning and I think I've found the vehicle the victims were driving. Actually, Lizzie saw it while I was cleaning up after the damn cat."

With a tilt of the head she says, "You have a cat?"

"Well, he's not ours, but he might as well be given the amount of time he spends in our house and eating our food. Anyway, he vomited on my shoe, so I told Lizzie to keep an eye on my phone while I dealt with it." He smiles. "She enjoys helping her old dad. Summer, on the other hand, would rather put pins in her eyes, or mine come to think of it." He shakes his head as he thinks about it. "I just can't understand how twins can be so different."

Madison should be surprised that Adams can't focus long enough to watch important surveillance footage, but she isn't.

He pulls his phone out and hits play on a video. "Watch this."

She immediately recognizes the area. The camera is located at a used-car dealership just a ten-minute drive east from here. The footage is good quality and shot in color. It's date and time stamped: Sunday at 9:03 a.m. Most people are home at that time, some will be getting ready to go to church.

She watches a Chevy truck drive by the dealership, heading out of town toward nearby Gold Rock. A couple of seconds later a dark blue sedan pulling a utility trailer drives by the camera. This vehicle is heading in the opposite direction.

Madison looks at Adams. "Dawn Freemantle said she saw a dark-colored sedan here the day the family moved in."

"Right, I remember you told me," he says. "It's got to be them. If I zoom in, you can see two adults in the front."

She leans in to his phone as he replays the footage. At the right moment he pauses it to enlarge the image. A male can be seen in the driver's seat, with a female next to him. The top halves of their faces are obscured by the car's sun visors as well as the baseball caps they're wearing. The lower parts of their faces that are visible are just a beige blur with no identifying features. Not unlike how they ended up.

"Can we read their license plate?"

"No," he says. "Not from this angle as the plates never face the camera head-on. Maybe someone else captured the car en route to Lost Creek, but there's not much this side of town business-wise, so this is probably the only camera they passed once they got here and made their way to the house."

"That's annoying. If we had their license plate, it would be easier to track their journey backward using traffic cameras and figure out where they traveled from." She sighs. "You should head to Gold Rock and see if any cameras or locals there spotted them, because they had to go through Gold Rock to get here."

"That shitty place?" says Adams, disappointed. "It's a ghost town. No one there would even notice if aliens camped outside the saloon."

He's not wrong there. "It's still worth pursuing. In your footage does the car appear again later on?"

"I don't know yet, I need to go fetch the next video. The dealership owner wasn't forthright in providing everything, so I had to coax this much out of him."

Madison shakes her head in frustration. "Why are some people so damn unhelpful? You'd think they'd want us to catch the bad guys." She turns to look at the house. "You'll be able to get a warrant for it now we know the vehicle drove by the dealership. Go get everything they have, and Adams?"

"What?" He looks at her.

"Your daughter might be helpful, but she's not a cop. Watch it yourself. All of it."

Amused, he lets the dig slide. "I will."

"I'm serious. Even if we don't get their license plate and just capture their car on camera at various locations along their journey, we can track their route backward and find out where they were living before they moved here."

"Which means we can interview their neighbors. Got it." He springs into action, rushing to his car. It's the first time Madison's ever seen him enthused about something.

CHAPTER TWENTY-FOUR

When Nate arrives for work, Brody runs ahead of him into the building. Owen and Richie don't appear to be around, leaving just Richie's office manager, Janine Blake, to greet him.

"Morning," he says.

Janine looks up from her computer behind the reception desk. "Jeez, what happened to you? You look like you haven't slept in a week. Was there a party I wasn't invited to? 'Cause you know how I hate missing out on a good party."

Nate smiles faintly. Janine's like one of those small dogs whose larger-than-life personality makes up for what they lack in size. She's an older lady and petite, but you usually hear her before you see her. "I wish," he says. "No, it was just a bad night. I couldn't sleep."

He doesn't tell her that he had a reckless coke binge after learning of Father Connor's death. Scoring drugs in Lost Creek is just as easy as scoring drugs anywhere in America. Using a few lines to help him cope with stress is something that started after he was freed from prison, but he hadn't touched the stuff this year. Until last night.

Being high used to make him feel better, but not this time. This time he felt like a complete loser for letting himself be affected by the priest. He vowed to make it his last time. Things have got to change.

"Lucky for you there's coffee in the kitchen," says Janine. "You may as well top me up while I say a special good morning to a special good boy." She holds up her chipped coffee-stained mug and winks at him. Brody sits next to Janine's chair, eagerly awaiting his morning greeting.

"Sure." Nate takes it from her. While in the kitchen he hears her fussing over Brody. It makes him smile. Brody used to hate being fussed over when Nate first discovered him at the summer camp in Shadow Falls, California. Things sure have changed since then. For both of them.

Once both mugs are full of coffee he returns to the front office and places Janine's on a stack of paperwork. "Is it okay to use Richie's office?"

She nods. "He's in court all morning. He'll never know. I don't know where young Owen is though. He promised me he'd shred all this today." She nods to the paperwork.

Owen's been working on turning the office paperless. It's not the most interesting job, so Nate can understand why he's bailed on her. "I'm sure he'll be along soon."

He leads Brody into Richie's cramped office. The dog smells of Janine. Her perfume is so strong it could be used as a fire accelerant. "Settle down, buddy."

Brody hovers by Nate's side as he gets comfortable at Richie's desk. The dog has been keeping a close eye on him after last night. Maybe it's because he's a former K9 but Brody doesn't approve of Nate's sporadic drug use. Eventually he slides his paws out and settles on the floor next to the desk with a loud yawn.

Checking his phone, Nate sees a text from Madison about

Lena. It seems the medical examiner might be looking for more than just friendship. He replies with a thumbs-up. He hadn't realized Lena was interested; he thought she was just being friendly.

After getting news about Father Connor's death last night, he'd considered calling Madison to let her know. She has a vested interest as she's been caught in the madness of the priest's homicidal games. What put him off was knowing she would've dropped everything to come straight over to be with him. She would've wanted to comfort him and make sure he didn't do anything stupid.

That's not what Nate wanted or needed. He wanted to release his anger and disappointment in the situation. Over Connor dying pain-free in his sleep. Nate knows from experience that if he didn't get that out of his system, it would've built up and eventually destroyed him. It's not that he's in favor of capital punishment—he'd be the last person to agree with that after sharing death row with so many other innocent people— but he wanted justice. He wanted the world to finally accept that Father Connor was the cold-blooded killer he'd made Nate out to be.

But life doesn't work like that. At least, not for him.

Madison will find out about Connor's death eventually. It'll be all over the news soon. Nate pulls open his laptop to google the priest for the fourth time this morning. He knows that once the news breaks, the media will try to find him for comment. Thanks to some of the high-profile cases he's worked on with Madison over the previous year, it won't take long for them to locate him here in Lost Creek.

Google has no results about Father Connor's death, just information about his scheduled trial. The Feds can't have released a statement yet. Nate leans back in his chair. Maybe he has time to vanish before they announce it. He was going to leave town anyway, so why not go today?

He sighs heavily as he logs in to his new website. He needs a client who lives anywhere but Lost Creek. It would give him a place to disappear to. Something to occupy his mind. More emails have come in overnight from people wanting help. He spends a half hour reading them while sipping coffee.

When Janine appears at his door Brody looks up and gently wags his tail before going back to sleep.

"Huh." She appears confused and amused as she looks at a large brown envelope in her hands.

"What is it?" asks Nate.

"Marty just dropped this off for you." She hands the envelope over. Marty is the mail guy who Janine has been flirting with for months. He's got to be half her age, if that.

Nate reads the address on the envelope:

Nathanial Monroe
Lost Creek
Colorado

It has a Department of Corrections stamp across the top.

"You're like Santa Claus," says Janine. "You don't even need an address for mail to reach you."

It isn't the first time Nate's received letters like this, because it isn't the first time a prisoner has requested his help. Like Madison when she was incarcerated, a lot of inmates followed his case and saw his exoneration as something that could happen to them. Because, once he was released, they thought he could help them get out too, as if he had some magic solution. Madison had waited until she was released before tracking him down to seek his help in finding out who framed her for murder. Eventually he'd agreed to help her.

He smiles as he remembers she didn't really give him much choice.

Nate would do the same for anyone if he thought he could

help. Especially if they were wrongfully convicted because of a crooked cop, like he was.

"Thanks, Janine. It'll be someone asking for help."

She nods before returning to the front desk.

Intrigued, he tears open the letter.

Mr. Monroe,

For over fourteen years I've been serving time for the murder of a baby I did not touch. I was sentenced to death until the governor commuted my sentence earlier this year to life in prison without the possibility of parole, along with everyone else sentenced to the same fate.

Now I'm no longer scheduled to die, I have a new yearning for life. My old life. From before I was wrongfully convicted.

My case was handled badly. I was the victim of a detective who was closed to all other plausible suspects, and a lawyer so useless he screwed up my defense. The poor girl's body was never found. There's no real evidence linking me to her disappearance. I know you've been through something similar. I'm praying that you can find it within yourself to at least read the enclosed legal documents that explain my case, or point me in the direction of someone who will.

I need to get out of here, and this is my last attempt at getting out alive.

Dennis McKinney

Colorado State Penitentiary

Nate gets a familiar flutter of excitement in his chest. He's been in this guy's place. He knows the desperation that goes with it. Maybe he can help him.

He starts reading the enclosed documents. The more he reads, the more he shakes his head in disgust. The lack of evidence against the guy, together with the lack of a body, means Nate knows pretty fast that he's going to try to help this man in his bid for freedom.

CHAPTER TWENTY-FIVE

Madison checks her phone while waiting in line at Ruby's Diner. She's hoping to hear from Doug Draper's wife and has told dispatch to forward Nancy through to her if she calls. Madison has a feeling Doug might stop his wife from doing that though.

With no messages or missed calls, she puts her phone away and waits to fetch coffees for the search party. It's hot inside the diner, and the salty aroma of bacon makes her wish it were lunchtime already. She appears to have come during a midmorning rush as the diner is full of other people desperate for caffeine. She spots Dawn Freemantle's elderly neighbor, Richard, parked at the counter with his back to her. He's passing the time of day with the diner's other frequent resident, Jim. Sensing her eyes on him, Richard idly glances over his shoulder and, when spotting her, raises his coffee cup in greeting.

She smiles awkwardly, thinking of her untimely breakdown in his living room. He probably thinks she's unhinged. Maybe he's right.

"What can I get you, Madison?" asks Carla, head waitress.

She ignores the three people in line ahead of Madison and when they protest, Carla says, "Oh shush. She's got places she needs to be, unlike you people."

Madison stifles a laugh. "Eight black coffees and nine white, please."

"Wow, you have a serious caffeine addiction," Carla says with a glint in her eye.

The TV above the counter shows reporters feeding speculation to the public about the Doe Family homicides. It cuts to a shot of Madison giving her press conference yesterday. She looks washed out and in desperate need of a haircut.

She looks away with a sigh and spots Alex's ex-girlfriend heading toward her for the exit. "Hey, Sam."

With a tentative smile, Sam stops. "Hi. How are you?"

"Good thanks. Better than Alex, anyway. He's a little hurt about what happened." She knows she shouldn't get involved but she can't help herself. They made a good couple and Alex is so shy that it could take him years to meet someone else he likes as much as he likes her.

"I'm sorry about that. I didn't mean to screw with him." Sam nervously lowers her eyes. "I guess he told you everything."

"Not everything." Madison feels sorry for her. Breaking up with someone sucks no matter what the reason. And she's probably worried the whole police department is going to be baying for her blood. "He's a big boy. I'm sure he'll be fine. I think he was just taken by surprise, that's all. You shouldn't feel bad."

Sam glances around before quietly asking, "Have you found that little girl yet? I heard about what happened on the news. I don't mean to pry, but I guess because of my job it's difficult not to when something like this happens."

Madison can understand her professional interest. "Not yet. We're doing everything we can. If you happen to overhear anything suspicious while you're visiting people's homes..."

Sam catches her drift. "Of course. I know just how many

creeps there are in this town, so I'll be sure to stay alert." She pulls her purse over her shoulder. "If you need anything from child services, just call and ask for me. I don't want what happened between me and Alex to get in the way."

Madison's impressed. "Thanks. I appreciate it."

Glancing at her phone, Sam takes a deep breath. "I need to get to work, I have a family waiting for me. They're adopting a little boy today, so I don't want to keep them waiting."

Madison steps out of her way. "Sure. Have a good day."

Sam leaves and when Madison turns around, she sees Carla has completed her order.

With the volunteers caffeinated, Madison sits in her car on the victims' driveway with her door open. The morning is pleasantly warm with a reassuring breeze. She pulls out the hard copies of Alex's crime-scene photos for another look.

One photo in particular has her wondering if they're missing something obvious. It's of the couple on the bed. The woman has her left leg hanging off the mattress, and her partner's back is to her. He's naked apart from boxer shorts, but the woman is wearing a black T-shirt and black yoga pants. It seems odd to dress in black on a hot day, but maybe that's the first clean outfit she found in the unopened boxes. Perhaps she went for a run at some point.

Maybe she jogged by Dawn and Kai's house on Sunday afternoon or evening. If Kai was out doing yard chores, he could've seen her. He could've followed her home. Maybe he wanted to see whether she'd moved to town alone, just her and her kids. He doesn't have a rap sheet for sexual assault and there was no evidence the female was assaulted, but that doesn't mean he didn't consider it. He could've thought she was easy prey and then stumbled across her partner inside before he could make a move.

"Detective?"

Madison jumps, dropping the photograph into her lap. She hadn't heard anyone approach.

Officer Sanchez smiles at her. "Sorry. I didn't mean to scare you."

"That's okay."

He nods over his shoulder. "There's a guy turned up who says he moved all the previous owner's belongings out of here a few weeks ago."

Madison steps out of the car, intrigued. "Where is he?"

"Over here. Name's Jerry Clark. Sounds like he clears houses for a living." Sanchez leads her to the edge of the property and lifts the crime-scene tape so the guy can step closer to them.

Madison ignores the reporters and their questions. "Thanks, Luis," she says to Sanchez as he walks away.

She assesses Jerry Clark. The guy's a little rough around the edges with dirty jeans, messy shoulder-length brown hair and week-old stubble. He's only about thirty, if that. She's surprised into shaking his hand when he holds his out after a cursory wipe on his stained jeans.

"Hey, Detective," he says enthusiastically. "Jerry Clark. I saw it on TV—what happened—and just knew I needed to come on by and speak to you." He crosses his arms, businesslike. "What do you need to know?"

Amused that he's so eager to help she says, "Start at the beginning." She pulls out her notebook and pen. "Who hired you to clear this place and when did they first make contact?"

"Sure, sure." He takes a deep breath and when he expels it, Madison can smell weed and sour coffee. "So, I got an email to my website from someone named Mrs. Hendricks. That was six weeks ago to the day."

Madison pauses him. "Mrs. Hendricks?"

He nods.

That was the name of the woman who owned this place, but she's dead. Whoever organized the clearance didn't want to give their real name. "Go on. What did the email say?"

"Well, it was brief. It said something like"—he looks up as he recounts the contents—"the property needs clearing of everything except the couch and the double bed in the master bedroom. She didn't want anything else left behind. Not even a painting on the wall or any garbage in the trash cans, so I took it all." He grins for a second. "Although I might have left a couple of items that didn't fit in my truck. It was a hot day, I was tired, and I didn't want to have to come back..."

Madison thinks. "Like the old closet in the spare room?"

"Right. It was just too big. I can't remember if I took the washing machine either now I come to think of it. They're a pain in the ass to dispose of and tricky to lift on my own."

"You work alone?"

"Right." He nods enthusiastically while tucking his hair behind his ears.

He reminds Madison of a stoner, one from the West Coast who spends all day surfing and never really grows up. It makes her think of Kai Bishop as he gives off the same energy, although she suspects Kai's shiftier.

"I can't afford employees yet," he says. "But one day." He holds up crossed fingers and smiles.

Madison almost laughs. He's a likable guy. "What did you do with the items you removed?" she asks.

"Well sometimes people can't afford to pay me, so I give them the option of having me take the items in lieu of payment, which means I can sell what I want and keep the proceeds. You can get real lucky on some jobs. This one wasn't great; it was mostly junk."

Madison tilts her head. "The person who emailed you didn't pay you?"

"No. They wanted the house cleared ASAP and said I

could do whatever I wanted with what I found. They didn't want an itemized list or valuation or anything."

That seems odd to Madison, but as Linda's family were estranged from her it's not completely surprising that they wouldn't want to visit the property and sift through her things. That's got to be stressful no matter whether you miss your loved one or not. It sounds to her like they really didn't want anything to do with it. They didn't even want to know whether she owned anything of value, suggesting they weren't interested in inheriting anything. Maybe they already knew she owned nothing of value. That could explain why the house was empty and not up for sale. They washed their hands of the whole estate.

Which means the couple who died here with their children were effectively squatters. Unless Jerry here is lying and he actually robbed the place.

"You still have a copy of the email?" she asks.

He shakes his head. "Nope. Deleted it. From my deleted folder too. I checked."

Madison eyeballs him. "Are you usually that thorough, Jerry?"

He grins. "Hey, you call it thorough, my doc calls it OCD."

She does laugh this time. Still, it's frustrating that she can't contact the person who emailed him, but it's also highly unlikely they know anything about the Doe Family. "So where's the stuff now?" she asks.

"Oh, long gone. That was six weeks ago, Detective. I sell stuff online and to random places I know. The highest priced item was an old, cheap laptop, which went to a computer geek I know on Facebook. He wipes them and then sells them to schools. The TV went to my neighbor for forty bucks. It wasn't great. She didn't have much jewelry, just one gold ring, which went to a pawn shop, the rest was costume. And the salvage yard over in Gold Rock bought her Toyota. It was pretty beat up."

She makes a note of that. It's a link to Doug Draper.

"Yo, Jerry!"

Madison and Jerry turn at the voice yelling from the road. It's Kai Bishop. He's alone.

"Hey, brother!" shouts Jerry, his face lighting up.

Madison gets his attention. "You know Kai?"

"Oh sure. His good lady—Dawn—says we're long-lost brothers or something, on account of us being so alike. I don't see it myself, but I do love him like a brother."

Madison sees it. "He ever help you with your clearance jobs?"

"No, ma'am," says Jerry. "He's not business minded like me. If he can spend all day lying in the sun, drinking beer and getting high, he will. It makes the poor bastard unreliable. Excuse my French." With a grin, he looks back at his friend, who waits patiently at the crime-scene tape. Jerry waves. They're like two schoolboys who haven't seen each other for weeks.

Madison passes him her notebook and pen. "Would you write down your contact details for me, Jerry? Name, address, cell number. Just in case I have any follow-up questions."

"Sure," he says, taking the notebook from her.

Behind them Kai shouts, "You getting the detective's number already, Jerry? Damn, you work fast!" He laughs at his own joke.

Jerry snickers as he writes.

Madison rolls her eyes.

CHAPTER TWENTY-SIX

Once Madison's done questioning Jerry, she thanks him for his help and approaches Kai before he disappears. "Got a minute?" she asks.

Kai high-fives Jerry as he passes and says, "Catch you later, bro."

Jerry heads to his truck.

After leading Kai to a quiet corner of the plot, Madison stops and turns. She's wondering if these seemingly amiable friends might be hiding something. It could support the idea that there were two people involved in the murders. "I'll get straight to the point, Mr. Bishop. I did a background check on you and it flagged up your prior conviction for domestic battery."

His smile fades immediately. He pulls the sunglasses that were sitting atop his head down to cover his hazel eyes. "It was over something stupid. I served my time."

She stares at him. "Where were you Sunday afternoon and evening? And did you join Dawn and Timmy when they came here to introduce themselves to the new neighbors?"

Rubbing the back of his neck he says, "No. I was busy in the yard all day, same as always. Dawn wants to buy an RV when her husband passes, so I'm clearing some space where we can keep it parked. You've seen the state of the yard, it needs a lot of work. Her husband let it all go to seed."

"Well, he has dementia, so it's probably been too much for him to manage," she says.

"Sure, I get that. And I'm happy to help out."

A cloud obscures the sun, putting them in shade. "What time did you finish working in the yard? And did you see anyone driving past a little slower than usual? Anyone who could've been scoping the neighbor's place out?"

"Nah, when I work I wear earbuds and listen to music. I didn't notice anything. I stopped work around eight and went inside to have a shower and a beer before watching TV."

She writes it down. "What did you watch?"

He appears surprised by the question and lets out a long sigh as he tries to remember. "Some crime documentary on Netflix about a female serial killer out in Maple Valley, New Hampshire—Dawn loves 'em—followed by a crappy Denzel Washington movie from the nineties on Channel Nine. It was so bad I fell asleep and missed the end."

He appears to be telling the truth but it should be easy for Madison to check what was on TV and at what time. "And the next day, did Dawn tell you that Timmy freaked out when they stopped by here to introduce themselves? Because I'm surprised you wouldn't offer to come over and take a look for yourself to see what freaked him out."

Kai laughs unkindly. "That kid's a weirdo, so he's always freaking out over something. Dawn babies him, letting him get away with murder." He pulls his sunglasses off. "We don't exactly get on. I find it hard to warm to the boy. I blame his weirdness on all the drugs his folks were taking when they made him."

Madison's heard enough. "So your alibi is that you were home with Dawn, Timmy and her husband on Sunday night?"

"Right. Sorry I can't be more help. I've gotta go."

Madison nods and watches him leave. She has a gut feeling about him. About the whole household, if she's honest. She's considering whether they could be hiding the missing toddler in that house. She's not sure. She needs to delve further into Doug and Nancy Draper first, because right now she doesn't have enough to obtain a search warrant for Dawn's property.

She checks her phone for the time. As it's past eleven and Madison still hasn't heard from Nancy Draper, she gets their landline number from dispatch and calls the house. If Doug's working in the salvage yard, she might catch Nancy alone. If no one picks up, it'll mean another trip out to Gold Rock.

"Hello?" A woman's voice answers.

"Hi, Nancy? This is Detective Harper. I stopped by yesterday evening."

"Hello, Detective." The woman sounds hesitant.

"I'm sorry to bother you but I'm working a homicide case; the Doe Family murders. Have you seen it on the news?"

"No."

That's surprising considering that when Madison came by yesterday, the woman inquired whether the little girl had been found. She ignores it for now. "Well it occurred Sunday evening and when I asked your husband where he was during that time, he stated he was home with you. Is that correct?"

"That's correct. Yes." She doesn't elaborate.

"Care to tell me what you were doing all evening? And did you have any visitors or phone calls from anyone who can confirm you were both there?"

"I don't understand why you're asking these questions," says Nancy, clearly affronted. "We're not killers. We live a quiet life and try not to upset anyone."

"I'm certainly not accusing either of you of anything, ma'am. It's just that, as part of our investigation, we're speaking to anyone who had contact with Linda Hendricks, who was the owner of the property where the murders occurred. Your husband's name came up. I'm sure you can understand I'm duty bound to clear him from my list of inquiries, and I'm hoping you can help me do that." Before the woman protests Madison adds, "Did *you* know Linda Hendricks?"

"No, I did not. I don't believe Doug did either, so I don't know why you would think he did." She sighs heavily down the line. "On Sunday evening we did what we do every evening; we ate dinner, then watched TV. I went to bed first, like usual."

Madison makes a note. "Did you fall asleep before your husband came to bed?"

Nancy scoffs. "I don't sleep, Detective. I have problems with nighttime."

Madison frowns. "I'm sorry to hear that. Can you think of anyone who could confirm you were both home that night?"

She hesitates before answering. "Doug's employees. They would've worked in the yard until dusk. Try Al Peters and Sonny Felton. If Doug left the house at any point, which he didn't, they would've seen him."

That doesn't rule out the fact Doug could've traveled to Lost Creek after they finished work for the day. She'll get Adams to speak to them. "Thank you, Mrs. Draper. You've been very helpful."

"Yes, well. Maybe one day you'll return the favor," says Nancy before hanging up.

Madison looks at her phone, confused. As she goes to put it away it rings and Adams's name flashes on-screen. Before she can answer, someone from behind the house calls out to her.

"Madison?"

She walks around the house to find who it is and is greeted by Shelley running toward her, radio in one hand.

"What is it?" asks Madison.

"I just got word from the volunteers over at Lake Providence that they've found something."

Madison declines Adams's call. "What have they found?"

Shelley tries to catch her breath by leaning forward, hands on knees. She must've run some distance as she's usually fit. When she stands straight, she says, "A dark-colored sedan submerged in the water."

Madison's heart pounds a little harder.

CHAPTER TWENTY-SEVEN

By the time Madison arrives at Lake Providence—just a five-minute drive from the crime scene—there's a crowd. No reporters yet thankfully, just police and search volunteers. Madison spots Vince Rader standing near the shore. She asked him to meet her here and, despite being busy running his late wife's diner, he dropped everything to come straight over.

"Hey, Vince," she says approaching. Tall and skinny with cropped hair, he had a long career in the US Navy followed by time spent working as a commercial diver. He's sixty now but he's always open to helping LCPD with water searches.

"Afternoon," says Vince. "Your friend here was just filling me in."

Steve nods at her. "One of the volunteers noticed a reflection in the water," he says. "So he threw a couple of large stones over there. When they bounced off of something he waded in as far as he could go and dunked his waterproof cell phone under to record it. He quickly realized there was a vehicle submerged under there."

Madison raises her eyebrows. "This is huge. If this is our family's car, we could have their identity in a matter of hours."

"Right," says Steve.

"Did he manage to read the license plate?" she asks.

"Unfortunately not. It was too murky down there."

Madison turns to Vince. "Did you bring your diving gear?"

"Sure did." He nods. "I'll suit up." He heads over to his car.

If Vince can get them the license plate, Steve can arrange for the car to be recovered. It may be water damaged but there could be something inside that helps her build a case against whoever killed that family. But more importantly, it could lead her to the missing toddler.

She has a sudden sinking feeling as she realizes there's something she hasn't considered in her excitement at locating the vehicle. She sighs heavily.

Steve looks at her questioningly.

"What if the girl's in the car?" she says.

Steve turns to glance back at the water, his expression darkening. "If she is, then we'll have to deal with it. But I pray to God she's not." He turns back to face her. "I'll call the coroner's office. Lena needs to be here when we get the car out, just in case."

It's times like this that Madison wishes she weren't a cop. Knowing what the killer did to the girl's family doesn't give her any reason to hope the little girl is still alive, but she's also worked enough cases to know that, sometimes, miracles do happen.

"Get Alex down here too," she says.

"Sure."

Her cell rings. It's Adams again. "Hey," she says. "I have news."

"So do I," he says. "Which you'd know if you ever answered your damn phone."

She ignores his attitude. "Go ahead."

"I found the victim's car on different surveillance footage and managed to get a partial on the license plate."

Madison smiles. "That's great news. Well done." She feels a little sorry for him as she says, "We think we've just found the actual car."

"What?" he says, dismayed. "You've gotta be kidding me? So I've been wasting my time?"

"No, not at all. Your footage will help us track their journey."

He sighs. "Where are you? With the car?"

"Yeah, at Lake Providence. Know it?"

"I'll find it." He ends the call.

Madison's phone rings again immediately. She thinks Adams must've forgotten something but when she answers she's greeted by a female voice.

"Madison Harper?"

"Yes. Who's this?" she says.

"Special Agent Lisa Baxter. I'm calling you with an update on the Father Jack Connor case, although I'm assuming your friend Mr. Monroe has probably already told you by now. Regardless of that, as you're a witness for the prosecution, I need to scratch you off my list of notifications."

Madison turns her back on Steve and walks a few steps away from the lake. "I'm not sure what you're talking about. Has the trial date changed?"

"No, Detective. The trial's been canceled."

Madison's mouth drops open. Her first thought is that the asshole has escaped from prison, or been released on health grounds. She feels anger building in her chest as she thinks of Nate's reaction. "Why the hell has it been canceled? That man deserves to spend the rest of his miserable life in prison. You guys need to—"

"Whoa!" says Lisa. "Calm down a second before you get all righteous on me, would you?" She sounds amused. "Detective, I'm calling to tell you Jack Connor's dead. He died in his sleep. I'm sorry, I thought Nate would've mentioned it by now."

Madison is stunned into silence. *Father Connor's dead.*

Her throat clenches with emotion and she's not sure whether that's from relief that Nate's ordeal is over, or anger that the bastard got off scot-free in the end. "How did Nate react?" she asks.

The special agent inhales deeply. "It's hard to say. I think he was pissed. But I'm hoping this is the end of his own life sentence, you know? That guy really screwed with him. Once Nate's over the shock, he should see the priest's death as a good thing."

Madison nods. She hopes so. She's still in shock and can feel her hands shaking slightly. "I'll pay Nate a visit as soon as I get a chance."

"Probably a good idea."

"Thanks for letting me know."

"No problem. We'll issue a press release tomorrow morning. You might want to tell him to lay low as it's going to stir up interest in his case again."

Madison closes her eyes briefly. Because she knows Nate's going to be hounded. And that might tempt him to disappear.

After all, it wouldn't be the first time.

CHAPTER TWENTY-EIGHT

FIFTEEN YEARS EARLIER

17 hours remaining

Mike tries not to spill coffee as he descends the steps leading down to the holding cells. It's his last job before he clocks off for the evening. At almost eleven o'clock, it's two hours after he was due to finish. When a child goes missing, everyone works longer and nobody complains about it.

The holding cells aren't full right now. They only contain a couple of small-time drug dealers and a woman who was driving under the influence and is now sleeping off her hangover from the looks of it.

At the end of the row of cells, Dennis McKinney is seated on a thin mattress atop the metal bunk, his head in his hands. He better get used to this confined space as he's probably not going to see much daylight once he's charged.

Dennis looks up when Mike unlocks his cell door. "Has my lawyer arrived yet?" he asks.

"No," says Mike, handing him the plastic cup. He can already tell the coffee is barely lukewarm. Their vending machine hasn't worked properly in years. "In my experience they don't tend to rush, so you could be waiting awhile."

Dennis shakes his head and doesn't attempt to drink the coffee.

Mike hovers. "Detective Ramsey is hell-bent on finding Grace. If you know anything, it'll go in your favor to speak up now rather than wait. Even if she's dead, it would be something to tell the girl's mother. She could plan the funeral."

He's met with silence, but he can tell there's a lot going on in this guy's head. Usually when people are arrested, they're weighing up how to play it. They're replaying all the cop shows and crime documentaries they've ever watched on TV and trying to decide whether to talk without a lawyer present—to make them appear helpful and therefore innocent—or to do the smart thing and refrain from saying a single word that could be twisted by the cops.

Men like Dennis are also considering how bad it looks just to be a male who lives close to the crime scene. Especially one who knew the victim. In some parts of the country those factors alone can see you incarcerated for the rest of your life.

Mike doesn't think Detective Ramsey is incompetent, or one of those cops who wants to look good by closing the case fast no matter who gets sent down for the crime. But he's not always good at thinking outside the box.

"Tiffany broke down on TV and said she's going to kill herself within twenty-four hours if her baby isn't brought home to her alive," he says. "Did you know that?"

Silence.

"I think she'd do it too. And there's only"—he glances at his watch—"seventeen hours left until she makes good on the promise. How does that make you feel, Dennis? Your victim count would double then. Which means more chance of death row."

With weary eyes, Dennis looks up at him. "I've told you a million times; I did not touch that baby. I've never hurt a child or a woman in my life. You're on the wrong track. You should be out looking for her because she could still be alive. If her mother kills herself because you guys didn't find her daughter in time, that's on *you*. Not me."

Something about the way he says it makes Mike think he could have a good chance of convincing a jury. Except for the evidence. "We know you're lying because we found something on your property."

Dennis jumps up, spilling coffee all over the place. He grips the cup so hard it implodes. "There's nothing on my property that could make me look guilty for this. *Nothing*!" he yells. "I know that for a fact."

He's up in Mike's face, but Mike holds his ground. "I wish that were true, but the facts don't lie."

Reddening with rage, Dennis doesn't blink. His stare is intense. "If Ramsey has planted something to frame me for this, I'll sue every single one of you and I'll win, because me and my family will sell everything we own to hire the best lawyers we can afford." His voice rises. "Your careers will be over. I'll never stop shouting from the rooftops about how you let a little girl and her mother die because you were all so crooked you didn't do your jobs properly!"

Mike's never seen him this way. And he seems so sure of himself. So sure that he didn't do it. He's convincing too. He turns away from Dennis, meaning to leave. "Planting evidence only happens in the movies."

"So tell me what it is," says Dennis. "If you're so sure it's real evidence, tell me. Let me explain it."

Mike's tempted, just to see his reaction, but it's not his place to do that.

"Just as I thought." With a shake of his head Dennis adds, "You're either bullshitting me or it was planted. Why are you even down here, Mike? You're not leading this case, you're just a uniform who thinks he's detective material. Why aren't you looking at the girl's dad for this? Where was Ronnie Russo when she went missing, huh? What about all the other men Tiffany brings home?" He sounds desperate now.

Mike leaves the cell, locking it after him.

As he walks away his gut feeling has changed. He considers how, if he *were* leading this case, he wouldn't be focusing solely on Dennis McKinney for Grace's disappearance. It all seems too convenient somehow. How the friendly neighbor who happened to be home alone at the time Grace was taken— giving him no credible alibi—supposedly left the girl's sandal in his pickup to be found. That's sloppy. Too sloppy. And the guy has no prior convictions for anything. He's squeaky clean.

It's almost like Dennis *was* framed. But Mike knows Ramsey wouldn't do something like that. No one in the department would. At least he doesn't think so. Besides, suggesting the guy was framed to Detective Ramsey or Chief Sullivan could cost Mike any chance of a promotion in the future. He'd promised his wife, Viv, that he'd make more money one day. That they could afford to start a family and buy a bigger home.

And for that reason, Mike knows he has to keep his mouth shut.

Still, he can't help wondering whether there's someone else among them who is responsible for this. And if there *is*, who are they? And what the hell have they done with baby Grace?

CHAPTER TWENTY-NINE
PRESENT DAY

Nate has spent all morning researching Dennis McKinney and the sixteen-month-old girl he was accused of murdering. He learned the child's shoe was found in his pickup truck at the property Dennis shared with his father. Apparently, his father was out of town at the time, meaning Dennis made a perfect suspect.

What Nate doesn't like is that the shoe was the only evidence ever found in the case. There was nothing to put him at the location she vanished from—her front yard—and there were no witnesses other than Grace's mother. Tiffany was adamant she saw Dennis in the area around the time, but no one could corroborate that and the guy was convicted based on those two things alone.

The only thing that does bother Nate is that one of Dennis's fingerprints was found on Grace's sandal. But he could've touched her shoe another day. The girl's mother already admitted he used to stop by to say hi to them sometimes, just being neighborly. Nate's been around enough small kids in his time to know that when they have a visitor, they like to pass them everything they own: their toys, their shoes, their food.

Nate doesn't think the fingerprint is that significant given the lack of other evidence.

He's waiting to be connected to Dennis in the Colorado State Penitentiary and, when the inmate finally comes on the line, he sounds weary. After introductions, Nate says, "I'm interested in investigating your case, but I don't want to give you any false hope."

Dennis sighs heavily. "Any hope would be a good thing right about now, Mr. Monroe. I've been in here over fourteen years already and I fear I may never get out. It doesn't get any easier either, the longer I'm locked up. I've never gotten used to it like some of the guys in here have."

Nate hadn't either.

"I feel like my entire family will die while I'm here."

"Have they been helping you with your case?" he asks.

A moment passes before Dennis replies. "In the beginning, yes. My brother even sold his house to pay the lawyer's fees, which caused his marriage to break down. I don't hear from them too much anymore. It's just too stressful for them. They've had to live in the shadow of their brother being a convicted child killer. The cops tried to make out I molested the girl first. Do you know how hard that is for my family to live with?" He's silent for a second.

Nate doesn't reply. He knows all too well how a felon's family is affected after a conviction.

"They hate how they can't talk about me to anyone, ever, because of the response they get," continues Dennis. "So they have to pretend they're not related to me when they meet new people. It sucks. I'm literally being wiped from everyone's memories for something I didn't do."

Nate hears the familiar sounds of other inmates in the background. It brings it all back to him: the constant yelling of obscenities, the banging of cell doors opening and closing, and the hostile environment where the corrections officers treat you worse than vermin. His heart pounds a little too hard as he imagines himself back in Dennis's position, holding out hope that just one person would not just listen to him, but *believe* him when he explains he didn't commit the crime he's in for.

"I want to help you," he says. "I want to see if I can find out what happened to baby Grace."

Dennis sighs with relief. "You don't know how much that means to me, Mr. Monroe." He takes a second before continuing, "Okay, time is short, so let me give you some names you should start with. You ready?"

Nate has a pen in hand. "Go ahead."

"Ronnie Russo is Grace's biological father. He was just a young guy when he got Tiffany pregnant. Now, I don't *think* he killed his baby, but I'm desperate, and Tiffany could've pushed him over the edge."

"I'm guessing they had a poor relationship?"

"Volatile," confirms Dennis. "They never lived together or anything, it never got that serious, but because of their young age, they were both jealous of each other's new partners and used to wind each other up."

"You witnessed this for yourself?"

"Oh sure. Ronnie was good with his daughter though. Little Grace was only just learning her words but she jabbered about her daddy all the time. I can't see him hurting her, but he might know who did."

Nate makes a note. "Anyone else?"

"Bruce Cullen. My old lawyer. See if he'll give you everything he's got, or at least allow you access to it. He knows he did a bad job. I sometimes hear from him, asking how I'm doing, although it's been a few years since his last call. He feels guilty, I just know he does. I've always wondered whether the police had something to do with my lack of defense. Whether Cullen took a bribe from Detective Ramsey."

Nate wouldn't be surprised. "That would be difficult to prove."

"It would, but fifteen years have passed. Maybe Cullen's ready to do the right thing and speak out."

Nate doubts it. Bruce Cullen's a lawyer, after all. Perhaps he's being too harsh. "I'll contact him."

Someone yells in the background that Dennis's time on the phone is up.

"I've gotta go," he says. "Can I call you in a day or two? It's a little hard for you to get in touch with me at a moment's notice, what with the schedule they have us on."

"Sure," says Nate. He gives him his cell number and they say their goodbyes. Nate thinks Dennis sounds a little brighter than he did at the beginning of the call.

He slips his phone into his pocket, invigorated to begin a new case, especially as it has possible police corruption at its core. The only problem with the case is that it happened here in Lost Creek. Which means it will delay him leaving town.

His back aches from sitting all morning, so Nate decides to take Brody for a long walk in the White Woods in order to help him plan his investigation. By the time they pull into the parking lot, the sky is clouding over. They could be in for some summer showers.

Brody jumps out of the back seat and immediately runs ahead to sniff the trail. It's quiet out here while everyone's at work. The peace gives Nate time to think about the demise of his former mentor. His anger over Father Connor dying a peaceful death hasn't lasted as long as he thought it would, and he's grateful for that. He doesn't want to remain bitter forever. It could be that the Dennis McKinney case came at the right time. It should provide a much-needed distraction.

As voices reach him, Nate notices Brody has disappeared well ahead of him, out of view. One voice sounds familiar and he realizes Madison's up there and she's talking to Brody.

He emerges from the woods where it separates for Lake Providence, close to Fantasy World amusement park. The screams of happy children and fairground rides reach him, and the Wonder Wheel is lit up in the distance as it slowly turns.

Brody runs back to Nate, bringing Madison with him. She looks flustered. He notices the crowd of cops, near the shore of the lake. He knows what that means. "Everything okay?" he asks as she reaches him.

Madison pulls him in for a hug and he can sense she's holding back tears.

He's confused. It takes him a second before he realizes she must've been notified of Father Connor's death. When she pulls away, she studies his face, especially his eyes.

"You look terrible," she says, not unkindly. "Your eyes are bloodshot, you clearly haven't slept... You've been using again, haven't you?"

He doesn't bother to deny it. He nods.

Madison backhands his bare arm so hard it hurts. He's wearing a T-shirt that offers no protection.

"Hey!" he says, rubbing his forearm with amusement. "What was that for!"

"You're such an asshole," she says, crossing her arms. "When will you learn drugs will make you feel worse, not better? I mean, what are you, stupid? Do I really have to keep repeating myself to a grown man? Not to mention the fact I could arrest you for buying it in the first place. And let's talk about who's selling it to you, shall we?"

He holds his hands up in surrender. "Alright, alright, I get it. I'm sorry, okay? I didn't use much and I've learned my lesson. I don't intend to do it again. I shouldn't need to anyway." He sighs. "I guess you heard about Father Connor?"

She softens at last. "Yeah. Thanks for telling me, by the way. It's not as if I have a vested interest or anything."

He feels bad because she's right. He should've called her. "Sorry. You know what I'm like when it comes to him."

"Yes. Infuriating." She nudges his elbow affectionately. "So how do you feel about it? I was pretty angry when I heard he died in his sleep. It was too good for him."

The truth is, he feels numb to it right now. "It's frustrating for sure. And I wish, with every bone in my body, that he'd held off until we secured that murder conviction." He sighs. "But I'm trying to focus on the positives. He'll never be able to hurt anyone else. And I won't have to return to Texas. I won't have to relive the last twenty years on the stand, with my every word being recorded for the whole world to tear apart and discuss. That's got to be a good thing, right?"

She nods. "Of course it is. But it also sucks to know that some of the worst people out there never get what they deserve. It kind of makes me wonder why I bother doing my job."

He glances over her shoulder and spots Vince getting out of the lake, head to toe in diving gear. Lena and Steve watch as a tow truck reverses up to the lake. "What's going on?"

She follows his gaze. "The search party found a vehicle in the lake. We think this is the car of the family who were killed. It could be the break we need."

"No sign of their daughter yet?"

She shakes her head sadly. "I'm hoping she's not in there."

Nate raises his eyebrows. It's unthinkable. "I have a cold case I'm working on. I was contacted by a guy in prison for the murder of a baby, despite no body and limited evidence."

"Sounds interesting. You know I love working cold cases."

He does. The two of them had worked together to find out what happened to Vince Rader's wife, Ruby, and their grandson, Oliver, when they vanished seven years ago. That case had a bittersweet ending and it resulted in Vince becoming a close friend of the pair. He shows up unannounced at Nate's place all the time, with beer in one hand and diner leftovers for Brody in the other.

"I'm glad you have something to keep you busy." Madison glances behind her before adding, "Have you spoken to Lena yet?"

He looks over at the ME and catches her eye, forcing him to wave. She waves back before returning her attention to the lake. "Not yet."

Exasperated, Madison rolls her eyes. "Men." After patting Brody's head, she starts walking away from them. "I need to get back to work. Good luck with your cold case."

He watches her walk over to Lena and Steve and feels a tug of guilt. She has no idea how close he is to leaving town. If he can find some lead that will help Dennis McKinney secure an appeal as fast as possible, Nate can vanish into obscurity and forget Father Connor ever existed.

He can finally start living the rest of his life.

CHAPTER THIRTY

Madison watches the tow truck reverse, coming to a stop with its rear end facing the lake. When she sees who gets out of the truck, her eyes widen. She turns to Steve. "What's Doug Draper doing here?"

He shrugs. "He was the first company to pick up the phone. Why? Don't you like his alibi for Sunday night?"

"He says he was home with his wife."

"Did she corroborate that?" he asks.

"She did, but I don't know... I have a funny feeling about them."

"Want me to call it off and try to find someone else?"

Madison watches Doug work. He's wearing greasy blue coveralls. With gloved hands he reaches across the water to pass Vince chains to fix to the front of the submerged car. Madison's torn. They can't afford to delay any longer. She needs to see what's inside that car.

She considers whether he could claim at trial, should he ever be charged, that his DNA was on the vehicle because he helped pull it out of the lake. But he's wearing gloves and he doesn't need to touch the car. Besides, it's likely any DNA on the vehicle has been destroyed by the water. "As long as he stays away from the vehicle once it's out and loaded onto his truck, it should be okay."

"We need him to take the car to the station so Alex can check it for evidence," says Steve. "But I'll go with him. Make sure he's not alone with it."

She nods. That puts her mind at ease.

With the tow truck ready, Doug pushes a lever and it loudly kicks into action. It takes seconds for the chains to pull taut. A little longer for the submerged vehicle to start moving. Slowly, the bumper appears first, revealing the license plate. Madison immediately writes it down then steps away to call dispatch.

Stella runs the plate for her. "Looks like it's registered to an Eric Bailey," she says, checking his personal details. "Says here he's forty years old. No outstanding tickets. His place of residence is a town called Buford."

"Where's that?" asks Madison.

"North of Denver. I have a landline number for you."

Madison makes a note of it. "Do you have his photo?"

"No, but I have a description. Five foot nine, black hair and brown eyes."

The height and hair color match their male victim. His eyes weren't intact, so there was no way of knowing his eye color, but it's enough for Madison. Her shoulders drop with relief. "Finally we have a name for one of the victims. This gives us a starting point."

"Want me to release it to patrol and the press?"

She hesitates. "Not to the press. I want to notify his family before they see it on TV."

"Sure," says Stella. "Anything else I can help you with?"

"Not right now. Thanks."

Once the call has ended Madison immediately dials the landline number for Eric Bailey, hoping he has a roommate or someone picking up his calls so she can finally get some answers.

As the phone rings, she watches the dark blue sedan appear from underwater. At the same time the heavens open and fat summer rain starts pelting down. She doesn't have a jacket with her, so she resigns herself to getting wet.

The vehicle is in good condition. Rain bounces off the hood and she can see all the windows are down, spilling water as it rises out of the lake. Whoever pushed it in there wanted it to remain hidden for a long time. It also means anything that was inside the car before being submerged is now likely spilled out across the bed of the lake. They might never find all of it. Including the toddler's body.

She doesn't dwell on the thought. She wants to find her alive.

The hum of a car engine behind her makes her turn. Reporters are arriving. "Dammit," she mutters.

Just when it feels like no one is going to pick up, Madison's surprised by a voice on the other end of the line.

"What?" The woman's tone is hostile and followed by an irritated sigh.

"Sorry to bother you, ma'am. I'm Detective Harper from Lost Creek Police Department down in southwestern Colorado and—"

Before she can finish her sentence, the woman on the other end laughs bitterly. "Why doesn't that surprise me?"

"What do you mean?" asks Madison.

"You're after Eric, right? What's the asshole done now? All I know is, he's skipped town on me and bailed on his last rent check."

"You're his landlady?"

"Right. Or I *was*. I won't be letting his sorry ass back in here anytime soon. He left all his shitty furniture behind, and the fact I'm talking to you on his landline suggests he didn't even bother canceling it."

It sounds like Eric left in a hurry, which confirms the team's suspicion that the family were running away from something. "Did he live there with his partner and children?"

"What are you talking about?" The woman becomes confused. "He doesn't have kids. Or a girlfriend that I know of. Not that I ever got involved in his business. I only came by today because he's late with the rent. I would never have known he'd skipped town otherwise."

Madison's confused. "If his furniture's still there and his phone's still connected, what makes you think he's skipped town?"

She snorts. "When you've been in this game as long as I have you know when you've been screwed. Besides, I found his keys in the mailbox outside. He's left the place a mess and most of his clothes are gone. I can't find any personal items at all."

The fact he left his keys behind suggests he left of his own free will. But how come this woman doesn't know about the female he was traveling with, and the kids? "Do you have a cell number for him?"

"Yeah, but it's dead. Disconnected probably. You still want the number?"

"Please." Madison waits while the woman retrieves her own cell phone to find the number. Even though his cell is disconnected, she should be able to get his call records to see who Eric was interacting with in the days leading up to his death. She'll request his landline records too. Once she's made a note of his number she asks, "Can I take your name and number for my records in case I have any follow-up questions?"

"Donna Betts. I've been his landlady for a year." She reels off her number. "I haven't seen or heard from Eric since I swung by last month for his rent."

"Do you have emergency contact details for Eric's next of kin?"

"Nope. I don't have a clue who his relatives are. But I know there were no kids living here. It's a one-bedroom apartment and there's nothing to suggest any kids spent time here."

Madison thinks this adds weight to her theory that Eric was having an affair with the woman he was found dead next to, and together they took her children away from her husband. Maybe they were trying to save the kids from a volatile situation.

Although, there is another possibility.

Eric might have been the threat. He could've kidnapped the woman he was found with, and her kids.

But that wouldn't make sense. Dawn Freemantle said she heard the boys playing happily outside the house shortly after they moved in, suggesting they weren't afraid of him. Besides, he was murdered too, so it clearly wasn't a case of murder-suicide because no one could bludgeon themselves to death. Lena also said she believes Eric was killed first.

"What are you after him for?" asks Donna.

Madison hesitates. She doesn't know whether to tell this woman her former tenant is dead. If she does, the woman could go straight to the press. She decides against it for now. "I can't divulge that information right now, I'm afraid."

The woman sighs heavily again. She's a real charmer. "Can I at least dump his furniture and re-let the apartment?"

"I'll need to get the local police to check it over first. There could be some important evidence in there. I'll give them your number and ask them to call you with a time to swing by. That okay with you?"

"Do I have a choice?"

"Afraid not. But the sooner you let them into the apartment, the sooner you can look for new tenants."

"Fine," says Donna. She ends the call.

Madison's phone rings right away. It's that kind of day. "Hey, Alex. What have you got for me?"

"Hi, Detective. My colleagues at the lab expedited the DNA tests for me. They're not finished yet but they've discovered that our male victim isn't related to the two boys found at the house with him."

So he's not their father. "That fits with what I just learned. We've identified him as Eric Bailey from Buford, Colorado. Did Steve tell you about the vehicle we found?"

"Congratulations on identifying him. I'll pass that on to the lab. Yes, Steve told me. That was a stroke of good luck."

"Right. Eric's landlady just told me he skipped town and she doesn't think he had kids or a partner."

"Interesting. The lab also checked whether the two adults were related, because I wondered if he could be a concerned brother helping his sister flee a domestic violence situation."

Madison smiles. She hadn't thought of that.

"But they're not related either," says Alex.

"Doesn't surprise me. This case isn't going to be that simple. I assume the female is the mother of the boys though, right?"

"That's yet to be confirmed. Nora from the lab is drip-feeding me results as she gets them."

She nods. "I'm working on the assumption that the couple were having an affair. Maybe they fled the woman's husband."

"They could've just been friends. I know I'd help a friend flee a bad marriage."

"That's because you're a good guy," she says. "Speaking of which, I bumped into Sam in the diner earlier. If it's any consolation, she looks as miserable as you about your breakup."

"Thanks," he says. "I'll get over it. In a way I'm glad this case is complex. It gives me something else to focus on. I bet it's stopped you thinking about Owen leaving town?"

Madison frowns, because she realizes he's right. Her chest suddenly feels heavy with dread and she has an overwhelming urge to speak to her son. "It has. Think the lab will confirm anything else for you today?"

"I doubt it, but I'll keep my fingers crossed."

"Sure." She knows how it is. "Thanks for the update. Steve should have the victims' vehicle at the station within the next hour. Think you can prioritize that?"

"Of course. Just don't hold out too much hope. Water damage is unforgiving when it comes to evidence."

Madison's hopes vanish. Doubt starts to creep in and she wonders whether this will be one of those cases that goes cold.

"I'm going to head to the lake shortly," says Alex. "To see if I can find any shoe prints in the earth around the water. You never know, we might get lucky if we can compare the killer's shoe prints with our suspect's footwear."

Madison doubts it. That would be too easy.

CHAPTER THIRTY-ONE

After a quick bite to eat, Madison has Detective Adams meet her at the station so she can update him at the same time as Chief Mendes and the rest of the team. She feels a chill run through her as she approaches the dispatchers. The showers have let up for now, but the A/C is cooling her damp clothes against her skin.

Adams joins her as she questions Stella and Dina. "Have any calls come in about the missing toddler?" she asks.

Dina shakes her head but Stella says, "I've had three potential sightings but patrol managed to rule them all out."

"Think they were deliberate time wasters?" asks Adams. "Could it be the killer trying to divert our attention?"

"They were from different callers," says Stella. "So it's unlikely."

"What are their names, just so I know," he says.

Madison glances at him, impressed by his attention to detail.

Stella checks her notes. "Sandy Halstrom, Brian Idle and Jerry Clark."

Madison stands straight. "Jerry Clark? He called? What did he say?"

"You know him?" asks Adams.

"I met him earlier today. He cleared the victims' house of possessions six weeks ago. Came by to tell me himself."

Adams considers it. "So he knows the house layout *and* he inserted himself into the investigation."

Stella says, "He told me he thought he saw a girl at his neighbor's house, and that his neighbor doesn't have kids."

"Has patrol checked it out?" asks Madison.

"They sure did. The owner had his granddaughter visiting. Nothing untoward." Stella turns her back to them to take another call.

Dina's busy with what sounds like a drunk caller because they hear her saying, "No, sir, we do not offer a ride home from a bar to anyone, let alone someone who has lost his own license for driving under the influence." She manages to keep her cool.

Madison walks to her desk, with Adams following. "Jerry's involvement bothers me," she says. "He's friends with the victims' neighbors, Dawn and Kai, and they bother me too."

Chief Mendes approaches from her office, so Madison updates her and Adams on everything she learned at the lake. When she's done the chief says, "Good work on getting a name. Now we need to figure out who Eric Bailey's companion was."

"Want me to run a background check on Jerry Clark?" asks Adams.

Madison nods and tells him to look into Kai Bishop's alibi for that night too. "He says he was watching a Denzel Washington film on TV. Check the listings online to see what was on that night and at what time. Also, get the Buford police to check Eric Bailey's apartment for evidence. Stella has his address. Oh, and also, here's Eric's cell and landline numbers. See if you can get his call records as fast as possible. That should give us a clue as to who his partner was."

He rests his hands on his hips. "Why don't you stick a broom up my ass and have me sweep the floor while I'm at it?"

Chief Mendes appears unimpressed but Madison laughs as she says, "Trust me, if I thought you could multitask, I would."

Adams goes to his desk with a faint smile on his face. His desk is opposite Madison's. Their computer screens are back-to-back.

"So what's next?" asks Chief Mendes.

"I have a few potential suspects," says Madison, looking up at her from her seat. "A couple of the neighbors, the guy who emptied the property after the owner died and, perhaps less promising, a couple who took over my sister's ranch and salvage yard business."

Mendes nods. "At least you have leads. When's Alex checking the victims' vehicle?"

"Now, I hope. I saw him return from the lake about twenty minutes ago. He stopped by to check for shoe prints."

"Let's pay him a visit," says Mendes. "I'd be interested to see what state the car is in."

They find Alex in the station's large outbuilding. As the afternoon is gloomy thanks to the building rain clouds, he has the overhead lights on. He doesn't notice their presence right away. Head to toe in protective gear, he's in the front passenger seat, sitting on top of some clear plastic sheets to keep dry.

Madison steps closer to get his attention. He looks deep in thought, his expression solemn. He must be thinking about Sam. "Alex?" she says. "How's it going?"

He jumps before coughing awkwardly. As he gets out of the car he says, "I have something to show you."

Leading Madison and Chief Mendes to the trunk, he opens it. A small, rectangular safe sits inside, the kind you'd find in a hotel room. "This is the only item in the entire car."

Madison pulls on some latex gloves before leaning in for a better look. The safe isn't big enough to house a toddler, thankfully. Or the weapon that was used to bludgeon the adults. It could just be money in there, but they still need to check inside. The safe is robust, with no digital display. It requires a key to open it. She looks at Alex. "I'm guessing you don't have the key?"

He smiles. "Wouldn't that be nice? I can contact the manufacturer to try to get one. It shouldn't be too difficult."

"Can't you just smash it open?" says Mendes.

Alex looks at it. "I could probably cut it open with an angle grinder, but that would risk destroying whatever's inside."

"Right. No, don't do that," she says. "Not unless we get desperate."

"This car's tires match the impressions I took from the driveway at the victims' property," he says.

Relieved, Madison nods. "Good. That's something at least. Did you find any traces of body decomp in the car?"

"I haven't got that far yet," he says.

"Sorry, I'm being impatient. We'll leave you to it. Let me know the minute you find anything."

"Of course." Alex slips back into the passenger seat as Madison and Mendes walk away.

CHAPTER THIRTY-TWO

Working from Richie's office, Nate googles the name of Dennis McKinney's former defense lawyer, Bruce Cullen. He needs to find his office number so he can pay the guy a visit. But he isn't expecting the headlines that greet him. Turns out Bruce took his own life three and a half years ago, passing away from a self-inflicted gunshot wound.

"That's not good."

He scours the various articles for reasons behind the lawyer's suicide. Friends speculated his business wasn't doing well. Others said he suffered with depression. Nate can't help wondering whether guilt played a part in his decision to end things. Did he take a bribe in order to help the prosecution secure a conviction against Dennis?

Nothing here suggests that, so it's a dead end. Dennis won't be happy.

Needing refreshment, Nate goes to the small kitchen, disturbing Brody, who was asleep at his feet. Brody yawns loudly and then lazily follows him, probably in the hope he'll get a snack from the fridge. "Not yet, buddy. It'll be dinner time soon enough." He checks his watch. It's six o'clock. He thinks about calling it a day but first he needs to make contact with the other person Dennis mentioned during their phone call: Ronnie Russo. The missing baby's father.

As he hunts for a clean cup in the kitchen cabinets, he hears someone arrive in the reception area.

"Hi, I'm looking for Nate Monroe. Is he here?"

Nate stands still. He can't see the front office from here, but sound travels in this old building.

Janine's voice comes through and she sounds apprehensive. "That depends," she says. "Who's asking?"

"I'm a friend of his. He'll be pleased to see me."

It takes a couple of seconds before Janine enters the kitchen, but Nate hears the click-clacking of her high heels long before he sees her. She likes to add four or five inches to her height. Brody's tail thumps the floor in anticipation.

Closing the door behind her so their visitor can't hear, Janine says, "Some guy's asking for you. I'm getting reporter vibes from him. Want me to get rid of him?"

The guy could be here because he's heard about Father Connor's death, but it's unlikely since the Feds haven't released a statement yet. "That's okay, I'll see him."

Janine leads him out to the reception area, where the stranger holds out his hand for Nate to shake. "Bobbie Jackson. Pleasure to meet you."

Janine eyeballs him. "I thought you said you knew Nate?"

He laughs good-naturedly. "Sorry about that. Little white lies are an occupational hazard in my line of work. Nate, have you got a minute?"

"What for?" says Nate. "And which paper do you work for?"

"I'm a reporter with Channel Five news. I wanted to get your reaction about Father Jack Connor's death."

Someone's leaked the news. Nate feels the blood drain from his face. "No comment." He turns to walk away.

Brody sniffs Bobbie's shoes, making him back up. "Your dog friendly?" he asks.

Nate turns. "Friendlier than me. I suggest you leave."

"Listen," says Bobbie, "I get it; the priest traumatized you. He ruined your entire life. But this story is of public interest and the public is rooting for you now! They no longer believe Connor's claims about you murdering your fiancée. Which means you could make some serious money from a sit-down interview. My producer is willing to offer you whatever it takes. Within reason. I mean, you're already a millionaire thanks to this case, so you don't need that much financial persuasion, right?"

Nate closes his eyes against this guy's arrogance. He's met some good reporters over the years. People who do the job to find the truth and deliver it in an unbiased, sensitive manner. But he's also met a lot of Bobbies. Too many in fact. He doesn't even know what to say to the guy without blowing up.

Brody notices his change in body language. He looks from Nate to Bobbie, and within seconds he emits a low growl.

"Take a hike, asshole," says Janine, approaching the reporter. "Or you'll be dog food before you know it."

Bobbie doesn't back down. He fixes his eyes on Nate's. "Can't you see that until you pass comment on Father Connor's death, it won't be over. Guys like me will be following you around, trying to get a reaction. Trying to get a shot of you in tears, or lashing out, or hugging your girlfriend with 'palpable relief.'" He actually makes air quotes. "Just give me one line I can use to feed the public's hunger. Just enough for them to move on to the next sensational story." He sounds desperate now. "People need an end to this case, Monroe! They've followed it for *twenty years*! Once they hear your reaction in your own words, they'll forget all about you, your late fiancée and the priest. You'll be allowed to move on for good."

Nate's fists are clenched. How dare this asshole try to

emotionally blackmail him into saying something he doesn't want to say? He doesn't owe anyone anything.

He takes a step forward but Brody places himself between him and Bobbie.

His jaw tense, Nate says, "People like you and your ignorant viewers were the ones calling for me to be executed twenty years ago like some kind of blood sport. Why the *fuck* would I want to give them the happy ending they crave? If you want a quote from me, this is it—"

"Nate, don't," says Janine. "Don't give him the satisfaction."

Bobbie's clearly hungry for Nate's final word on the matter. He leans in, transfixed.

Nate was about to tell him and his viewers to go fuck themselves, but he realizes Janine's right. If he says that, it'll be all over the press. He'll be accused of being a hate-filled, angry person. One filled with rage so deep that they could imagine him killing Stacey Connor all those years ago. They'll start speculating again about whether his exoneration was misguided. Whether he managed to fool them all into believing he wasn't a killer and that, actually, poor, recently deceased Father Connor was right all along.

Nate can't win. Everything he says is twisted. It always will be because of *public interest*.

Not wanting to feed the media monster, he simply says, "No comment."

Brody barks loudly, making Bobbie jump. The disappointment on the reporter's face is evident, and that gives Nate more satisfaction than yelling profanities at him ever could.

He walks to the exit, with Brody close behind. The heavens have opened again. Rain pelts down hard. They rush into Nate's car. Nate knows Bobbie will be the first of many vultures looking for his reaction. They're not happy for him that Connor's dead. They just want viewers for their shows and hits on their websites. And he's determined not to give them what they want.

As he starts the engine, he realizes it's time to ditch the Dennis McKinney case—maybe ditch being a PI altogether—and leave Lost Creek right this minute, and for good. The thought brings him some relief. Relief that he'll never have to talk about the priest or his time on death row again.

He can start over. Change his name. Maybe even leave the country. Why not? He can afford to live anywhere in the world. Something good might as well come from his wrongful conviction payout. Isn't that what it was for? To make up for what happened to him.

As if it ever could. Money doesn't buy time. And he lost seventeen years. Twenty if you include those since his release, which were spent dealing with the aftermath.

Thoughts of Madison cross his mind, but he hardens his heart against them. She's made it clear she's not interested in him, and why would she be? He comes with more emotional baggage than anyone she's ever met. She doesn't need that in her life. If he leaves town, she could start fresh too, without him dragging her down.

With a clearness he's not had in a long time, Nate speeds away from the office.

CHAPTER THIRTY-THREE

Exhausted, Madison drives home through the evening's downpour. The sun has vanished behind heavy, dark clouds. She hopes the rain doesn't stick around. It's put a dampener on her mood.

Traffic builds downtown as everyone slows their speed during the heavy shower. Car horns blast for the few who don't. Madison sighs as she waits at a red light. A quick glance at her phone shows no messages from Owen. He normally checks in at least once a day. Richie must be keeping him busy, squeezing every last minute out of him before he leaves.

When the lights turn green only a few cars get through, allowing her time to call her son. But his phone is switched off. Madison frowns. Maybe he's picking something up from court. She shoots him a quick text.

I'm making lasagna for dinner. Attendance is not optional!

She smiles as she imagines him rolling his eyes when he reads it. What can she do? It's Wednesday night already, so they only have three more evenings together. Three more opportunities to make her son ready for the dog-eat-dog world he's about to enter. How will he cope without her and Nate around when he has problems? Who will make sure he studies and makes the most of the opportunities he's been given? Who will stop him from underage drinking and making poor decisions when all those around him are succumbing to the peer pressure that comes with being a college student?

A horn behind her alerts her to the green light. She gets through this time and races home, her wipers working hard to clear her vision of the roads.

As she lets herself into the house, she heads straight to the kitchen to get a towel to dry her hair. Bandit is sitting on the counter. He meows pathetically in greeting.

"Hey, kitty. I'll feed you in a second."

With her hair almost dry she runs her fingers through it to straighten it out and then goes to the bottom of the stairs. No backpack in the way, which means Owen's not home yet. She calls out to him just in case he—for once in his life—took it upstairs with him.

She's met with silence. He hasn't responded to her message yet either. She sighs as she returns to the kitchen. "He better be home soon or his ass is grass," she says to the cat.

Bandit meows in agreement.

Madison leans in to kiss the cat's head. She feeds him before starting dinner. When he's happy, she goes to open the refrigerator. That's when she sees a note on the door, held on with magnets. She recognizes Owen's handwriting.

"What the?" She pulls it off to read it.

Mom,

First of all: don't be mad!

Her heart sinks.

I left for college this morning. I know you'll be upset that we didn't get to say goodbye, but I couldn't do it. I don't want to see you upset. It's too much. I have enough anxiety about moving away already, so I'm wimping out.

I know you love me and I'll be back to visit real soon, OK? And before you break down in tears: Don't worry! I'm going to be fine!!

I'll call you tomorrow because I need a minute to settle in.

Love you, Mom.

BTW Nate and Richie don't know I've left early, so don't blame them for not telling you.

PS. Take care of Bandit for me. Remember to keep your door open at night so he can sleep on your bed. His treats are in my nightstand. And make sure he's with you whenever you video-call me!

Madison sobs hard. She can't believe he'd do that to her. He's denied her a goodbye. There was so much left to tell him before he moved out. He doesn't even know how to use a damn washing machine. That's *her* fault.

Tears run down her face as she slides to the floor. It feels too similar to the last time she lost him, when he was only ten years old. Images of the little boy she left behind consume her. She could only watch from the back seat of a cruiser after the police led her away from her home, closing the door on her son in his pajamas as he desperately tried reaching for her.

She can't believe he's gone. Moved out for good. In the blink of an eye, everything has changed.

Ten minutes pass on the cold floor as her tears slowly ebb away. Bandit wanders into her lap, where he gets comfy before cleaning himself. She takes comfort from his body heat.

"He screwed you over too, huh?" she says, her voice thick with emotion.

Bandit purrs as she strokes his neck. After some time, she's able to put things into perspective. She realizes this isn't a normal reaction to her son going to college. If they hadn't lost each other for seven years, it might've been easier. But still emotional.

Maybe he did the right thing. He wouldn't have wanted to see her like this.

It came as a shock though. He must have planned it. How long did he know? What did they last say to each other?

She thinks back to this morning, which seems days ago now. She was drinking coffee outside, watching the sunrise. Owen had passed her the newspaper. He looked like he wanted to say something, but didn't. Maybe he was second-guessing himself. Or maybe that was when he realized he couldn't face their goodbye and made the decision to leave early.

It feels so unfair. She thinks she could've contained herself until he'd been driven away by Jason's dad. Just the image of him driving away to start a new life elsewhere fills her eyes with more tears.

No. She couldn't have contained it. He did the right thing.

Madison becomes aware of how quiet the house is. She's already lonely. She needs to get out of here. She gets off the floor and cleans her face at the kitchen sink. In front of the hallway mirror, she dries it with a hand towel. She looks like a hot mess. Her eyes are bright red, her eyelids puffy, all makeup gone.

She'll go back to the station and work. It will distract her. It's better than sitting around here on her own all night, thinking about Owen.

Grabbing her car keys, she heads for the front door.

CHAPTER THIRTY-FOUR

Madison pulls up in the dark and switches the car's engine off. The rain makes it difficult to see the house through the windshield. She hadn't meant to come here. She intended to go back to work. But how could she?

She focuses on her breathing, trying her hardest to compose herself before leaving the car. She had to come here. To Nate's house. Nate's the only person who will understand. He'll be disappointed by Owen's swift departure too.

With her eyes dried she takes the deepest breath she can manage. She forces herself out of the car, instantly soaked by rainfall. Summer has vanished, along with her son.

The thought stops her in her tracks. She gulps back a sob and closes her eyes tight. She didn't even make it to Nate's porch before breaking down again. She feels so stupid. He's not dead! He'll be calling her tomorrow!

Aware she's being ridiculous but unable to stop it, she cuts herself some slack, if only to pull herself together.

Nate's car is outside and the kitchen light shines from within the house. She hasn't been here for months. She shouldn't have stayed away. Grief has a way of isolating you from people. She can see that now. Has she treated Nate badly and added to his own loneliness? Is that why he accepted Lena's coffee date?

She suddenly doubts her decision to come here. What if he's entertaining Lena? Or what if he has someone else in there? If he was open to seeing Lena, he could be dating others.

She hesitates, letting the rain soak through her clothes. She hadn't even worn a jacket. It was so hot earlier. She doesn't even know where her rain jacket is.

Madison turns back to her car, doubting herself. She should leave. This isn't Nate's problem. As she takes a step forward, she hears Brody bark behind her. He might have spotted her from the window. She digs her car keys out of her pocket, feeling like she should rush to get away before Nate sees her. A door opens.

"Madison?"

Too late. She slowly turns around. Brody excitedly runs up to her, ignoring the rain. He loves getting wet. Frozen in her overthinking, she doesn't pet the dog.

Nate stands in his doorway. He looks like he was about to go out. He's wearing a jacket over his T-shirt and jeans and he's holding a box. When she meets his eyes, she sees concern for her.

"What's going on?" he asks, placing the box on the floor inside.

Madison's face crumples. She covers it with her hands.

Within seconds Nate's there, pulling her into his warm embrace, his hand stroking the back of her head. He's getting as soaked as she is. Into her ear he says, "What's wrong? Is Owen okay?"

She tries hard to control her tears. "He left me a note," she says into his neck. "He's gone already. He left for college without saying goodbye."

Nate pulls back and looks at her. His hair is soaking wet. Rain runs down his face. "He's okay though, right?"

She nods. "He couldn't face seeing me upset."

Nate tenderly kisses her forehead. "I'm sorry. That sucks." He takes her hand in his and leads her into the house.

Brody follows them inside before Nate closes the door and removes his jacket and shoes. Madison stands in his kitchen, dripping water all over the floor. She feels so sad. She can't imagine her tears ever stopping.

Nate comes to her, his T-shirt and jeans soaked through. She can make out the rosary around his neck. It's the one she bought him as a gift last Christmas after he finally removed his dead fiancée's. He takes both her hands in his. When his cell phone rings on the kitchen counter, he doesn't glance at it. It's as if he doesn't even hear it.

Madison doesn't know whether it's the close proximity to him or whether it's his A/C making her damp clothes cold, but she shivers.

He pushes a strand of her wet hair away from her face. "You need to get out of those clothes before you catch your death." Taking her hand, he turns and leads her upstairs.

She lets him.

Nate runs the shower hot while she waits in his bedroom, unsure what to do. The room is almost empty apart from his bed and some boxes. "Are you moving?" she asks as he returns.

He fixes his eyes on hers, his expression serious. She knows she has his full attention. "I was thinking about it," he says.

Before she can question him further, he moves close and slowly unbuttons her damp shirt, revealing her bra underneath.

Madison wipes her eyes, unsure what's going to happen. She's acutely aware of every move he makes. Every time his warm hands skim her body. She realizes she's wanted this since the first time he showed her she could trust him. Her life, and that of her son's, has been in his hands. He's never let her down. Not when it mattered.

When he leads her to the bathroom, she goes willingly.

Steam from the hot shower quickly warms the room. He turns to her. "You're shaking," he says.

"So are you."

Nate slowly runs his warm hands down her arms before removing her shirt. Madison pulls off his T-shirt. His rosary rests on his toned torso. She touches it, glad he was able to believe again. Glad that Father Connor didn't take that from him, despite trying so hard.

When they're both naked and within inches of each other, Nate touches her face, gently brushing his thumb over her lips. It makes her shiver harder.

He kisses her. His lips are soft and she can feel stubble from his jaw against her skin.

Madison closes her eyes. The electricity between them is overpowering. She pulls away and looks into his deep blue eyes. She sees the intensity of his feelings for her. She sees her future.

She steps under the shower, letting the warm water wash away her tears. Nate joins her and, as he begins kissing her entire body, she closes her eyes and forgets all about what brought her here tonight.

CHAPTER THIRTY-FIVE

Madison wakes to someone stroking her back. She couldn't be more confused. At first, she thinks she imagined it, but it's followed by a kiss on her neck. It all comes back to her.

Nate. The shower. What happened afterward.

There's a second when she feels awkward at having to turn and face him in his bed the morning after the night before. Brody soon quashes that, because when she opens her eyes, he's sitting on the floor next to the bed, staring at her with a quizzical expression. Maybe he's not used to his dad having visitors.

As her eyes open fully, the dog's tail thumps harder.

Madison smiles. "Hey, Brody. Sorry for stealing your side of the bed."

Nate laughs behind her, so she turns to face him. He's leaning on his elbow with a smile on his face. Like her, he's naked under the blanket. It's weird. His hair is a little messy but otherwise he looks wide awake. She wishes she felt the same. She must look a mess with no makeup.

"Morning," he says.

Madison smiles sheepishly, trying to keep herself covered.

With just her shoulders visible she says, "Morning." She doesn't know what else to say and is relieved when his cell phone rings.

Nate glances at it quickly and when he sees who's calling, he laughs.

"What are you laughing at?" she says, confused.

"You'll see." He holds it up and Madison sees Owen's face on the screen. It's a video call.

"No! Don't answer!" she yelps.

It's too late. Nate has already accepted it. When Owen sees them in bed together, he grimaces. "Dude! That's my *mom*!"

Madison dives under the cover but Nate seems to find the whole situation amusing.

Owen sighs. "I've literally been gone less than twenty-four hours and you're already screwing each other?"

"What can I tell you?" says Nate. "I'm a fast worker."

Madison pops her head out and shoves his bare shoulder. "What are you talking about?" To Owen she says, "It's not what you think."

Nate raises his eyebrows at Owen and mouths, "It's exactly what you think."

Madison could die of embarrassment, but Owen sees the funny side of it.

"And here's me calling Nate to ask him to check on you because I thought you'd be in the middle of some kind of emotional breakdown..." He shakes his head. "I'll call you later, Mom." He pauses. "Actually, maybe I'll text."

"This doesn't let you off the hook for leaving without saying goodbye!" she says.

Owen grins as he ends the call.

Madison rests her head back against the pillow. "Well *that* was awkward."

After putting his phone back on the nightstand, Nate leans in to her. "It's not awkward, it's funny. And now you don't need to worry about how to tell him about us."

She looks into his eyes. "It would've been nice to get used to the idea myself first."

"Come on," he says playfully. "You always knew we'd end up here." He looks at the bed and then adds, "Well, not right here, but you know what I mean."

She sighs. She enjoyed last night and she's relieved Owen isn't upset about it, but she doesn't want to ruin her friendship with Nate. He's literally all she has now. "We have to take this slow."

Nate strokes her arm. "Madison? You're lying naked in my bed and I'm paying for your son's education. I think we're past taking things slow."

She laughs, realizing how ridiculous this all is. "Oh my God. I can't believe we're really doing this."

Tired of being ignored, Brody jumps on the bed, trying to get between them. Nate gently forces him off and tells him to go downstairs. "Go on! You're too young to witness what's about to happen in here."

Shocked, Madison says, "Nate! I have to get to work!"

He comes in close and says, "You will. I just want to start your day off right first."

Madison relents as he kisses her.

After the shame of having to dress in yesterday's crumpled clothes—now dry, thankfully—Madison heads downstairs, where Nate has coffee waiting for her. He's in nothing but pajama bottoms and she's left wondering not just how she resisted him for so long, but why she did.

She sips her coffee, noticing the entire house is packed up. "What's going on?"

He looks around. "This place is too big for me. I was thinking of downsizing." His expression turns serious. "You know what? That's a lie. I want to be completely honest with you."

Madison gets a horrible feeling in the pit of her stomach. "You're skipping town, aren't you?"

He comes to her, sets her coffee on the counter and holds her hands in his. "I wanted to—yesterday. If you'd arrived ten minutes later, I would've been gone."

It doesn't bear thinking about. "But why? What's going on with you?"

He sighs. "I had a visit from a reporter. News of Father Connor's death has leaked and the reporter basically told me I owed it to the great American public to give them a happy ending to my story by doing a tell-all sit-down interview."

Madison can't be too mad. She knows how much that would've upset him. "And today? Are you going to be gone by the time I finish work tonight?"

"No." He kisses her fingers. "I promise."

She studies his face. He seems lighter than she's seen him in a while. "You've got to stop running away from your problems, okay? If any more reporters turn up, just give 'em hell!"

He smiles. "Yes, boss."

"Ooh, I like that. Keep that up and we're going to get along just fine."

Her cell phone rings and she sees Steve's name. Nate fixes himself coffee while she answers.

"Morning, Madison," says Steve. "Sorry to bother you this early but I've heard back from the manufacturer of the breast implants from our female victim. Lena's idea for tracing the serial numbers appears to have worked."

Madison's intrigued. "Really? What did they say?"

"They gave me the name of the clinic they sold them to, and the manager of that clinic is calling me as soon as he gets into work in an hour or so, around nine o'clock. He's agreed to disclose the name of the recipient."

Madison's mouth drops open. "No way?"

"I know, right? Tracking down a victim through their cosmetic surgery has to be a first for me."

"Steve, that's amazing," she says. "I'll be in as fast as I can."

"Understood. See you shortly."

Madison turns to Nate. "I have to go."

He walks her to the door. "Something tells me you're going to have a long day ahead."

"Right. I might not be in touch for a while. Sorry."

"That's okay. I'll be working anyway. On that wrongful conviction case I told you about. But don't stay away too long."

"Okay, bye." She opens the front door and is about to leave when he turns her to face him.

"Where's my goodbye kiss?" he asks.

She reddens. "Oh God, you're one of those needy guys." She's joking, to hide her embarrassed delight at the amount of attention he's lavishing on her. She's not used to it.

He kisses her lovingly until she pulls away. "Seriously, I have to go change before I can head to work!"

Nate laughs as she rushes to her car. Madison slips inside thinking about how much things can change in the space of twenty-four hours.

CHAPTER THIRTY-SIX

Madison sits next to Steve as they patiently wait for his desk phone to ring. The clinic's manager should call any minute with the identity of the patient who received the breast implants.

As they haven't been able to find Eric Bailey's next of kin, learning the female's identity should help them to track down the pair's loved ones so that Madison can finally notify them of their deaths. That's not something she's looking forward to, but it will provide her with answers as to who this couple's inner circle were and that, hopefully, will lead her to their killer.

Steve glances at her. "If he doesn't call within the next ten minutes, I'll call him."

Her stomach is in knots with anticipation. "I just hope he doesn't decide he'd rather we get a warrant for his patient information." Once they know the female's name, they'll also be on their way to naming the children and looking into potential custody battles.

"I don't think he will," says Steve. "Once I told him why I was calling he said he'd be glad to help. Seemed like a good guy."

She hears Dina on dispatch fielding calls from reporters for updates. Apparently, the media want another press conference as soon as possible. Madison can at least inform them of Eric Bailey's identity and the car they found.

Detective Adams arrives ten minutes late for his shift, one takeout coffee in his hand. He approaches them with Alex trailing behind him. Alex looks like he's been working all night.

"Morning." Madison nods to them both.

Adams goes to his desk to fire up his computer and down his drink. Maybe one day he'll bring her coffee, but she doubts it.

"Morning, Detective," says Alex. "How are you today?" His hands are full.

Madison checks out what he's holding. It looks like a bunch of identifying documents. "I'm good. What have you got there?" she asks.

Alex smiles. "The identity of both our adult victims."

Madison and Steve exchange a surprised look. She takes the documents from Alex. There are also two wallets. Everything is sodden and water damaged. "From the safe in the car?" she asks.

"Correct," says Alex. "I took an angle grinder to it in the end. The door came off easier than I expected. I almost took my hand off too, but that's another matter." He leans in to point to the documents. "Sorry about the water damage. No safe is water resistant for as long as this one was submerged, but the damage has been limited somewhat by the fact the safe was protected for some time by being in the boot—sorry, trunk—of the car."

Madison kisses Alex on his cheek. "It's official: you're my favorite forensic technician ever!"

He blushes. "That's kind of a given, considering I'm the *only* forensic technician ever employed by this department..."

"Was this everything?" she asks.

"No. We also have the steak knife used on one of the twins.

I've bagged that to send to the lab but, again, the water probably ruined our chances of pulling DNA from it."

It's good to have the knife but Madison's still holding out hope they'll find the weapon used to bludgeon the parents to death, because that would've been held by the killer for longer than the knife was, and it wasn't in the lake, so it should have DNA all over it.

"And..." Alex pulls out two cell phones in evidence bags from the back pocket of his jeans. "These."

Madison glances at Steve and Adams with a grin on her face before saying, "You've outdone yourself this time, Alex."

"Well, don't get too excited. It's likely they're useless due to the water. But I'll see what I can extract from them. Phones aren't my specialty so I may need to call someone I know for their advice."

Detective Adams takes some of the paperwork from her. Madison has a passport for Eric Bailey. It appears to have fared much better than the other documents. She finds Eric's photograph inside and for the first time is able to see his face. He was pretty average looking. A face you'd likely forget, if it hadn't been bludgeoned and covered in bugs the first time you saw it.

Adams shows her Eric's birth certificate. The text is faded.

When Steve's phone rings he immediately spins around to answer it.

Distracted by what's in her hands, Madison opens one of the wallets to find a driver's license. It's for the female victim. Her photo shows a somewhat attractive woman who clearly had a love of fillers and possibly Botox. However, because she doesn't appear to be very old, the cosmetic surgery makes her look oddly mishappen, as if she's been attacked by a swarm of bees. Her long platinum hair is considerably sleeker than it was when she was found dead.

Madison reads out the information on the license. "Tammy Smith. Says here she lived in the same town as Eric, but at a different residence." She's filled with relief. "Finally, we know who they both are."

She realizes then that the date of birth has been scratched out by someone. Running her thumb over the rough scratches, she frowns. It's yet another attempt to conceal the victim's identity. But why?

She turns the driver's license to Adams. "How old would you guess?"

He peers at it for ages. "Thirty-three, thirty-four?"

Madison nods. She'd guess mid-thirties too.

There's nothing to identify the children; no birth certificates or passports. The DNA testing so far has revealed Eric isn't the father of the boys, but the lack of birth certificates for them has Madison questioning whether or not Tammy is the children's mother. Could this couple have abducted all three children? The wounded boy she found dying outside the house asked for his mom before he died. Madison has to consider the possibility he wasn't referring to Tammy. Maybe he hadn't seen his actual mother for days.

Detective Adams's phone rings and he walks away to answer it. The whole office appears to be buzzing with activity this morning. It fills Madison with hope that they could find the missing child by the end of the day.

Frustrated she can't run a background check on Tammy Smith without her date of birth, she tries anyway, using approximate years of birth: 1984, 1985 and 1986. She gets several responses thanks to the common last name, but unfortunately none of the photographs match Tammy's. She wonders if Tammy's known to child protective services and thinks of Alex's ex-girlfriend, Samantha, who has access to CPS records. Looking over at Alex she says, "I need Sam's phone number. I want to see if she can check whether Tammy or Eric are known to child services up in Buford."

Alex pulls out his phone and then hesitates. "I can call her if you like?"

Madison frowns. "Are you sure? I didn't think you'd want to speak to her."

"To be honest, it would be a good opportunity to clear the air, especially if I start with a work-related issue." He's trying to come across casual but Madison can tell he's desperate to speak to his ex.

"Okay," she says. "I'm trying to see if there was a custody battle ongoing, or maybe even whether they've ever had any children removed from them in the past. Until the lab's DNA results come back for Tammy, we won't know whether she's the boys' mother, so CPS might be a quicker route to finding out. Sam might not have access to another town's records, but she might know who to call to find out."

Alex nods. "Give me ten minutes." He heads to his office for some privacy.

When he's gone, Steve finishes his call and punches the air. "The clinic says the recipient of the implants was a woman named Tammy Smith back in 2014."

Madison smiles. "That's the name we have too thanks to these." She shows him the documents from the safe. "It's always good to have more than one source of identification though."

Detective Adams approaches. "Just spoke to a Sergeant Corcoran from Buford PD. They searched Eric Bailey's home and found no signs of a disturbance or anything of significance. While they were there a neighbor came forward and disclosed he had a girlfriend."

"Did they name her as Tammy Smith?" says Madison.

"They didn't know her last name, but yeah, they called her Tammy and they knew where she lived," he says. "So the cops checked out Tammy's place too; a small apartment. She'd not long ago moved in apparently. But now the place looks like it's been abandoned. Tammy's neighbor confirmed she had twin boys and a little girl."

Madison's eyes widen. "So the kids *were* living with Tammy before she and Eric moved here. Which means the little girl's definitely missing."

Adams nods. "Sergeant Corcoran said there were no personal belongings left behind or signs of a struggle. None of Eric's or Tammy's neighbors knew much about them, so the cops couldn't get a next of kin from anyone."

Madison thinks for a second. "This suggests all three children are Tammy's. She didn't abduct them. She probably fought hard to save them the night she died."

"The clinic took emergency contact details for Tammy," says Steve, checking his notes. "Maria Smith, same last name as Tammy. She was listed as Tammy's sister-in-law."

Madison frowns. "So Tammy *was* married? That must be Eric's sister."

"But Eric's last name is Bailey," says Adams. He looks as confused as Madison feels.

"Maybe Tammy was married more than once," says Steve. He tears off Maria's contact details before handing them to Madison. "They only had a landline number for her and no address."

Madison goes straight to her desk phone to call the woman. Her hands dial the wrong number twice in her excitement for answers. Once the call is placed, she waits patiently for someone to answer, but no one does and there's no voicemail service. "Dammit." She hangs up.

"Given we're drawing a blank with next of kin," says Adams, "we should release the couple's name to the media to see if anyone comes forward."

Madison agrees. "I would've liked to have spoken to Maria first, but there's no telling when she might be home and I don't think we should delay any longer." She sighs. "I wish we'd found the murder weapon." Then something occurs to her. "Hang on a minute. Why were their personal documents locked away in the safe?"

"The killer must've done it before pushing the car into the lake," says Steve. "To make it harder to identify them."

"Which means he must be linked to them somehow," she says, "given the pains he went to in order to conceal their identities."

Adams has a different theory. "If Tammy and Eric were on the run with her kids because of a custody battle, they could've come prepared to hide their own identities. Maybe they bought the safe in case anyone came after them. Or maybe they were intending to keep something else in there, like a stash of cash they'd stolen."

It's so confusing to Madison. She needs to find out why they were on the run in the first place. "We need to know what they were fleeing from, because something obviously caught up with them."

Adams nods. "Want me to hold the press conference?"

She'd rather do it herself but doesn't want to upset him. They are supposed to be a team, and he appears to be fully invested in this case now. "Sure. You know as much as I do."

He beams at her, clearly surprised she's agreed to it. "I'm waiting on Eric's call records to come through but the cell provider said it could take up to a week."

Madison shakes her head. She's never understood why something that is so easily accessible to the phone companies takes a week to be sent to *them*, especially in high-risk cases like this where a little girl is missing.

"By the way, I checked Jerry Clark out," he says. "He's clean."

Madison's surprised. She was hoping Jerry might make a good suspect given he cleared the victims' house just weeks before their murder. "What about Kai Bishop's alibi that he was home all evening?"

"I mean, I checked the TV guide," says Adams, "and there *was* a Denzel Washington movie on that night. Not one of Denzel's best, but yeah, it was on. Whether or not Kai was home watching it is a different matter. I don't know how we'd prove that."

"We could try to get a warrant for *his* cell phone," suggests Steve.

"We need probable cause first," says Madison. In her eyes Kai and Dawn are still potential suspects due to their weak alibis, their proximity to the crime scene and the fact Dawn admits she saw the family moving in on the day they died. She's one of the few people who knew they were there. "It's odd that Dawn didn't go into their house despite being a nosy neighbor, right?"

Adams crosses his arms. "You think she knew they were dead in there and didn't want to see them?"

"Possibly," she says. "That would mean she knowingly sent her grandson in to find them instead."

Shaking his head in disgust Adams says, "What kind of person would do that?"

"The kind of person who would move a younger guy into her home while her poor husband is left to rot in the spare room with no specialist care or attention."

The more she thinks about that couple and their friend, Jerry, the more Madison thinks they're hiding something. She just needs to figure out what.

CHAPTER THIRTY-SEVEN

FIFTEEN YEARS EARLIER

5 hours remaining

Mike stands with his back to the door of the interview room while Detective Ramsey interrogates Dennis McKinney for the second time. The first time, yesterday evening, the guy had his lawyer present. This time he hasn't bothered as he feels he can do better without him. Mike knows that's a bad decision. It never works out well when someone forgoes a lawyer. But it could work in their favor, so he's not about to offer the guy any legal advice.

Dennis didn't sleep at all last night. The overnight officer regularly checked on him and reported back this morning that Dennis spent hours writing pages and pages of notes. Mike suspected it was a handwritten confession. Turns out he was writing to his family and the press, denying any involvement in Grace's disappearance.

The press is already getting antsy about the baby's father, Ronnie Russo. They think he makes a better suspect, but Ramsey's fixated on Dennis for this. So much so that when Ramsey arrived for work early this morning and was made aware of the letters, he tore them up in anger. Dennis doesn't know that yet.

With just an hour to go until noon, Detective Ramsey has brought Dennis a sandwich and a soda. They sit on the table between them, untouched. Dennis looks drained with tired eyes. His weary expression is that of a man who feels he isn't being listened to.

Ramsey looks just as tired. He worked overnight and even joined the search party. But the trail is completely cold other than the sandal found in Dennis's truck with his print on, and the mother's witness testimony.

"Listen, Dennis," says Ramsey, his elbows on the table between them. "We only have five hours until Grace's mother potentially kills herself over this. If you could at least tell us what you've done with her daughter's body, we could bring her some kind of closure."

Dennis stares at Ramsey. "Tiffany's suicide will be on you, not me."

Ramsey shakes his head in frustration. "You know the only thing that's worse than a child killer?" He waits a beat before answering his own question. "A child killer who never lets the family bury their child. Is that what you want to be known as, Dennis? Because those guys get special treatment in prison. You'll be ranked even lower than the pedophiles, and that's not somewhere you want to be, my friend."

Dennis takes a breath. With complete conviction, at least in Mike's opinion, he says, "You're not listening to me. I didn't touch that girl, I didn't abduct that girl and I did not kill that girl. My DNA is on her sandal because I briefly touched her foot to greet her when they arrived to buy eggs. If her sandal was found in my truck, like you say, then it was planted there." He glares at Mike before continuing. "You're wasting your time if you think you're going to get me to confess to something I didn't do, and in the meantime, you're letting her abductor roam free." He leans back in his seat. "What are you going to do when another child goes missing while I'm locked up in here? Because you sure as hell can't blame me then, can you?"

Unfazed, Ramsey moves his chair around the table and closer to Dennis, their knees touching. Mike would hate that. He'd feel claustrophobic, which is exactly what Ramsey wants. But it's embarrassing and not something he'd ever do. He doesn't want to be one of those cliché TV detectives who plays good cop-bad cop, which is exactly what Ramsey reminds him of.

Dennis pushes his seat back to get away from Ramsey but the wall stops him moving far.

"Tiffany is adamant she saw you talking to Grace in her front yard just hours before she disappeared," says Ramsey. "Are you calling Tiffany a liar?"

"She's mistaken. It wasn't me."

"Oh, sure, it was just some guy who looked *exactly* like you. *Exactly* like the neighbor who lives just a stone's throw from where the missing child was abducted. I mean, come on, man! You've got to give me something to work with!" He leans in closer. "Did you talk to the girl and now you're afraid to tell me because it looks bad? If so, I can deal with that. It puts you at the scene but it doesn't mean you took her. If you were at the scene, maybe you saw someone else in the area who looked like they could've done it, huh?"

Ramsey's just trying to get Dennis to admit to being there. Not so he can rule him out, like he implies, but so he can use it against the guy.

"I wasn't there," says Dennis.

"Maybe it was an accident." Ramsey's relentless. "Maybe you said hi to little Grace, took her home with you to play together, or whatever, and she accidentally died. Is that how it happened? Did you freak out and realize it would look bad, even though it was an accident? Is that why you've hidden her body?"

Dennis closes his eyes and rubs them. "I'll repeat this one last time as you don't appear to be getting it," he says, "and this is my last word on the matter." He opens his eyes and exhales. "I am *not* responsible for Grace's disappearance. Charge me or let me go because I'm done with this bullshit."

Detective Ramsey stares at the guy with such venom that Mike thinks he might punch him. Instead, he stands. "Congratulations, McKinney. You just secured yourself a death sentence."

He motions for Mike to open the door and then angrily brushes passed him.

CHAPTER THIRTY-EIGHT

PRESENT DAY

Nate spent the morning unboxing some of his belongings while thinking about how close he and Madison came to missing each other last night. Ten minutes later and he would've been on the road to who knows where by now. He's glad she showed up. He feels completely different today than he did yesterday, which tells him he needs to work on his fight-or-flight response. He needs to do better, for Madison.

Brody comes in from the yard and goes straight to his food bowl, which is ready for him. He noisily wolfs down some kibble as Nate takes a seat at his dining table, phone and legal pad in hand. He's tracked down Ronnie Russo's number. He knows the media thought he made a good suspect for his daughter's disappearance fifteen years ago, so he wants to find out whether the police ever considered him a person of interest. If Ronnie *is* guilty, it's unlikely he'll agree to speak to Nate.

The phone rings four times before someone answers. "Hello?"

"Hi, my name's Nate Monroe. I'm a private investigator hoping to speak with Ronnie Russo. Is that you?"

Understandably, there's a few seconds' hesitation where Ronnie must be wondering whether to hang up now or see what Nate's investigating. His curiosity wins. "What do you want with me?"

"I've been employed by Dennis McKinney to look into what happened to your daughter. He claims he wasn't responsible for her disappearance and would like to get out of prison."

Ronnie snorts. "He would say that, wouldn't he?"

Nate knows the best way to play this conversation is to remain neutral. "I don't know whether he's innocent or guilty, but the case against him was weak. I was hoping to find out what you thought."

"You want my opinion?" says Ronnie, some surprise evident in his voice.

"Right. Do you have any theories about what happened to Grace? Or do you think the police have the right guy?"

Ronnie sighs heavily. "Look, man, this whole situation ruined my life. I don't like being reminded of it."

"I understand that, and I'm sorry for bringing it up. I just want you to have your say because this is your daughter we're talking about, and I know cops don't always do their job properly. You've had a lot of time to think about what happened to her. All I'm asking is that you share your opinion with me. If you think McKinney is the guy who took her, then tell me that and I won't bother you again."

Nate hears what sounds like a beer bottle being opened. It's only eleven a.m.

"You know," says Ronnie, "I never touched alcohol until my daughter went missing. Drugs? Sure, I smoked weed. But alcohol? No. I wasn't interested. I'd seen what it did to my dad. He was an abusive asshole who loved liquor more than his family."

Sensing he's going to open up, Nate remains silent.

After a few seconds, Ronnie's ready to reminisce. "I hadn't

seen Grace for a couple of days. Tiffany said she'd been ill with a stomach bug, so I was planning to visit the day after Grace was taken."

Nate silently takes notes.

"When the detective showed up at my door, I thought he was there to arrest me for marijuana possession. I had no idea he was there to tell me someone had taken my daughter."

"Did he ask you where you were at the time?"

"Of course. I had prior arrests for drug use and possession, so Detective Ramsey implied I sold my daughter to pay for my habit. He interviewed me for it, twice. But I'd been at work at a construction site that day. They interviewed everyone and then searched the whole damn site looking for her body!" He gulps back his drink, clearly still affected by what happened. "To this day I *still* have to see a therapist. Even after all these years. But none of them can help me. None of them know what it's like to live with losing a child."

Nate can tell he's struggling, so he changes the subject slightly. "How did you and Tiffany meet?"

"I don't want to talk about her."

Raising his eyebrows, Nate says, "You don't have a high opinion of her?"

"Listen, we were young and we screwed around, that was it. I never lived with her, dated her, proposed to her or nothing. We had sex a few times and she got pregnant. I helped her out with money after Grace was born, and I had to stay in touch with her because I wanted to be in my daughter's life. That's as far as our relationship went."

There's clearly a lot he's not saying. Nate asks, "Was she a difficult person to get along with?"

"I'm done talking about her. It's too hard. I can't help Dennis. Neither can you. Don't call me again. You don't realize what this does to me."

The line goes dead.

Nate looks at his phone. Now he knows Ronnie had an alibi and the police even searched his place of employment, it's likely he wasn't involved.

Which leaves Nate questioning whether Dennis McKinney belongs in prison after all.

CHAPTER THIRTY-NINE

Madison watches from the doorway of the station's conference room as Detective Adams updates the press. He confidently explains what they've learned since she spoke to them outside the murder house. Once the reporters get Tammy's and Eric's names, they have many follow-up questions, all of which Adams handles well.

With their victims' identities finally being released, it should be only a matter of time before someone comes forward with information about them, and possibly about Tammy's missing daughter. It's alarming that the little girl hasn't been spotted by anyone in a town this size. It could mean she's either been killed already, or the killer fled town straight after murdering Tammy, Eric and the boys, in which case it will be a lot harder to locate him.

"Madison?"

She spins around.

Chief Mendes approaches with Dina. Steve follows behind them, glancing in at the press conference.

Dina has her headset in one hand and a piece of paper in the other. "I've just had an anonymous tip that Doug and

Nancy Draper might have the missing girl." She keeps her voice low so no reporters hear.

Madison freezes. "What did the caller say?"

"It was a guy. I think he was putting on a fake accent, so I don't know how good the information is, but he said he'd seen Nancy Draper playing with a female toddler this morning in the paddock beside her house. Claims he saw them together as he drove by."

Madison frowns. "If the Drapers took her, would they really have her out in full view of passersby?"

Dina shrugs. "Criminals are stupid."

She can't argue with that. Madison gets a surge of adrenaline. "I'll head out there right away."

As Dina returns to her cubicle, Chief Mendes says, "What do we know about the Drapers?"

"They're not very friendly. Apparently Doug's a loan shark and there's a possibility Linda Hendricks owed him money when she died."

"And Linda owned the property our victims were found in?" says Mendes.

"Right. I considered whether Doug might have sent someone to the house to collect what he was owed, and the deaths could be the result of mistaken identity, but it's unlikely given Linda died months ago. Presumably he would've heard about it."

Mendes considers it. "Unless he thought the new residents were related to her and expected them to pay up on her behalf."

Steve jumps in. "I did find a brief newspaper obituary for her online so, yeah, it's likely Doug would've heard she passed. There's an appeal in the obituary for any relatives to come forward to claim her remains. I found it when I was looking into whether or not she had a will, but she didn't as far as I can tell. She'd lived there her entire life and it was paid for, so no one cared what happened to the place."

"You haven't found any of Linda's relatives?" asks Madison.

"I chased it with the paper, to see if anyone came forward, but no one did, so an old co-worker of Linda's arranged a cremation in the end. The paper wouldn't give me the co-worker's name but they did agree to pass my details on. All I can do is wait to see if they're willing to speak to us."

Madison sighs. "Everything's so much harder when a family's estranged." Turning to Chief Mendes she asks, "Think you could persuade a judge to sign a search warrant for Doug Drapers' property?"

Mendes shakes her head. "Not based off one anonymous tip-off and the rumor that someone unrelated to the murders owed Draper money. Find me something else."

She nods. "I'll try."

Chief Mendes and Steve return to their desks.

Madison remains hovering by the door waiting for Adams to finish his press conference. Eventually Alex joins her. "I've spoken to Sam," he says.

"And?"

"She doesn't have access to anything that we need, not unless she breaks some rules, which I told her not to do."

It's a shame, but it was a long shot that this couple was known to child services anyway. "Did you two resolve anything?" she asks.

"As far as she's concerned, there's nothing to resolve." He looks downcast as he says, "She told me again she's sorry and we agreed there were no hard feelings. It was all very amicable, which makes it harder to understand."

Madison feels for him.

"Anyway, I've had some interesting lab results back," he says, changing the subject. "Some items are still being tested but the DNA results confirm that Tammy *is* the mother of the twin boys."

"It's good to know for sure." It feels like everything's starting to come together.

"As for the missing girl, the clothes we took from the utility trailer were sent off later than everything else, so we'll have to wait a little longer to see if the lab can pull any DNA to confirm whether Tammy is her mother too."

Madison nods. "Sure. You know, it sounds to me as if Tammy and Eric brought her children here to start a new life together. Maybe they didn't flee their old town; they could've simply been moving in together."

"Why Lost Creek though?" says Alex. "And how come someone killed them?"

She chews her lip. "That I don't know. But I know where to look."

The minute Detective Adams steps out from the conference room, and before the reporters follow him out, Madison grabs his arm. "We're going to Gold Rock. Doug Draper might have the girl."

They take separate cars and pull up outside the Drapers' ranch within twenty minutes, thanks to exceeding the speed limit.

Adams gets out of his car and walks over to her as she steps out. "Isn't this your sister's place?"

"It was."

Adams studies her face. "You ever visit her in prison?"

Madison scoffs. "I don't think I'm invited." He'll know some of what went down between them, but only what he can learn online. The rest, he doesn't need to know. "Stay alert." She moves toward the house. "Let's see who's home."

Several men in blue coveralls are hard at work in the salvage yard, but they don't notice Madison and Adams approaching the house. And a knock at the door goes unanswered.

"Are these guys dangerous?" asks Adams.

"Doug and Nancy have no prior arrests, but I'm willing to bet some of those guys do." She nods to the yard. "Places like this attract drifters eager to work for cash with no questions asked about their employment or criminal history. As a result, they work hard for low pay and they're usually loyal to their boss, so I doubt they'll be friendly." She remembers the shady characters her brother-in-law employed.

Adams touches his service weapon as he heads over to the yard. "Only one way to find out," he says over his shoulder.

Madison follows.

CHAPTER FORTY

Adams approaches the first person he sees, a younger guy in his twenties who's stopped work to enjoy a cigarette. As he reaches him, Adams says, "Hey, we're looking for your boss."

"Who's asking?" he responds, eyeing them suspiciously.

An older man joins them. He rubs his hands on a grease-stained towel as he casts a critical glance over Madison.

She holds up her badge. "LCPD detectives. And you two are?"

The older man's gaze is untrusting, suggesting he has beef with the police, although Madison doesn't recognize him. "I'm Al. This is Sonny." He doesn't reveal their last names.

"Where's Doug?" asks Adams.

Al shrugs. "How should I know? I'm not his keeper."

"When did you last see him?" presses Adams. "Or his wife."

"We don't see Nancy much around here," says Sonny, stubbing out the cigarette under his shoe. He makes no attempts to pick it up after, but the whole area is filled with mud puddles after yesterday's rain, so it quickly vanishes into the ground. "She's a little agoraphobic if you ask me."

"Shut up, kid," says Al with a scathing glance. "They're both out. Care to leave a message?"

Madison looks around the yard. Nothing has changed since her brother-in-law died here. It's still full of cars stacked high around the perimeter, ready to be crushed or stripped of parts. This is also the last place she saw Detective Mike Bowers, just over a year ago. She remembers the sun was shining during their last devastating conversation. The memory of what happened next makes her shudder. This place is cursed.

"Do you know if Nancy and Doug were home on Sunday evening?" she asks.

Sonny doesn't move but Al nods. "All night. I left here after midnight and Doug's truck was still out front."

She doesn't know how much weight to give his statement considering the hostility in his voice. "Do the Drapers have kids?" she asks.

Sonny looks like he wants to say something, but Al jumps in. "It's not our place to talk about our boss or his wife. I'll tell Doug to give you a call." He turns to Sonny. "Break's over. Get back to work."

Both men walk away as Adams turns to Madison. "Friendly guys." His gaze drifts past her and they listen to the sound of an approaching engine. A delivery truck pulls up, stopping outside the Drapers' driveway.

They watch as a woman in a brown uniform gets out. She's listening to music but nods to them before opening the back of her truck where she locates four large parcels. She places them on the ground, closes her truck and then carries two parcels at a time to the front door. After knocking loudly on the door, she doesn't wait for an answer. Her truck disappears as fast as it arrived.

Madison approaches the porch, climbs the steps and looks at the labels on the parcels. They're for Nancy. One of the boxes has a sticker of its contents on the side. It's a kitchen playset suitable for a young child.

She gasps. Turning to find Adams she waves him over. "These are toys."

He climbs the porch steps and leans in. "My girls loved this when they were little."

The front door suddenly opens making them both jump. Nancy appears. She's deathly pale and still wearing her pajamas. "Go away," she says.

"Sorry to bother you, ma'am," says Madison. "We knocked but got no answer."

"I don't have to answer the door if I don't want to. Now leave me alone." She reaches down to pick up the first parcel.

"I understand from your employees that you don't like leaving the house," says Madison, "So if you won't talk to us out here, can we at least come inside for a second?"

The speed at which Nancy retrieves the packages is impressive. "No. I don't want to talk to you. Leave me alone!"

She goes to slam the door shut but Adams wedges his foot in the way. "Just one question before we leave. Do you have a child in there?"

Nancy's expression immediately turns to disgust. Tears spring to her eyes. "Leave me alone!" She uses all her strength to push the door shut and Adams only just removes his foot in time.

"Wow," says Madison as they walk to their vehicles. A nervous excitement builds in her chest. "That's not good. I think it's safe to say she's hiding something, or someone. We need a search warrant immediately."

"I'll talk to Chief Mendes," says Adams. "And I'll inform patrol they need to locate Doug Draper."

She nods. "Try to track down the woman who claimed Draper was a loan shark too. She made a complaint before dropping it so we should have her details. We may need her statement in order to get a warrant."

"Got it." Adams gets into his car and speeds off.

Madison turns back to the house, where she sees Nancy watching her from a downstairs window. Within seconds the woman disappears behind the blinds.

Madison checks her phone and sees a missed call from Steve. She returns his call as she heads to her car. After updating him on what just happened, she says, "Adams should be back at the station in twenty minutes or so. Make sure Mendes knows what he's coming for. I really think this could be the break we need."

"I'll let her know," he says. "I called about two things. First, I have a message from Alex. He said he's identified a shoe print from the shore of Lake Providence that could belong to the person who pushed the car into the water."

She smiles. "You know, I'm starting to think he works even better when he's heartbroken."

"I know, right?" Steve laughs. "There were about seven people who stepped in the exact location where the print was found, so Alex checked it against my shoes, Lena's and the search party's shoes and it doesn't match. He just needs to check it against yours before he can rule you out. If it's not your print, it could be the killer's."

Excitement builds in her chest. Every small piece of evidence collected helps them build their case, which brings them closer to their missing toddler. "I'll send him a photo of my shoe prints so he can compare them before I return to the station."

"Great." He takes a deep breath. "The second reason I was calling is because I have some interesting news."

Intrigued, she says, "What's that?"

"It's about Linda Hendricks. I just found out that Linda's

granddaughter went missing fifteen years ago from the front yard of her house."

She frowns. "From the murder house? You're kidding?"

"Nope, and what's interesting is that her daughter Tiffany gave the cops an ultimatum. She told them—at a press conference for everyone to hear—that if she didn't get her child back safe within twenty-four hours, she'd kill herself."

Madison's speechless. She can't imagine the kind of pressure that would put the investigating detective under. "Who was working the case?"

"Detective John Ramsey," he says.

She remembers him well. He's retired now.

"Our old friend Mike Bowers had some involvement too, but he was in uniform at the time."

Madison swallows. "That's a coincidence. I've been thinking about him today. I'm at my sister's ranch, which was obviously the last place I saw him."

"Shit. You okay?" he asks, concerned.

"Yeah. I still have some fond memories of him, despite everything that happened."

Steve sighs down the line. "That's because he was a good guy... Until he wasn't."

Mike worked his way up from officer, to sergeant, to detective. If things had worked out differently, she and Mike could've been partners. Instead, he chose to ruin her life. "Did Ramsey find the missing girl?" she asks.

"No. There was a huge investigation but she was never found. Her name was Grace Hendricks."

"That's awful. I'm assuming Tiffany didn't make good on her threat and it was just an attempt to get Ramsey to work harder?"

"Actually, she did."

Madison gasps. "No!" She gets goosebumps. "Please tell me she didn't kill herself?"

"Afraid so. She left her home once the twenty-four hours were up, once Ramsey told her he thought Grace had been murdered. She was never seen again. Ramsey searched for weeks, but eventually had to close the case. He figured she'd killed herself somewhere her body wouldn't be stumbled across by anyone she knew, to try to minimize their suffering. Her mom's quoted as saying Tiffany's death is on the police department's conscience and that Ramsey and his team should be ashamed of themselves."

Madison's heart breaks for Tiffany Hendricks. She must have been completely overwhelmed with grief. Madison's never heard of someone issuing such a threat and then making good on it. She knows from previous cases that some people can just about cope with losing a child, continuing their lives as ghosts, or shadows of their former selves. But others can't even begin to deal with their loss and eventually take their own lives, whether intentionally, or over time with new addictions triggered by their harrowing ordeal.

It means Linda didn't just lose her granddaughter; she also lost her daughter at the same time. No wonder she became reclusive. She was probably severely depressed.

"Some guy named Dennis McKinney was sent down for Grace's abduction and murder," says Steve.

"Wait. McKinney?" She's shocked when she recognizes the name. "Nate's working that case! McKinney contacted him from prison. He wants Nate to find out what happened so he can be released."

"Interesting. Your friend likes cold cases, doesn't he?"

"We both do. Maybe I should see what he's learned so far. It might have some relevance to our case."

Despite the cases being fifteen years apart, Steve agrees. "Anything's worth a try at this stage."

When they finish the call, Madison immediately messages Nate.

Dennis McKinney's name just came up in our hunt for the Doe Family's killer. Meet me at my crime scene?

She gets into her car and pulls her seatbelt on.
Nate replies within seconds.

Any excuse to see me, huh? On my way.

She rolls her eyes affectionately as she starts the engine.

CHAPTER FORTY-ONE

FIFTEEN YEARS EARLIER

0 hours remaining

Detective Ramsey has asked Mike to accompany him to Tiffany's residence. Ramsey has the unenviable task of telling the girl what he thinks has happened to her baby, and just the thought of it must be getting to him because he's been silent the whole ride here. Normally the guy never shuts up.

Once outside the property, Ramsey looks over at Mike. "You better come inside with me. You never know how they might react to the news."

Mike nods before getting out of the car. He's starting to doubt whether he still wants to make detective one day. A career spent delivering bad news to good people is looking less enticing the longer he's in uniform.

Tiffany's mom, Linda, has the front door open before they've even climbed the steps. A heavy-set woman with brown curly hair and thick lenses in her glasses, Linda has multiple health problems linked to her diabetes and depression. Mike clocks her eagerly looking at their hands, and then at the cruiser behind them, as if they've forgotten to bring her granddaughter with them.

Her smile fades when she sees Ramsey's solemn expression and realizes that's not why they're here.

"Oh God." She feels for the small crucifix around her neck and squeezes it. "You'd better come in."

She leads them into the spacious living room where they first spoke to Tiffany and her mom just yesterday. It feels like a week has gone by since then, because no one in the department has stopped in their search for Grace. They've worked long hours, and when he finally did manage some sleep, Mike had nightmares about what could've happened to the baby. He'd seen Tiffany's distraught face as he tried to sleep. As a result, his caffeine intake has tripled today and he's had heart palpitations.

The living room floor is still covered in Grace's colorful baby toys. Tiffany has made no attempt at tidying up, and who can blame her? Mike's eyes go to the couch where he sees the young mother huddled against the far end, her feet pulled up underneath her, still in yesterday's clothes. Her expression is pained. Maybe she's already accepted the inevitable.

They've kept a close eye on her since her threat, and it hurts to look at her right now. Mike can't maintain eye contact. He holds back and stands near the doorway as Detective Ramsey crosses the room to her. Ramsey waits as Linda takes a seat next to her daughter.

"Hi, Tiffany," says Ramsey.

"Where is she?" Tiffany's eyes are red. She looks defeated. Her mouth barely moves as she speaks.

With no armchair in the room, Ramsey crouches down in front of her. "I've arrested someone today."

She remains expressionless.

"Who?" says Linda.

"Dennis McKinney."

Linda closes her eyes briefly as she realizes Tiffany's suspicions were correct; their neighbor has betrayed them in the worst possible way. "What did you arrest him for?" she asks.

"Suspected abduction and first-degree murder."

Linda groans with pain. "No, no, no. She's not dead, she can't be! *Please?*" She looks over at Mike to see if Ramsey is serious. "Have you checked his barn? His attic? His brother's house?"

Mike breaks eye contact. It's difficult to watch her clutching at straws.

Tears leak from Linda's eyes as she starts gasping for breath and then sobbing. She removes her glasses and grabs a tissue from her pocket.

Tiffany is yet to react physically. "What makes you think he killed her?" she asks quietly.

"We have our reasons," says Ramsey.

Tiffany doesn't like that response. She leans forward and repeats her question with such intensity Mike takes a step closer in case she's about to lash out at Ramsey.

Ramsey stands. "We found Grace's sandal in his truck."

Tiffany leans back and lowers her eyes. Silently she nods.

In a bid to offer some kind of hope, Ramsey says, "I want to assure you we're still trying to find Grace and this investigation won't stop until you have her back with you."

In between sobbing, Linda says, "We need to bury her. *Please!* We need a funeral!"

Tiffany turns away from all of them. "You can go now."

Ramsey glances over his shoulder at Mike, who nods. They should go. Give the women time to come to terms with things. Ramsey can return tomorrow to answer the questions they're bound to have. It's all too fresh right now.

"Call me if you need anything at all," says Ramsey. "I'll be in touch." He looks at Linda, who is furiously dabbing her eyes with a balled-up tissue. "Would you see us out, Mrs. Hendricks?"

With some effort, Linda stands before following Ramsey into the hallway to the front door.

"Officer?"

Tiffany's voice makes Mike turn back to look at her. They're alone.

She leans forward to hand him a folded piece of paper. He has to cross the room to take it from her. "Thanks for being nicer than the detective," she says.

He looks at his hand.

"Don't worry," she adds. "It's not a suicide note. I wouldn't do that to my mom."

When he goes to open the note, she says, "Read it when you get home later."

He looks at her questioningly, but she turns away with a tear rolling down her face.

Mike joins Ramsey outside the house where he's questioning Linda on whether they keep any firearms on the property.

Linda's eyes widen in shock. "No. Why?"

"I just wanted to check," says Ramsey. "Obviously we're concerned about your daughter's state of mind, what with the comment she made yesterday. And she's rejected all our offers of extra support."

Linda shakes her head. "She wouldn't do anything like that. She was just desperate. I'll be here. She'll be fine. I'll see if Ronnie will come over."

"I thought they didn't get along?" says Mike, probably overstepping his role.

Linda looks at him. "They get along for Grace's sake. Ronnie's a good boy. He tried being with Tiffany after she got pregnant, but she wasn't interested." She wipes her nose with the tissue. "He'll come over if I ask him. He's been calling nonstop since Grace..."

Mike nods. That's something.

"It would be good to keep a close eye on Tiffany," says Ramsey. "Make sure you have plenty of visitors around her. I'm sure she'll be fine, like you say, but if you think she's at risk of harming herself, call 911. Okay?"

The woman nods. "Thank you. I know you tried your hardest to find my granddaughter before anything happened to her, but I guess the truth is she was probably dead before we even called you, wasn't she?"

Ramsey squeezes Linda's clasped hands but refuses to confirm one way or another. Instead, he says, "We'll make sure McKinney pays for this. That should bring some relief to you and your daughter."

Linda offers a weak smile before turning her back on them and disappearing into the house.

Ramsey turns to Mike and sighs heavily, clearly affected by the women's reactions. "Man, I can't believe I chose to do this for a living." He wanders back to the car, his shoulders slumped.

Mike absently slips the piece of paper Tiffany gave him into his pants pocket before climbing into the passenger seat.

CHAPTER FORTY-TWO

PRESENT DAY

When Nate arrives at the victims' house, he can't see Madison anywhere. The sunshine reflects off of the house, blinding Nate for a second. With a wave of his hand, Officer Sanchez lets him drive past the small crowd of reporters so he can park in the driveway before letting Brody out of the back.

There's some buzz from the reporters behind him. "How do you feel about Father Connor's death, Mr. Monroe?" shouts a male reporter, taking his opportunity despite being here to cover the murders. "Do you wish he was convicted before he died?" he adds.

Cameras go off, getting a shot of his back.

Nate shakes his head in disgust, but he's determined not to let them rattle him.

Brody hears voices in the backyard and races around the side of the house. Nate follows, where he finds Officer Shelley Vickers talking to Madison. He notices Madison's changed her clothes since she left his place earlier this morning. Her shoulder-length blonde hair is highlighted by the sun and her arms are tanned. He approaches her, sliding his hand against the small of her back and pulling her in for a kiss.

After a second Madison pulls away, her face a deep red color. "Nate, I'm at work," she says, embarrassed.

"So am I," he replies.

Shelley's staring at them with raised eyebrows and a wide smile. She looks like she's about to comment, but Madison leads Nate away from her for some privacy.

"Seriously, you can't do that when I'm at work."

Nate takes a deep breath. "Madison? I'm always going to greet you like that, so you may as well get used to it."

She turns away from him but he sees the hint of a smile on her face. "What's Brody doing?" she asks, changing the subject.

Brody's lounging on the same patch of lawn he sat on the last time he was here. He's sniffing the air as if he can smell grilled ribs coming from someone's backyard. "Enjoying the sunshine from the look of it."

"I'll go help Sanchez," Shelley yells over to them. "I'm sure he needs me for something." The grin on her face says it all.

Madison rolls her eyes. "I don't want everyone talking about us."

"Why not?" He slips his hands around her waist and pulls her closer. "We're the hottest new couple in town. Let them talk."

She laughs as she pulls away. "You're going to get me fired!"

"Good. Then you can come work for me again and I can be your boss. Remember how much fun we had in Shadow Falls? You loved working for me as a PI."

Madison shakes her head. "You're crazy! Listen, I'm glad you're here, but now we need to focus, because I just learned that this was the address of the baby that your guy Dennis McKinney is in prison for murdering."

He looks around. "Seriously? I knew it happened on this street, but not at this exact house." His investigation would have led him here eventually but he hadn't gotten that far yet. "So Tiffany Hendricks lived here with Grace?"

"And her mom, Linda. You know Tiffany killed herself shortly after Dennis was arrested, right?"

He nods. "Because of that the DA tried to add an involuntary manslaughter charge on top of Dennis's other charges, but it didn't stick." He considers the implications. "Do you think the Doe Family murders are linked to Grace's disappearance?"

Madison sighs. "I mean, it's a long shot given the time difference, but that involved a missing child, and I have a missing child. I just think it's worth considering. Mainly so I can rule it out."

"Was the family who died related to Linda or Tiffany?" he asks.

"I don't believe so, but we've only just learned their identities and we're struggling to track down anyone who knew them. Plus, Linda died a recluse, with no family around her, so I'm drawing blanks everywhere. How about you? How far have you gotten with your investigation into Dennis McKinney?"

Nate crosses his arms. "Dennis's lawyer took his own life, so I can't speak to him, and Ronnie Russo—Grace's father—won't go into much detail. It sounds like he's suffered a lot since his daughter's murder, turning to alcohol for comfort. I don't think he had anything to do with it."

Madison uses her hand to shield her eyes from the sun as she looks up at him. "You don't have any other suspects yet?"

He pulls off his sunglasses and slips them on her face. "Not yet. I was thinking about speaking to Detective Ramsey to see if he ever had suspects other than Dennis. Did you ever work with Ramsey?"

"I wasn't a cop when Grace vanished, but I did work with Ramsey for a year or two later on, before he retired. I obviously worked with Mike too."

"Mike?"

"Mike Bowers was involved in the search for Grace apparently."

Nate knows Madison's haunted by what happened between her and Mike Bowers. She had trusted him and not only had he let her down in the worst possible way, he wound up dead because of it. "Want to check if Ramsey's still around so we can visit him together?"

She nods, pulling out her cell phone. "Let me call Steve to get Ramsey's address."

While she talks to Steve, Nate approaches Brody. The dog lies back, ready for a belly rub, so Nate crouches down. Brody's thick fur feels warm. "You know you can get fired for sleeping on the job right, buddy?"

Nate stands and wanders to the front yard, keeping his back to the reporters. None of them bother him this time. He looks around the overgrown plot. So this is where Grace Hendricks was playing when she was abducted. The road beyond is pretty secluded, with only a handful of properties on either end. It would be easy to pull up outside and grab the girl, before absconding unseen. Or maybe the cops were right and the abductor lived nearby, making his journey on foot. Dennis McKinney was one of Grace's neighbors.

Nate thinks walking the girl along the road for any passing cars to see them together was too risky for her killer. It's more likely that whoever took her made their way through the backyard and out to the woods beyond.

He feels a warm hand on his back as Madison approaches. Brody follows her but continues ahead to Officers Sanchez and Vickers, where he sits between them, looking up and down the street almost mimicking them. He appears perfectly at home, as if he's a cop himself.

Nate's always wondered whether Brody misses his original owner, an officer who died in the line of duty, because the dog loves being surrounded by cops. Which is the complete opposite to Nate.

Nate looks at Madison and smiles to himself at the irony

that he's involved with a cop. Not just involved with, but in love with. If someone had told him how his life would turn out back when he was on death row—the owner of a former K9 and the partner of a detective—he would have laughed, or maybe spat, in their face.

"Apparently, Detective Ramsey owns the hardware store downtown," says Madison. "Want to see if he'll talk to us?"

Nate nods. "Let's go."

CHAPTER FORTY-THREE

Madison peers in through the window as she waits for Nate to arrive. Ramsey's hardware store isn't busy at one thirty on a weekday afternoon. Madison would guess DIY lovers flock here on weekends though. It's not something that appeals to her. She can paint walls and fix a few things, but she's not into home improvement. She's only a homeowner because she was left the house in her ex-girlfriend's will.

Nate pulls up behind her. He leaves Brody in his car with the windows wide open while they enter the store together, confident that Brody knows how to deter potential car thieves.

The building is spacious and filled with rows of tools, wallpaper, paint and even houseplants. It smells strongly of sawdust, a strangely reassuring aroma. It makes Madison think of her father for some reason, although she doesn't remember him being interested in DIY.

A young male store employee wearing a brown apron over a white shirt and black pants approaches them with a wide smile. "Hi, I'm Brian. How can I help you folks today?"

Before they can speak, an older guy appears behind him. "They're here for me," he says.

Brian makes himself scarce as Madison looks at retired detective John Ramsey. He's scowling at her, not a good sign. Maybe he blames her for what happened to Mike last year. Or maybe he believes she should never have been released from prison and allowed back in law enforcement.

"I knew it was just a matter of time before you came looking for me," says Ramsey.

Madison offers a smile and holds out her hand. "How are you, Detective? It's been a long time."

He shakes her hand, then Nate's and when introductions are over he says, "I no longer go by detective. Call me John."

He leads them to the back of the store, to an employee area with a beat-up couch and a small kitchen. "Coffee?"

Madison's about to decline but Nate says, "That would be great."

They both sit on the couch while Ramsey busies himself. Eventually he turns to face them. With his back against the counter he crosses his arms. "Your victims were killed in the very same house, huh?"

Madison nods. He's been watching the news. And he's made the same link between the cases as they have. "Obviously I need to check whether it's a coincidence or not," she says.

Rubbing his chin, Ramsey says, "You know how they say all cops have that one case that really gets under their skin and they can never forget?"

"Sure," she says.

"Well it's bullshit. There's at least fifteen of them by the time you retire. All of them keep you awake at night, and every single one that you never managed to solve haunts you like your worst regrets in life. I don't mind admitting the disappearance of Grace Hendricks is one of them." He turns back to the coffee machine and pours three cups.

When he's placed them on the small coffee table and taken a seat opposite them on a hard plastic chair, Nate says, "If

Grace's disappearance still haunts you, does that mean you don't believe you have the right guy for it?"

Ramsey looks at Madison instead of Nate. "LCPD's hiring private investigators now? Chief Sullivan would never have approved that."

Chief Sullivan was an asshole. "No," she says. "Nate's a friend. It's a coincidence that he's working on Dennis's case at the same time as I'm trying to find out who killed the family that moved into Linda's house."

Nate says, "Dennis McKinney has asked me to find out what really happened."

Ramsey stares at him. "I've read about you and your history on death row. When Harper returned to town it was all over the news, especially when you helped her clear her name." He says *clear her name* with some disdain, as if the very thought leaves a bad taste in his mouth. "How did you two meet?"

Nate sips his coffee before responding. "With all due respect, that's none of your business and it's not why we're here," he says flatly. "Is there a reason you don't want to talk about alternative suspects for Grace's disappearance? Did you put the wrong guy behind bars?"

Ramsey's jaw clenches.

Sensing she should step in before Ramsey throws them out, Madison says, "He's not trying to insult you, John, he's trying to help his client. Maybe there's a chance we can find Grace's body in the process, and that of her mom's. Wouldn't that help you sleep at night?"

He doesn't reply but his expression conveys his dislike of private investigators.

"Think about it," says Madison. "If we can find Grace's body, we might learn who killed her. If the evidence points to Dennis, then you'll know for sure you arrested the right person."

"And if it doesn't, I'm the asshole who imprisoned an innocent man," he says.

"Look, it happens," she replies, downplaying it.

She feels Nate's eyes on her, probably disgusted she's excusing something as serious as a wrongful conviction. But this isn't about what they experienced. It's about saying the right thing in order to find the missing toddler *and* the person who killed her entire family. "Is there anyone you want us to look at for this? Did Mike like anyone else for it?"

With the mention of Mike's name, Ramsey takes a deep breath before leaning back in his seat. "Mike didn't think Dennis did it. He thought it was too convenient the way we found the girl's sandal in McKinney's truck. But Mike was young and inexperienced, and he focused too much on Tiffany's threat to kill herself. I didn't take that seriously."

Mike was obviously more intuitive than Ramsey since Tiffany did go on to kill herself. She doesn't say that though.

"Have you watched it yet?" he asks.

"Watched what?" says Nate.

"The press conference where she made the threat."

"I didn't know we had a recording of it," says Madison.

"It's on YouTube. At least it was a few years ago. You can find anything online these days, even graphic crime-scene photos. It's sick." He sighs. "I've watched it over and over again, trying to figure out how I missed it. How I couldn't see that she meant to make good on her threat. I didn't take her seriously because I never completely trusted her."

"What do you mean?" says Nate.

"Oh, I don't know. It was just a gut feeling that she was inherently cold, but obviously I was wrong. She was only young, so I guess she just didn't know how to convey her emotions. With more experience I learned that the people who mask their true feelings are the ones who go on to hurt themselves." He shakes his head with a sigh. "Some days I wish I'd never become a cop at all."

Madison can understand how he feels. Most cops find themselves wishing the same thing at some point in their career.

Nate's on his phone, searching for the video. "Here it is. It's only two minutes long."

"Two minutes too long if you ask me," says Ramsey. He gets up and walks to the sink, not wanting to watch it again.

Madison leans against Nate's arm to peer at his screen. After an infuriatingly long commercial for life coaching, LCPD's conference room appears. An officer has his back to the camera, obscuring the view. He leans in, handing someone tissues. As he turns away, Madison sees Mike's face. She grips Nate's forearm in surprise. Mike looks so young. He probably wasn't married to Viv at this point, and he certainly didn't have a daughter yet.

On-screen, Detective Ramsey takes a seat next to Tiffany Hendricks. Her long brown hair obscures her face, and her eyes are lowered as he talks to the press. It's obvious she doesn't want to be in front of the cameras. When her eyes finally meet the camera's lens, Madison finds herself transfixed.

"If I don't get my baby home safe within the next twenty-four hours," says Tiffany, "I'll kill myself."

They don't get to see what happens next as the video ends, going straight to another commercial.

Ramsey turns to look at them. "What do you think? Would *you* have taken her seriously?"

Nate nods. "Of course. She's clearly exceptionally vulnerable in this moment."

Madison probably would have, and she feels sorry for the young mother, but there's something she doesn't like about the fact she issued an ultimatum. Threats don't sit well with her. It's manipulative. She understands why Tiffany thought it would be a good tactic to get the police to work harder and faster to find her daughter, but it suggests the woman is used to getting her own way.

Regardless, the fact she followed through on her threat shows just how desperate she was. "If someone's determined to take their own life, there's little anyone else can do about it," she says diplomatically. "You're not responsible for her death."

He scoffs. "Try telling that to the press. I took a lot of heat for that case. Even though we offered her all kinds of support, she refused our help, and the chief—as well as her own mother—didn't think she needed to be held for her own safety. Sullivan thought she was just trying to get us to find her daughter. But once the press made us look bad, it sealed the deal for me. I knew then that I wouldn't last much longer in law enforcement." He checks his watch. "I need to be somewhere. Are we done?"

Madison stands. He's already been generous with his time.

Nate stands too but before they leave he asks, "In my second conversation with Dennis, he told me he has a brother, Jim. Jim wasn't living with Dennis and their dad when this happened, but he knew Tiffany. Did you ever look into Jim's alibi?"

Ramsey grimaces. "Jim McKinney is an asshole. Once I arrested Dennis he threatened me every time we bumped into each other. Said he'd get me fired for framing his brother. Their dad wasn't happy about it either, but you'll know that's not unusual, Harper. A perp's family always blames the cops and accuses them of being corrupt, right?"

She nods. "It happens. Is his brother the same Jim who hangs out at the diner most evenings? Wears a cowboy hat?" She was hiding behind him at the counter the night Nate and Lena went on their coffee date.

"That's him. I seem to remember he had an alibi."

She hadn't realized Jim was Dennis's brother. He's always been cordial to her, and she's never heard anything negative about him. "What about Doug Draper, did you ever look into him?"

Ramsey frowns. "No, his name was never brought up during the investigation. Why?"

The door to the break room opens and Brian enters. "Marjorie's here for you, Mr. Ramsey."

"We'll let you get on with your day," says Madison, heading for the door. "Thanks for speaking with us. I'm sorry for bringing back memories from that time."

Ramsey shrugs. "Like I could ever forget."

Madison feels for him.

As she walks toward the store's exit, she thinks about how she doesn't want to end up like him; with cases unsolved, bodies left undiscovered and a life full of regrets.

CHAPTER FORTY-FOUR

Once they're out on the sunny sidewalk, Nate turns to Madison. "I'm going to try to speak with Dennis's brother. Want to join me?"

She shakes her head. "No. I shouldn't focus on the cold case. The only link between that and my case is the fact that both crimes happened on the same property fifteen years apart. It's obviously concerning, but I'd need something else. Otherwise it's just a distraction from finding the missing girl."

"I agree," he says. "If I find anything to link them, I'll let you know."

"Thanks. I need to check in with Adams. We're trying to obtain a search warrant for Doug Draper's property. Someone said they saw Doug's wife with a young girl earlier today." She sighs. "I'd really rather not go inside Angie's old house, but if we get that warrant, I'll have no option."

"Have you heard from your sister lately?" he asks.

"Not since we visited her in prison about Ruby Rader's disappearance. I called the prison to get a message to her about Dad. She never called me back, so I don't know how she feels about his death."

"Knowing Angie, she probably doesn't care."

Madison nods before opening her car door. "I better go." When Nate leans in to kiss her goodbye she backs away and glances around to see who's watching. No one appears to be interested in them, but she's still self-conscious.

With a smile she says, "Listen, Monroe. You can't just go kissing me in public whenever you want, at least not when I'm working. I need to maintain some kind of professional appearance when I'm on the job, so just rein it in, okay?"

Nate raises his eyebrows. "You're limiting my affection?"

"No! I'm limiting your PDAs!" She squeezes his hand to show him she's still interested. "I've got to go. There's plenty of time for affection when we've solved our cases." She slips into her car and watches as he walks to his.

She never expected him to be overly affectionate. His time in prison gave him an aversion to physical contact, because he went so long without any. She remembers how his whole body would tense the first few times she ever hugged him. Now he's the complete opposite. It's satisfying to think he's willing to trust her, but now she's the one who needs to get used to it.

Nate waves with a smile as he drives past her. She can see Brody seated in the back of the car. Before she can pull away her phone rings. "Hello?"

"Hi, Detective, it's Stella. I've got a caller named Maria Smith holding for you. She says she's the sister-in-law of Tammy Smith, so I thought you'd want to talk to her."

"Absolutely. Put her through." Madison's intrigued. This could be the break she needs to learn more about her victims. After finding out Maria was listed as Tammy's emergency contact at the clinic, Madison hadn't been able to leave a message on the woman's landline. She wonders how Maria knew to get in touch.

"Maria? This is Detective Harper. I tried calling you yesterday."

"I didn't get a missed call." The woman sounds defensive.

"We got your landline number from the clinic where Tammy received breast implants. You were listed as an emergency contact."

Maria sighs heavily. "She never asked my permission first. I'd be the last person to come to her aid."

Taken aback, Madison says, "Care to explain that, ma'am?"

"Sure, but first I want to know what's going on down there, because I'm in Utah and quite frankly I don't know what to believe." Her voice is filled with anxiety. She sounds a lot older than Tammy was, maybe in her sixties.

"I saw something on the news," she continues, "and my ears pricked when I heard Tammy's name mentioned, but Smith is a common last name and then I didn't recognize the name of the man who was killed with her—Eric something—so I figured it wasn't the Tammy I know. Besides, I've never heard of Lost Creek, so I figured it's nothing to do with me and switched channels. But it's been eating away at me because the Tammy I know has vanished, along with my beautiful niece and nephews, and now I'm too scared to google it in case it *is* them and something has happened to those poor, sweet children."

Madison's heart sinks. It's up to her to deliver the bad news. It's interesting Maria's never heard of Eric though. "In order to make sure we're talking about the same person, would you confirm how old she is and tell me how old your niece and nephews are?"

Maria says, "Tammy's thirty-four or thirty-five, I don't remember her actual date of birth. CJ and Joey are twins. They'd be almost seven and a half now. I haven't seen them in two years thanks to *that woman*."

The venom in her voice tells Madison everything she needs to know about her relationship with Tammy. Still, it's good to have names for the boys at last. "And your niece?"

"Annie's just over two years old." She takes a deep breath

while working it out. "Maybe twenty-six months by now. I've only seen photos of her. I live in hope I'll get to meet her one day and stop her from turning out like her awful mother."

Oh God. Madison shifts position in her seat, preparing herself. "Is anyone with you right now, Ms. Smith?"

"I'm at work in the library. I have my closest friend standing right next to me. We've worked together for almost forty years, so if she can't help me no one can. Just say what you've got to say, Detective."

Madison would prefer to tell her to go home and be somewhere she can absorb the news without interruption, but she knows from experience that people want to hear bad news immediately. They don't want to delay the inevitable. "It appears that Tammy very recently moved here with her three children and Eric Bailey." She inhales. "I'm sorry to have to tell you that on the same day they moved in, Tammy, Eric and the two boys were murdered by an unknown assailant."

She's met with silence.

"We don't currently know where Annie is, but there's no evidence to suggest she's dead. We believe the killer took her when they fled the scene."

"Did you hear that, Daphne?" says Maria to her companion. "Tammy's gone and got everyone killed." She lets out a stifled sob. "I told you she was wicked."

Madison gives her a minute and listens to Daphne trying to comfort her in the background.

After a short time, Maria composes herself. "What are you doing to find my niece?" she says, clearly upset. "There's still hope I take it?"

Madison nods. "We've launched a search; we've released details to the press; and my chief is organizing an Amber Alert. We didn't know the children's names until you just told me. Is Annie's last name Smith?"

"Yes."

"Can you give me a description of her?"

Maria sighs shakily as she tries to focus. "The photo I saw was taken last year, so she was still small. She had brown hair, brown eyes and a goofy smile." A sob breaks out.

Madison feels her pain and wishes there was something she could say to lessen the blow. "Are you able to send me that photo?"

"No, it wasn't mine. I was never given a photo to keep."

That's frustrating. "Does Annie have any identifying features?" she presses gently. "A birthmark? A distinctive mole anywhere?"

"I don't know. I don't remember."

"Sure, that's fine. Give me just a second so I can text my chief the details." Madison lowers her phone and opens a new text message.

We know the missing girl's name: Annie Smith. Approx. two years two months old, brown hair and eyes.

Let me know when Amber Alert goes live. I'm currently talking to Tammy's SIL.

Once sent, Madison asks, "One of the boys has a mole on the side of his nose—"

"That's Joey. Oh my God," she moans. "What will happen to the boys? Who will bury them?"

"They're safe with us for now," says Madison. "We can discuss what happens next as soon as we have Annie, and the killer is in custody." She tries to move the conversation on as she doesn't think Maria will give her much longer. "I take it Tammy married your brother? Can you tell me about him?"

"Wade was seventy-one years old when he met her. That was eight years ago."

Shocked, Madison checks she heard correctly. "*Seventy-one?*"

"Seventy-one and suffering with ill health. He's since passed, but it took just months for her to weasel her way into his life and convince him to marry her. The old fool thought she loved him. What she loved was the fact he was a self-made millionaire."

Madison tries not to react. A younger woman after an older man's money isn't unusual, but who's to say Maria wasn't just jealous of Tammy for the fact she was much younger and spending time with her brother? Tammy came to Lost Creek with barely any belongings, so it's not as though she was living a lavish lifestyle after his death.

Unless Wade listened to his sister's concerns and kept his younger wife out of his will. "How old was Tammy at the time they met?"

"Twenty-five or twenty-six. The very next year she gave birth to their first children, knowing full well she'd be set for life if they had kids together. Despite my feelings for her, I loved those boys. CJ and Joey were—" Maria stops as the shock finally wears off and the floodgates open.

Daphne comes on the line. "Detective? I'm going to take Maria home. She's causing a scene in the library and she'll need some time to come to terms with all this."

"Of course, I understand. Tell her to call me when she's ready to talk again."

"I will. You just make sure you find little Annie. I don't know if Maria's heart could take it if her niece dies as well as her nephews." She ends the call.

Madison leans her head back and exhales. That was tough. She can't imagine how Maria will begin to cope with losing so many family members in one go, regardless of the animosity between her and Tammy.

CHAPTER FORTY-FIVE

At midafternoon Madison gets a text from Detective Adams informing her he's secured the search warrant for Doug Draper's house. She races to Gold Rock to meet him there. Adams has asked for backup, so by the time Madison arrives, Officers Vickers and Sanchez are waiting in their cruisers a short distance away from the ranch.

Madison pulls up alongside Shelley's car, rolling down her window as Sanchez gets out of his car and approaches. "Where's Adams?" she asks.

"He should be here any minute," says Shelley. "How come we're here? Do you think Doug killed that family?"

"We're not sure," says Madison. "We got a tip to say Nancy was seen with a young girl, and when I was here earlier she took delivery of some kids' toys."

"They could have grandkids," says Sanchez.

Madison's assuming Adams has already checked into that before obtaining the warrant. "I need you both to keep your eyes on the guys who work in the salvage yard. I don't know how loyal they are to Doug, or whether they're armed."

"Sure," says Shelley.

They hear a car engine approach. Adams overtakes them and pulls up outside the ranch, with Madison and the cruisers following. He's out of his car fast and waits for Madison to join him. "You ready?" he says.

"Did you find the woman who claimed Doug was a loan shark?"

"No. Steve couldn't find her name; for some reason it wasn't entered onto the system. We got the warrant based on the urgency involved and the fact a child was spotted here."

She nods, letting him lead the way. At the top of the porch steps he bangs loudly on the front door before taking a step back, one hand on his weapon in case they're greeted with trouble. They listen. They're met with silence. No signs of life inside. But that's been their experience every time they've come.

Adams bangs again. "Lost Creek PD, open up! We've got a search warrant."

Shelley and Sanchez walk toward the salvage yard, where workers have started appearing to see what's going on. Five men watch with hard stares and crossed arms. Madison thinks things could quickly turn bad if they're loyal to the Drapers. She recognizes Sonny near the back.

"Doug's out doing business," he yells.

"Is Nancy home?" she asks.

He nods. "I told you; she's always home." He pulls out a cigarette, obviously figuring now's a good time for a break.

Madison approaches the door of the house and raises her voice. "Nancy, we just want to take a look around. It won't take long and the sooner you let us in, the sooner we can leave you in peace."

The door opens a fraction. "Why are you doing this to us?" asks Nancy, barely visible.

"We're looking for a young girl," Madison explains. "I'm

sure you've seen it on the news. Someone said they saw a little girl here with you. Is that right?"

Nancy opens the door an inch or so wider. Her expression is strained. "You're torturing me. My daughter's not here."

"Daughter?" says Adams, coming closer. "So you have a child living here?"

She stares at him, her eyes clouded with confusion.

"Nancy, who were the toys for?" asks Madison gently. An uneasiness settles over her. "Do you have grandchildren?"

Tugging at her hair in frustration the older woman pleads, "Why are you doing this to us? I don't understand. Haven't we suffered enough?"

Madison takes a step toward her. She's starting to think Nancy could be vulnerable, perhaps suffering with some kind of dementia. "Detective Adams and I are going to come in for ten minutes. You can call your husband to join us and you can watch us the whole time, okay?" Her foot is over the threshold now and Nancy finally relents, turning her back on them.

Madison tries to push the door wide open but something behind it stops her. For a second she thinks it's a person, maybe Doug. She feels for her weapon and a terrible smell reaches her. Covering her nose, she looks back at Adams with confusion. There's something seriously wrong here.

Once she carefully squeezes past the door and sees there's no person there, she quickly realizes what's going on.

Nancy's a hoarder.

The large hallway is filled from floor to waist with... she doesn't know exactly. A mixture of unopened packages, newspapers, soda bottles, trash, clothes and purses, for starters. She has to step over a foot's worth of trash just to follow Nancy into the living room.

She hears Adams struggling behind her. "This is disgusting," he says. "I'm going to lose my shoes if I'm not careful. There better not be any needles in here."

"Ssh!" Madison hisses over her shoulder. "Don't let her hear you." She has a lot of sympathy for the woman, and she doesn't want to offend her. Hoarding to this extreme is difficult to understand, and Madison's no psychiatrist, but she has to assume it's linked to some kind of trauma or mental health issue.

The living room is even worse, with just a narrow route to reach a leather couch beyond. Madison feels the room closing in on her. Her chest tightens in panic. It's taken so much effort to get this far that she's sweating. The day's too warm for this. She can't imagine how Nancy and Doug move around day to day. How do they shower? How do they cook? What's even more disturbing is that the Drapers have lived here less than a year, because the previous occupiers were here until their downfall last July.

How on earth could all this build up in such a short time?

The couch has three seats but the middle seat is covered in clothes. Nancy takes the closest, falling backward and catching her breath once seated. Madison stands some distance away, not wanting to overcrowd her.

"Nancy, we had no idea what we were walking in to," she says.

With lowered eyes the woman says, "No one does. Doug hides it from the world. He hides *me*. No one's allowed in here. He's going to be mad."

That doesn't sound good. "Are you saying he's violent?"

Nancy finally makes eye contact. "Not at all. He's trying to protect me. People will think there's something wrong with me if they see this. He hates it. He thinks I need help, but when I needed help, no one did anything."

She's talking in riddles and Madison's struggling not to gag at the smell of whatever rotten food she's disturbed underfoot. She can only imagine what this couples' fridge smells like. A rustle off to her left makes her shudder. An old newspaper moves. "Do you have pets?" she asks.

"Not pets. *Rats*. They live in the salvage yard but every now and then they find their way inside."

Adams groans loudly behind her.

Containing her alarm, Madison keeps an eye on her feet in case anything gets too close. "I can get you out of here. There are services that will clear all this away and help you to start fresh in a healthy, safe environment. It wouldn't take them long to return your home to some kind of normality."

"No."

"But Nancy, all this is a massive fire risk. If one of your workers dropped their cigarette in the wrong place, your entire house would go up in flames in seconds, killing you and Doug."

Nancy keeps her eyes lowered. "What does it matter? I'm dead already."

As she's not getting through to the woman, Madison decides it's best to ignore the condition of the house for now. She can try to persuade Nancy to let her contact someone on her behalf another time. She needs to find Annie first. "Nancy, this is very important. If we search your home, are we going to find the missing girl we're looking for?"

Nancy scoffs. "Police don't find missing people. That's my experience."

Madison thinks of what Nancy asked her the first time they met each other. *Have you found her?* She had thought at the time that Nancy was talking about the missing girl, but now she realizes what she was really asking. "You've lost a child?"

"I didn't lose her. Your department did. She was just a young woman when she disappeared."

Madison swallows. Why didn't they know that? Steve did the background check on Doug for her. The investigation into his daughter's disappearance should've been on their system. Overcome with sadness at Nancy's hopeless expression, Madison steps closer and crouches down in front of her. "I'm so sorry. I didn't know. I wish you'd told me on my first visit. We could have avoided all this."

Nancy pulls a tissue from her nightgown and dabs her eyes. "I thought you were here to tell me you'd found her at last."

"What happened?"

"Becky had a love of hiking. She and some of her friends went for a hike on Grave Mountain." She stares intently into Madison's eyes. "Becky never returned."

Madison touches her hand. It's cold. "I'm sorry. That must be devastating."

"If you genuinely cared, you'd reopen her case for me." Nancy's eyes mist over. "I need to find my daughter, Detective. Then I can rest easy. Then I can stop living like this."

Without knowing the details of the case and what was done to find Nancy's daughter, Madison can't make any firm promises. "I'll see what I can do. But right now my focus has to be on finding someone else's daughter, because Annie Smith is just a toddler, Nancy, and she's in the hands of a killer. Do you know anything about that?"

The woman shakes her head. "We're not child abductors. Doug spends all his spare time with me. That's why he bought this place; he knew he could work nearby in the salvage yard. He thought that would stop me getting into this mess again."

It sounds like Nancy hoarded at their previous residence too. "Does Doug try to tidy the place?"

"He used to. But he's given up, like me. Our bedroom is the one room he insists on keeping empty. He escapes up there to watch TV." She straightens her bathrobe. "He won't come in here anymore."

Madison hears tires skidding outside. She stands. Through the front window she can see Doug arriving home and his expression warns her he's not happy. One of his employees must've called him to tell him the cops were interrogating his wife.

Upon exiting his truck he yells over to his employees, "What the hell do they think they're doing in there?"

Adams disappears backward into the hallway. "We have a search warrant," he explains out of Madison's view.

"For what? You guys couldn't find a damn needle in a haystack. Get out of here!"

Madison looks down at Nancy and sighs. This woman needs help, but it's not something she can get involved with right now. Not until they've found Annie.

CHAPTER FORTY-SIX

It's early evening and still warm as Nate arrives at the apartment complex where Jim McKinney lives. The brick building is surrounded by mature trees, with a large parking lot out front. Jim lives on the second floor and Nate decides to leave Brody behind. The dog is currently circling the parking lot, stopping only when a car speeds past. To Brody, every speeding car is a possible hot pursuit that he should be involved in.

There's no answer when Nate knocks on Jim's door the first time, so he tries again. Nothing. No sounds of movement from inside. He probably should've phoned first. On his way back downstairs he's met by a tall, skinny guy wearing a cowboy hat who nods as he passes. Nate takes a chance. "Jim McKinney?"

The man stops on the step above him before turning back. He eyes him suspiciously. "Who wants to know?"

"The name's Nate Monroe." He holds his hand out and shakes Jim's. "Your brother's hired me to look into his case. He might have told you?"

Jim leans against the exposed brick behind him. "No, he

didn't. But it doesn't surprise me Dennis has hired another PI. He's been doing it for years."

That's interesting. Nate wants to know why he's still in prison if his case has been investigated more than once. "Mind if we talk for a few minutes?"

After glancing at his watch, Jim brushes past him, down the stairs instead of up to his apartment. "There's a picnic bench outside," he says. "I only have five minutes. I'm expecting visitors."

Brody joins them at the picnic bench, inquisitively sniffing Jim's boots. Unfazed, Jim says, "Attractive dog. He half wolf or something?"

"Shepherd-husky mix, I believe."

Jim nods, impressed. "Bet no one comes for you with him around."

Brody lets him pet the top of his head briefly before losing interest and wandering away.

"I didn't know Dennis had hired other investigators before," says Nate. The sun is bright, making him wish he had his sunglasses. He'd given them to Madison. "Nothing came of it, I take it?"

"He's still inside, ain't he?" Jim sighs. "I try to stay in contact with him but God knows it's draining. All he wants to talk about is his innocence and getting out. I can't help him with that. I can't afford more lawyers and no one's going to listen to me without one." He pulls out a cigarette and shakes his head. "I sold my house to pay for his defense. Turns out it was a waste of money."

"So you *do* believe he's innocent?" says Nate.

Jim breaks eye contact and stares at the horizon instead. "At first I did."

"But not now?" Surprised, Nate asks, "What makes you doubt it?"

Straightening, Jim says, "He's innocent, alright? Tiffany

Hendricks was lying when she said she saw Dennis there that day."

"Why would she lie?"

"To make the police search his home... To distract from the fact she was a bad mother... I don't know! Women like that are evil for fun. They get a kick out of seeing a man suffer. I always felt she knew exactly what had happened to her baby. She was just pointing the finger of blame somewhere else."

Nate's unsettled by the flippant accusation. "With all due respect, Tiffany *killed* herself over all this. Doesn't sound like she was having much fun to me."

"She killed herself over guilt, probably!" says Jim, before taking a long drag on his cigarette. "That's what Dennis says. I mean, she had to live with knowing her negligence caused her baby to get abducted, and then her lies caused an innocent man to spend years behind bars. Hell, I'd kill myself if I were that evil." He shakes his head. "Besides," he spits, "she was a whore."

Nate's taken aback at the venom in his tone. Ronnie Russo hadn't had a high opinion of Tiffany either but to call her a whore is out of line. "She was a young, single mother trying her best from what I can tell."

"You're wrong." Jim exhales a mouthful of smoke. "She loved male attention as long as she got something in return like money or gifts. She might as well have been a hooker. She used her looks to entrap men."

Nate rolls his eyes. "Come on. Are you seriously blaming her for her looks?"

"No, I'm blaming her for her deviance. She was always out partying and causing trouble. It could've been any one of her conquests who abducted her baby. She probably didn't even care. With Grace dead it meant she'd have more time to sleep around."

Disturbed by his attitude, Nate says, "Jim, have you seen

her press conference? The look on her face as she pleads for her daughter's safe return? I can show it to you right now..."

He waves a dismissive hand. "I saw it at the time. Made no impact on me. Not once she lied about my brother. Just because someone killed her kid doesn't mean she was a good person all of a sudden."

The fact that Jim has such an intense hatred of Tiffany is worrying. Nate wonders whether she ever spurned him when they were younger and that's where his hostility is coming from. If so, he had a motive to take her child and make her suffer. "Did Dennis ever sleep with her?"

"Absolutely not." He looks disgusted at the suggestion.

"How do you know?"

Jim locks eyes on him. "My brother is gay, Monroe. He's not interested in females of any age."

Nate's shocked that this is the first time he's hearing this. "Why didn't his lawyer use that as his defense?"

"Bruce Cullen was a useless piece of shit. He thought the jury would take against Dennis just for being gay. He advised they'd want to see him sent down for anything if it meant getting him off the street."

Nate doesn't doubt homophobia is still a massive problem in small towns, but with Dennis's life at risk, it was worth a try. "He could've put one of Dennis's ex partners on the stand to testify."

"Dennis didn't want anyone he knew to be dragged into it. I understood that his most recent partner had been a married man with a couple of kids. It would've caused more upset than it solved. So Dennis agreed with Cullen that they shouldn't open that can of worms."

Nate thinks this is a potential new angle that could help get him out of prison. That and the fact Jim is looking like a much better suspect right now than Dennis ever was. "How well did you know Tiffany?"

Jim's stare becomes intense. "If you're asking whether I ever slept with her, the answer is no. I date people my own age, not that it's any of your business."

"Dennis was thirty-two when Grace vanished, right?"

Jim nods.

"How old were you?"

"Thirty-six. Tiffany was twenty. Like I said, far too young and far too trashy for me."

Nate thinks he's telling the truth. "Once Dennis was arrested, did the cops talk to you? Ask where you were at the time Grace vanished?"

"Why would they? I didn't live with my brother, and our dad was out of town at the time."

"Does your father believe Dennis is innocent?"

"He's never doubted it. He took the conviction hard."

A Honda pulls into the parking lot and a young redhead carrying a couple of grocery store bags gets out. Nate doesn't know her. She approaches but keeps some distance away, perhaps afraid of dogs as Brody's now resting at their feet while watching her with interest.

When Jim sees her, he nods before standing. "You won't get Dennis out of prison, Monroe, and you won't find Grace's body. Too much time has passed. But I guess you don't care as long as you still get paid, right?"

Without waiting for a response, Jim and his visitor head up to his apartment.

CHAPTER FORTY-SEVEN

"I've never seen a home that bad in all my life," says Adams once he and Madison are at the station. "I can smell rat droppings on me."

Madison rolls her eyes. "Give it a rest, Adams. Nancy can't help it."

He actually reeks of deodorant, having sprayed his entire body at his car.

"They could have the girl in there and we'd never know," he says. "Maybe that's what the smell was."

"No, the smell was rotten food. Can't you tell the difference between that and a rotting corpse yet?"

She hurries ahead to her desk, where Stella approaches her. It looks like she's getting ready to leave for the evening.

"After I heard the Draper tip was a bust," says Stella, "I traced the call."

Madison smiles. "Good thinking. And?"

"It came from the landline of Jerry Clark."

Madison's mouth drops open. "Son of a... He's the guy who cleared the victims' home of Linda's belongings before they moved in."

"Well, he lied about seeing Nancy with the child." Stella hunts for her keys in her purse. "Want me to send an officer out to scare him off doing it again?"

They get false tips all the time during investigations, but this one is particularly annoying for Madison. "Why the hell would he insert himself into the investigation like that?"

Stella shrugs. "He's probably just an idiot. The world's full of 'em."

"You can say that again." Madison sighs. "I'll speak to him."

Stella swings her purse over her shoulder and says her goodbyes.

Madison sits at her computer and searches Doug Draper's name. She can't understand how the investigation into his missing daughter wasn't obvious when Steve did a background check. But she finds no missing person case files linked to his name. She tries Nancy's name next, and they appear. "Shit." Whoever uploaded them only attached them to one parent, not both. She sighs. She wishes the admin error hadn't been made, as she could've saved both the Drapers some upset, but she also knows how easy it is to make mistakes when working under pressure.

Next she locates Jerry's number and calls it while Adams sits at his desk opposite her. He's fetched himself coffee and is sanitizing his hands for the fourth time.

Jerry answers almost immediately. "Hello?"

"Jerry this is Detective Harper. Do you have a minute?"

"Sure, Detective!" He sounds surprisingly happy to hear from her. "What can I do for you on this fine evening?"

Madison can't tell if he's high on something or just a happy imbecile. "Tell me something, Jerry. Why did you call the station to inform us you saw a little girl with Nancy Draper?"

When she's met with silence she continues.

"Because we've been out to the ranch and there's no child

there. Why would you lie about something like that? Is it because *you* have the missing toddler?"

"No way!" he says. "Shit, I'm sorry, Detective. You got me. I'll admit it. It was me who called." He laughs nervously, adding, "Jeez, you've got me sweating like a snitch."

She can picture him grinning. "Jesus, Jerry."

"I know, I'm sorry." He sounds like he's been caught stealing a person's last chocolate, not accusing someone of child abduction.

Madison has to contain her temper. "Why would you do that? You've wasted our time *and* you've made us upset the Drapers."

"I wanted to help! Besides, they make good suspects to me." He becomes excited as he explains his theory. "Think about it, their daughter's been missing all these years and they're still devastated. Something like that could really fu—, I mean, screw with your head. It makes sense they'd want to replace her with a younger version. That Doug would want to make his wife happy."

Madison's not buying it. "Did you try to get a job in the salvage yard and Doug turned you down? Is that it? You're holding a grudge?" The business Jerry's in isn't that different to Doug's. Maybe he got tired of being self-employed and never knowing where the next paycheck was coming from.

Jerry laughs. "Wow, you're really good. How did you guess that?"

She rubs her temple. "Jerry? If I roll my eyes any harder, I'm going to detach a retina. So help me out here. Do you know where the missing girl is?"

"No, ma'am."

"Do you know who killed the family who moved into Linda Hendricks's house?"

"No, ma'am."

"So with that being said, are you going to phone in any more false tips?"

"Absolutely not. You have my word."

"Excellent. You have a good evening." She ends the call before he can reply with any more inane comments. "Some people are morons," she mutters.

Adams smiles. "Lost Creek sure attracts a type."

Madison looks at him sternly. For some reason he thinks he's better than everyone else who lives here, probably because he came from Denver. "You moved here voluntarily. What does that say about you?"

To his credit, he laughs. "You can blame my wife for that. I'm pretty sure she googled the worst place to live in the United States and found this hell hole."

"Come on," she says. "It's not that bad."

He sips his coffee, preferring not to comment further.

As frustrating as it is to learn Jerry made a false tip, Madison considers whether there's something more sinister behind it. Perhaps he was hoping to divert attention from his friend Kai. Maybe Kai told him to do it. She looks at the clock. It's only a little after six.

"I'm going to visit Kai Bishop. See if I can't get him to slip up about his alibi."

Adams nods. "Kai and his old lady make good suspects now the Drapers are off our list. I mean, their age gap alone is criminal."

Madison sighs. "Truth be told, they're our only suspects now."

"Want me to come with you?" he asks, glancing at his fresh coffee.

"No. I'll be heading home once I'm done there." Her stomach flips with excitement and she can't tell whether that's because she can call Owen once she gets home, or the thought that Nate might come over.

"I'll check in with Alex," he says. "See if he's had any more results from the lab."

"Check in with the search team too. We need the murder weapon." Madison heads for the exit.

CHAPTER FORTY-EIGHT

The sun is low in the sky as Madison heads to Dawn Freemantle's house. The street, emptier than it's been for days, has just a single reporter and news truck outside the murder house. It's becoming old news already, despite the missing toddler. It's around this stage of an investigation that the public loses hope and starts assuming what they've learned from countless crime documentaries: that the girl is inevitably dead by now.

Lucky for Annie Smith, Madison can't think like that or she'd never come to work.

She slows as she approaches the house before Dawn's. She hears adults shouting, along with some furious barking. The homeowner is in the front yard yelling loudly at his neighbor. Madison parks and gets out, rushing over to Richard. His face is flushed bright red. He glances at her over his shoulder before taking a few steps away from the property line.

Madison sees Kai Bishop on the other side, partially obscured by trees.

"What's going on?" she says.

Kai looks at his neighbor. "I can't believe you called the

cops, man." His eyes betray his anger and he shocks them by throwing something at Dawn's house in a fit of rage. An ax. It barely misses the front window. If young Timmy had been standing there, he'd likely be dead.

Madison wonders if Kai would've thrown it at Richard if she hadn't turned up. The guy clearly can't control his angry outbursts. His laid-back demeanor has finally slipped.

"He didn't call anyone," she says. "I was passing and heard the hollering. Do we have a problem or are you going to aim that ax in our direction next time?"

Kai gives her a look of pure hatred and it would be easy to picture him harming someone when he's this upset. After a long pause he plasters a smile on his face. "I don't have a problem if you don't."

Madison's not buying it, but she's alarmed at Richard's condition—he's sweating profusely—so she takes his arm. "Join me in my car for a minute, would you? The A/C will cool you down."

The old man pulls his arm free of her grasp but follows her. Once they're both inside the vehicle, Madison looks at him. "Tell me what's going on."

"Those guys are assholes, that's what!" He pulls a handkerchief from his pants pocket and wipes his brow. "I can't get any rest since she moved that damn hippie in!"

"Why not? Does he play loud music?"

"No, it's the hens and the dogs, they never shut up! Those bitches bark all day long, upsetting everyone. I just want some sleep. I'm too old for this shit."

Madison feels for him. He's got himself so worked up he looks like he's on the verge of a heart attack. "Want me to get animal control out to pay Dawn a visit?"

He shakes his head, slightly calmer now. "The rottweilers... they're beautiful girls but Dawn doesn't take care of them. I feel like stealing them and letting them come live with me, but Sassy wouldn't like it." He nods to his small dog, who's sitting in the front window of Richard's house, intensely peering out at them. "She'd be jealous."

Sensing there's some acrimony between Richard and Dawn, Madison asks, "You have a low opinion of her?"

"Sure I have," he says. "Me and her husband, Duke, were good friends. Went to school together. His first wife was a beautiful person before she got what he's got now. Alzheimer's. After she passed, he married Dawn, even though I tried to talk him out of it. Duke's one of those people who can't be alone. Needs female energy in the house. Dawn knows I can't stand her, so she doesn't shut the dogs up." He shakes his head in disgust, getting agitated again. "The audacity of the woman to move that guy in when Duke can't do anything about it is disgusting. She won't even let me visit him anymore. And what kind of name is Kai, anyway?"

Madison can tell he misses his friend, but she's only hearing one side of the story. She looks over at Dawn's property, where Kai is on his phone, keeping an eye on them. She wonders what he does for a living. "Does he work?"

"She works, he doesn't. He lives off Duke's money in Duke's house. All he ever does is mow that damn lawn over and over, which is probably just so he can watch out for his drug dealers arriving."

Madison doesn't react. Richard wouldn't be the first person to accuse a neighbor of using drugs just to get them into trouble.

"And I never see the poor grandchild. I don't even think he goes to school. It's getting to be like a commune in there. Or a cult."

She agrees they make a strange family unit, but that doesn't mean they're criminals or up to anything nefarious. Still, something about Kai's cold stare leaves her feeling uneasy. "Do you happen to know if they were both home Sunday night?"

Richard looks disinterested now, like he just wants to get

inside and nap. "I don't know and I don't care." He opens the door and slides out, not bothering to say goodbye.

Madison finds her cell phone and messages Adams.

See if we can get a search warrant for Dawn Freemantle's place. I'm guessing "gut instinct" won't do it but that's all I've got, along with an alibi we can't corroborate for Kai Bishop.

Before he replies, her phone rings. It's dispatch.

"Sorry to bother you after you've left for the day," says Dina, "but I've got Maria Smith on the line, Tammy's former sister-in-law. Says she wants to talk to you urgently."

Madison takes a deep breath. She has a feeling she's never going to make it home tonight. "Fine. Put her through." Once connected Madison says, "Hi, Ms. Smith. What can I do for you?"

"I want you to exhume my brother's body."

Madison blinks. That's not what she was expecting to hear. "Care to explain that?"

"It's my opinion that my brother Wade died under suspicious circumstances. Tammy pushed for cremation but I wouldn't allow it. I told her I'd go to the police with my suspicions if she didn't organize a burial for him. I wanted to preserve his body in case I could ever get anyone to take me seriously. She eventually relented, which confirmed her guilt in my eyes."

Madison's so confused she doesn't even know where to start. "What was listed as Wade's cause of death on his death certificate?"

"Pneumonia, but that was baloney."

"How do you know?"

Maria exhales as if she's explaining something to a child and they're not quite getting it. "Listen, he'd been getting steadily better the longer he was in hospital. Then she collected him, took him home and he died within hours."

It sounds to Madison like a case of a sister not wanting to accept her brother's death. She doesn't say that though, as she fears the woman's wrath. "Remind me how long Tammy was married to Wade."

"Eight years."

"That's a long time." If Tammy was a gold digger, as Maria previously suggested, it's unlikely she'd have three children with him and stick around for eight years until he passed away. "Do you know her maiden name?"

"She was already a Smith when they met," says Maria. "Wade used to joke that's because they were meant to be together."

Sounds like he was truly in love with his wife. "And do you know any of Tammy's family?"

"No. She never talked about family. She had a friend, Kerry something. That pair acted like teenagers together. I wouldn't trust Kerry any more than I did Tammy."

Madison makes a note of the name. "Can you remember Kerry's last name?"

"I don't believe I ever knew it."

Another dead end. She changes the subject. "Did Wade want children? What with him being older than Tammy, I guess I'm questioning whose idea the kids were."

"He always wanted children but his previous wife was infertile. I strongly believe that's what attracted him to a younger woman. He told Tammy from the outset that he wanted at least three kids so he had someone to pass everything on to. I always got the impression she wasn't that keen on the idea, but I guess she proved me wrong. Just over a year after they got married they had the boys, CJ and Joey, before having Annie. But since hearing Tammy was found with another man by her side—this Eric person—I checked the dates, and it doesn't add up."

Madison pulls out her notebook and pen. "What doesn't add up?"

"Annie would've needed to have been conceived during the month that Wade was hospitalized for pneumonia. Which means Tammy was sleeping around, cheating on my brother. Probably with this Eric guy. That gives her motive for murder if you ask me."

She's not wrong. "Did Tammy claim his life insurance?"

"He never had life insurance, even before Tammy came along. And Tammy wasn't that stupid to take a policy out on him in the months before his death. She would've known that would be an obvious motive for murdering him. Hell, everyone who watches TV knows that'd be stupid."

"Did she inherit everything?"

"She sure did. Wade left everything to Tammy and the kids. He was wealthy enough for her to live comfortably for the rest of her life. But for some reason she put their wonderful home up for sale right away and moved into a small apartment. I received nothing, not even family heirlooms."

Something doesn't add up to Madison. Tammy and Eric moved to an empty, dilapidated house in the middle of nowhere and with no signs of living an extravagant lifestyle: no jewelry, cash or expensive belongings. If Tammy inherited a lot of money, where is it? What was she spending it on? Once Madison can get more information about her, she needs to look into the woman's finances.

Perhaps she moved down here in order to get away from Maria's murder accusations. Fearing her sister-in-law would go to the police and secure the exhumation she wants would be a powerful motivator.

"Did Tammy know you thought she killed Wade?"

"Yes, I told you; I threatened to tell the police unless she opted for a burial over a cremation. It didn't go down well as we were already hostile toward one another by that point."

In cases where family members are at war, especially when there's money involved, Madison knows it's important to hear both sides of the story. Maria's painting Tammy in a negative light, but what would Tammy say about Maria? "Listen, Ms. Smith. When we find your niece, we can confirm who her father was through DNA testing. But as far as Tammy's concerned, having an extramarital affair isn't a crime, I'm afraid."

"Maybe not, but murdering my brother is. She and Eric probably plotted together to kill him for his money. Why else would they skip town together? I want Wade exhumed."

Madison takes a deep breath. "That would be up to the Buford PD. I suggest you contact them. And unfortunately, even if Tammy did kill your brother, she's dead now. She can't exactly stand trial for murder, neither can Eric, so I'm not sure what you're hoping to achieve."

"She died a victim when everyone should know she was a killer who evaded capture!" Maria seethes. "I wish I would've killed her myself, at least then I'd get some satisfaction. And where's my brother's money now? Whatever's left after that woman spent thousands on crap like motorcycles, breast implants and Botox should be mine. *I* should be entitled to it. I was Wade's only surviving family member."

The motorcycle found at the murder house must've been Tammy's. Regardless, the older woman sounds so bitter that Madison's left feeling *she* could've been involved. Maybe she hired someone to track Tammy and the money down. But would she really allow her nephews to be killed too?

With serious money involved, maybe. It wouldn't be the first time someone's put money over family.

"You live in Utah, right?" asks Madison.

"Right."

"Think you could drive to Lost Creek in under ten, maybe eleven hours?"

"Maybe," she admits. "What's that got to do with anything?"

Madison knows her next question won't go down well. "What were you doing on Sunday evening?"

The line goes silent.

"Ms. Smith?"

Maria hangs up.

Madison looks at her phone. "I think I hit a nerve."

CHAPTER FORTY-NINE

Instead of questioning Kai after calming Richard down and talking to Maria Smith, Madison decides to call it a night. She's exhausted, so she drives back past the murder house with the intention of heading home. But when she spots Nate's car in the driveway, she can't resist seeing what he's there for. She parks her car behind his, intrigued.

"Evening, Detective," says Officer Sanchez. He's drinking a takeout coffee.

"You ever get any sleep?" she asks, surprised he's still here.

"Not really, you?"

She laughs. "Wouldn't that be nice?" She looks at the house. "Have you noticed whether Kai Bishop or Jerry Clark have been by much today?"

"I saw that Kai guy driving by earlier on his way home from somewhere. He took a good look, even slowed down as he passed. But I can't say I've noticed Jerry in the area. He's something else, ain't he?"

"You can say that again. Is Nate inside?"

"Nah," says the young officer. "He wanted to go in but I didn't think he was allowed, so he's taking a look out back."

She's glad Sanchez is being cautious. "Just for the record, he's allowed inside now the forensic exam is over. He's helping me with something."

Sanchez nods with a grin. "Helping you with something. Right."

Madison figures news of their relationship is spreading. She ignores him and heads around the back of the house to find Nate. His back is to her, so she touches his shoulder. "What are you doing here?"

He turns, leaning in for a kiss. "Hey. Look at Brody." The dog is lounging on the grass again. "That's odd, right?"

Madison shrugs. "He's probably just tired. Why? Think he needs to see a vet?"

Nate shakes his head. "No. I think he can smell something. Just not very pronounced. He keeps returning to that exact spot. This is the third time in a row."

She thinks about it. "Is that why you came back?"

"Yeah. It bothered me the second time he chose that spot, so I thought I'd come back one more time."

"He'd be alert and barking if he smelled blood or a body though, right?" she asks.

"He should do. But..." He trails off.

She looks at him. "You think it's an old scent? Something that's been there a while?"

He considers it. "Grace Hendricks vanished fifteen years ago from this very property. What if she was buried here all along and that's why no one found her? Because no one was looking *here.*"

Madison glances over at Brody. "He wouldn't detect a scent that old, surely?"

Brody yawns before lying on his side. With his nose close to the earth, he sniffs it, before closing his eyes to snooze.

The more she thinks about it, the more sense it makes. She gets goosebumps. "Oh my God. We need to dig." She immediately gets her phone out to call Chief Mendes for permission.

Mendes takes some persuading. "That's a cold case, Madison. I think our focus should be on our current missing child."

Nate's eyes are on her while Madison pleads their case. "With all due respect, Chief, Brody's never been wrong before. And Grace Hendricks was never found. Besides, we're assuming it's Grace but it could be someone else, maybe someone we don't even know about."

"But you said the earth wasn't disturbed, so it's not going to be Annie Smith, right?"

"No, it's not. I just think it's worth investigating. I don't like the fact two children have gone missing from the same property, years apart. If there are bodies buried on this property, we could be dealing with a serial killer and just an hour or so's effort can tell us whether the dog's right or not."

Mendes exhales loudly down the line. "Fine. I can be contacted at home if you find anything."

Madison smiles at Nate as she pockets her phone. "We can dig."

She finds Officer Sanchez and tells him to locate a couple of shovels. He radios Shelley, who's downtown on patrol. She arrives within twenty minutes after purchasing shovels at Ramsey's hardware store. Sanchez takes one and Nate takes the other.

They have to move Brody out of the way first. As Nate ruffles his fur he says, "Come on, boy. Let's see what you've found."

The dog gets up, wagging his tail excitedly. When he realizes what they're doing he tries to help by digging up the soil. He's alarmingly quick.

Nate stops him. "Sorry, buddy. We've got to be meticulous about this hole. It's not like the ones you make in my yard." Brody barks before going to sit between Shelley and Madison.

They all watch as Nate and Sanchez carefully begin removing the earth one shovelful at a time.

"We need to be careful not to disturb any potential remains," says Madison. "If you notice anything at all down there, stop and let me look."

"Got it," says Nate.

Sanchez works slowly, appearing slightly afraid. It seems as though he doesn't want to find anything, which is understandable. Not all cops can handle discovering human remains. Especially not a child's.

After only five minutes of digging, Brody moves closer to the hole in the ground. He looks interested, sniffing the air in front of him. After another few minutes, he barks louder than normal. He peers over his shoulder at Madison, and barks again.

The hairs on her arms stand up. Because Brody's never wrong.

Nate stops digging, knowing what this means. He drops the shovel and gets on his knees as Madison joins him. She gently brushes her hand over the disturbed soil and her fingers find something poking out from underneath.

A plastic bag.

"Okay, stop everything!" She leans back, filled with dread. "We need to get Alex down here immediately. Lena too." She swallows hard. "I think we've found someone."

CHAPTER FIFTY

Alex arrives first and uses several different tools to push the earth back from the white plastic bag. He's painstakingly slow, and all the while Madison has her fingers crossed it's a false alarm. No one should end up in an unmarked grave. Especially not a child, if that's what this is.

Nate rests his hand on the small of her back as they watch. Madison glances at him. His attention is on the ground. He probably doesn't even realize he's touching her. No one's paying them any attention, so she doesn't mind. The sun is fading fast, leaving a chill in the air, but she can feel the heat emitting from his body. She'd give anything to be home with him right now, instead of waiting to identify potential remains.

Footsteps approach. Lena appears from the side of the house. She's dressed casually in jeans and a T-shirt, having finished work a couple of hours ago. She glances at Nate's hand on Madison's back. A fleeting look of contempt passes over her face before she looks away.

Madison's surprised by Lena's response but pretends not to notice. She moves away from Nate slightly. "Thanks for coming, Lena," she says. "We think Brody might've discovered remains."

"Bingo." Alex pulls his face mask down and leans back on his feet. He has the plastic bag in his hands. It's empty. But when Madison sees what it was hiding, her stomach leaps with dread.

It's the top of a skull. A small one.

"There could be a full skeleton, or it could just be the skull," says Alex. "I'll photograph every item as I unearth it. I want to document the position the child was in. This"—he gestures to the bag—"may contain the killer's DNA, so I'll get that to the lab as soon as possible."

Lena sighs heavily. "I'll call my office and get someone down here ready to transport the remains."

She walks away without making eye contact with Madison or Nate but her body language oozes hostility.

Madison can't worry about her feelings right now. She needs to figure out who put this child here. Turning to Nate she says, "This has got to be Grace Hendricks, right?"

He nods. "It's likely. Given it wasn't a fresh grave and this is where she was last seen."

"So who do you like for her murder?" asks Madison. "Is Dennis McKinney telling the truth when he says he's innocent?"

Nate considers it before answering. "I spoke to his brother, Jim, earlier. He said Dennis is gay. He thinks that means his brother had no reason to abduct a little girl."

Madison tucks her hair behind her ears. "She wasn't abducted though, was she? She was here all along."

"Which suggests someone in her family killed her."

"Right." She looks at the skull. "It can't have been Tiffany or she wouldn't have issued an ultimatum to the police. She must've genuinely believed her daughter was taken given the fact she killed herself once Dennis was arrested for suspected murder. But could her mother have done this?"

Nate crosses his arms. "Didn't you say Linda's neighbors only had bad things to say about her?"

It's true that Richard referred to Linda Hendricks as a dragon and a real piece of work. Even her family abandoned her. Other neighbors didn't know her well at all. "I thought she became reclusive because of what happened. She had to come to terms with the fact someone in her community killed her granddaughter. Besides, what motive would she have to kill the baby?"

Rubbing his jaw as he thinks, Nate says, "I'd put my money on Jim McKinney before Linda Hendricks."

Madison looks at him. "Why?"

"Turns out he despised Tiffany. He spoke so poorly of her I could see he had strong feelings. I don't think that's only because her testimony imprisoned his brother. He called her a whore and basically implied she slept around."

"Interesting. Focus on him then. See what you can find."

Nate smiles at her. "Are you telling me how to run my investigation, Detective?"

Before she can reply Lena returns. "My team's on its way. I'll take a look at the bones first thing tomorrow, but I can't stay tonight."

"Sure," says Madison. "Thanks for coming."

The ME turns away and disappears around the side of the house.

"So what if Tiffany slept around?" says Madison, picking up where she and Nate left off. "She was young. And single too, right?"

Nate nods. "Twenty years old."

"Twenty?" Madison frowns. Something comes to her. "Huh."

"What is it?" he says.

"You told me the cops didn't find Tiffany's body, right? They concluded she'd killed herself somewhere remote in order that her family didn't stumble across her body."

"Right." With an inquisitive look he says, "What's going on in that brain of yours?"

Madison gets a creeping sensation. If what she's thinking is true, the consequences don't bear thinking about. She hesitates to tell him until she's given it more thought, but she doesn't have the luxury of time. "If Tiffany were alive today, she'd be thirty-five."

"And?"

Her mouth goes dry. Something about the way Jim described Tiffany makes her think of the way Maria described Tammy. "My female victim, Tammy Smith, was the same age Tiffany would be now had she lived. And she died in the same house as Tiffany's daughter disappeared from."

He considers it. "You don't think..."

Madison fixes her eyes on his. "What if Tiffany didn't kill herself? What if she skipped town and changed her name to Tammy Smith?"

Nate's stunned for a second. "You think the woman who was murdered here with her partner and sons is *Tiffany Hendricks*?"

She doubts herself. "I mean, I'm just thinking aloud."

"Why would a twenty-year-old girl stage her own suicide and skip town?"

"The same reason anyone skips town: to avoid capture for something she'd done. Something bad." Madison looks at the tiny skull in front of them. "She could be the one who killed her baby."

Shocked, Nate rubs his jaw as he considers it.

"Maybe it wasn't murder," she says, clutching at straws. "Maybe she hurt Grace accidentally and didn't want to fess up. I've seen that before. The mother pretended her baby had been snatched by a mysterious abductor to take the heat off herself. But that case didn't go as far as to put someone else in prison for it. The woman's parents made her come clean in the end."

Normally supportive of her theories, Nate's unconvinced. "I don't see it. That video of Tiffany in the press conference was harrowing. She was genuinely upset. And where would she find the money to skip town? It sounds to me like she was financially dependent on her mom."

Her mind buzzing, Madison says, "I agree it's a long shot. I mean, why would she ever return to this house knowing her baby's buried in the backyard? It would take a real piece of work to be comfortable with that."

"Exactly," says Nate. "It's more likely Jim McKinney was involved, given his hatred of her. Perhaps he wanted a relationship and she didn't. For all we know he could've been obsessed with her and he couldn't handle the humiliation of being rejected." He sighs. "I was on death row with a guy who was there for the same reason. A woman he liked turned him down and it enraged him so much he said he had to teach the woman a lesson by killing her baby."

Madison shakes her head in disgust.

"If that's the case with Jim," says Nate, "that could be why the baby was buried here; he was trying to frame Tiffany for it and it backfired."

"Although that wouldn't explain why Grace's missing sandal was found in Dennis's truck," she says.

He thinks for a second. "Maybe Detective Ramsey planted it, in a bid to get Dennis to confess in time to stop Tiffany from killing herself. I mean, he knew he'd take a lot of heat if she followed through on her threat. It was all over the media."

Madison rests her hands on her hips and gives him a stern look. "You really believe a detective would plant evidence, don't you?" She shakes her head. "I can't believe you still think most cops are crooked, even now." She wants to say *even though he's screwing one*, but she can't with Alex around. Nate catches her meaning though.

He smiles. "Fine, I'll discount that. Who knows, maybe both McKinney brothers are responsible."

Madison doesn't know what to believe. She approaches Alex who's still crouched at the grave. "We can extract DNA from these remains, right?"

He stands. "It's a little harder with bones than with tissue and blood, but yes, it's possible. It'll take longer than usual though. Why? Who do you have in mind as a comparison?"

"Tammy Smith," she says. "I have a wild theory I want debunked, just to put my mind at ease. Age-wise it's possible, although not likely, that she might be this child's mother."

Alex raises his eyebrows. "Intriguing. I heard you mention Grace Hendricks. Is that a case I need to research?"

She nods. "Nate's working on the cold case. I think this might be her."

Adrenaline races through her. If Tiffany and Tammy are the same person, Madison could be close to solving two cases at once.

CHAPTER FIFTY-ONE

Madison calls the rest of her team to the murder house to update them on the remains found, despite the late hour. It's ten o'clock and she's had to message Owen to say he won't be able to call her tonight due to her having to work.

He didn't seem too bothered and said he's out partying with new college friends already. The very thought raised her blood pressure. Her son's in a new state mixing with new people, some of whom won't be trustworthy. She just has to hope he stays smart.

Chief Mendes arrives at the house the same time as Detective Adams, who lets Madison know more reporters are turning up on the road out front in the hope of an update about the killer or the missing child. Interest is building quickly. The press must've seen the flurry of activity. She just hopes it doesn't make their killer go on the run before she can figure out who they are.

Being at the rear of the property means the team is shielded from the reporters and their cameras. Despite it being pitch black now, the uniforms have brought in crime-scene lighting so Alex can see what he's doing.

Chief Mendes has pulled some of the case files from the Grace Hendricks investigation so they can see what was done to find her. Madison, Nate and Adams lean in as Mendes holds up one photo of the backyard they're currently standing in as it looked fifteen years ago. "I was wondering why Detective Ramsey didn't see the freshly dug grave after Grace went missing," she says. "I guess this explains it."

In the photograph the whole yard is in better condition than it is now. Linda obviously took pride in her property, as there's a vegetable garden off to the left with a small potting shed near to where they stand. It looks newly erected; the wood is pristine and the windows are clean. Several large ceramic flowerpots sit in front of it. Sunflowers, dahlias and wildflowers all give the illusion of a happy home.

"Someone bought the shed and flowerpots to cover the patch of ground where the baby was buried," says Madison.

Mendes nods. "And with Tiffany claiming her baby was taken from the front yard, only a cursory search would've been done back here. We're lucky we even have a photo of it."

Their attention turns to Alex as he, with the help of one of the medical examiner's assistants, lifts the child's bones from the ground one at a time, carefully placing them on a sheet of black tarpaulin. It's hard not to be saddened by the sight. Being so small and vulnerable, the child stood no chance against their attacker.

"How old do you think the child was when they were killed?" Mendes asks Alex.

He takes a second to assess the bones. "This is a baby, no doubt. But Lena's better qualified to provide an approximate age. I can't identify any fractures to the skull or any obvious injuries to the bones. I think it's fair to assume they were suffocated with the plastic bag, but again, I'm no expert." He notices something in the earth and carefully extracts it. "The remnants of clothing. A small T-shirt. Looks like it was once a shade of yellow."

Nate takes a deep breath. "That's what Grace Hendricks was wearing when she vanished."

Detective Adams shakes his head before turning away, probably thinking of his girls.

"Something else," says Alex, leaning forward again. He unearths something plastic. As he pulls it out Madison sees it's a small white sandal.

"The other one of those was found in Dennis McKinney's truck," says Nate. "It's what got him convicted, along with Tiffany's eyewitness testimony placing him at the scene hours before Grace allegedly vanished."

Chief Mendes turns to Nate. "I take it you don't think Dennis was responsible for this?"

He looks at her. "It's not impossible, but from what I've learned about Dennis, it's unlikely."

Madison says, "We have to assume this is Grace Hendricks. We won't know for sure whether Tiffany Hendricks and Tammy Smith are the same person until we compare this child's DNA with Tammy's. But say Tiffany *is* Tammy. It's highly likely she fled town because she killed her baby, whether intentionally or not. That means by pointing the finger at Dennis McKinney, she effectively framed him for murder." She has everyone's full attention, so she continues. "Now, fifteen years later, someone kills Tiffany the minute she arrives back in town at her late mother's house." She looks at each of them in turn to see if they're understanding where she's going with this. "I think it's fair to say we should work on the idea that the motive for Tammy's and Eric's murders is revenge for putting an innocent man behind bars fifteen years ago."

"But why would she come back here?" asks Adams. "The whole town thought she'd killed herself."

Madison shrugs. "Her mom recently died. It's likely she saw

the news online. Steve said he found an obituary for Linda, so it wouldn't be difficult for Tiffany to find. Just because she fled town doesn't mean she didn't keep tabs on her mom. And once she saw her mom had passed, she knew she could live here rent free because, technically, it's hers."

"But I thought Tammy Smith was a wealthy widow?" says Adams. He's clearly not buying Madison's theory. "Why not buy a mansion somewhere? Why choose to return to this shithole?"

Madison sighs. She doesn't mind her ideas being tested, but his attitude stinks. "Listen, I never said I had all the answers, okay? It's just something to investigate. Maybe they're not the same person and I'm wildly off! But I want to find Annie and to do that I need to go where the evidence leads me."

Chief Mendes looks at him. "You have any better suspects in mind, Detective?"

He appears affronted. "Not without having time to review the case. I don't know anything about Tiffany Hendricks and her dead baby. I was focusing on the guys who were murdered here last Sunday."

Mendes turns to Madison. "Whether or not Tiffany and Tammy are the same person, she clearly didn't bludgeon herself to death, so who do you like for the murder of her, Eric Bailey and the twin boys?"

"Well," says Madison, thinking things through. "That really depends on whether they *are* the same woman. Because if they're not, then our pool of suspects increases to include anyone who saw the family move in here on Sunday. Kai Bishop and Dawn Fremantle were aware of them, and Jerry Clark cleared the property of furniture just weeks before, presumably for Tammy or Eric." She suddenly remembers what Jerry said. "When I asked Jerry who hired him to clear the place, he said it was done through a—now deleted—email and the person called themselves Mrs. Hendricks. It's likely it was Tiffany, using her mom's name."

Nate nods along.

"Regardless," she continues, "I also have a bad feeling about Maria Smith, Tammy's former sister-in-law."

Mendes frowns. "How so?"

"Because Maria hated the fact her brother married a much younger woman. She accused Tammy of being a gold digger and was unhappy that Tammy got everything after Wade died. She's an older woman who lives in Utah, so I'm not suggesting she traveled here and committed the murders herself, but she could've hired someone. As we know, money's a powerful motive for murder."

"It's definitely worth pursuing," says Mendes.

"What if our victim *is* Tiffany?" says Adams.

"Then Tiffany framed an innocent man who might want revenge. Although Dennis McKinney is still incarcerated, so it can't have been him."

Adams says, "But he could easily have hired a hitman if word got to him that Tiffany was back and living under a new name. I mean, she was bold enough to move back into the same house!"

She nods. "It's possible."

Nate says, "Maybe his brother, Jim, took it upon himself to kill her, without even being asked."

"Right. Which means Jim McKinney is the best suspect we've had yet. But he would've had to witness Tammy moving in here that day, and he would've had to recognize her. From what was left of her body, Tammy looked a little different to when she was Tiffany. Her hair was platinum-blonde instead of dark and she'd had breast implants."

When no one speaks, Madison continues, "If it *was* Jim who killed this family, the question becomes, what did he do with Tammy's youngest child? The condition of Tammy's and

Eric's bodies tells us the killer acted in a fit of rage so bad that he thought nothing of killing her sons too. So, why he took Annie with him instead of killing her is confusing. Kids are difficult to hide for long. And Annie was too young to be able to provide a description of him to the cops, so he didn't need to kill her. Why not just leave her behind unharmed?"

"Revenge does funny things to people," says Adams. "Maybe he figured his brother lost fifteen years of his life for the murder of her first child, so why not kill all her children out of spite?"

"But if that's the case," says Madison, "how come we haven't found Annie's body?"

Chief Mendes appears thoughtful. "Lack of a body doesn't mean she's still alive. We might never find her, or it might take fifteen years like this little one." She looks at the tiny bones on the ground.

Madison doesn't want to believe they'll never find Annie. "The only way we'll know if we're on the right track is if we interview Jim McKinney. Let's see if he'll talk." She looks at Mendes. "Can I bring him in for questioning?"

Mendes doesn't hesitate. "Do it right away."

CHAPTER FIFTY-TWO

The station smells good. Chief Mendes has ordered a selection of takeout pizzas to sustain the team while they work late. Madison finishes her second slice while she waits for Jim McKinney to be brought in for questioning. She follows Nate into the station's small kitchen as she thinks about everything that needs doing.

While the baby's bones are taken to the morgue ready for Lena to examine in the morning, Alex is on his way up north to visit the forensic specialists at the crime lab. He'll hand-deliver the evidence he collected from the baby's unmarked grave, including the plastic bag used to suffocate her. Having a close working relationship with a couple of the forensic specialists has its perks. One of them, Nora, has agreed to expedite the DNA testing for him on certain items, which means she'll be working overnight, like the rest of them.

Madison knows that if they can pinpoint who put that bag around the baby's head all those years ago, they can narrow down their pool of suspects for the so-called Doe Family homicides.

"Coffee?" Nate pours himself a cup. Chief Mendes has

HER LONELY BONES 301

allowed him to join them at the station only because he has knowledge of the Grace Hendricks case and he's already spoken to both Dennis and Jim McKinney. He can watch Madison's interview with Jim from the next room and tell them whether Jim deviates from what he told him earlier.

"Please," she says. "Steve's talking to Buford PD to see if they'll exhume Wade Smith's body in a bid to autopsy it. If Wade's sister is right about Tammy and she did have a hand in Wade's death, then we know she was capable of murder."

"Murdering your vulnerable husband for his wealth isn't the same as murdering your baby though," says Nate, passing her a cup.

"I know. I guess we'll see what the DNA reveals."

They head to her desk at the same time as Shelley arrives. She's escorting Jim McKinney. He's missing his cowboy hat and there's no hint of a smile. Instead, the scowl on his face tells her he's not happy about being brought in for questioning.

Madison doesn't care. "Interview room one," she says to Shelley.

She watches them go before approaching Detective Adams at his desk. "Did we get warrants for Dawn Freemantle's place and Kai Bishop's cell phone?"

He nods. "We did."

She's relieved, but with it being past eleven p.m., the search will have to wait for the morning now. And if Jim McKinney confesses, it might not need to take place at all. "Ready for the interview?"

Adams finishes sending a text and then stands. Slipping his phone away he says, "Selena's mad at me for working late."

"It can't be helped," says Madison. "Remind her we're trying to make the streets safer for your girls."

He scoffs. "She's sick of hearing that one."

He follows her and Nate to the interview rooms. Nate joins

Steve in the room next door to where Jim is waiting. They'll watch it all play out on-screen.

Madison opens the door to the other room and enters, dropping some case files on the table. "Hi, Jim. Thanks for coming. Have you met Detective Adams before?"

He briefly glances at Adams. "I've seen him around town."

"Can we get you a drink?" asks Adams.

Jim shakes his head. "Let's get this over with. I have work in the morning."

Madison and Adams take seats opposite him.

"What do you do for work, Jim?" she asks.

"I'm a truck driver, mostly Colorado based."

Madison thinks that would be a good job if you wanted to abduct a child. He could've driven Annie anywhere.

"Nice," says Adams. "I hear that pays well."

"You hear wrong." Jim crosses his arms. "What am I here for?"

Not wanting to waste time, Madison looks him in the eye. "We've found human remains buried in the backyard of Linda Hendricks's home."

A flicker of surprise flashes across his face before he controls it. "What's that got to do with me?"

"You tell us," she says. "It looks like the body has been there some time."

Jim quickly understands what she's saying. "Is it a baby?"

"We believe so. We're working on the assumption it's Grace Hendricks, but that's between you and us. If the press finds out, I'll know where they got their information."

Jim leans back in his seat. His scowl vanishes and he turns pale. "Son of a bitch. Tiffany killed her all along."

"What makes you say that?" asks Adams.

Raising his eyebrows as if they're fools, Jim says, "Who else could get away with burying a body in her backyard?"

Madison says, "Well, we don't know—"

"Oh, come on!" exclaims Jim, leaning forward. "The way I see it, there's only three people who could've buried that child in that yard: Tiffany Hendricks, Linda Hendricks or the child's father, Ronnie Russo." He shakes his head. "I knew it. This is why Ronnie's never been able to look me in the eye, not since Dennis was arrested."

"You think Ronnie knew she was buried there?" she asks. She remembers Nate saying that Ronnie was less than forth-coming about Tiffany. Maybe this is why.

"That's *your* job to find out. You've brought the wrong guy in for questioning, Detective. I don't know what happened to that child, neither does my brother. He was framed by someone."

"By who?" asks Adams.

"Now I know the baby was buried in her own backyard, my money's on Tiffany and Detective Ramsey. Maybe she was offering him sexual favors or something in order to divert atten-tion from herself. I wouldn't put it past her."

Madison doesn't believe Ramsey's capable of looking the other way in return for sex. It's a ridiculous and lazy accusation. But she has to admit it's a possibility, no matter how slim. "Where were *you* the day Grace vanished?"

"I was alone in my apartment. It was my day off."

"Huh," says Adams. "You and your brother both had the same day off. Was that intentional? Did you go visit him?"

"No. I slept late, ate lunch at the diner and returned home by two o'clock. The rest of the day I stayed indoors."

"Can anyone corroborate that?" asks Madison. "Your neigh-bors, any visitors you had?"

He gives her a stern look. "It was so long ago that I couldn't even tell you who my neighbor was at the time."

Closing the file in front of her Madison says, "I thought maybe the day before your brother was arrested for murder would stick in your memory. I mean, you just said you remember what time you returned from the diner. It's odd that you'd remember that but not who your neighbor was."

He glares at her tight-lipped.

"What about your father?" she presses. "I believe Dennis lived with him." She pulls out the crime-scene photos taken the day Grace vanished. So far she's only seen the one Chief Mendes showed them, of Linda's backyard. As she goes through them, they're intentionally visible to Jim and she catches him looking.

"Our father was out of town working."

"Does he drive trucks too?" asks Adams.

"He did then. He's retired now."

Madison picks up one of the photos for a closer look. It shows the interior of Dennis's house, with cops searching the place. Mike Bowers is there. He glanced at the camera just as the shot was taken, leaving him forever frozen in time.

"Wait a minute." She recognizes the interior because it hasn't changed much at all. She checks the next photo. It's of the front of the house. Something comes to her as she realizes she's been in this house recently.

She recalls Tiffany's statement about what happened in the lead-up to Grace's disappearance. It said she and Grace had gone to Dennis's place to buy some eggs before Grace vanished.

"Chickens," she mutters. "Why didn't I realize?"

Adams says, "What's that?"

Madison could kick herself for being slow to put two and two together. Dennis kept chickens fifteen years ago. Madison heard chickens while she was at Dawn's house. The rottweilers were antagonizing them. She had assumed they were Dawn's, but she never saw them. They must've been in Richard's backyard.

She looks at Jim. "What's your father's name?"

"Richard McKinney."

Dawn's elderly neighbor. Madison leans back in her seat. "I didn't realize."

"What's that got to do with anything?" says Jim.

Adams looks puzzled too.

"I paid him a visit earlier this week, right after the family were found dead," she says. "I asked him about Linda Hendricks and whether she had any family. I'm surprised he didn't mention one of his sons was in prison for the murder of her granddaughter."

"Why would he?" says Jim defensively. "Dennis's wrongful conviction isn't relevant to that family being beaten to death all these years later."

Madison isn't so sure. Jim's acting as though he didn't know the murdered family. But could he have known Tammy was Tiffany?

If that's what the DNA results eventually confirm, then Jim could've sought revenge for his brother's conviction. And it's likely he would've told his dad about what he'd done, as it sounds like the whole family was pissed at Tiffany. Maybe Jim thought he would bring his father peace at last by killing her.

Either way, Richard would be keen to make sure Madison didn't realize Jim had a powerful motive for this family's murder.

She thinks back to her first visit to Richard's home earlier this week, when she asked for his name. He definitely hadn't given her his last name or she would've realized he was Dennis and Jim's father right away. Instead, he'd made some wisecrack about not calling him Dick, possibly to distract her.

She curses herself for not pressing him on his last name. It doesn't help that she'd been distracted by the wave of grief she'd experience at his house. It had caught her off guard, leaving her embarrassed. She was also worrying about Owen leaving for college. Looks like Adams isn't the only one making mistakes.

"Think your dad would come down and answer some questions?" she asks.

Jim's face drops. "You leave my father alone. He's an old man and he's suffered enough thanks to this police department." He abruptly stands, making Adams shoot up too. "If you're not arresting me," he says, "I want to leave. Next time I'll have a lawyer present. So will my father. In the meantime I suggest you bring Ronnie Russo in for questioning."

Adams looks over at Madison. "Shall I escort him out?"

She reluctantly nods. "Thanks for your time, Mr. McKinney."

When they're gone, she exhales heavily. This case is exhausting.

CHAPTER FIFTY-THREE

After going home to catch some sleep, Madison returns to the station early. It's not even six thirty when she walks past the front desk. The sun is just creeping up over the mountains. There's an early morning chill in the air, which is a nice change from the recent stifling heat.

Steve greets her from his desk. "Morning." His eyes are puffy and his shirt is crumpled.

"Hey," she says. "Did you even go home?"

"Yeah, but I couldn't sleep, so I went to the gym before coming here. I saw Lena there. We had breakfast."

Madison breaks out in a smile. "Oh yeah? You and Lena?"

When he realizes what she's insinuating he says, "Breakfast, Madison. Not sex."

She laughs.

"Is Adams coming in early too?" he asks.

Madison snorts. "What do you think?"

He smiles before getting straight to business. "So Nate listened to your interview with Jim McKinney and apparently the guy didn't deviate from what he'd already told him. Could be Jim's not our guy."

She chews on her lip as she thinks. She'd dreamed about the missing toddler last night. Annie had been crying nonstop and Madison had to wake herself up in order to stop the sound of Annie's cries piercing her brain.

"By the way," says Steve, "I heard from Buford PD last night. Their chief has decided exhuming Wade Smith is not a productive way to spend public funds, given the guy's age and medical condition, and the fact his potential killer is dead and can't stand trial. So his sister will never know if he was murdered."

"That's a shame for Maria," she says. "I wouldn't want to be the person to tell her."

"I checked whether there was a protective order in Eric's or Tammy's name," he continues. "I thought it could tell us whether they were running from someone, but I couldn't find one."

"It was worth checking." Madison turns to look around the station. It's just them and Dina in right now, with a few uniforms coming and going. The station's phones are quiet so Dina's keeping busy knitting something.

"Before you ask," says the dispatcher, catching Madison's eye, "there haven't been any tips or sightings overnight of Annie Smith."

Madison's stomach lurches with dread. The longer Annie's missing the quieter the public goes. She has to hope the Amber Alert will get people calling in. She can ask Adams to hold another press conference this morning, to remind the community to keep their eyes peeled. The only problem with that is that increased media coverage puts more pressure on her abductor to get rid of the toddler in order to evade capture. But at this stage of the investigation it's a risk they have to take.

"But you did get a call from Maria Smith," says Dina.

Madison's surprised the woman called back after hanging up on her. "What did she want?"

"To apologize. She says she hung up on you because she was offended when you asked her for an alibi."

Madison's not surprised the woman was offended. She's that kind of person.

"She was indignant telling me about it." Dina laughs before doing an impression of Maria. "'I've never been accused of something so heinous in all my life,' she said. And, 'You've added to my distress at this trying time.' I thought I'd never get rid of her but eventually I persuaded her to go make herself an herbal tea."

"Thanks," says Madison. "I'm glad I didn't have to deal with her. I get she's upset and all, but she's more worried about her brother's money than the fact her nephews have been murdered."

Dina shakes her head in disgust. "What's that British expression Alex uses... 'There's nowt so queer as folk.'"

Madison snorts. As she goes to switch her computer on, she gets a call on her desk phone. She picks it up. "Hello?"

"Good morning, Detective. How are you?" It's Alex, and he sounds wide awake.

"I'm good. Where are you?"

"I'm still at the lab. Nora and I worked through the night."

She's impressed. "I'm going to put you on speakerphone so Steve can listen in." Steve comes over to sit on her desk. "What have you got for us?" she says down the line.

"Well," says Alex with a deep breath, "with regards to the infant remains we found at the Hendricks's house, it'll take some time to extract the DNA in order to compare it to Tammy Smith's. That's a specialism Nora can't help us with unfortunately, so she has a colleague coming in later to begin the process."

Madison's disappointed. They don't have the luxury of time.

Chief Mendes appears and after dumping her purse in her office she joins them and listens in to the call.

"However," Alex continues, "Nora *has* compared DNA taken from the plastic bag found wrapped around the baby's skull to a sample I took from Tammy Smith's body." He falls silent.

"And?" says Madison. "Come on, Alex, you're killing me here!"

"Oh, sorry, I got distracted there for a minute. This lab is full of fascinating—"

"Alex!" she says sternly.

"It's a match," he says.

Madison gasps and glances at Steve and Mendes, who both look just as shocked. "No freakin' way," she says.

"Afraid so," says Alex. "Tammy Smith must have placed that bag over the baby's head, as there are only two different people's DNA on it. The other DNA must belong to the baby, given the bag's close proximity to her skin and saliva. This means Tammy was at the Hendricks's house fifteen years ago, which suggests it's highly likely that Tammy Smith and Tiffany Hendricks are the same person, and the remains are those of her firstborn baby, Grace Hendricks."

Madison closes her eyes. *She killed her own baby.*

She's shocked Tiffany managed to get away with staging her own death, and how everyone working the case back then just accepted it to be true, even though they never found her body. And it's interesting that Detective Ramsey, Mike Bowers and even Nate were taken in by Tiffany's performance at her press conference. They all believed she would kill herself once the twenty-four hours were up. Although Ramsey eventually admitted he'd had his reservations.

Would they have believed a missing child's father in the same position?

Madison hadn't been completely fooled. She's met women

like Tiffany before. They're able to manipulate men so well they can literally get away with murder. They find it harder to control other women in the same way though, which usually means they have fewer female friends.

"Detective Ramsey will be devastated when he finds out," says Steve. "He let Tiffany run rings around him."

Madison knows she'll have to tell Ramsey at some point, and before the information is released to the media. "What about Dennis McKinney?" she says. "He just spent fifteen years of his life in prison for something he didn't do."

Chief Mendes speaks up. "That's going to be a tough conversation. I'll call the DA and explain what we've found. Dennis needs to put his lawyer to work ASAP."

Madison knows it might not be that easy. Just because you're innocent, doesn't mean the justice system works in your favor. It depends on the DA's office and how they want to proceed. Still, at least she knows neither Dennis nor Jim killed Grace Hendricks.

It doesn't mean Jim didn't kill Tiffany and her family though. "That means Tiffany planted Grace's sandal on Dennis's truck. Probably that day she went to buy eggs with her daughter." She looks at Steve. "Why not plant Grace's body on his property? Why just a sandal?"

Alex answers that one. "Because she would've known Dennis's DNA wasn't on the baby's body. No one else's DNA would be on it but hers. She had to hide it."

"Of course." She sighs, suddenly depressed at how depraved people can be. "I wonder if Linda knew what her daughter did?"

"I highly doubt it," says Chief Mendes. "From what I've read, Grace's murder followed by Tiffany's disappearance destroyed Linda's life."

Madison agrees. Linda was just another of Tiffany's

victims. "Alex? Is there anything else you can get expedited while you're up there?"

"Well, with regards to Sunday's homicides, Nora's currently working on the fingernail scrapings taken from Tammy, I mean, Tiffany's body." He pauses. "Shall we refer to Tammy as Tiffany now? I think it'll be less confusing for everyone."

"I agree," she says. There's no reason not to now.

Steve and Mendes both nod.

Alex continues. "If we have enough for a DNA comparison, we may be able to figure out who killed her, assuming they've had a prior arrest and their DNA was collected at some point."

Although Madison has a gut feeling Jim might've killed Tiffany, Eric and the boys, she still wants to search Dawn Freemantle's place, seeing as they already have the warrant. There's just something not right about Kai Bishop, but she can't put her finger on what. And the fact that three different methods were used for the family's murders suggests there could have been more than one killer. Maybe Jim paid Kai to help him. Or maybe Kai and Jerry did it, while high on drugs.

Either way, any one of them could be hiding Annie Smith, so she intends to exhaust all possibilities.

"Did you get any matches from the shoe print you took from the lake?" asks Chief Mendes.

"No," says Alex. "Which means it wasn't from any of our shoes. It could've been a walker's print, or it could be the killer's."

Frustrated, Madison's shoulders slump. "What about the cell phones found in the car's safe?"

"I haven't even had a chance to look into those yet. All I know is they wouldn't switch on, suggesting we'll need to extract the data another way. It's on my to-do list."

Madison feels for him. He has enough work to keep three full-time forensic technicians busy, but the department can't afford any more employees.

"Hold on a second, Detective." Alex has a discussion with a woman next to him, presumably Nora. It seems to go on forever and Madison senses a flirty tone from him, followed by a shy laugh from Nora, who sounds younger than her name suggests.

She shoots Steve a look and his smile suggests he heard it too. Alex has obviously moved on from his heartbreak real quick.

Eventually Alex returns on the line and says, "We have some DNA results just come back for various other things. Let me see—" He rifles through papers. "Ah. So the toddler's clothes found in boxes stored on the trailer, which we're assuming are Annie's clothes, have provided a rich source of DNA for comparison to Tiffany's and Eric's. And the results confirm..." A pause while he reads. "They were both Annie's biological parents."

So Maria Smith was right: Tiffany was cheating on Wade with Eric. "But CJ and Joey are Tiffany's, right?"

"Correct, but not Eric's."

She nods. "They must've been Wade's children." With a sigh she says, "At least Wade wasn't alive to know what happened to his little boys."

"Quite," agrees Alex. "I think that's all we have for now. I'll be heading home shortly."

"Okay. Well, drive safely. And tell Nora thanks. I appreciate the fact she worked through the night for us."

"I will."

Madison ends the call with the suspicion that something's blossoming between that pair. Selfishly she hopes not because if he falls in love with someone who works at the crime lab, he might leave his job here to go work with her. It sounds like he found the lab impressive, which isn't surprising considering his own office here is nothing but a glorified broom cupboard. Plus, none of the team here know what he's talking about when he launches into the more complex forensic explanations. He'd probably appreciate being surrounded with more intelligent co-workers.

Adams surprises her by arriving for work sooner than she expected. Steve fills him in on everything as Mendes gets Madison's attention. "I had an irate call from Doug Draper last night."

Madison grimaces. "A complaint about me and Adams trying to search his property?"

"Right," says Mendes. "He actually threatened to sue the department for causing his wife severe mental anguish. He tried to blackmail me into agreeing to reopen his daughter's cold case in order to call off his lawyers."

With raised eyebrows Madison says, "So let's reopen the case, once we've found Annie Smith. Their daughter went missing during a hike on Grave Mountain. I'm sure we could find out what happened to her." She knows Nate and Brody would be open to helping her.

"I don't take kindly to blackmail," says Mendes.

Detective Adams approaches them, open-mouthed. "Is Alex seriously suggesting Tiffany faked her emotion in that press conference?" He shakes his head, incredulous. "She deserves an Oscar for that performance."

"She was a good actor," says Madison. "The whole twenty-four-hour countdown to killing herself was a set-up to stage her own disappearance."

"It was certainly a clever way of stopping people from looking at her for the baby's disappearance," says Steve.

To Adams, Madison says, "Could you get the press in and release the news? Tell them about Tiffany and the fact we've found remains at the house, but don't confirm Grace's identity yet. I want the results from her remains to come back before we do that."

Adams nods.

Her cell phone rings. It's Nate, so she walks away from the

group to answer it. "Morning," she says, a hint of a smile on her lips.

"Morning. Did you get any sleep?" he asks.

"Some. I've had some DNA results back and it confirms Tiffany and Tammy are the same person."

"They are? That's interesting," he says. "Because I've just had a call from Grace's father."

"Ronnie Russo?"

"Yeah. He wants to talk. I'm about to meet him at the diner. Want to join us?"

She'll have to tell Ronnie about the discovery of his daughter's remains, which she'd prefer to do somewhere private, but she might not have a choice. "I'll head there now."

CHAPTER FIFTY-FOUR

From inside the diner, Nate watches Brody waiting in the parking lot. The dog stares at anyone who exits the building to see if they've brought him something to eat.

Madison arrives before Ronnie and, once out of her car, Brody excitedly approaches her for some attention. Nate smiles as he watches them interact. She never used to be a dog person.

Once inside she approaches his booth with a bashful smile. He chose a seat at the quieter end of the diner, allowing them some privacy. He stands, leaning in for a quick kiss before catching Vince Rader's eye over Madison's shoulder.

Vince stops what he's doing and heads straight to them, open-mouthed. "Are you telling me..." He doesn't finish the thought.

Madison takes a seat, embarrassed, while Nate nods. "Yeah."

A wide smile breaks out on Vince's face. "*Finally!*" he says. "I thought I'd be dead and buried before you pair came to your senses. I think this calls for breakfast on the house. What'll it be?"

They order a selection of bacon, eggs, toast and coffee. "We'll be joined by someone else soon."

"Oh yeah?" says Vince, disappointed. "Not the medical examiner, I hope? I mean, unless that's what you're into..."

Madison laughs nervously. "No," she says. "Not Lena. Ronnie Russo."

Vince looks at Nate. "Russo? Interesting. Does that mean you're working his daughter's cold case?" Having his own true-crime podcast means Vince has an interest in, and knowledge of, local crime.

Nate smiles at him. "You know we can't tell you that."

"Not even for a free breakfast?"

"Sorry."

Vince shakes his head before walking away. "Hey, Carla?" he yells across the floor. "Wait 'til you hear this!"

Madison lowers her head and cringes. "Shoot me now."

Nate sees the funny side of it. "We'll be old news by next week. Have you heard from Owen?"

"Yeah, he called really late last night," she says. "He's doing fine. It's so weird but because I'm busy, I haven't had a chance to miss him yet. Not properly. It just feels like he's on vacation."

"He called me too. I got introduced to his new friends. He had his arm around one of them. A cute blonde."

Madison leans in, shocked. "He has a girlfriend already?"

Nate laughs. "I don't know if they're dating but they looked comfortable around each other."

"He's only been there two days!" She leans back and adds, "He sure works faster than you do."

Before Nate can defend himself the door to the diner opens and Ronnie steps inside. Ronnie's in his mid-thirties but grief has aged him. His graying hair and heavily lined face suggest he's not in good health. When he glances around the diner to find them, Nate stands and waves him over.

Ronnie approaches but slows once he sees Madison. "I

didn't know the cops would be here," he says. He's softly spoken.

Madison moves to sit next to Nate as she says, "I have an update to share with you." When he doesn't sit, she adds, "Do you really think if I was going to arrest you for something I'd do it here? Take a seat, breakfast is on us."

Ronnie looks back and forth between them before sliding into the booth.

Vince returns with coffee. "Morning, Ronnie. Food's on its way." He heads back to the counter once their cups are filled.

"What update?" says Ronnie, nervously picking at his nails. The fingers on his right hand are stained yellow from years of nicotine. He's wearing dirty sweatpants and a well-worn T-shirt. It's clear he hasn't shaved in days.

Nate says, "Why don't you tell me why you wanted to see me first?"

Ronnie glances over his shoulder. His back is to the door, which makes people like him nervous. Maybe he owes someone money. Or maybe he's waiting for his past to catch up with him. "I've been thinking about Tiffany a lot since you called me," he says. "And I keep seeing you guys at her old house on the news. It's making me drink more."

"I understand you had a difficult relationship with her," says Madison gently.

Ronnie lowers his eyes. "That woman ruined my life. She was evil."

"In what way?" she asks.

Vince and Carla bring their food. Carla gives Nate a discreet wink to show she approves of him and Madison.

Once they're gone Ronnie relaxes a little and picks up a slice of bacon, chewing on it slowly. "I've been googling accessory to murder." He looks at Madison. "And what that actually means."

Madison acts as though this is a perfectly normal topic of

discussion in a bid to keep him relaxed. She won't want to spook him. She bites into a slice of toast as Nate sips his coffee. "Why's that?" she asks. "Do you know something, Ronnie?"

He nods, lowering his eyes. "I know too much. That's why I drink."

"Why don't you unburden yourself? A problem shared and all that."

He drops the half-eaten bacon back on his plate. "What did you want to tell me?"

Madison glances at Nate. He's guessing she needs to tell him they found his daughter's remains.

"Why don't you come out to my vehicle so we can talk in private?" she says.

"Why? So you can arrest me?" Ronnie keeps shifting position. He might be on something or it could just be nerves.

"No," she says sadly. "I just don't want to tell you in public, that's all."

He leans on his elbows and keeps his voice low. "You know, don't you?"

Madison doesn't answer.

"You know she killed our daughter?"

"Tiffany? Yes. Are you telling me you've known all along?"

He answers with his own question. "Does that mean you've found Grace?"

Slowly, she nods. "I'm afraid so. She was located on Linda's property."

He puts his palms to his eyes and leans back, barely containing a sob.

Nate finds it tough to watch his reaction. Ronnie clearly has demons, but was he involved? They've already seen how Tiffany fooled them all with her fake display of grief. Maybe Ronnie's just as good at acting.

Ronnie removes his hands and looks at them. His eyes are red-rimmed. "Can I bury her now?"

"She's with the medical examiner," says Madison softly. "It will take some time, but yes, soon."

Ronnie nods, before sipping his coffee. The cup shakes in his hands.

"How did you know Tiffany killed her?" asks Madison. She keeps her voice down.

"She told me," says Ronnie. "That's what I mean when I say she was evil! She took sick pleasure in hurting me. She wanted me to know what she'd done. She even had a smile on her face as she told me I'd never see my daughter again. But she refused to tell me how she'd done it or where she'd buried her."

"Did she say *why* she did it?"

He waves his hand. "Stupid, stupid reasons."

"Like what?" she presses.

"Like she felt fat and frumpy after the birth. Said she was losing her looks and she resented me and the baby for that. And she didn't want the burden of taking care of a baby. She wanted to do something with her life and thought Grace would hold her back. Her mom kept telling her she couldn't go out like she used to anymore because of the baby. Tiff hated that. She hated being tethered. She hated parental responsibilities. Linda looked after Grace far better than Tiffany ever did. I liked her mom, but once Linda knew Grace was dead and thought Tiffany had killed herself, she became bitter. She didn't want any visitors. Her daughter ruined so many people's lives." His expression is pained. "Tiffany always said she'd be rich one day. She was so good at manipulating guys."

He pauses as he looks out of the window. "I don't think she ever loved Grace. I don't think she ever felt anything for anyone. You know, most people assume only men can be psychopaths, but Tiffany could teach Ted Bundy a thing or two." He quickly swipes away a tear.

Madison's eyes are full of sympathy. "I'm so sorry."

He looks away. "I wanted to kill the bitch."

Nate clears his throat. "Why didn't you tell Detective Ramsey what she'd done?"

Ronnie looks at him with desperate eyes. "She told me she hid one of Grace's sandals in Dennis McKinney's truck to frame him for it. Apparently, Dennis touched Grace's shoe the last time he saw her, as he was saying hi. So Tiffany figured his print or DNA or whatever would be on it." He swallows before continuing. "I was so upset she'd killed our baby. I couldn't figure out why she didn't just allow me to raise her if she didn't want to. I got the hell away from her before I could choke her. I went to my truck, intending to go straight to the police station. But she stopped me."

When he falls silent, Madison asks, "What did she say?"

"She said she could just as easily frame *me* for it. She could tell Ramsey that I told her how *I'd* planted the sandal there. How *I* was the one who killed our daughter. And then it would be me sitting in Dennis's cell instead of him." His voice is rising and they're catching glances from other diners now. "She used to flirt with Dennis but he never seemed interested. He was one of the few who turned her down. I guess she thought he had money or something."

Nate says, "Dennis is gay. That's why he wasn't interested."

Ronnie seems surprised. "I never knew. He should've told the jury that."

Madison lowers her coffee cup. "Tiffany didn't kill herself. Did you know that?"

Looking increasingly uncomfortable, Ronnie nods. "She had a plan to fake her own death and skip town. I couldn't believe it when the cops just accepted she'd topped herself."

"There was no search?" asks Nate.

"Oh, sure there was, but they gave up too quickly. Detective Ramsey said a jogger or a dog walker would likely find her bones years from now. I wanted to leave an anonymous tip but I know they can trace those things, and if they did, they'd think I had some involvement in everything. I literally had nowhere to turn! My life has been stuck ever since that point, and I was trying to grieve for my daughter at the same time." He's struggling to contain a sob.

A few minutes pass in silence before Madison speaks. "Tiffany's dead now, Ronnie."

He stares at her for a full thirty seconds before responding. "How do you know?"

"The family murdered at Linda's place on Sunday? That was Tiffany, her boyfriend and her sons. After leaving Lost Creek she'd changed her name and married a rich old guy up north."

Ronnie breaks down in front of them. The relief coming off him is evident. He can finally begin to grieve properly for Grace.

Madison tells him to take a breather and sip his coffee. He does, but he's too worked up to sit still. He stands. "You find any evidence on my daughter's remains to prove Tiffany did it?"

She nods. "We believe so."

He balls his fists. "Did my daughter suffer, Detective?"

Nate looks at Madison. She's tense and her eyes are watery. Under the table, he slips a reassuring hand on her thigh. She's been working nonstop this week. Add to that the fact she knows the baby was suffocated and another young child is missing, it's clearly taking a toll on her.

"Answer me, Detective," says Ronnie, his tears about to spill over. "Did my daughter suffer?"

The girl was suffocated by her own mother. Nate knows that method takes time. Of course she suffered. He's about to say something when Madison looks up at Ronnie and says, "Not for long."

It's the most diplomatic answer she can give him, and it might offer this man small comfort.

A single tear escapes from Ronnie's left eye before he turns and stalks out of the diner, slamming the door shut behind him. Through the window they watch him go to his truck and sit in the driver's seat, his forehead resting on the steering wheel.

Nate looks at Madison who takes a deep breath. "You okay?" he asks.

She pushes away the plate of food in front of her. "Yeah."

"What do you think about Ronnie?"

"I mean, I obviously feel terrible for the guy, but on the other hand, he just became a person of interest for the murders."

"Really?"

"Sure! What better motive is there? She killed his child all those years ago so, when he saw her back in town, his rage kicks in and he kills her. Eric and the boys were collateral damage, in the wrong place at the wrong time."

"But he didn't kill Annie," says Nate.

She looks at him. "No. Because Annie would remind him of Grace. The child they had together. The child he dearly misses, even to this day."

Nate hadn't thought of that. His heart skips a beat. "You think he has Annie? That he's keeping her to raise?"

They watch Ronnie hit the gas and screech out of the parking lot.

"It's a possibility," she says. "Which means I need a search warrant for his place immediately."

CHAPTER FIFTY-FIVE

Before she leaves the diner's parking lot, Madison calls Chief Mendes and explains why she wants a warrant for Ronnie Russo's place. The chief gets right on it, so Madison slips her phone away and looks at Nate. "We may as well head to Ronnie's to wait for the warrant to come through."

"Let's go."

Nate goes to his car and before Madison can get in hers, she hears the rumble of a truck pulling into the lot. Detective Ramsey parks next to her vehicle. He drives a silver Chevy pickup and it's covered in sarcastic bumper stickers. When he gets out, he nods to them but doesn't say anything.

"John?" she says as he walks away. "Do you have a minute? I have news."

He hesitates, which confirms her suspicion that he doesn't like her much. She can almost understand that—she was convicted of killing a fellow officer after all—but she's since been exonerated, so he should accept her innocence and move on.

Guys like Ramsey can't though. They're incapable of maturity because they have an underlying misogyny that makes them want to believe the worst about a woman. Especially as she dared to rejoin law enforcement after her release. It also doesn't help that he was friends with Mike Bowers and he probably blames her for what happened to Mike last year.

"What is it?" he asks, his back to her. "I don't want to talk about Tiffany damn Hendricks again if that's what you're after."

"She didn't kill herself."

He turns around, his eyes mistrusting. "Of course she did."

"No," says Madison. "She didn't. She wanted everyone to believe that, but the fact is she skipped town and started fresh somewhere else under a new name."

Ramsey's eyes flicker to Nate. He holds his gaze while gesturing to Madison. "Is she drunk or high?"

"You're out of line," says Nate.

Madison's blood boils. That's disrespectful.

Brody comes over to sit by her, eyeballing Ramsey, as Madison takes a step closer to the retired cop. Keeping her voice low so no one might overhear them, she says, "We have DNA proof that Tiffany killed Grace. It wasn't Dennis McKinney."

"Bullshit." Doubt creeps across Ramsey's face. "If she's still alive then where is she?"

"Right this minute? In the morgue," says Madison. "She was going by the name of Tammy Smith. She was one of the victims from Sunday's homicides."

Ramsey looks like he wants to laugh. "That's a wild theory. You like being on the news or something?"

She raises her voice, her fists balled in anger. "Listen to me, Ramsey! I get that you're embarrassed you let her escape, but you have to accept reality. We're working on the assumption that whoever killed Tiffany, her boyfriend and her sons did it out of revenge for what she did fifteen years ago. I'm only telling you now out of respect. The whole town will know shortly, as my partner's about to hold a press conference." She turns away from him, barely containing her anger.

"You ever think about Mike, Harper?" he says scornfully.

She stops and turns around. "Of course. He was my friend."

Ramsey nods. "He was a fine officer back then, and he made an even better detective. Better than you'll ever be."

Nate steps forward but she stops him.

"*What?*" She's stunned that a fellow police officer could claim Mike was a good detective after everything he did. Mike was in deep with the wrong people and it was Madison who paid the price. Ramsey either has a selective memory or he's the kind of guy who'll always side with his crooked male buddies over a female co-worker. She's glad he retired early. It's better for the women of this town that they don't have someone like him in the department anymore.

With a smirk Ramsey says, "If you hadn't come back here after your release, Mike would still be alive today."

Nate speaks up. "You're not just out of line, you're wrong. Mike Bowers turned into the worst kind of cop, and the fact you'd ignore what he did to Madison tells me everything I need to know about you." He takes her hand and they turn their back on him to walk to her car.

Ramsey thinks twice about entering the diner now he knows the whole town is about to find out he put away an innocent man. The press conference will be shown on the diner's TV. Madison knows he won't want to be there for that.

She's right. He turns back, gets in his truck and skids out of the lot.

When he's gone, Nate turns to her. "You okay?"

She nods, but she's bothered by what happened. "He's such an asshole. There was no need to say any of that."

"The guy's ego is bruised. It may have been unintentional but he let Tiffany get away with murder. He's not the hotshot detective he thought he was, and everyone else is about to learn that."

She knows Nate's right. "If he thought he took a lot of heat for letting Tiffany kill herself, he's going to hate the shitstorm Adams's press conference will bring." She's been in the media spotlight many times. It crushes your confidence and destroys your reputation. But you have to deal with it.

"Wouldn't surprise me if he books himself a vacation," says Nate. "And remains out of town until all this blows over."

She frowns. "He didn't even ask whether we'd found Annie Smith. It's like he doesn't care about the repercussions of letting Tiffany get away back then."

Based on his behavior here today, Madison thinks of Jim's earlier comment. In his interview, Jim McKinney had suggested Tiffany could've offered Ramsey sexual favors back then, to turn a blind eye to her guilt. Or to help frame Dennis for murder.

The thought leaves her cold.

Because she doesn't want to believe anyone from LCPD would have helped Tiffany get away with killing her baby.

CHAPTER FIFTY-SIX

FIFTEEN YEARS EARLIER

+10 hours

Mike sits in the pitch blackness, questioning what he's doing out here at the lake at two a.m.

It's been ten hours since Detective Ramsey broke the devastating news to Tiffany and her mom that he'd arrested Dennis McKinney for child abduction and suspected homicide. Ten hours since they failed to bring Grace Hendricks home in time to stop Tiffany making good on her harrowing promise.

Mike had finished the rest of his shift half expecting a call over the radio saying someone had found a young female body out in the woods.

Until he'd read her note.

At first, he'd forgotten about the piece of paper Tiffany slipped him in her living room, as Ramsey walked outside with Linda. He'd had an urgent callout to a domestic violence situation downtown afterward that took forever to get under control. But once he'd gotten home, showered and changed, he checked the pockets of his uniform and found the note.

He reads it again now, using the light from his cell phone.

Officer Bowers, I just want to say thank you for your care and attention. It's been comforting during this horrendous time. Comforting enough to save my life? Maybe. Maybe if I could get out of here and start again someplace new. Someplace where no one knows me, and no one knows I was negligent enough to lose my own baby. To let her be abducted.

I won't be able to bear the shame and the judgmental glances from the other mothers. They all judge me. I know they do. They think I should've been watching her 24/7.

I can't stay here. One way or another I have to leave. If you think you can help me with that, meet me at Lake Providence at 2 a.m. I promise I won't tell a soul you helped me.

If you don't show up, you won't see me again. I've chosen my final resting place and no one will ever find my remains. Grace and I will both be lost forever.

He runs his hand through his hair. What could he do? He couldn't just leave her hopeless. He wants to tell her there are organizations that can help her with her grief. She could see a therapist and try to build a way forward. A way out of her pain.

Even as he thinks it, he doesn't believe a therapist could help in this situation, not this early on, but it's the best that he can offer her. That and the suggestion she leans on her faith, if she has any.

Movement behind the car sends his eyes to the rearview mirror. He'd brought his own car, and he's not in uniform. He didn't want to be spotted.

It's too dark to see anything outside the vehicle.

The passenger door suddenly flies open and Tiffany slides in, shoving a full backpack into the back of the car. Once she closes the door the internal light goes out, shrouding them in darkness. But he can see enough to know she's been crying. The moon's reflection in the lake illuminates her tears.

"Thanks for coming," she says before shyly leaning over to kiss him on his cheek.

She smells of candy. It must be her shampoo.

Mike pulls away. "Listen, I don't know why you think I came but it isn't to squirrel you away into the night. That would be irresponsible of me."

She appears hurt by the comment and lowers her eyes. "You don't want to help me?"

"Yes, I do. The whole department does." He keeps his tone gentle, not wanting to upset her. "But that means suggesting support groups and finding your daughter. I don't understand why you want to leave town. Think of your mother, she'll be devastated."

She slowly shakes her head. "Not as devastated as me if I have to stay here. You don't understand. I can't remain in the same house my poor baby was taken from, and in the same street her killer lived in. They'll be a constant reminder of what happened. I'll never be able to forget." Her breath quickens and she becomes upset.

She looks at him. "I just can't. Not right now. Maybe later, once I've had some time to grieve, I can come back. But for now I need to disappear. I need out of the town that's killed my baby. Can't you see that?" Her eyes are imploring. "I thought you understood. I thought you were different to the rest of them."

Mike can see she's desperate to try to run away from what's happening. It's probably a knee-jerk reaction that will fade with time, but he genuinely believes that if he doesn't help her get out of town, she might take the other way out, and then her death is on him.

"Please?" she says. "Just take me as far as Denver and I swear I'll spend some time at a motel to clear my head. If I don't get out of here it's going to end badly because my entire soul is telling me to run away, and if I can't run away..." She sobs before finishing. Her whole body trembles as she says,

"Then I only have one other option to stop me from feeling this way."

She lifts her sleeves. A crisscross of angry, fresh cuts covers her arms.

Mike's heart breaks for her. He can understand the impulse to try to outrun grief, but experience has taught him it always catches up with you in the end. He's never been in Tiffany's horrific situation but he remembers having very few coping mechanisms at her age. She's left him with no doubt that she'll seriously harm herself if he doesn't help her.

Glancing over his shoulder at her backpack he says, "What have you brought?"

She pulls out a tissue from her pants pocket and wipes her nose and eyes. "Clothes, mainly. Food too. And I emptied the piggy bank I was using to save for Grace's college education." She squeezes her eyes shut against more tears.

He places a reassuring hand on her shoulder. "How much cash do you have?"

She takes a deep, steadying breath. "Three hundred bucks. It won't last long but I'll be careful. I just need time to think. Time to breathe. I can't get that with the press outside my door, my daughter's beautiful face all over the news, and my mom wailing in pain. That's what she did all evening; wailed while clutching onto me as if I could help her somehow." She fixes her eyes on his. "But how can I help her if I can't help myself?"

Trusting his instincts about her—that she's a kid who needs short-term help to stop her doing something drastic—Mike pulls out his wallet. He has two hundred bucks in cash meant for two new tires. He hands it to her along with an LCPD contact card.

Shocked, she looks up at him and wipes her eyes. "You don't have to do that."

He puts his wallet away. "I'll take you as far as I can get you in two hours. But I expect you to come back once you're feeling stronger."

She slowly nods. "I'm sure I will. Just don't tell anyone. I don't want anyone but you looking for me, okay?"

He can't stop Ramsey from getting a search party together once Linda realizes she's missing. But there's no way they'd look outside of Lost Creek. "You can't tell anyone I helped you," he says. "It's more than my job's worth."

"Thank you. I hope you understand that by taking me away from this place you're saving my life."

Mike starts the engine and stares directly ahead. The car's headlights illuminate the shadowy lake in front of them. In order to help Tiffany he has to ignore the creeping uneasiness building in his chest.

He glances at her. "You better buckle up."

Before she can leave the diner's parking lot Madison gets a call from Detective Adams. "Hey," she says. "How did the press conference go?"

"Oh, man," says Adams. "You should've seen their reaction when I told them Tiffany Hendricks was alive all this time!" He sounds more upbeat than she's heard him in months. "They were stunned into silence. An intense hush went over the entire room before they exploded with questions! And when I told them we believe Tiffany is one of our Doe Family victims, they were incredulous! This news is going to be *everywhere*. Honestly, Harper, they took so many photos of me I'll probably get invited onto *Oprah* or something."

Madison smiles faintly. "Sounds like you're going to be famous."

"Right? If I go viral, maybe the chief will give me a raise," he quips.

Bringing him back to earth with a bump Madison says, "Now we need to focus on finding Annie."

"Sure. What's our next move?"

"Well, instead of narrowing down suspects my list keeps

getting bigger." She sighs as she thinks of everyone they've spoken to so far. "Why don't you and Steve execute the search warrant on Dawn Freemantle's place? I'm not as convinced she and Kai were involved anymore, but we've already got the warrant, so we might as well rule them out properly."

"Sure. You don't want to come?"

"No, I'm waiting for Mendes to give me the okay to search Ronnie Russo's home. He's the father of Grace Hendricks." She fills him in on what Ronnie told her and Nate in the diner.

After hearing Madison's theory that Ronnie could've taken Annie to replace Grace, Adams says, "Holy shit, he sounds like our best suspect yet."

"I know."

"Why don't I join you there? Let Steve handle Dawn's place."

She glances at Nate who's leading Brody to his car. "I'm going to take Nate with me, because of his dog. Brody might be able to locate Annie's scent in Ronnie's place."

"Oh. Okay, fine." Adams sounds hurt.

"Don't take it personally, it's purely because of the dog, and besides, I need you to rule out Kai Bishop. He's weird and even if he's not involved in this case, I'd put money on him being involved in *something*. See if you can talk to Dawn's grandson, Timmy. See what he thinks of his grandma's boyfriend. Kids are usually honest when it comes to their opinions of someone and they don't miss a trick. If Annie was ever in their home, I'd bet Timmy would know about it."

"Got it," he says. "Keep me updated with what you find."

"You too. Catch you later." She slips her phone away.

Nate approaches. "Are you speeding off somewhere?" he asks.

"Actually, I want you and Brody to join me at Ronnie's house. That okay with you?"

He smiles. "Sure."

Madison drives the three of them the short distance to Ronnie's trailer park, but stops far enough away to make sure he can't see them from his windows. The search warrant could take a while to get signed off, assuming it does, but she wants to keep an eye on him in the meantime in case he decides to skip town. Maybe with Annie.

While they wait, they see other residents come and go from their trailers. Madison recognizes Tina Jackson, the mother of Nikki Jackson who was killed last year at Fantasy World amusement park. She briefly wonders whether Nikki's mother ever left her deadbeat husband, but when he follows her out of their trailer, she gets her answer. Mr. Jackson scowls at her as he passes.

She ignores him. There's no movement from Ronnie's place. The sun is strong this morning, burning her arm through the car window. She glances at the rearview mirror. Brody sits between them on the backseat. If he tries to chew on her headrests like he does Nate's, he'll be banned from ever riding in her car again. At the moment, he's focused on watching every movement outside the car.

An old lady walks past, eyeballing them with a hostile glare. She doesn't appear to have any teeth as her mouth has a sunken appearance.

"Madison, look." Nate points to Ronnie's trailer.

The door has opened, but he's yet to appear. She grips her door handle, ready to leap out.

"Maybe he just wanted some air," says Nate. "It can get hot inside those things."

She keeps her eyes on the trailer as Brody leans his head into the front of the car to watch the door. Madison feels a wet drip on her hand. He's drooling in anticipation of some action.

Ronnie suddenly appears and he's moving fast, heading to his vehicle. He doesn't even close, never mind lock, the trailer's door behind him.

"Let's go," says Madison, opening her door and letting Brody squeeze out of the car. She turns to Nate as he gets out. "Keep Brody back for now. I don't want to scare Ronnie."

He nods.

Madison's phone beeps, so she risks a quick glance.

Got the warrant. Wait for backup.

It's from Mendes. Madison races over to Ronnie's vehicle and steps in front of it. He starts his engine anyway, so Brody jumps up at the driver's door, barking loudly. He looks and sounds menacing.

"Switch your engine off, Ronnie," says Madison loud enough for him to hear through the windshield.

His face is red and strained. He's either upset to learn his daughter's remains have been found or he's stressed about getting Annie out of here undetected. He stares at the dog. "Get that thing away from me."

Nate approaches Brody. "Switch off the engine and I'll call him off."

Ronnie looks from the dog to Madison to his trailer. She thinks he might take off, running over her as he speeds away. She knows Brody would chase the truck for miles if he did, but ultimately, Brody can't outrun the vehicle.

Nate walks to the front of the truck to stand beside Madison. She's considering pulling her weapon but she'd rather handle this differently. If she's wrong about Ronnie being the person who abducted Annie, pulling her weapon on him could push him too far after everything he's had to deal with today.

Eventually Ronnie rests his head on the steering wheel as if beaten. He switches the engine off. Nate goes to Brody and gently pulls him away by the collar.

Madison opens Ronnie's door. "All we want to do is search your home. I have a warrant."

He doesn't look up.

"Do you have Tiffany's little girl, Ronnie? Is she here?"

He finally looks at her. "What are you talking about?"

Something about his expression has her doubting herself. "Whoever killed Tiffany took her youngest child."

"I didn't kill anyone! I thought you were here to arrest me for withholding evidence because I knew she killed Grace. I didn't even know she was back in town until you told me earlier!" His expression is full of fear.

Madison stands straight. "If that's the case, you won't mind us searching your home for the murder weapon and for the missing child."

Sirens reach them. Shelley's first on the scene. Her cruiser skids to a halt behind Madison's car and she gets straight out. Officer Gloria Williams arrives shortly after.

Ronnie climbs out of his truck, letting Madison search his body for weapons. It's clear. "Go take a seat in the cruiser," she says. "I'll try to make this quick."

Shelley approaches to lead him away. "Handcuffs?" she asks discreetly.

Madison shakes her head. "No. He won't give you any trouble."

Nate approaches. "Ready to go inside?"

She turns to the trailer, secretly hoping Ronnie had nothing to do with this. "Let's go."

CHAPTER FIFTY-EIGHT

Madison, Nate and Officer Gloria Williams hold back in the doorway while Brody searches the entire trailer. It's hot inside, causing beads of sweat on Madison's brow. The dog is thorough and his heightened sense of smell means he's quick at ruling areas out. If there's a dead body in here, he'll find it. And if there's a live person hiding or being hidden in here, he'll find them too.

Once he's gone over the small space three times, he returns to where they stand and flops onto the floor at Nate's feet. Nate looks at her. "Nothing."

Madison finds her relief outweighs her disappointment. Of course she wants to find Annie, but at least they haven't found her dead. "Check his vehicle next."

Nate leads Brody outside just as Chief Mendes arrives.

"Want me to see if I can find anything?" asks Gloria.

"Sure." Madison knows there are some things Brody can't be expected to find: child abuse images; Google searches about how to hide a body; any recent letters between Ronnie and Tiffany; and the murdered family's personal belongings, just for starters.

Gloria gets to work, so Madison steps out of the trailer to greet Mendes.

"Anything?" asks the chief.

"Nothing. Brody's going to check the vehicle, but I don't think Ronnie was involved."

Chief Mendes appears disappointed. "While Detective Adams and Sergeant Tanner are at Dawn Freemantle's property, I think you should search Jim McKinney's home. I'm just waiting for yet another warrant to be approved before we can do it. I'm not very popular with Judge Hoyle right now. He says we're a drain on his time."

Madison smiles. "It must look as though we're running around like headless chickens." The mention of chickens reminds her of Tiffany and Grace's visit to Dennis McKinney in the days before Grace's supposed disappearance. That must've been when Tiffany planted one of Grace's sandals in his truck, while she was waiting for him to fetch the eggs she bought. It was probably the only real purpose of her visit.

She watches Brody sniff the entire truck. He doesn't pick up any scents. Ronnie can't have Annie, which means it's unlikely he was involved in Tiffany's murder.

Her cell phone rings. "Hello?"

"Hey, Detective. It's Stella. I have a woman who wants to speak to you but she's calling from a penitentiary, so I don't know if you want to speak to her?"

Madison's stomach lurches with dread at the thought of it being her sister, Angie. "What's her name?"

"Kerry Wood. Says she was a friend of Tammy Smith until they had a major falling out."

Madison raises an eyebrow. Kerry is the friend Maria Smith mentioned when Madison asked her if she knew any of Tammy's acquaintances or family.

"Detective?" says Stella. "Alex has just arrived. Says he needs to speak to you urgently."

Intrigued, she says, "Put him on first. Then I'll speak to Kerry Wood."

"Sure."

"Hi, Detective," says Alex.

She's told him a million times to call her Madison but he never does. "I have Chief Mendes with me," she says, "so I'm going to put you on speakerphone, okay?"

"Of course." Once done he says, "Sorry to jump in like that but I've made a fascinating discovery."

"Go ahead."

"Let me catch my breath, I ran all the way here from my office." He takes a minute, leaving Madison desperate for whatever he's about to tell her. "Okay, phew. So, I was analyzing the blood spatter patterns from our crime scene."

"I take it you mean Sunday's crime scene?" she says, to make sure they're on the same page.

"Exactly. Specifically the bedroom our two adults were found in. I've discovered something rather disturbing."

Chief Mendes leans in to hear more clearly.

"You see," he says, "the blood spatter that comes from the bludgeoning of Eric Bailey and the blood spatter that comes from the bludgeoning of his partner Tam—, Tiffany, suggests, and I can't quite believe I'm going to say this... In fact I can't believe I didn't see it sooner. Nora thinks I was distracted by my breakup with Sam but—"

Madison rolls her eyes. "Stay focused, Alex!"

"Oh, sorry. My mind's buzzing with all these revelations. I'll get to the point. The blood spatter pattern suggests *Tiffany* was the person who killed Eric Bailey."

Mendes glances at Madison, confused.

Madison's mouth drops open. She can't believe what she's hearing and is rendered speechless while she thinks about the logistics. Goosebumps cover her arms. "How is that possible?"

"Well, remember Dr. Scott said she believes Tiffany was

killed last?" he says. "Maybe an hour or two after Eric and the boys? This would explain that. She wasn't being mentally tortured by her killer during that time. I believe she was killing her sons."

"You've got to be kidding me?" She blinks, unable to believe it. "But why would she do that?"

Alex scoffs. "Why did she kill her first child? Why does anyone kill anyone? If you listen to the experts—"

"Now's not the time to discuss why people kill, Alex," says Madison.

They already suspect Tiffany killed her firstborn child, but could she really be capable of killing her twin boys too, years later? Madison remembers little Joey, in his dinosaur pajamas, dying in her arms outside the Hendricks's house.

His last words were, "Where's my mom?" He'd looked terrified and Madison thought that was because he wanted to be comforted by his mother in his dying seconds.

She was wrong.

He wanted to know if his mother was still around in case she tried to stab him again. The thought sends an icy shudder through her. "Alex?" she says. "Explain the blood spatter thing to us as simply as possible."

He takes a deep breath. "Nora checked both Tiffany's and Eric's clothes for DNA, blood, trace evidence, etcetera, and she found that Tiffany's clothes contained Eric's blood spatter, as well as her own."

Madison frowns. "Well, yeah, she died next to him, so it makes sense she'd get some of his blood on her, doesn't it?"

"No, actually," he says. "Because if Eric was killed by someone else, and Tiffany was killed an hour or so later, how did his blood spray all over her clothes and in the manner that suggests she was standing directly *in front* of him on the right-hand side of the bed?" He pauses. "Her body was found on the left side of the mattress. The blood spatter doesn't match up.

I've recreated several scenarios and the results show that Tiffany would've had to be standing in the *exact* location the killer would've been standing when delivering the fatal blows to Eric."

Clutching at straws, Madison says, "Maybe the killer made her come close to watch Eric's bludgeoning?"

"While not impossible, it *is* illogical," he replies. "Because if she was that close to the killer when he killed Eric—and I mean she'd have to be almost in front of the killer to get Eric's blood on her the way she did—then she could've been a real threat to the killer. Would he really take that risk? Knowing she could've fought for the sledgehammer to save her own life? And if she loved her boys, she *would* have fought tooth and nail to stop them from being harmed."

A silence falls over them as Madison and Mendes consider what he's saying. The implication—that she killed Eric and her own sons—is horrific.

"Maybe she was tied up?" suggests Mendes. "And therefore not a threat to the killer."

"I'm afraid not, Chief," says Alex. "No ligature marks were found anywhere on her body, and she wasn't tied up when she was discovered. There was no binding material at the scene at all."

Madison lowers herself onto the step outside Ronnie's trailer. "I can't even get my head around this. You're saying Tiffany killed Eric and her boys, but then someone killed her before she could get away with it?"

He clears his throat. "I don't have any proof yet that she killed her boys, it's just a theory, but as for Eric, that's what the evidence suggests. Nora's working on DNA taken from the knife that killed Joey. If we can prove Tiffany touched it it will certainly add weight to our theory, although a defense lawyer could argue it came from her house so that explains the presence of her DNA on it."

She shakes her head in disbelief, but she knows she needs to trust Alex's and Nora's expertise. And, actually, it fits with her original suspicion that more than one perpetrator was involved in the murder of this family. She thought the killer had an accomplice, but it turns out there were two separate killers.

She's suddenly reminded of the car in Lake Providence, and the shoe print Alex photographed that doesn't match any of the team's. "Alex? Tiffany was wearing sneakers when we found her. Have you checked whether the shoe print from Lake Providence matches her shoe prints?"

"No, I'd forgotten about that in my haste at examining the blood spatter. I'll check that next."

"Thanks. If that matches, that means she was the person who tried to hide their identities."

Mendes nods along. "In order to make it harder to find *her* when she fled, disappearing into the night for the second time in her life."

Madison sighs, suddenly overwhelmed by the level of depravity they're dealing with. "The problem we're left with now is that, if it *was* Tiffany who killed Eric and the boys, that doesn't tell us who killed her and took Annie."

Alex agrees. "No, it doesn't. We need the sledgehammer. That will confirm whether Tiffany bludgeoned Eric, and then, as she suffered the same fate as him, who took that weapon from her to end *her* life."

A little dazed by this turn of events, Madison nods. "Thanks, Alex. Keep me updated."

"Will do."

Stella comes back on the line. "I'm afraid our caller hung up. Probably ran out of credit. Want me to call the prison?"

"Not just yet. I need a minute to think."

"Sure." Stella ends the call as Madison stands.

Chief Mendes gets on her cell phone to make a call to the

judge. Probably to expedite the search warrant for Jim McKinney's place.

Nate approaches Madison. "Everything okay?" he asks.

Running her hands through her hair Madison says, "Not really. This case is more messed up than I could ever have imagined."

CHAPTER FIFTY-NINE

Madison drives north, intending to join Adams and Steve while they search Dawn Freemantle's property, but her phone rings when she's directly outside the Hendricks's house, so she pulls over to answer it.

"I have Kerry Wood on the line again," Stella informs her. "She's impatient. Says it's difficult to get phone time inside."

Madison remembers those days. "Fine. Put her through." When the line clicks, she says, "This is Detective Harper."

"Oh, hi. My name's Kerry. I, er, need to tell you something about Tiffany Hendricks, although *I* knew her as Tammy Smith." She sounds young, maybe in her late twenties, and she has a strong Southern accent. "I only found out her real name when I saw it on the news this morning." She sounds shaken.

"Thanks for calling," says Madison. "I appreciate any information you have. First of all, how do you know Tiffany?"

"We were friends up here in Buford. At least I *thought* we were friends. Until she tried to poison me that is."

Madison blinks. "She *what*?"

"I know, right?" Kerry snorts like it's funny. "I spent a week in the hospital thinking I was going to die. Doctors realized I'd been unknowingly drinking antifreeze. Talk about clichéd." She scoffs. "I mean, the stupid bitch couldn't come up with anything *original*?"

Astonished by her thought process Madison says, "You're disappointed she didn't try a more original method to kill you?"

"Oh don't mind me," says Kerry. "I use humor as a defense mechanism. How else are we meant to get through life, right?"

Madison takes a deep breath. She has a point. "So you think Tiffany spiked your drinks?"

"Well I didn't do it myself!" Something distracts Kerry from the call for a second and Madison hears voices behind her. It's noisy. Prison always is. She remembers how hard it was to get any sleep inside and shudders at the memory.

Eventually Kerry comes back on the line. "When Tam—, I mean Tiffany, realized I wasn't going to die, do you know what she did? She planted a huge bag of cocaine at my house and called the cops on me! Told them I was feeding it to my *baby*! That's how I wound up inside."

Madison might not have believed Kerry if she hadn't recently discovered what Tiffany Hendricks was capable of. She considers whether Kerry could have gotten someone to kill Tiffany in revenge for landing her in prison.

But then why would she call LCPD and implicate herself?

"When did you last see her?" she asks.

"Before I went into the hospital. About a month ago. She poisoned me because I know too much."

"Oh yeah?" says Madison. "What do you know?"

Sounding jittery, Kerry says, "That'll cost you. I want out of this place. You've got to get me out or I'll lose my baby. CPS will have her adopted; I just know it."

Knowing she has no control over that, Madison says, "I'm sorry but that's not up to me. Have you told the DA's office the drugs were planted?"

"Of course, but now the bitch is dead I can't prove it."

"Look, I'm sorry about your situation, but if you're not willing to talk to me, then I need to end this call because I'm looking for a missing child. Tiffany's youngest."

"Annie," says Kerry sadly. "She's Eric's child, not Wade's."

Madison pauses. The fact Kerry knows about Eric suggests she could be useful. "That's right. There's a chance she could still be alive."

Kerry sounds emotional as she says, "She was meant to be dead. Tiffany didn't want any of her kids."

Madison's mouth goes dry. She doesn't understand why the woman would want to harm her own children. "If you tell me what you know, it might help Annie. It might help me find her before the worst happens."

Kerry composes herself and takes a deep breath. "I really liked her husband, Wade. He was so kind to me and my daughter. He loved kids, unlike Tiffany..." She falls silent. Until, "Tiffany got real high one night and told me what she'd done. She and Eric came up with the idea of killing Wade for his money. She justified it by pointing out how old and ill he was, and she made it sound like they did him a favor by ending his suffering. I was shocked, but I thought it was the drugs talking, so for once in my life I just listened with my mouth shut."

"How long after Wade's death was this?"

"About a month. But that's not the worst of it. She later learned online that her mom—Linda I think her name was—had died, which meant she knew her mom's place was empty. She tricked Eric into agreeing to move away, down to Lost Creek. The poor sucker truly thought she wanted to start fresh with him. He was totally in love with her and the baby, Annie. The boys didn't like him much. CJ gave him hell, but that's because they were missing their dad. They were devastated when Wade died."

Madison's heart breaks for those poor boys. They went

through a lot in their short lives. "Why did she want to move down here instead of fleeing the state, or even the country? She must have inherited Wade's entire estate?"

"Right," says Kerry. "And from what she told me that was worth just over a million bucks once taxes and loans were paid off." She exhales heavily, sounding full of regret. "You know when you become friends or lovers with a person and there's a moment when you realize, oh shit, this person ain't who I thought they were?" She doesn't wait for a response. "That's what happened with me and Tammy. Sorry, Tiffany."

"So why did she move down here to her mom's house if she was wealthy?" Madison looks up at the dilapidated home in front of her. "Because I've got to say, this place is barely livable."

"Two reasons according to Tiffany. First of all, she said she knew for a fact the local cops down there were useless. No offense."

Madison doesn't take it personally as she wasn't in law enforcement back when Tiffany killed Grace. Ramsey had been. And he let Tiffany escape.

"Also, because it was convenient for her. She said she needed to get rid of some baggage. *Baggage.* That's the word she used. She said Lost Creek is isolated and no one would be able to connect her to what she was about to do." She goes quiet.

"Which was?" presses Madison.

"She didn't want to share her new wealth with Eric. She took him away from his family on the pretense of starting a new life when, really, she was planning to kill him and..."

"Kerry?"

The young woman sobs down the line. "She told me she was going to make sure the kids died peacefully."

Madison leans her head back. Tiffany Hendricks was evil. "She wanted to kill all three children and Eric?"

"Right."

"And then what, flee the country?"

There's a pause while Kerry blows her nose. "Tell me something, Detective Harper. Was there a motorcycle at Tammy's house?"

"There was. Why?"

"Tammy had a contact who was preparing a fake passport, and Wade's cash was in her bank account. Eric had to die because he knew she'd killed Wade. The kids had to die because they were a burden. She was completely emotionless as she said it, which made me think she was full of crap. But then, even if I only so much as had a *thought* like that about my kid, I'd get upset. But not Tiffany." Kerry sighs heavily.

Madison doesn't want to interrupt her so she remains silent. She's learning a lot.

The woman continues. "She said she just had to do it someplace no one could easily trace the kids and Eric back to her. That would give her a head start in terms of escaping. She knew her mom's house was empty and remote, and she thought she could be in and out of town quickly—within twenty-four hours —leaving no trace of her true identity behind. It sounded to me like she had it all meticulously planned."

Madison swallows. Tiffany was clever. But in the end, not clever enough. Because even with fifteen years away from home and some cosmetic surgery, someone still recognized her in the short time she was back. And she did leave a trace of her true identity behind. Her first daughter, Grace.

"She was planning to take off on her motorcycle once she was finished," says Kerry. "Then she'd go collect her fake ID and head south to cross the border into Mexico. Ultimately, she was planning to disappear in South America. She said her lifelong dream of being free from all parental responsibility *and* being rich would finally come true."

The conversation leaves Madison feeling drained. The

depravity of Tiffany's actions, from the very day she killed her firstborn child to the day she killed her sons, might just be the worst she's ever encountered. "Why didn't you go to the police with this information at the time?" She wants to add that if Kerry had done, she could've saved Eric's, CJ's and Joey's lives, but she doesn't. The woman already knows that.

"I guess I didn't want to believe the crazy bitch would go through with it. When someone tells you something like that you have to assume they're pulling your leg. And cops don't always listen to concerned friends." She scoffs. "Or they'll say they can't do anything until a crime's been committed."

Madison's not buying it. "Sounds to me like you took her seriously enough to stop hanging out with her afterward. Is that right?"

Kerry's silence speaks volumes. Eventually she says, "I left her house soon after she told me and tried to stay away from her, but she kept showing up unannounced for coffee. Now I know why; she realized she'd told me too much and wanted to kill me. Way I see it, I'm lucky to be alive. But since I saw on the news that she'd gone through with killing everyone, I haven't stopped shaking. I know there'll be no sleep for me for a long time."

Madison wonders how she'll live with the guilt.

"I gotta go," says Kerry. "My credit's run out. I want the world to know what a vile human being she was, Detective. And I hope you find Annie safe. Although..."

Madison frowns. "What?"

"I don't know. I guess I'm wondering what happens if she grows up to be just like her mother."

The line goes dead. Madison looks at her phone before dropping it her lap to try to process everything Kerry just told her. She doesn't get long enough. Within seconds her phone pings with a text from Adams.

We've got the sledgehammer.

Her eyes widen. Another ping.

It was in Dawn Freemantle's backyard.

"*What?*" Madison immediately reverses out of the driveway and drives the short distance to Dawn's house. She arrives in time to see Steve forcing an angry-looking Kai Bishop into the back of his car. He's wearing cuffs.

"This is bullshit!" shouts Kai. "You planted that there!"

Dawn rushes up to Madison. "What the hell are they doing? Kai wouldn't hurt a fly!"

Steve slams the door shut and turns to Dawn. "If that's the case, then why is the murder weapon we've been searching for all week in your backyard? And if you're saying he's innocent, that leaves us with *you* as our main suspect."

Dawn steps back, shock on her face. "Don't be ridiculous. I'm not capable of murder."

Her grandson watches them from inside the house. Timmy stands expressionless in the window.

Madison's worried all this police drama is going to traumatize him. "Why don't you stay with Timmy," she says to Dawn. "We're just going to question Kai, see what he says."

She hasn't ruled out Dawn's possible involvement, but someone needs to take care of the boy for now.

The older woman turns and hurries into the house, slamming the door shut behind her. Madison watches Steve drive Kai away.

Detective Adams approaches her. "No signs of Annie Smith on the property. The sledgehammer's in the trunk of my car."

"Get it to Alex immediately," she says. "It needs to be checked for prints."

"Got it." He gets into his vehicle and drives away.

Madison turns to face Dawn's house and through the window she can see the older woman hugging Timmy.

If Kai killed Tiffany and took Annie, then where is she?

Pulling out her phone, she texts Nate.

I need Brody's help again.

CHAPTER SIXTY

As officers finish a lengthy search of Dawn's house, Brody meticulously scours the backyard for the missing toddler's scent while Madison and Nate stand watching in the hot midday sunshine.

"You think Dawn could be involved?" asks Nate, batting away a persistent fly.

Madison glances at the older woman, who's nervously perched on a plastic patio chair. She's been chain-smoking ever since Kai was taken away. "Who knows? Nothing would surprise me these days. Adams has taken both their phones, so we'll see what we find on those."

She fills him in on her conversation with Kerry and about Tiffany's murderous plan to escape to South America with her late husband's money.

"Holy crap." He shakes his head. "She was a real piece of work."

The search of Dawn's yard appears to be fruitless, as Brody rejoins them without finding anything. Nate fetches a bowl of water meant for the two rottweilers, who have been kept inside while Brody did his thing. Brody goes to the water and makes a mess as he drinks from it.

"This is so frustrating," says Madison. "Where the hell is that little girl?"

They hear trucks outside. Reporters are probably showing up.

She runs a hand through her sweaty hair. "I better go interview Kai. Thanks for your help."

"Sure." He leans in for a quick, discreet goodbye kiss. He's getting the message.

Before she reaches the front yard her phone rings with a call from Detective Adams. "Hey, Adams. I'm on my way."

"You still at Kai's place?" He sounds energized.

"Yeah, why? Has he confessed?"

"No. Alex took prints from the sledgehammer. He found two sets. One of them matches Tiffany's."

"And the others are Kai's?" she says expectantly.

"That's a negative."

Disappointed, she glances at Dawn. "We need to take Dawn's then."

"No," he says excitedly. "They're not hers. Alex ran them through the system and got a match. You'll never guess in a million years whose prints they are."

Madison hates it when people leave her hanging. She pinches her forehead with her spare hand. "Adams? For the love of God, just tell me."

Nate must've heard her talking, as he approaches her.

"Alright, alright!" says Adams. "They belong to Kai's neighbor. Richard McKinney."

Madison almost drops her phone in surprise. She enters the front yard and looks over the hedge that separates the two properties. It's not far from the spot where the sledgehammer was found. Did he throw it over in an attempt to frame Dawn and Kai? "No freakin' way."

"Honestly!" says Adams. "I'd get Alex on the line but he's disappeared. I think he went to make a call."

Madison sees movement behind the blind in Richard's front window.

Nate follows her gaze.

Her heart is beating out of her chest. "But he's way too frail to have bludgeoned someone to death. And I turned up at his house unannounced earlier this week. There were definitely no signs of a child in there."

"So what do you think?" asks Adams.

She goes cold as she realizes what this means. She looks at Nate as she speaks. "He's covering for his son. Jim must've killed Tiffany out of revenge for putting Dennis in prison, and then his dad probably offered to hide the murder weapon for him. Richard despises Kai and Dawn, so why not frame them?" Her mouth is dry as she asks Adams, "Has Mendes got that search warrant for Jim's place yet?"

"It's just been signed."

Nate leans in and says, "When I went to introduce myself to Jim, he wouldn't let me in his apartment. He had me sit outside on a bench with him."

Madison nods. "He must be hiding her. Get over there, Adams, and be careful." She swallows. "I just hope he showed Tiffany's daughter more mercy than he showed her."

Adams takes a deep breath. He has daughters. He knows he could find the missing toddler's dead body at Jim's apartment. "Me too."

"Tell Mendes I'm bringing Richard in for questioning."

"Understood."

Madison ends the call and looks at Nate. "One way or another, we're about to learn what happened to Annie Smith."

CHAPTER SIXTY-ONE

Richard McKinney didn't say a word when Madison charged over to his house and explained she'd like to question him at the station. He simply topped up Sassy's water bowl, placed the dog on a blanket on the couch and then came willingly. He didn't say a word during the entire journey to the station either.

Madison decided against arresting and cuffing him and she took him in her car instead of placing him in the back of a cruiser. She wants the old man to open up to her, so she's treating him with respect. If he doesn't talk, that'll change.

He's already lost one son to the prison system and is about to lose another the same way, so this will be devastating for him. But, regardless, she needs him to tell her what Jim did, and where he's hiding Annie Smith.

Her phone pings with a text from Nate.

No sign of her at Richard's place.

Disappointed, she can only hope Adams finds her at Jim's apartment.

She leads Richard into the station and past the front desk,

with the hope that she can make him see he needs to do the right thing in order to save a child's life.

At the end of the hallway she opens the door to interview room one before turning to face him. That's when she realizes that, while her back was turned, Richard was busy sending messages on his phone. Quickly grabbing it from him, she's too late to see what he sent and who he sent it to, because he's switched his phone off.

"You're warning Jim we're on our way, aren't you?"

He silently breezes past her and takes a seat at the table.

Madison's disappointed. Upon first meeting Richard McKinney she'd thought he was a good, albeit somewhat grumpy, person who put her at ease when she experienced a wave of grief for her father. So she was hoping she could appeal to his softer side in order to find Annie.

It looks like that won't be the case. He's going to put his son's best interests before Tiffany's child's, even though the little girl isn't responsible for what her mother did.

Madison decides to read him his rights. He needs to realize the seriousness of the situation. When she asks if he wants an attorney present, he shakes his head.

With Steve and Adams on their way to search Jim's apartment, Chief Mendes joins Madison in the interview room to help with questioning. Mendes brings two plastic cups filled with water, but nothing for Richard to drink. She doesn't say a word, possibly in a bid to play bad cop. Madison isn't sure, so she introduces her.

"This is Chief Carmen Mendes."

Richard doesn't even glance at her. He's become sullen like a schoolboy in detention.

Madison takes a seat next to Mendes and opposite Richard. "I want to cut to the chase, Mr. McKinney. We believe your eldest son, Jim, killed Tiffany Hendricks on Sunday night."

She waits for a flicker of recognition at Tiffany's name.

There's nothing. Which tells her he already knew Tammy Smith was Tiffany. The question now becomes, did he know that because Jim confessed to him that he killed her, or did he see Adams's press conference on the TV earlier?

When he doesn't speak, she says, "Let me tell you what *I* think happened." She takes a sip of water. "I think Jim visited you during the daytime on Sunday, and on his way either *to* your house or *from* your house, he recognized Tiffany Hendricks moving back in to her mom's place."

Richard's hands are clasped over his chest. He's expressionless.

She continues. "I think Jim's held a lot of rage toward Tiffany ever since she framed his younger brother for Grace's murder."

He raises an eyebrow. He's probably never heard anyone from the police department acknowledge the fact that Dennis was framed before now.

"We've recently learned that Tiffany committed the murder that put Dennis behind bars." She pauses. "Which means your son could eventually be freed."

The old man's mouth drops open in surprise. He looks from Madison to Mendes and back again. "Are you just saying this to get me to talk?"

Madison can't help but feel bad for the guy. His family has been through a lot because of Tiffany. "Not at all. We've found Grace. She was buried in Linda's backyard all this time."

Richard's eyes well up. "And you have irrefutable proof that woman killed her own baby?"

She nods. "The justice system works slow, but we'll be making sure the DA knows they put the wrong guy in prison."

A sob escapes his mouth and he pinches his eyes with one hand. "That woman ruined our lives."

"I know," she says gently. "She was a despicable person. Which is why I can understand Jim wanting to kill her."

Mendes shoots her a sharp look, which she ignores. She gives Richard a moment and passes him Chief Mendes's untouched water.

When he's composed, Madison softens her tone. "I imagine that once Jim saw Tiffany was back in town, it was a shock, and all his old resentments came to the surface. It would've made sense to him to confront her about it." She leans forward. "But what I can't understand is why he took her youngest child with him. Annie is just two years old, Richard. She doesn't deserve to pay for her mother's crimes."

He won't make eye contact.

"I know you love your sons and I'm sure they love you just as much. They know they can trust you with anything. So I'm guessing Jim told you what he'd done, didn't he? I imagine he thought you'd be proud of him for killing the woman who—as you just acknowledged yourself— ruined all your lives."

Richard shakes his head. Wiping his eyes he says, "No, he didn't."

Gently she says, "He did, Richard. He asked you to hide the weapon he used to take out all the rage he had for her. Because he knew you'd cover for him, or hide the evidence for him. Because he knows you're a good father and he could trust you."

Silence.

"There was a struggle with Tiffany before she died," she says. "We're going to find Jim's DNA on the fingernail scrapings we took from her."

Richard finally looks her in the eye. "Neither of my sons are killers. You can't put Jim away for this. You can't set one of my sons free while imprisoning the other. It's not right!"

Chief Mendes clears her throat. "At the moment, all we care about is finding Annie alive. If Jim gives her up now, a judge will look more favorably—"

"He didn't kill Tiffany, *goddammit!*" His tone is forceful, surprising Madison.

"So who did?" she presses.

Pulling out a handkerchief, Richard coughs. The act makes him wince and he grabs his shoulder in pain.

A creeping realization sweeps over Madison as he opens his mouth to speak. She knows what he's going to say.

"I did."

Madison stares in silence. Last time Richard grabbed his shoulder in pain he said it was his arthritis giving him trouble. Could it really have been caused by bludgeoning Tiffany to death? Sounding uncertain of herself she says, "With all due respect, I don't see how you'd have the strength to deliver the blows—"

His steely gaze cuts her off. "Hate gives you strength, Detective. Just as love does." He pulls his sleeve up, revealing a deep scratch on his forearm. A wound made by Tiffany in her bid to defend herself.

Madison blinks. She's lost for words. She considers whether he's just trying to cover for his son, so that he can serve Jim's sentence. But she doesn't think he is. His expression is deadly serious. "So tell us what happened," she says.

He takes a deep breath and leans back in his seat. "I wish I hadn't driven past the damn house and seen her in the yard. She looked older, and she had two damn melons stuck to her chest and hair down to her waist, dyed porn-star blonde. But I knew her instantly. I recognized the smirk on her face and the evil in her eyes." He coughs. "I almost crashed when I realized she had the nerve to come back here. Back to the town that held vigils for her and prayed that she hadn't hurt herself."

"Did she see you looking?" asks Madison.

"I don't think so. I was shaking with anger by the time I got home. I wanted to march straight back over there and yell at her."

Mendes shifts in her seat. "What stopped you?"

"I heard a man's voice on the property."

"So you went back when it was dark," says Madison. "Did you think you could get her alone and kill her without being seen?"

He looks at Madison with disappointment in his eyes. Disappointment that she's not understanding him perhaps. "I didn't go there to kill her, and that's the God's honest truth. I took nothing with me, no weapon. The sledgehammer was already there." He shudders.

"So why did you go there?" she asks.

"To finally have it out with her. To tell her what I thought of her. To tell her how she ruined our lives. And to make her leave. I didn't want that woman as a neighbor. I never wanted to see her again."

"But you ended up killing her. So what happened?"

He takes a sip of water before lowering his eyes. "I'll never forget what I walked into. The upstairs of that house was like hell on earth."

Both Madison and Mendes lean forward, eager to watch the crime scene unfold through Richard's eyes.

CHAPTER SIXTY-TWO

SUNDAY NIGHT

Having worked himself up all day, Richard feels like he might have a heart attack if he doesn't get some things off his chest. He saw Tiffany arrive home from a late-night jog. Her boyfriend is nowhere to be seen; he must've retired to bed early.

Richard's been watching from outside the house, hidden behind some trees, for twenty minutes now. It's given him time to fume about how, fifteen years ago, Tiffany managed to fool everyone into thinking *she* was the victim.

He can't understand her thought process for returning to Lost Creek. Does she really think the town is going to welcome her back with open arms? Something about her return doesn't add up to him. He suspects she's not intending to stick around for long. Maybe she's on the run and needed her mom's empty house to hide out for a couple of days. It wouldn't surprise him.

It doesn't matter what she's here for. While she *is* in town, he needs to get her alone and make her see sense. She could get Dennis out of prison if she does the right thing and admits she lied back then. She could tell the cops she hadn't seen Dennis anywhere near her house when her baby went missing. His son could come home at last. Dennis's bedroom remains as he left it and would just need a quick spring clean in preparation.

When his old bones won't let him stay still any longer, Richard creeps around the back of the house. All is quiet. Eerily still.

He knows there's no chance she'll talk to him if he simply knocks on the door, so he's going to take her by surprise. The back door is ajar, which isn't unusual. The evening is stiflingly warm and Linda's place doesn't have A/C, so the open door is to allow the slight breeze to circulate.

Once inside the kitchen, Richard stops and listens.

A child's cry reaches him.

"Shut up. Mommy's busy." Tiffany's voice. Cold and uncaring.

He creeps toward the staircase as that's where her voice is coming from. Adrenaline pumps through his body as he has a moment of clarity.

What am I doing here? What if she calls the cops on me?

The child yells, "Daddy!" Sounds like a girl.

"Daddy's dead, baby. Just give me a minute, would you?"

Richard's blood runs cold. The guy's *dead*? That can't be.

The toddler keeps screaming. Something's upset her. "I want Joey!" Her voice is desperate, like she wants to be comforted by someone.

"Joey's dead too. And CJ. Don't worry, you'll be joining them in Heaven real soon."

Richard's frozen to the spot. Tiffany talks about her family being dead as casually as if she's telling her daughter it's bath time.

And she means to kill the little girl next.

His legs tremble as he's compelled to climb the stairs. He can't let her kill that child. He just can't.

At the top of the hallway he looks left and sees a young boy asleep on his bed, facing away from him. But his torso isn't moving with steady breaths.

He's dead.

Richard's heart hammers against his chest in horror. There's no sign of the third victim Tiffany mentioned. Movement ahead makes him look toward the next bedroom. The little girl is stumbling backward, out of the doorway. She hasn't seen him but it's just a matter of time before she raises the alarm.

Richard knows he has two choices; flee the building and hope Tiffany doesn't catch up with him, or charge ahead and take her by surprise.

He's no runner, so before he can rethink anything he charges ahead, pushes the child backward—out of the bedroom and out of harm's way—before slamming the door shut behind him.

On the other side of the door, the little girl screams in surprise. Tiffany looks up and sees him. She's standing at the end of the bed, and when their eyes lock, she immediately recognizes him.

"What do you want, old man?"

Her face is strangely smooth, with no wrinkles. Her lips are fat, like two slugs. She's had cosmetic surgery.

Richard's gaze is drawn to the shape on the bed. It's a man's body. It looks as though his head is missing and has been replaced with a sack of blood. Richard tears his eyes away to look at the monster in front of him. "What the hell have you done, Tiffany?"

There's no remorse on her face. She looks as though it's her God-given right to kill whoever she wants. It angers him. Because it reminds him of the day Dennis was convicted of Grace's murder. Of the first time he visited his son in prison. It was an agonizing day that left him feeling hopeless. Because he couldn't help his son. He couldn't serve his sentence for him.

A surge of rage and adrenaline runs through his veins. He wishes he'd brought a weapon.

Tiffany must sense she's in danger as her eyes flicker to something beside her. He realizes too late it's a sledgehammer. It must be what she used on the guy on the bed.

She grabs for it, so Richard lunges forward, trying to knock her over. She's strong, but he's determined not to let her kill that little girl outside.

The toddler's screams can be heard. She wants her daddy.

Richard forces Tiffany backward, against the wall.

"Get off me, you crazy old bastard!" she yells.

They're both clutching the sledgehammer's handle, but it's slick with blood spatter and sweat, and difficult to keep a grip on it. Tiffany gains strength from the wall and pushes him away hard.

He takes a second to catch his breath before she lunges forward, swinging the weapon. The heavy end cuts through the air but takes her off balance and Richard uses his opportunity to push her onto the bed. She drops the sledgehammer, giving him a split-second opportunity to take control of it.

He pulls it toward him and looms over her, panting so hard he thinks his heart will burst out of his chest.

Tiffany catches her breath too as she lies back on the mattress next to her dead boyfriend's body.

"Why?" he says between breaths. "Why would you kill the children?"

She scoffs. "Why wouldn't I? They were stopping me from living my life." She smirks at him. "You don't have the balls to hurt me. You'd go straight to prison. Or maybe you'd like that. You'd get to see Dennis every day." Her voice is mocking and it enrages him even more.

Without another word, he lifts the sledgehammer over his shoulder. Tiffany screams until it makes contact with her head.

The dull thud it makes on impact makes him want to throw

up, but he can't stop. He needs to know she'll never hurt anyone else. He hits her again, and again, until his shoulder protests and he's sure he's going to drop dead.

When he's finally done, he sinks to the floor and tries hard not to pass out.

CHAPTER SIXTY-THREE

When Richard's done talking, the interview room falls silent for a full minute. Madison's lost for words. Chief Mendes abruptly stands and excuses herself. Madison's surprised. She thought Mendes was a seasoned pro. But everyone has their limits.

Richard looks equally as surprised. With Mendes gone he says, "You want to hear more?"

No, she wants a stiff drink. "I have to," she says.

He eyes her while mopping his brow with a handkerchief. He's beginning to sweat profusely. "How can you do this job? How can you listen to things like this every day? Doesn't it get to you?"

"More than you'll ever know."

His story answers important questions for her. To disguise the identities of the victims in order to buy herself time to escape the country, Tiffany must have driven the vehicle containing all their personal documents to the lake and pushed it in, and then jogged the short distance back to the house. That's why she was dressed in black. So she could move around undetected.

She also knows now that Tiffany left her daughter at home

while she hid the car. Annie was alone with the dead bodies of her brothers and father. She would've been terrified.

The thought of what she went through makes Madison feel sick.

Tiffany Hendricks was a psychopath.

It's deeply unsatisfying that they can't put her behind bars for what she's done, but ultimately, she's paid a higher price. They can't get justice for Grace but they can give Annie a good start in life. She's sole beneficiary to whatever her mother inherited from Wade's estate. That could be put in a trust ready for when she becomes an adult. But she would only benefit if they can find her.

To Richard, Madison says, "If you'd alerted us when you first realized what was happening inside that house, we could've found the little boy outside sooner and saved his life. His name was Joey. He was seven years old. He bled out from a knife wound to the stomach." She swallows the lump in her throat before continuing. "We could've arrested Tiffany and you'd have had the satisfaction of seeing her locked up for the rest of her life."

He shakes his head. "I'm sorry about the boy, I truly am. I had no idea he was in the backyard until I saw the news reports. He must've escaped before I got into the house. But I'm not sorry about killing Tiffany. Who's to say she would've been found guilty? Who's to say she'd even make it to trial and not trick some rookie guard into helping her escape? No. People like her always get away with their crimes. She needed to be stopped. She needed to die."

He rubs his temple as if he feels unwell. "And if I'd come to you after I killed her, you wouldn't have believed me. No one would've believed Tiffany killed her own children. Because mothers don't do that, right? Fathers do, but not mothers."

"You're wrong," she says. "We know now that Tiffany killed Grace. We have evidence to prove she killed Eric. We would've got there in the end, and your testimony could've helped us get there a lot faster."

He sips some water, but he's sweating profusely. "And I'd die in prison for my trouble. No. I don't regret anything. I saved the little girl. I'll take my solace from that."

After a deep breath she asks, "What did you do with Annie?"

"I picked her up and got us the hell out of there."

Her heart pounds with anticipation as she asks the all-important question, hoping with everything in her being that he didn't take his rage out on the innocent child. "Where is she now?"

"She's alive and well, I can tell you that much." He coughs hard and his face drains of blood.

Alarmed, she leans forward, desperate to get the answers she needs. "I can't take your word for that, Richard. I need to see the child for myself."

He leans back in his chair and clutches his left arm. "Oh shit, something's not right."

Within seconds he collapses onto the floor.

Madison rushes to the door just as Mendes comes out of the adjoining room. "We need EMS!" she yells.

CHAPTER SIXTY-FOUR

Once Richard's stabilized, he's rushed to the hospital by ambulance, refusing to tell Madison anything else. He looks so ill she worries he might die before she can find Annie. She's beyond frustrated to be so close to knowing where the child is. The only consolation is that Richard said she was safe, but Madison doesn't think she can trust the promise of a killer.

Alex, who has been hovering ever since Madison opened the door to the interview room, asks if he can speak to her urgently.

But Madison's trying to get her head together, and Chief Mendes is on the phone with Detective Adams, filling him in on what Richard told them.

"Just a second," she says, walking away from Alex. "Chief? Did they get Jim McKinney?"

Mendes lowers the phone to answer. "No, his apartment was empty and there's no sign of Annie."

"Dammit!" If Richard's hidden her unattended somewhere, she could die from a lack of water, or heatstroke.

Her phone pings. It's Nate.

Someone told Dennis his dad was being questioned and he wants to know what's going on. I don't think he has a clue what his brother did.

Madison quickly replies.

It wasn't Jim. Their dad killed Tiffany. You can break the news to him. Tell him to speak to his lawyers about getting out. Might as well get the ball rolling ASAP.

"Detective?" says Alex. "I really need to speak to you."

She spins around to face him. "Sorry, Alex. What is it?"

"Two things." He talks fast. "First of all, the shoe print from the lake matches the shoe Tiffany was wearing when found."

She nods. "Good to know. What else?"

Alex hesitates, a perturbed look on his face. "When I checked whose prints were on the handle of the sledgehammer, I recognized the face that came up."

"Whose? Richard's?"

"Yes. I realized I met him once, but I only knew him as Richard. I didn't know his last name."

She's confused at his point, which isn't uncommon as he sometimes talks in riddles. "What's that got to do with anything? We already know he's Jim's and Dennis's dad."

"Yes, but what you don't know is who his granddaughter is."

Her stomach flips with dread. "Who's that?"

He looks pale as he says, "My ex-girlfriend. Samantha Slater."

At first Madison fails to see the relevance, but not for long. Sam's a social worker. It makes perfect sense that Richard would give the child to her to take care of. "Oh my God, that's why she dumped you."

He nods. "I think so. She didn't want me to find out she was hiding the child."

"But why hide her? Why not bring her to us?"

"Because it would implicate her grandfather."

"Which means she knew what he'd done. She covered for him." Something doesn't make sense. "So, wait, who's her father?"

"Jim McKinney. But in the short time we were together she never introduced me to any of her family other than her mom, who she lives with, and her grandfather, and that was only because we bumped into him in the diner. I got the impression she was embarrassed of her family, which makes sense given her uncle is in prison for murdering a baby."

"But Sam's last name isn't McKinney?"

"No. Her mom and Jim are divorced and Sam goes by her mom's maiden name. Now we know why."

Madison thinks back to the times she's bumped into Sam at the diner recently. She was sitting next to Jim at the counter the night the family were discovered dead—when Nate was on his coffee date with Lena. The next time, Sam had been walking away from both Jim and Richard, who were sitting next to each other at the counter. She had stopped to ask Madison whether she'd found Annie yet. She actually had the audacity to look concerned, and even volunteered to help. On neither occasion had Madison gotten the impression they were there together as a family.

Because they didn't want her to know they were related. That's why Sam walked away on both occasions.

Adrenaline races through Madison's body. "What's her address?"

Alex gives it to her on a piece of paper. "I tried calling but she's not answering her phone, and she's not at work either."

"Don't try her again," she says. "I don't want her to know we're coming."

He nods. "Can I recommend you don't go in guns blazing? Sam would never hurt a child."

Madison looks at him. He's visibly upset that someone he trusted has deceived him so badly. "Understood. Update Mendes for me, would you? And arrange for backup to follow me there."

Madison races out of the station.

CHAPTER SIXTY-FIVE

Madison arrives at Samantha's house alone, but she knows it won't be long before backup arrives. She's hoping she won't need it, and that Samantha's levelheaded enough to know she needs to hand the child over. That she should have put the toddler's well-being before her grandfather's. Isn't that what she's trained to do?

There's no way Sam can keep her job after this. And if she realizes that, it might make her desperate and unpredictable.

As Madison gets out of her car, Sam appears at the front door with an older woman behind her. Their striking resemblance to each other suggests this is Sam's mother.

Madison approaches them.

Before she can say a word the older woman steps forward. "My name's Peggy Slater. I'm Sam's mom. I need to tell you I had no idea the little girl we were caring for was the missing girl from the news. Sam lied to me from the start. She told me her name was Belle and that we were to care for her while her parents were investigated for child abuse. I wasn't to take her outside the house in case her parents tried to abduct her." She looks at her daughter. "Tell her, Sam. Tell her I didn't know anything."

Madison trusts the fear in the woman's eyes. "I believe you, ma'am."

"We *were* caring for her," says Sam. "We would never have hurt her."

"But you knew who she was, didn't you, Sam?" Madison studies her expression. "You knew what your grandfather had done."

Tears escape the young woman's eyes. "He told me everything when he brought Annie here Sunday night. Mom was already asleep when Grandad called me to meet him outside. He was covered in blood and holding a petrified child. *Tiffany's* child." She wipes her face with her hands. "I couldn't believe what he'd done to Tiffany. I was stunned."

They don't move from the entrance, and Madison wonders if that's because they don't want her to come inside and take the child away.

"You should've called the police," she says. "I mean, you're a *social worker*, Samantha. What were you thinking?"

She's clearly distraught. "I panicked. I didn't know what to do. I didn't want him to go to jail and I didn't want to see my dad upset again. Grandad made me promise not to tell my dad. He said he'd been through enough." She pauses. "I'll lose my job over this, won't I?"

Madison can't offer her any reassurance and besides, she deserves to lose her job over this. She's supposed to care for vulnerable children, not endanger them. What would've happened if Richard had come back to harm Annie?

Madison tries to peer over the women's shoulders. She's nervous about Jim's current location. Maybe he's inside.

Maybe he's armed.

Resting her hands on her hips, she discreetly feels the butt of her weapon. "Alex is disappointed in you."

"I'm sure he is. He always wanted to meet my family but I knew he'd dump me if he found out my uncle was in prison for murdering a child. It's not an easy thing to explain to someone and there's no guarantee he'd believe Dennis is innocent."

"Alex wouldn't have blamed you for whatever your uncle did or didn't do." She sighs. "I need to see Annie. Would you fetch her for me?"

Peggy groans and exchanges a worried look with her daughter.

Madison gets a bad feeling. "What's wrong?"

Sam lowers her eyes. "Please don't hurt him. I can't lose my dad."

Madison gets a sudden sinking feeling. "Sam? What's going on? Where's Annie? Has your dad taken her?"

Peggy speaks up. "Jim didn't know what his father had done. Not until he was through with you at the station yesterday. When you started asking him about his dad, he got suspicious. He went to Richard's house to confront him. When Richard confirmed it, Jim panicked and made him hide the sledgehammer on his neighbor's property. He said they could frame the neighbor for it, but he didn't think to wipe it clean first, and by the time Jim thought of that he couldn't retrieve it without the rottweilers giving him away. And then he got a message from Richard this afternoon saying he'd been taken in for questioning."

So, as Madison suspected, that's who Richard was messaging from the station.

"You have to understand," says Peggy, "Jim has a long history of depression and suicidal thoughts ever since his brother was locked up. He's never been able to get over it. It's why we divorced. And once he found out his dad was being questioned for Tiffany's murder, Jim came here and flipped out. He said if his dad gets arrested, he'll kill Annie."

Oh God.

"We tried to stop him from taking her," says Sam, her eyes desperate. "But we couldn't. He pushed us away."

Madison gets her phone out. "Where could he have taken her?"

With a shake of the head Peggy says, "He wouldn't tell us."

Samantha's sobbing now. "Please don't shoot my dad. *Please!* Our family has suffered enough."

Madison races back to her car while phoning Detective Adams. He answers right away and she tries to explain what's happening but he cuts her off.

"I know where he is," says Adams. "Someone's called in about a guy matching Jim's description. He's standing on top of the shopping mall. He's threatening to jump."

Madison's heart sinks. If Jim jumps to his death, they might never find Annie.

"And, Madison?" he says, his voice grave.

"What?"

"He's holding the little girl."

She's floored for a second. Her mouth goes dry and she has to fight back tears of hopelessness. She clears her throat and starts the car's engine. "Send everyone we have, but absolutely *no sirens*, understood? I don't want to spook him."

"Got it."

Madison steps on the gas. "I'm on my way."

CHAPTER SIXTY-SIX

A crowd is forming outside the mall. Everyone is staring or pointing upward, most people filming on their phones. Madison doesn't even want to think about Annie's murder being captured on video for the media to show repeatedly on TV for the next few weeks.

She gets straight out of her car and shouts over to Officer Sanchez, who beat her here. "Confiscate their phones or get them out of here! This should *not* be recorded."

"Got it," he yells back.

Madison looks up. Blinded by the sun, she leans into her car for Nate's sunglasses. She needs to be able to keep her eyes fixed on Jim at all times without being distracted by glare.

A fire escape at the side of the building gives Madison a more direct route to the rooftop than going through the mall. She runs over there and makes her way up. It takes forever.

She's both sweating and out of breath by the time she reaches the top step, making her wish she'd given up cigarettes years earlier than she did.

A glance over her shoulder to the ground tells her Adams

has arrived. She also sees Nate's car approaching at high speed. Chief Mendes must've kept him in the loop.

She gets vertigo from looking down, feeling as if she's about to fall.

Stepping onto the rooftop she realizes she's first on the scene. Her heart pounds hard against her chest as she spots Jim McKinney pacing back and forth near the edge. He's holding the toddler.

Annie appears unharmed. Her fine brown hair is tangled over her face and she's sucking her thumb, probably self-soothing. Being held by a man she doesn't know, and being so close to the edge of this tall building, the poor child must be terrified.

Jim hasn't stepped onto the waist-high narrow ledge yet.

Madison can only hope he doesn't spook when he sees her.

Slowly approaching him, she tries to assess whether she can reach him unseen, but he turns and spots her.

"Stay back!" he yells, his eyes wild.

About fifteen feet away from him she stops and raises her hands to show him they're empty. Her holster is unclipped, ready, and she won't hesitate to shoot him if it means saving the child. But then Jim does the unthinkable.

He steps up onto the ledge.

Her heart is in her mouth as she realizes he might actually jump. "Jim! Stop! You're scaring her."

Annie clutches his chest, wide-eyed now. Somehow, she's not crying. She must be traumatized and in shock by this point. She witnessed her father's and brothers' murders, then she spent almost a week living with strangers. Now she's been grabbed from her new safe haven to find herself over a hundred feet up in the air with a desperate stranger.

"If you want her," says Jim, "I need you to promise me you won't put my dad in prison."

Madison's heart sinks. "Get down and we'll discuss it."

"Promise me!" he yells. "I understand he'll be convicted,

I'm not stupid. But he's old. He should be considered for home detention. I know you can arrange that with the DA's office if you really want to. They owe my family for putting Dennis away. We wouldn't seek financial compensation for that. We just want Dad to stay out of prison."

Madison swallows, unsure what to say. She's not experienced in hostage negotiations. She just knows she can't upset him because, in order to stop him from jumping with Annie in his arms, she needs to give him hope.

She thinks she hears footsteps climbing the fire escape behind her. It must be Adams. Her heart sinks as she worries he might say or do something stupid that literally tips Jim over the edge.

Turning back to Jim McKinney she says, "We want to help you."

"No you don't. You're going to put my father behind bars, just like you did my brother."

"I wasn't responsible for that," she says. "And I agree Dennis should never have been arrested, never mind convicted. That's all going to be fixed now. Please, Jim. Give me the little girl. You don't really want to hurt her."

"Are you kidding?" he says. "The mother of this child ruined my life. What if this one has bad blood and turns out just like Tiffany? What if *she* destroys people's lives too? I'd be doing everyone a favor by killing her before she gets the chance."

Madison hates it when people assume children will become criminals just because their parents are. It's bullshit and unfair to the kids. But she has to stay focused. "Jim, your brother's going to get out of prison now. You can be reunited. You can't miss that. He's going to need you to help him readjust to life on the outside. Trust me, I know. I've been there."

He shakes his head. "It's too late. We won't get the last fifteen years back. It's just going to start all over again: the court case, the conviction, the visiting hours. Except this time it'll be for my father, which is even worse because it'll destroy him to be locked away at his age."

Madison's sympathetic but Richard killed Tiffany. He's a murderer, no matter what his motive, or the fact he saved Annie's life. She struggles to find any comforting words, because Jim's right; his situation is dire. And it all stems from what Tiffany Hendricks did as a young woman. The minute she took baby Grace's life, she also destroyed the lives of all those around her: Ronnie Russo: her mother, Linda; as well as the McKinney men.

Madison's hands are slick with sweat. She's way out of her comfort zone.

Jim's gaze is distracted by something behind her.

Madison risks a quick glance over her shoulder. Adams has arrived, and next to him the door that leads inside the mall opens a crack and Madison thinks she sees Brody's nose poking out, but it closes again. Nate must be in there, waiting for the right moment to help her.

But if Brody runs for Jim, he could accidentally push both him and Annie off the ledge.

Her mind buzzes with a million different thoughts as she tries to figure out how to end this safely. She turns back to face Jim, who looks hopeless now. He can tell more cops are going to arrive and he's going to be arrested.

"You're not going to help my father, are you?" he says.

Madison decides the situation is dire enough to warrant a lie. "I'll do whatever's in my power to keep your father out of prison, Jim. I promise you. But this isn't helping. You're endangering a child's life right now. Just hand her over and we'll talk about what I can do for you and your dad. You can't help him if you're dead."

Jim silently stares at her, trying to judge whether she's lying.

She risks one slow step forward, followed by another. "I can talk to the DA and explain how this is all Tiffany's fault."

As she nears them, Annie reaches out for Madison to take her from her captor.

Madison has to resist as she doesn't want to spook him. But every bone in her body wants to grab the little girl.

"You can watch Dennis emerge a free man," she says softly.

He scoffs. "And while my brother comes out of one prison door, my father will enter another." He shakes his head. "I can't stick around to witness that."

Madison stares in horror as he slowly leans backward.

Something shoots by her so fast she doesn't understand at first.

Brody.

The dog grabs Jim's left ankle in his jaw as Madison runs toward them both, reaching for Annie. It feels as if she's moving impossibly slowly, that she's going to miss.

Finally, her hands clutch Annie's waist. And because Jim maintains his grip around the now-screaming child, she manages to pull both him and Annie off course so that they're moving sideways.

But Jim's determined to die.

He releases the toddler and uses his foot against the ledge to project himself backward again.

Brody refuses to release his grip on the guy's ankle.

They're both about to go over the edge as Madison tries to pull the child to safety.

Nate only just makes it to the dog in time. He pulls Brody back by his hefty torso. Brody's jaw doesn't relinquish Jim's ankle, which must be excruciating for both of them.

With some effort, Nate yanks hard, tipping Brody to safety.

Madison's able to fall onto her back, on the hot rooftop. Annie follows, safe—but stunned—in her arms, landing painfully on Madison's rib cage.

Madison looks over and sees Nate just as he falls backward, his head hitting the ground and Brody landing on top of his chest. She just has time to wince at the thought of how much weight Brody's put on Nate's rib cage when she realizes the dog only has a small torn-off section of Jim's jeans in his mouth.

She looks up.

Jim's gone.

Below, a noise reaches her that she knows she'll never forget. A devastating thud followed by the screams of onlookers.

Madison closes her eyes. "Oh God."

Detective Adams runs to the edge to peer over at the ground below. "Holy crap." He quickly turns away again, doubling over in shock. "Oh, Jesus." He shakes his head as he tries to calm his nerves. "This damn town..."

No one could survive that fall. Jim must be dead.

Annie lies still on Madison's chest, whimpering in fear. Madison looks down at the girl's big round eyes. She looks like Tiffany. She looks a little like Grace too, the sister she'll never meet.

Madison strokes her soft hair. "It's okay, sweetie," she says between breaths. "Everything's going to be okay now."

Is that a lie? Madison doesn't know. She swallows back her emotion as she can only hope Annie is placed with a loving family who will help her deal with her inevitable trauma.

Nate crawls over to them both as Detective Adams leans in to take Annie from Madison. Ambulance sirens reach them from below.

"I'll get her checked out," says Adams, walking away with the child in his arms.

Nate winces as he reaches Madison. "Are you okay?" He strokes the side of her face.

Madison can tell she's hurt her back but doesn't think it's serious. Her head is pounding though, and she can't bring herself to sit up just yet. She's both mentally and emotionally drained. "I think so. You?"

He rests his head against the ground. "I'll be okay. Who had the girl?"

"Jim's daughter. She's a social worker. And she was dating Alex until this happened."

Nate looks at her. "Dyed red hair, about five foot six?"

She nods.

"I saw her arrive at Jim's apartment complex when I went to discuss his brother with him. I didn't know she was his daughter."

Brody sits up, panting hard.

"I can't believe he jumped," says Madison. "Richard will be devastated." She knows Sam and Dennis will be too, but Richard's actions caused this. If he'd let the police know about Tiffany being back in town, and what she'd done in that house, he could've had both his sons by his side.

She swallows the lump in her throat. "I almost had him. But I had to take Annie. Maybe if I'd just—"

She feels Nate's hand reaching for hers. "No one could've stopped him, Madison. You saved the girl. Focus on that."

She still can't bring herself to get up, so they lie there alone, looking up at the clear blue sky and listening to the commotion coming from the ground below. Minutes pass as they come to terms with what happened.

Eventually Nate feels his ribs. "I think I cracked a few ribs when Brody landed on top of me."

Madison looks at him and realizes she has to focus on the positives from today. They saved Annie.

Nate looks like he's going to try to get up. "I need a stiff drink."

"Nate?" she says.

He looks over at her.

"You realize you chose to save Brody over me, right?"

He frowns. "I did?"

She nods. "Yeah. When we were all tipping over the edge you grabbed him instead of me."

Nate looks at the dog with a sheepish grin. "Well of course, it's Brody. I mean look at him! I can't lose my buddy."

Brody licks Nate's face and excitedly nuzzles his neck.

Madison rolls her eyes and surprises herself by smiling. She needs to or she'll fall into a deep depression doing this job. "Wonderful," she says. "Good to know you love him more than you love me." The L-word slips out before she realizes it. She turns away from him, embarrassed.

With some effort, and pain, Nate moves onto his shoulder and gently turns her to look at him, removing his sunglasses from her face so he can fix his eyes on hers. "Madison?" he says. "Don't be jealous. I'll never be able to love anyone more than I love you."

She feels her face redden. He probably wants her to kiss him, but others are arriving on the roof, waiting to talk to them. So instead she says, "Prove it. Take me away from all this. I need a break. It doesn't have to be far away or for long. Owen's settled at college, Uncle Vince can take care of Brody, and we can get away from all this and take some time for ourselves. We deserve that, don't we?"

Nate smiles. "I thought you'd never ask."

She rests her head back, thinking how it feels wrong to be hopeful for the future right now. A man just died, and she's going to have to break it to his father, brother and daughter. But this is the job she chose to do. And in order to be able to do this day after day, Madison needs to have some light in her life or she'd never cope with the overwhelming reality of facing human depravity every day.

She squeezes Nate's hand tight, knowing she can get through anything with him by her side.

A LETTER FROM WENDY

Thank you for reading *Her Lonely Bones,* book six in the Detective Madison Harper series.

You can keep in touch with me and get updates about the series by signing up to my newsletter here, and by following me on social media.

www.bookouture.com/wendy-dranfield

I hope you enjoyed this latest book in the series. Some of you will be happy about the development in Madison and Nate's relationship, others not so! I actually never intended for them to get together. From the very beginning I wanted them to be supportive friends only, and avoid any possibility of a romance, but their relationship developed into something that couldn't be ignored any longer.

I'm not too mad about it as they clearly make a good couple and need to be in each other's lives in some capacity. It will be interesting to see how it develops in the next book. I sometimes feel like a reader myself, as I usually have no idea what's going to happen, so when Madison turned up at Nate's house in the heavy downpour, I felt like I should make some popcorn while I watched the scene unfold in front of me!

If you haven't read books one and two in the series, you may be wondering what happened to Officer Mike Bowers in his past, and why he died. I can't give too much away about his past in *this* book as it will spoil book two (*Cry for Help*) for those who read the books out of order (a surprising amount of people!).

I would always recommend reading this series from the beginning with book one (*Shadow Falls*), as past books will make Mike's flashback chapters in this book more interesting for you. Also, I think Madison and Nate have such unique backstories that you can't really understand their motivations until you know what they've been through to get where they currently are.

And now, it seems, they have everything they ever wanted. It should make for plain sailing from here on out.

Unless something terrible should happen of course...

There's only one thing I can promise you about this series, and that is this: nothing bad will ever happen to Brody!

If you enjoyed this book, please do leave a rating or review (no matter how brief) on Amazon, as this helps it to stand out among the thousands of books that are published each day, thereby allowing it to reach more readers and ensuring the series continues.

See you next time!

Wendy

www.wendydranfield.co.uk

 facebook.com/WendyDranfield1

ACKNOWLEDGMENTS

Thank you to the advance readers and book bloggers who review my books with so much enthusiasm. I love reading your reviews and sharing your posts.

As always, thank you to everyone at Bookouture who worked on my latest book.

And special thanks to the reader of all my first drafts, my wonderful husband.

Printed in Great Britain
by Amazon